WHAT LIES BENEATH

Stephen Edger has been writing crime thrillers since 2010. An avid reader, Stephen writes what he likes to read: fast-paced, suspense thrillers with more than a nod to the darker side of the human psyche. He also writes under the pen name M.A. Hunter.

Stephen was born in the north-east of England, but grew up in London, meaning he is both a northerner and a southerner. By day he works in the financial industry using his insider knowledge to help shape the plots of his books.

He is passionate about reading and writing, and cites Simon Kernick and C.L. Taylor as major influences on his writing style.

www.stephenedger.com

/AuthorStephenEdger

@StephenEdger

ALSO BY STEPHEN EDGER

Snatched
Nowhere To Hide
Then He Was Gone
Little Girl Gone
Till Death Do Us Part
Future Echoes
Look Closer
Blood On Her Hands
The Prodigal Mother

The DI Kate Matthews Series
Dead to Me
Dying Day
Cold Heart

WHAT LIES BENEATH

Stephen Edger

This novel is entirely a work of fiction.
The names, characters and incidents portrayed in it are the work of the author's imagination. Any resemblance to actual persons, living or dead, events or localities is entirely coincidental.

All rights reserved. No part of this publication may be reproduced, stored in a retrieval system, or transmitted, in any form or by any means, electronic, mechanical, photocopying, recording or otherwise, without the prior permission of the author

Copyright © 2022 Stephen Edger

ISBN: 9798422925612

*Dedicated to my wife and children
whom I love more than life itself.*

Chapter 1

Joe

I shouldn't have come. Every bone and sinew in my body – every base instinct – is telling me to go home, and pretend like the last three months didn't happen. It was one thing to *think* about how I could snatch him, quite another to actually secure a cell to hold him in. Now that I'm here … Now that the moment is just seconds away, I don't think I can go through with it. That's not who I am. I'm not like *him*.

It's so dark inside the car I barely notice my breath as it drifts from my nose. Beyond the windscreen, I can just about make out the rear of the car a few metres in front. The street light overhead has been broken for several weeks, and the council are no closer to having it repaired. Thank God! This is the ideal spot to lurk without being noticed at this bewitching hour. That's why I came here first thing this morning and waited for the space to empty, before parking and jogging home.

Funny, I've only just noticed but the next street light along also appears to be faulty. Maybe it's like when a bulb blows on Christmas tree lights, knocking out the rest of the circuit? I don't know, I'm no electrician. In fact, I never was practical when it came to doing things with my hands. My wife would attest to that.

The silver pendant on the bracelet hanging around

the rear-view mirror catches my eye as a car drives by on the opposite side of the road. I turn my head long enough that the driver won't have seen me. I smeared enough mud over the licence plate that he won't be able to recognise the digits either.

Would he act differently if he knew why I'm just sat here waiting?

This is ridiculous! This isn't me.

I played the idea through my head over and over, until the plan started to form, and in those early days I think I almost managed to convince myself that when it came to it, I'd be able to do it.

What was I thinking?

I should just go. Now. Before he turns up.

My finger hovers over the engine start button, while my eyes focus on the tiny pendant again.

Is this what she would have wanted?

I adjust the mirror so that I can see the back seat, picturing her brown, button eyes, the way her blonde fringe curled to the left, and the spattering of freckles on her cheeks. What would she say if she could see me here now? Would she be appalled that I could have even considered breaking the law – becoming what I despise the most – or would she be disappointed to see me contemplating backing out?

Who am I kidding? There's no contemplation: I know I can't go through with it.

Hiring the Private Investigator, securing the house, ordering a weapon … I thought I was so clever, so tough, but I'm just a joke. If I was a real man then she wouldn't have …

A pair of white lights suddenly appear in the

passenger wing mirror. I'm amazed that this stretch of road is so busy at so close to midnight. Why is anyone out rather than at home in bed where it's safe and secure?

Where I should be.

The lights grow in the mirror, so I duck down as low as I can in my seat, pulling the hood of my black sweatshirt up around my neck.

The car slows to a stop two cars back, and idles there. What the hell are they doing? Surely they're not planning to double park?

What if they live nearby and I'm parked in their usual space? All the more reason why I should just go home and stop pretending to be someone I'm not. The last thing I need is for them to come over and leave a note on my car to then spot me hiding behind the wheel. How would I explain what I'm doing here?

The lights are still stationary.

Daring to straighten my neck a little, I glimpse back over my left shoulder to try and get a look out of the back window. The breath catches in my throat.

A police car.

What are they doing here? Do they know what I'm planning? Did Detective Andrews plant some kind of bug the last time he was in this very car? There's no other reason a police car would happen to be here when I'm waiting to pounce.

Surely it isn't too late? I haven't technically committed a crime yet. The intention was there, sure, but I haven't broken any laws yet. If I was to start the engine and drive home now, no crime will have been committed.

My finger once again hovers over the start button.

There is another possibility, of course. Maybe I've allowed my overactive imagination to get the better of me. Why would Andrews plant a bug in my car? And why would he send officers to arrest me before I've committed a crime? There's no logic to it. But that isn't to say some nosey neighbour hasn't spotted me hiding in the car and phoned to report a prowler. Oh wouldn't that be ironic!

If I start my engine and suddenly pull away, won't that draw attention to myself? What if they pull me over and search the car? How will I explain why I've emptied the contents of the boot onto the back seat?

I dare myself to have a second glance through the back window.

The headlights are too bright for me to be able to see inside the vehicle. What are they doing?

A figure in black moves in front of one of the beams, and I instantly duck back down.

Oh God, I hope they didn't see me. I know it's the adrenaline coursing through my veins that has me so on edge. But what if they did see me, and now come over?

I should just start the engine and drive away quickly. If I'm lucky I'll catch them by surprise and they won't be ready to give chase.

I remain hunkered down, waiting for a set of beady eyes to peer in at me along with an intense beam of torchlight. I haven't taken a breath since the figure stepped in front of the headlight, though they must be able to hear my thundering heart echoing off the rear windows.

What if they think I'm armed and are planning to take me down? If Detective Andrews did tip them off, then they're bound to suspect I would bring something with me to deter any resistance. That must be why they've approached without the tell-tale flashing blue lights and siren.

My heart is in my mouth, as I dare myself to sneak one final glance back at the headlights, but as I do I realise they're shrinking. The police car is reversing back the way it came, and is now turning around. I sit further up, keeping most of my head hidden behind the headrest, looking for any sign of whether this is some kind of trick to lull me into a false sense of security. I check my wing mirror for any sign of a secret assault approaching, but there is no sign of the officer who'd exited the car.

Opening my door, I slide out, and stand as tall as I can, but all I catch are the rear lights disappearing around the bend at the end of the road. I finally exhale, and suck in a breath of fresh air, willing my pulse to slow.

Their being here has to have been a sign: a sign that I shouldn't have come, and should just go home. I climb back into the car, my mind made up, and then I see the bracelet in the full glow of the internal light and my heart sinks. This isn't about me. I can see her reflection brushing the curly fringe from her eyes with her hand.

If it wasn't for her, I wouldn't be here now. No, wait, that's wrong.

If it wasn't for what *he* did to her, I wouldn't be here now. She needs me to be strong. She won't be at peace until we know one way or another.

I close the door, and focus my attention on the pavement outside the door, and that's when I see him. In the wing mirror, two long legs walking towards my car, and I immediately know it's the man I've been waiting for by the way he half limps and leans into the walking stick. He claims it's a war injury, when I know it's because he had his knee stamped on when serving his last prison term. Apparently, even criminals don't like sex offenders.

He's moving slowly, but I need to take him by surprise, so I'll wait until he's gone past the front wing before I make my move. Reaching into my door's storage pocket, I feel around until my fingertips brush the hardened plastic, and I slowly tighten my grip around the handle. The PYTHONTEC XB-400 Rechargeable Stun Gun should be all I need to subdue him. At least that's what the website I ordered it from claimed. It definitely fires a crackle of electricity, but I haven't been brave enough to test it on anyone yet. I did consider jolting myself, but feared I'd end up killing myself, so I'll just have to risk it now. The weight of it in my hand brings reassurance; it reminds me of a heavy-duty torch. So even if the electrical current doesn't subdue him, I can always hit him over the head with it. One way or another, he'll be coming with me.

His shadow shuffles slowly past the window, and I shrink myself as low in the seat as I can, my eye line barely visible above the lower rim of the window. If he stops and looks in, he'll see me, but I'm relieved that his attention is elsewhere. I tighten my grip on the stun gun.

I wait until he is just past the bumper before I reach over with my free hand and very carefully pull on the handle. The internal light suddenly fills the front of the cabin because I've forgotten to turn it off. The man with the limp halts and turns, and our eyes meet.

It's now or never.

Heaving the door open, I roll out of the car, driving forwards. The element of surprise is gone, and I need to get to him before he has chance to call for help. It's as if time has been paused, and everything is moving forward one frame at a time. My knees are bent, and my upper body is so low, that my face is barely a foot from the pavement. His eyes widen and his face morphs into a look of terrified panic as he recognises my face, and realises exactly why I would want to charge towards him.

His walking stick slowly begins to rise as he attempts to adopt a defensive position, but something is keeping his left hand from grasping the other end of the stick. I only spot the rope leash around his wrist at the last minute and as I drive the stun gun into roughly where his rib cage should be, my eyes meet the bewildered stare of the beagle puppy.

My velocity and trajectory has caught David by surprise and sends him toppling backwards, instantly releasing both the walking stick and the dog leash as he crashes to the damp pavement. I keep the stun gun where it is, my finger depressed on the switch. It almost feels like the current is flowing through me as he writhes and squirms into a lifeless heap at my feet.

I've never felt so alive.

***

When the idea for tonight first started to form in my head after that chat in Mike's office, I hadn't actually thought about how I would get David into the boot of my old Lexus. Maybe I should have spent more of the last few weeks working on my upper body strength, rather than over analysing whether I would have the courage to go through with it.

The beagle seems quite content to sit and observe as I push David into a sitting position, and then jab my hands under his armpits. I left him on the floor for sixty seconds after I pulled the stun gun away, just to check he was definitely passed out. It was a relief to find he still had a pulse in his neck, as I don't want him dead. At least not yet. That would defeat the object of all of this.

I count to three in my head, then, with a deep breath, I hoist David up, and drag him towards the boot of the Lexus. The heels of his shoes make a horrid scuffing noise along the concrete of the pavement, but maybe it just sounds louder to me because I'm closer to it. Hopefully it isn't loud enough for anyone in the row of semi-detached houses across the road to hear. There are no lights on in the five houses closest to us, so I'm hopeful the residents are all fast asleep by now.

I'm breathless by the time we make it to the rear of the car. I hadn't realised just how heavy he would be, but as he's passed out he's a dead weight. I rest his back against my knees, as I fumble beneath the boot lid for the release button, and then lift the lid. The empty space that stares back at me feels so ominous. I don't want to count how many laws I've already broken in the last three minutes, but locking him in the boot will add a charge of false imprisonment to my rap sheet.

It really is too late to be worried about any of that. Even if I just left him here – allowed him to go free – I know he recognised me, and will probably be only too happy to report my actions to the police.

There's no going back now.

Taking another deep breath, I return my hands to his arm pits and hoist him into a standing position, then bend him over so that his head and upper body are inside the boot. If anyone happened to glance out of their window now, there'd be no way to talk myself out of this compromising position. Thank God the council have yet to repair the street light directly above my head.

With a final heave, I manage to lift David's legs up and swing them into the boot with the rest of him. His body has fallen into the foetal position, but by the time I'm done with him, he'll wish he'd never been born.

Reaching into the boot, I run my hands over the pockets of his coat, extracting a set of house keys, and a packet of chewing gum. I continue my search, removing an old Nokia phone from the pocket of his jeans. I turn the phone over in my hands. I remember having this exact model, must be at least twenty years ago, back before phones were smart and capable of anything more than sending a text message and playing Snake. Odd that he wouldn't have something more modern. I pocket the items.

Lowering the boot lid, I use both hands to push it

shut to make sure the locking mechanism is engaged without slamming it. The beagle stares back at me from its position at the side of the kerb.

'Go on,' I say with quiet aggression.

The pup doesn't move.

I make my way around the car to my door, and try to shoo her again, but she comes over and sits at my feet, staring up at me expectantly.

'No, you need to go. I can't take you with me. You're free of that monster; go and find a new home where you'll be loved as you deserve.'

I open the car door and climb in. She ducks beneath the rim of the door and lies down. The stare she's giving me is breaking my heart. I can't leave her here in the middle of nowhere.

'Fine,' I quietly seethe. 'You can come with us for now, but in the morning I'm taking you to a shelter.'

I reach out and scoop her up. She's heavier than I anticipated, but doesn't resist my handling. I carefully place her on the passenger seat, and loop the seatbelt through the harness she's wearing.

Lydia always wanted a dog, but it wasn't practical for us to have one, what with Meg and I both working fulltime. I did promise her we'd get a family pet one day; another promise I failed to keep.

The beagle licks the back of my hand as I click the belt into the buckle.

'Lydia would have loved you,' I say, placing my hands either side of her face, and kissing the top of her head.

What am I doing? I can't afford to form any kind of emotional bond with someone else's pet. I psych myself back into the cold and hard image I need to maintain to carry out the necessary with David.

I stare up at Lydia's bracelet and pendant once more, and it's all the reassurance I need. This is the right thing to do. It's what we need.

Starting the engine, I'm about to pull out when something catches my attention. A figure is approaching my car, but it's like nothing I've seen before. Am I imagining things, or is that a skeleton?

Chapter 2

Hazel

Wiping the tears from her cheeks, Hazel emerges from the woods, more alone than she's ever felt. It's so dark and quiet that if it wasn't for the distant hum of traffic she could almost believe she'd fallen into a void. The branches of the trees behind her are frozen in time, protecting the secrets held within.

Is this what heartbreak feels like?

It wasn't supposed to be like this. She'd planned everything so carefully. Telling her parents she was going to bed at eleven, knowing it wouldn't be long before they followed her up. And then once she could hear Dad snoring, she'd pushed out her open window until it was wide enough for her to slip through, and land gently onto the roof of the garage, and then onto the soft grass. Coming out without a coat hadn't been smart, but then she'd thought Matt would keep her warm. She twists the end of her long, flowing, golden hair, and wraps it around her neck as a makeshift scarf.

She swipes at her eyes again.

Bloody Matt!

Any other teenage boy surely would have jumped at the chance to have sex with his girlfriend. She'd snuck out for him, had made the clearing in the woods so special with a blanket, tea lights and Bruno Mars playing on her phone's speaker. She'd even stolen a couple of cans of her dad's lager to help with the nerves and inhibitions.

He'd wanted to meet with her. He must have known what her plan was, so why come if he had no intention of stepping up?

She longs to be back at home, rather than trudging through the mud of the field feeling cold, unloved, and ridiculous. She'd only worn the Halloween outfit as she figured the glow in the dark parts would help light her way, but if it wasn't for her phone's light she wouldn't be able to see a thing. At least that means nobody will see her sneaking home and back in through her window.

As soon as she is home she's going to go back on the site and tell Auntie Answers about what had happened in the woods. She always knows how to cheer up Hazel, and it had been her idea for Hazel to invite Matt to the woods in the first place, so she'd want to know what had happened. Maybe she can explain to Hazel why her seduction plan has failed.

At sixteen, Matt is two years older than Hazel, but most people they meet assume they are the same age. Does it matter that she is below the legal age limit to have sex? That is in place to protect children, but Hazel doesn't feel like a child. She is a young woman, has been having periods since she was eleven, and feels ready to take the next step. Matt hadn't duped her; she loves him, and wants him to be her first.

Hurrying across the field, she takes several breaths when she makes it onto Stable Road, surprised at how dark and lifeless the street seems. None of the houses have lights on, and with a couple of the street lights broken by vandals, it is almost as dark as it was on the field.

Matt had offered to walk her home, and she'd told him to go to hell, but was now regretting that decision. When she'd imagined this night earlier in the week, she'd pictured the two of them strolling back arm in arm, both walking a little taller, knowing that what they'd shared could never be taken away.

The sound of a can scuttling across the pavement snaps her head round to where the sound has come from. Is there someone there? She can barely see her own hand in front of her face, but she's watched enough horror movies to know those that wait to see the killer's face are the first to die. Turning in the direction of home she begins walking quickly, but in her terrified head she is sure she can hear footsteps following, and breaks into a jog, before deciding she'll be home quicker if she runs. Sprinting along the road, she now desperately hopes someone in one of the houses might happen to glance out, see her and offer reassurance that the figure chasing her is nothing more than her tired and muddled mind.

A door opens, and she turns to check whether that's in her head too and almost trips over, just about managing to correct her course. She starts to slow as lactic acid burns in her calves and thighs. The breath just won't fill her lungs quickly enough. She's getting ready to look back again and cross the road, when two dead weights suddenly pin her arms at her side. She yelps but is too tired and weak to prevent the figure pushing her towards the open rear doors of the van.

Chapter 3

Joe

The skeleton figure races past my window, and I realise now it must be a teenager wearing a Jack Skellington Halloween costume. The costume wearer has long blonde hair hanging out over the back of the costume, and judging by her thin frame she can't be much older than fourteen or fifteen. Someone so young shouldn't be out at this time of night. God knows where her parents think she is. As a parent, I feel compelled to offer her a lift home, but I'm also aware of two flaws in the plan: firstly, if she has any sense she wouldn't get into this stranger's car; and secondly, probably best not to pick up hitchhikers when I have an unconscious man in the boot.

I open the door get out of my car, hoping to see the girl cross the road and dive into one of the houses, so at least then I'll know she's made it home. She's made it to the second broken street light, but it doesn't look like she's slowing. I'll lose sight of her any minute, but I'm reluctant to follow in case I freak her out.

My mouth drops open as a large figure appears from nowhere and scoops her into his arms. She yelps in panic, and I'm frozen to the spot as he opens the rear doors of the van parked beneath the broken street light and throws her inside.

This can't be happening!

I know in my heart that there's no way that hulking brute is a parent collecting his child to take home. I have to do something.

I charge from my car, breaking into a sprint as the figure climbs into the driver's side of the van. I stop as I'm never going to get to the van before he pulls away, and I won't be able to keep up on foot. I turn and race back to the Lexus, jumping in and starting the engine, pulling my seatbelt around me as I indicate and pull out. I can already see the van's taillights are moving ahead.

I need to stop panicking and think clearly. I should just phone the police and report what I've seen, but my mobile is back at home so if anyone checks my GPS they'll find it where my planned alibi says it should be. Where I should be now.

David's phone, presses against my leg in my trouser pocket as the road bends. Of course, that's the answer!

Pulling out the phone, I don't know his PIN, but I don't need it to make an emergency call. I keep my eyes on the road ahead as my thumb stabs 9 three times. The van is already drifting into the distance, so I increase my speed over the legal thirty limit.

'999 emergency. What service do you require?' the operator's voice says through the phone's loud speaker.

'Police.'

There is a connection tone.

'Thames Valley Police, what's your emergency?'

'Hi, I've just seen a girl being forced into the back of a van by the Stable Road Recreation Park.'

'Are you at the park now?'

'No, I'm following the van. We're still on Stable Road, approaching the junction with Mayberry Road. You need to send someone immediately.'

'Can you tell me the make and model of the van, sir?'

'It's a Ford Transit ... I think it's dark grey in colour.'

'Can you see the licence plate?'

'Hold on.' I press harder on the accelerator and the speedometer creeps up to fifty. I relay the digits as I see them.

'Are you driving while talking to me, sir?'

'You're on hands free,' I lie to avoid a stern ticking off. 'The van's reached the junction. He's turning right onto Mayberry Road. Are officers on their way?'

'Yes, sir, I've dispatched two units to your location. Can you continue to follow if it's safe for you to do so?'

'Sure. I'm about two car lengths behind the van, but it's travelling quite fast.'

'Can I take a few more details from you, sir? Can you tell me your name?'

I don't respond because I don't want her to know who I am, or what I was doing on Stable Road.

'He's approaching the traffic lights' I say, grateful for the distraction. 'They've just turned red.'

'Units are less than two minutes away.'

I pull into the right turn lane so I can pull up beside the van for a better look at the driver. It's difficult to see in as the bright lights around us are reflecting off the window. I don't know how long I have until the lights will turn green, but maybe if I'm quick, I can get to the rear doors and get them open, and save the girl.

Without a second's thought, my seatbelt is off, and I'm around the back of my car. I reach for the van's rear door handle, and prise it up, but it's locked. I stand on the bumper and press my hands around my face to peer in the rear window. The girl stares back at me, and I know I haven't misjudged the situation: there are tears on her cheeks, and terror in her eyes.

Jumping down, I hurry along the side of the van, determined to try the driver's door next, but the lights turn green, and the van pulls off with a screech of tyres. Hurrying back to my car, I dive in, and put the car into drive.

'I looked in the back of the van,' I shout at the operator, 'and the girl looked terrified. I tried to open the door, but it was locked. He pulled away before I could get to him. I'm pursuing again, but he's driving even faster. I think he knows I'm following him.'

He doesn't stop at the next set of traffic lights, careering across the junction, and against my better judgement I follow suit, relieved when I don't get rammed by an oncoming vehicle.

Where the hell are the police?

'He's passed through the next set of lights. We're still on Mayberry Road, approaching the junction with Nutbush Street. Where are your officers?'

'The nearest is on Nutbush Street, waiting to intercept.'

He tears through the red light again, and I'm about to follow suit, when an articulated lorry thunders across the street, and I slam my foot against the brake.

The car jerks and swerves as my knuckles glow white with the strain of keeping the wheel steady. The car stops just short of the yellow hatchings and I pant breathlessly as my brain tries to process how close I just came to crashing.

The beagle whimpers beside me, and I gently stroke her head, about to move on again, when I spot the blue flashing lights of the police car as it turns onto Mayberry Road in pursuit of the van.

'Sir? One of our units is now on Mayberry Road. Please stop your pursuit where it's safe to do so. If you can then wait by your vehicle, one of the officers will come and take your statement. What car do you drive, sir?'

I disconnect the call, and switch off the phone. Removing the back of the device, I extract the battery and slide the SIM out of its slot, leaving both in the tray beneath the stereo. The filter on the lights turns green, and I indicate, pulling onto Nutbush Street. The detour has put me ten minutes behind schedule, but if it means another family avoid the grief Meg and I have suffered, then it was worth it.

***

I'm careful not to drive straight to the house. Although I can't hear David moving about, enough time has passed that he might have regained consciousness and be trying to picture where we're going. That's certainly what I'd be doing if I'd been abducted and forced into a stranger's boot. That's why I've driven via the level crossing, driven around twelve roundabouts that could easily have been avoided and driven down part of the same route three times in different directions. Even the world's greatest mnemonist would be hard pushed to tell police where I've taken him.

Lydia stares back at me in the rear-view mirror. I'd give up all my remaining years just for that reflection to be real once more. To be able to turn around and actually see her grinning back at me as she covers her ears to block out my terrible singing.

The beagle opens its jaws and makes a low whine as she yawns. I pat and stroke her head.

'Past your bedtime, I suppose,' I say warmly, feeling the pangs of fatigue scratching at the sides of my vision, and having to stifle a yawn of my own.

I should have brought a flask of coffee with me. I would stop and pick up a cup from a petrol station, but then my alibi would be blown. At least with mud smeared on my licence plate any traffic cameras I have passed (and I've kept those to an absolute minimum) won't be able to identify my vehicle.

Tonight's escapade was months in planning, and I think I've covered all the bases, but I don't want to be naïve enough to start complimenting myself on a job well done, not when really this is only the beginning of my journey.

We arrive at the private road a little after one thirty, and I'm relieved to see there are no lights on in the properties behind private gates. I still remember the first time I came here, and how in awe I was at the luxurious estates hidden behind the wrought iron gates, wondering how many people the owners had had to tread on to afford such luxury. I would conservatively estimate that the average value of the properties on this road would set a buyer back at least three million pounds each.

There's no way Meg and I could ever afford to live somewhere like this. It's enough of a struggle to afford the mortgage on our three bedroom semi. It always felt like such a squash for the three of us, but now it feels too big. I don't know if there's much point keeping such a big house now. We could easily downsize with little effort, but I don't think either of us is ready to sell all those memories.

David is definitely awake now. I first heard a few quiet shuffles five minutes ago, but he's making no effort to hide the sound of his exploration now. Maybe he can sense that we've nearly arrived at our destination now that I've slowed the speed of our approach.

Pulling up at the gate I lower my window and punch the code into the pad. The LED glows green and the motor whirs to life, separating the gates in the middle wide enough for me to drive through. I raise my window back up as the shock of the early morning air bites at my face.

The tyres crunch the gravel as I follow the route alongside the large expanse of lawn. It was mowed before the owners went overseas, but the blades of grass are already starting to lean over with the weight of the morning frost.

David kicks and punches inside his small cell, but there's no way he'll be able to escape. I riveted a cover over the emergency lid release button, so he won't get out until I'm ready to liberate him. The constant banging is unsettling the puppy, so I continue to tickle her behind her ears to show that I'm no threat to her.

Parking up by the front door of the large house, I reach into my door's storage pocket, and pull out the PYTHONTEC XB-400. I depress the red switch to make sure it doesn't need charging yet, and the two prongs crackle at the end.

The beagle tilts her head at the noise but doesn't venture forward to sniff the device. Patting her head again, I open my door and step out. My body shudders at the ice cold temperature. David must have sensed we've stopped and I've climbed out as he's gone deathly silent again. Maybe he thinks he'll be able to play dead and surprise me when I lift the lid.

It's tempting just to leave him in there for the night, but it's safer to get him inside under the cover of darkness, and I don't want to have to clean the boot if he soils himself inside.

Taking a deep breath, the steam escaping from my mouth is so thick, it temporarily blurs my vision. At least it isn't raining.

My finger finds the boot lid release button, and I press it, taking a step back so I can stick out the stun gun.

The boot lid flies up, and I'm shocked when David leaps out at me, sending us toppling to the hard gravel. His face is in mine, as he opens his mouth and tries to bite at my face. He pins my wrists at the side of my head, and for an alarming moment he has total control. With nothing I can do to shift his weight from my body, I jerk my head forward and my forehead strikes the bridge of his nose with a satisfying crack. He immediately releases my wrists, and rolls off me. I don't delay, rolling over and driving the crackling prongs into the side of his chest. He jolts and shudders, before falling flat on his face.

I sit up and compose myself before stunning him for a second time so that he won't be able to get the better of me as I drag him to the last room he'll ever see.

Chapter 4

14 weeks ago

Joe looked out of his window as he reached the wrought iron gate leading up to the property. Every estate agent worth their salt knew about the country estates on this private road, but Harrington Manor truly was the cream of the crop. Commissioned by the head of the Anglo-Indian Shipping Company in the late nineteenth century, the rest of the estate had built up around it in the years that had followed. The original owner had allegedly built it to house his mistresses under one roof, whilst his wife tended to the children down the road in Portsmouth, from where he would conduct his business affairs.

The current owners – Lady Violet and Sir Percival – had supposedly contacted the estate agency firm and asked for Joe specifically to oversee a let of the property. But as he studied the numbered keypad outside the gate, he was now convinced he was the butt of some elaborate prank. Someone back at the office was probably chuckling to themselves right now. Without even pressing a button on the keypad, the gate sputtered to life and began to slide open. Joe pulled forwards onto the winding gravel drive, leading up and around the mounds of bright green lawn, until the ancient building took over the horizon.

This had to be some kind of mistake. Patrons of manors like this didn't hire nobodies from high street estate agencies to handle their lettings. Whoever did get to handle the sale or let of this place would rake in an enormous fee, and would have manager Mike drooling over the monthly commission figures.

Joe was half-expecting some forgotten grounds person to suddenly appear with a shotgun, demanding he leave, but as he finally stopped at the front of the building, the main door opened and a woman with a perm of silver hair emerged, her tartan jacket matching the skirt that hung down to her shoes. She had to be in her late seventies or early eighties at Joe's best guess, and he now regretted not carrying out a bit of research on the potential clients, rather than focusing on just the building and its history.

Applying the handbrake, Joe opened his door, and offered her his most winning smile. 'Lady Violet? My name's Joe Irons, and I'm –'

'Yes, thank you for coming, Joe,' she said, cutting him off.

She knew who he was. Maybe it wasn't a prank after all.

He quickly closed his door and hurried around the car, thrusting out his hand to be shaken, but then withdrawing it when she made no effort to engage.

Of course she doesn't want to shake your hand, he internally chastised.

'Quite the sight, isn't she?' Lady Violet said stepping back, and turning to take in the manor, which now seemed large enough to block out the sun.

Joe allowed his eyes to scale the perimeter of the

building, trying to picture what the inside would look like, how many bedrooms it held, as well as well-appointed sitting and dining rooms. It was like somewhere he'd expect to see at a National Trust site. The brickwork would benefit from a little TLC, but otherwise, it was a magnificent sight.

'It's a beautiful building,' Joe agreed. 'I heard it was built by the head of the Anglo –'

'I didn't invite you here for a history lesson, Joe,' she interrupted again. 'I'm sorry, but I have neither the time, nor the patience for small talk. I prefer to be direct. I hope that isn't going to be a problem for you?'

He'd been practicing his charm offensive all morning on the off-chance that he wasn't the only letting agent being auditioned for the task. He made a mental effort to rein it in now.

'Tell me what I can do for you, Lady Violet,' he said, fixing her with a straight, but sincere stare.

'My husband and I are due to fly out for safari in a couple of weeks. He thinks it's his idea, but it's been my lifetime ambition to see wild animals in their natural environment, rather than cooped up in a cage. Are you married, Joe?'

Joe's hand instinctively shot to his left hand, and he twirled the ring around his finger. 'Yes.'

She looked wistfully back to the house. 'My mother taught me that the key to a strong marriage is compromise, and so long as you can convince your spouse that your ideas are his, you'll stay on the same page.' She turned back to face him. 'We're to be away for at least three to four months, and I don't want to see my home go to waste. I want you to let it for us, maybe you can find a film company looking to film the next Downton Abbey or something. Some of the rooms will remain locked, as they're for private use, but I'll leave it to your discretion about the rest.

Joe opened his pad, and began scribbling notes of the conversation. 'Is there a price you want to set for the period?'

Her face folded into a scowl. 'Discussing money is so bourgeois. Get us a fair price is all I ask. You're the expert in the market, not me.'

Joe would have to double-check the going rate for a building of this size and history. It was certainly an upgrade on the studio apartment letting he'd just come from.

He didn't want to rock the boat, but one question burned at the forefront of his mind. 'Can I ask why you chose me, Lady Violet?'

She rolled her tongue around the inside of her cheeks as if sucking on a sherbet lemon. 'I heard about what happened to your daughter, Joe, and I thought if anyone deserved a break of good fortune it was you. I am sorry for what you and your wife are going through. I never had children, so I can't begin to imagine the pain you're suffering. I understand if you'd rather not take on this work –'

'No, no, no, no, no,' he cut in, fearing she was about to snatch away her offer of candy. 'I'd be delighted to undertake this letting for you, Lady Violet, and I appreciate your generous gesture.'

She didn't look impressed by the flattery, but nodded sharply. 'Then it's settled. Draw up a plan of prospective clients and costs, and email it over to me.'

She handed him a business card, which he pressed between the pages of his notebook.

The conversation was over as she turned on her heel and headed back to the front door without another word. Joe resisted the urge to punch the air, already picturing his name at the top of the sales leader board within the month.

Chapter 5

Joe

Leaning David's prone body against the brilliant white stone pillar, I unlock the two bolts, and hurry in through the door to the alarm panel in the cupboard under the stairs. I have thirty seconds to input the six digit code before the system automatically notifies the private security firm who will send half a dozen trained operatives to the address. Although Lady Violet emailed the company to let them know I would be looking after the place for her while they're overseas, I don't want to have to explain what I'm doing here in the middle of the night, or why I have an unconscious man in my care.

I press the numbers carefully, and submit the code. The LEDs on the panel flash red twice and then change to green. I breathe a sigh of relief, and close the cupboard door. It's the only momentary respite I allow myself, because I'm still against the clock to get David down to his cell before he wakes and tries to fight me off again. I learned from his last attack that he is stronger than I'd given him credit for.

Maybe I was naive not to think a man in his midsixties would be agile enough to leap at me from the boot of the Lexus. I certainly didn't think he'd be strong enough to keep my wrists pinned in the way that he did, which means keeping the stun gun fully charged and close to hand is a necessity. I suppose the good news for me is that at least I know to watch out for a surprise attack from David. He's played his only card too early.

Rubbing my hands together, I blow warm air into them. The atrium is enormous, with a high ceiling that I can't even see through the darkness. I remember how spectacular the atrium looked when Lady Violet showed me around the building three months ago. Ahead of me, the sprawling staircase in the centre of the space curls up to the half floor, before splitting and bending back around both ways. It looks more like a West End theatre than a home. The wall where the staircase splits is entirely covered by a sheet of mirror glass, which in the daytime reflects an enormous amount of light into the house. But in the darkness it looks more like an abyss, and I can't look at it for long without feeling like I might fall in.

Pushing my hands under David's arms, I hoist him up, wrapping my arms around his middle and clasping my hands together. Carefully placing my feet I move backwards into the house, pulling him over the two steps and across the large hessian doormat. His eyes remain closed but I can see small wisps of breath escaping his nose, so I know he's still alive.

Dragging him to my left, I heave him through the grand sitting room, past the enormous burgundy-stained, leather sofas and the full-size snooker table. This room is the size of my entire downstairs, and I'm sweating by the time we reach the far side, and turn to my right to drag him through to the kitchen at the back of the house. I'm tempted to stop to calm my breathing, but I'm worried that if I stop I won't have the strength to start again.

At least the floor in the kitchen is smoother and his shoes offer less resistance against the fresh sheen of polish. I'll have to check for scuff marks when all this is over, but I don't want to think about any of that yet.

Keeping him elevated with one arm, I raise my knee to take the extra weight, allowing my free arm to reach for the handle of the door to the basement. Opening the door, David murmurs slightly, but his eyes remain closed. I could just push him down the stairs here, but I'm not prepared to deal with broken bones, and I don't like the thought of having to clean his blood off the concrete steps. Returning my second arm to its place beneath his shoulder I nudge the light switch with my elbow. The single bulb hanging from the long cable flickers to life over my head, filling the narrow passage way with light.

With a deep breath I step backwards onto the first step, conscious that I need to get him down the stairs before he wakes, but also aware that one missed step will send the two of us hurtling headfirst to our deaths. I count each of the thirty-two steps as we take them, shuffling my foot around after the last one just to double-check I haven't miscounted. Once confident that I've reached the ground, I quickly haul him through the barred door and lower him to the floor. I removed the bulbs from this room, so the only light is what creeps down the stairs from the bulb at the top. I can just about make out the inflated airbed and blanket I left in one corner, and the ceramic pot and roll of tissue I left in the other.

It took me several hours to fully empty this dungeon, but now it much better resembles a prison. Of course there are no windows this deep below the ground, and I can understand why Lady Violet is so keen to keep her husband's hobby out of sight. I was shocked to find the room decked out with bars until I realised its real purpose, but I don't think I could have asked for a better venue to hold my prisoner.

Stepping out of the cell, I slide the door closed with a satisfying crunch of metal on metal, before locking it with the key. Pulling on the door to make sure it's locked; I'm pleased when it doesn't budge.

Hurrying up the stairs, I cross through the kitchen and sitting room, back out to the car where I collect the beagle and bring her inside. I hadn't anticipated having to find somewhere for a dog to rest, so I remove my hoodie and fold it into a makeshift bed for her, and leave a plastic bowl of water on the floor in the kitchen. Closing all the doors, she should be safe there until I can organise something more permanent. At least I won't have to worry about her messing up any of the other rooms in the property.

Back in the basement, I drop onto the wooden chair I borrowed from the dining room, I let out the sigh I've been holding all night and focus on releasing the tension from my shoulders. My arm brushes against the tripod stand holding the camcorder. It is fully charged and ready to record the moment he starts talking. All I can do now is wait for him to wake, and hope he sees reason. Turning on the portable electric halogen heater, plugged in next to the tripod, I angle it away from the cell door. The orange light it emits casts a tinted shadow onto the wall behind me.

Reaching into my pocket, I pull out the photograph of Lydia. She's wearing the same yellow dress I always picture her in, and the shiny plastic tiara she insisted on wearing all day on her sixth birthday. My eyes well as I remember the silly argument at bedtime when she was adamant she wanted to wear it while she slept. Meg said it wasn't worth falling out over, but I'd insisted that the plastic would dig into her head and make sleeping uncomfortable. I won in the end, but now that I'm replaying that memory I wish I'd caved, rather than being pig-headed and stubborn. Would it really have been that much of a problem to let her go to sleep still believing she was an actual princess? She probably would have taken the tiara off of her own accord eventually.

It's hard to believe it's been almost a year since the photograph was taken. If I'd known it would be the last picture I was going to take of her, I'd have insisted on it being a selfie of the two of us. I'd have put on my biggest smile to show the world just how special she was, and how I was lucky to be able to call myself her dad for six whole years.

I'll never forget the feeling of dread when we looked around in the park and she was gone. I thought Meg was watching her while she thought I was. But there's no way anything should have happened. There were so many other parents there, how did none of them see Lydia wandering off? I know it's my fault for taking my eyes off her, but I was complacent. Things like that don't happen to people like us. At least that's what I used to believe.

I ran up and down those roads, my heart beating faster and slowly splintering as the minutes ticked past, but she was nowhere in sight. It was as if she'd simply disappeared like a rabbit in a magician's hat; only this wasn't entertainment.

I remember Detective Andrews promising he'd do everything within his power to find her, but as the days turned into weeks, I realised he'd said that because it was what I'd needed to hear that first day. He never made a false promise that he'd definitely find her, or that he'd be able to bring her home in one piece. He never lied to me.

Knowing your child is lost out there somewhere and there's nothing you can do about it is the worst feeling in the world. I felt useless. The one job I'd had was to keep her safe and I'd failed. No amount of tears or 'what if' scenarios will ever change that. Lydia was taken because I wasn't watching her. And that's something I will have to live with for the rest of my life.

I knew she was dead the moment Andrews's car pulled up outside our house. I watched from the window as he just sat there in his car for what must have been two minutes before he got out. I think now he must have been psyching himself to break the news. But then our eyes met as he reached the gate, and the message passed silently from his mind to mine.

I ran out of the house, past Andrews, and didn't stop until my lungs burned and my legs would no longer carry me. I didn't want to hear him say the words. It felt like if I didn't hear him say she was dead then it wasn't real; that somehow I'd be able to undo what had happened and bring her back. But life doesn't work like that.

I don't know what David did to my daughter, or how frightened she was when she died, but I'm going to make him pay for what he did. I don't care what it takes, he *will* confess to me, and when I know everything that happened – every single last detail – I will exact my revenge on him.

Chapter 6

Hazel

Who was the man staring in through the window of the van? Was that the man who'd grabbed her and forced her in here? The figure hadn't allowed her to see his face and she'd been unable to turn and look at her abductor, but she'd definitely seen the face at the window. There was something so familiar about the kind eyes, soft cheeks, and slightly receding hairline, but she can't place if or where she's seen it before.

It had looked like he was trying to open the door, but had then disappeared from sight again and then the van had started moving once more. She's already tried opening the door herself, but it is stuck fast. Whoever has taken her, she is his prisoner for now.

It had all happened so fast. One minute she'd been about to cross the road, and the next he had her. She can still feel the weight of his arms around her own. He is strong, and had lifted her like she was a feather. Even if she'd anticipated his attack, she doubts she would have been able to do anything to prevent it.

She'd been so close to home, and she'd tried to scream, but he'd covered her mouth with his warm, gloved hand, and not even she was convinced that anyone would have heard the yelp.

That means nobody knows she's been taken.

This thought makes her gasp and brings fresh, warm tears to sting her eyes. She can imagine her parents calling her down for breakfast in the morning, and then frustrated with her lack of response will climb the stairs and find her bed empty and window ajar. Will they assume she's run away? How many days will be wasted before somebody realises that she's been kidnapped? What if they never do?

Suddenly desperate for escape, she crawls along the cold metal floor as the van bounces and bustles her. Making it to the doors she slams her hands against the windows, hoping to have the strength to break the glass. She balls up her fists and thumps them against the panes, screaming at the top of her lungs on the off-chance that somebody somewhere might just be alert enough to hear her.

He took her phone when he forced her inside the van, otherwise she would be able to phone for help. Still she thunders against the glass, but it remains firm, and her shouting hasn't brought anyone back to help.

She doesn't know how long she's been trapped in the van. Minutes? Less than an hour, surely? She has no clue where they are going, and the view from the rear window only shows her dark road with no sign of any other traffic. There are no street signs telling her where he is taking her.

This is all Matt's fault!

Why did he have to mess up her plan? Why didn't he insist on walking her home, despite how the argument ended? A proper boyfriend would have made sure she got home safely. She will tell him as much when she next sees him.

But what if I never get to see him again?

She pushes that thought from her head. She can't give up hope; that is the road to failure. Closing her eyes she tries to control her breathing. She's seen her mum doing yoga every morning for the last month on her latest fitness kick. Hazel now wishes she'd actually listened when her mum had explained what she was doing, or had agreed when her mum asked if she wanted to join in. Hazel had thought it was just dumb stretching and breathing.

Her face rolls into a ball as she pictures her mum's face, and the warmth of the hugs she always gives. Hazel would give anything to be back home with her now. She should have left them a note about where she was going and who with. She should have told Matt to call her to check she made it home.

The van's brakes whine, and the bustling suddenly stops. Hazel's eyes snap open, and she listens for any movement. The engine is no longer running, and as she strains to hear what's happening or where they might be, she hears the sound of a door being opened. He's coming for her.

She tenses, trying to figure out the best means of attack. The back of the van is so dark, but appears to be bereft of anything she can use as a weapon. She has her costume and that is all. Is there time to take it off and try to fashion some kind of … some kind of what? Her mind is blank.

The front door is slammed shut, and she scrabbles to get as far from the rear doors as possible, curling herself into a ball in the hope that he won't be able to see her when he opens the door, and will maybe think she's escaped. But she realises that plan is destined to fail, when she spots the glow of torch light being shone in through the windows, bathing her in its glow. Whatever he intends to do is about to happen, and there's nothing she can do about it. Her future is now in the hands of fate. She's never felt more terrified her entire life.

Chapter 7

Joe

It's almost three by the time David finally comes around. I was just dozing in the chair when I heard his breathing becoming more rapid, and realised he was close to regaining consciousness. I've switched off the light on the heater, but he should still be able to see me with the little light from the bulb at the top of the stairs.

He winces as he sits up and takes in his surroundings. There is a look of confusion on his face, like that of someone who has just woken from a dream and can't determine whether they're actually awake, or still asleep. I should know, I often wake now, and for the briefest of seconds believe that the last year was just a twisted nightmare brought on by too much cheese before bedtime. It's my favourite time of the day. For the seconds it lasts, it's a joyous feeling, until I find Lydia's room empty, and her bed unslept in. And then it's like someone is driving a pitch fork straight into my heart over and over again. I don't cry in front of Meg anymore, as I don't want to be the cause of further anxiety and emotional instability for her. She urges me to open up to her, but if I let her in, I don't think she'd survive.

David takes in the bars, and then his eyes fall on me.

'W-Where am I? Who are you?'

The still frame of his recognition when I leapt at him from my car plays before my eyes. He knows exactly who I am, even though we've never met. When Lydia was still missing, mine and Meg's faces were plastered all over the television news, social media and newspapers. Whatever his motivation, I know he's lying right now.

'You know who I am,' I say evenly. There's no reason for me to shout.

'I-I've never seen you before in my life.'

I can't say I'm surprised that this is the approach he's decided to adopt. In fairness, if I'd been electrocuted, forced into a car, and then thrown into a prison cell beneath the ground, I'd probably claim temporary amnesia as well.

'I'm Lydia's father.'

He's trying to pretend that that means nothing to him, but I was studying his shoulders, and he definitely tensed, even if it was momentary.

'I-I don't know anyone called Lydia. I don't know you.'

I stand and move towards the bars, which instantly has him scurrying to the back wall of the cell.

'Please don't treat me like an idiot, David. I know you know who I am, and I imagine you've probably already worked out why I've brought you here tonight.'

'You must have made a mistake. I really don't know who you are.'

I don't know which of us is least convinced by the lie.

I fix him with a sincere stare. 'Listen, I'm going to

level with you, David: this can go one of two ways. Either you tell me what I want to know, or I'll stop pretending to be so calm and unleash a fury the likes of this world has not seen.'

I deliberately keep my tone passive, so he'll understand just how much thought and planning has gone into this.

'Nobody knows where you are, David. I can keep you here for as long as I want, and there's really nothing you can do to stop me. If you choose not to cooperate though, it won't work out well for you. I've got the ability to be reasonable, and treat you like a human being, even though you don't deserve it. You see, David, you may claim not to know who I am, but I know all about you. I know that you were the one who abducted my little girl and smothered her six months ago.'

'Th-That wasn't me. I told that detective that I had nothing to do with what happened to that girl. That's why I'm not facing charges.'

At least he's stopped lying about not knowing about our situation.

I press my face against the bars so I'm as close as I can be to him without opening the cell door.

'Funny because that's not what he told me. He said you were released because they didn't have enough evidence to keep you in. You're still their prime suspect, and I don't know about you, but in my experience, the police are rarely wrong about these things. Detective Andrews knows what you did, David, he just can't prove it yet. But that's where you and I are going to help him.'

I move away from the bars, and switch on the camcorder, zooming in until David's face fills the screen.

'You're going to tell me exactly what you did to my daughter, and I'm going to record it, and pass the video to the police.'

'You must be crazy if you think I'm going to confess to something I didn't do.'

'I'm not crazy, David. In fact, if anything I've never been clearer in my own mind. I have one objective here, and I will take as long as necessary to achieve that.'

'You're wasting your time. I didn't kill your daughter, and while you're threatening me here, the real killer is still out there getting away with it.'

I start the recording. 'Tell me why you chose to take Lydia.'

'You're out of your fucking mind. I didn't take your daughter.'

'What was it about her that appealed to you?'

'You're not listening to me: I never met your daughter. I don't know what you're talking about.'

'Where did you keep her? The police said there was no trace of her DNA at your house, so presumably you have somewhere you kept her alive at first?'

He doesn't answer this time, folding his arms like a petulant school child.

'They said you kept her alive for at least a week before you smothered her. Why wait so long if it was always your intention to kill her?'

He stands and walks towards the cell door, forcing me to zoom back to keep him in the frame.

'You know there's no point in all of this. I'm not going to tell you what you want to hear, and even if I did, it would be inadmissible in court as it was obtained through oppression.'

I'm not surprised that someone as conniving as David is fully briefed on section 67 of the Police and Criminal Evidence Act, which deals with admissibility of confessions.

'Oppression includes torture, inhuman or degrading treatment, and the use or threat of violence,' I quote to show him I've versed myself in the statute too. 'But I haven't used violence or threatened you, David. Not yet anyway.'

He narrows his eyes. 'So, what's the point in all of this?'

It's a fair question.

I step out from behind the camera, but leave it running. 'Because my wife deserves to know the truth. Do you know how hard it is for her? Knowing that some bastard abducted and killed her little girl, but not being able to hold anyone accountable for the heartache she feels every second of every day. Do you want to know why I plan to use any means necessary to get you to admit what you did? Because she deserves the truth and she won't be able to move on without it. Neither of us can.'

He takes a tentative step forwards, his voice dripping with concern. 'Listen to me, I am sorry that you lost your daughter, but as I said before, I wasn't involved. Hurting me isn't going to change that. Now, as far as I'm concerned, there's been no harm done so far. Yes you assaulted me and forced me into your boot, but do you know what? I'm prepared to overlook that. I can see you're grieving and I can't imagine how difficult it must have been for you over these last few months, particularly as the police have failed to catch the real culprit. If you let me out now, I'm prepared to let bygones be bygones. What do you say?'

I stamp my foot in the direction of the cell and he shudders.

'That's very big of you,' I half-laugh, 'but the thing is, David, I know you took her and killed her, because I know all about you.'

I sit back on the old wooden chair, and reach down to the brown envelope on the floor, opening it and pulling out the stapled sheets of paper Edie supplied to me.

'David Edward Calderwood. Born 3rd December 1957 to Callum and Genevieve Calderwood. You grew up in Stockport until your dad was arrested for beating your mother to death in June 1970. How old were you then, David? Twelve, right? There isn't a picture of you, but the report prepared by social services back then mentions bodily injuries. How old were you when your dad first started abusing you?'

He closes his eyes, and turns his head. 'Stop it.'

'You know it's amazing what you can find online these days for the right fee. I hired a Private Investigator to dig up everything she could about you. I never expected her to find out that you were sent to a boy's home after your dad was sent to prison, or that you were physically abused there too. I mean, most of what happened to you was redacted from the pages, but from what I'm led to believe, you didn't have a very happy upbringing.'

It's interesting to see how appalled he is at mention of his own misfortune.

'Hardly surprising to see that you were first arrested in 1974 aged sixteen,' I continue. 'It says you were found on your knees in the cubicle of a public toilet in SoHo in London.'

'Just stop it. Just because I haven't lived a saintly life, it doesn't mean I had any–'

'You were arrested again in 1984,' I interject, 'when you were caught in a police undercover operation dealing with child pornography. You were sentenced to three years in prison that time. And then there's nothing until 2006 when you were arrested again following the abduction and brutal rape of a fourteen year-old girl. That's when they made you sign the Sex Offenders Register wasn't it?'

'None of this has anything to do with what happened to your daughter.'

'It was while serving a ten-year custodial sentence that your kneecap was broken wasn't it? I mean, that's why you walk with a limp and rely on that stick isn't it?'

'You're not telling me anything I don't already know. My father was a drunk and yeah he hit me when he'd been on a bender, and the night my mum tried to stop him, he killed her. It was her own fault for not stopping him sooner. The boy's home was brutal, and if your amateur psychology course has suggested that the abuse I suffered there had a direct influence on my own twisted sexual desires, then yes, you're probably right. I've been receiving counselling for those darker parts of my psychopathy, and will continue to do so. Yes, my name is on the Sex Offenders Register, but so are hundreds of others. I served my time and am free to get on with the rest of my life. You look at me like you're better than me, Joe, but ask yourself something: who is the one breaking the law right now?'

I spring from my chair and have my arm through the bars, grabbing him by the lapel of his jacket before he's moved a muscle. I push the photograph of Lydia against the bars so he can't see anything but her innocent face.

'I swear to God, you're going to tell me what you did to my little girl, you dirty, fucking paedophile, or I'm going to make you beg me to kill you.'

Chapter 8

12 weeks ago

'Joe?' Meg's anxious voice called from the kitchen.

He paused the video on the laptop screen just as Lydia was giggling excitedly at the arrival of her birthday cake. They'd wanted her sixth birthday to be one she remembered, and she looked like a princess in her bright yellow dress, with elasticated fairy wings strapped around her shoulders.

Standing, Joe carefully placed the laptop on the coffee table, and found his wife at the kitchen window, the net curtain raised, and staring out at a car parked at the kerbside.

'That's Detective Andrews's car isn't it?'

Joe studied the royal blue Mondeo with the dent in the front wing, and the key scratch along the rear door. The figure behind the misted window was slightly hunched over, but there was no mistaking the outline.

'Yeah, it is,' Joe acknowledged. 'Did he call to say he was coming over today?'

She continued to look out of the window but Joe caught the shake of her head in his periphery.

When the Family Liaison Officer was staying with them, back when Lydia was only a missing child, rather a murder victim, all visits from the Senior Investigating Officer would have been announced in advance. That had all changed the day Lydia's body was recovered on the banks of the River Kennet. It had been Joe's decision for the FLO to be reassigned, fed up of the constant scrutiny of their actions and words. It had felt as though they'd remained the prime suspects in what had been done to Lydia, but how could a parent ever be suspected of such a crime?

'I wonder what he wants,' Meg said rhetorically.

The last they'd heard, a suspect had been arrested and interviewed, and Andrews had high hopes of pressing charges, so he could only hope that this visit was to confirm the identity and charging of that person.

Joe left the kitchen, and opened the front door, standing there until Andrews eventually climbed out of his car and headed up the path to meet him.

'Hi Joe, do you mind if I come in? There's something I need to discuss with you and Meg, and it would be better done inside.'

Joe allowed him through, and Meg joined them in the living room, but Joe chose to sit in the single armchair, rather than beside her on the sofa. Andrews sat between them, and exhaled a loud sigh, before fixing them each with a look of sympathy.

'There's no easy way to say this, so I'm just going to come out with it, and then explain why the decision was reached. We've had to release our prime suspect.'

Joe sat there speechless, blinking as he tried to process the news, unconvinced he could have heard correctly. 'You what?' he said.

Andrews met his stare with a look of disappointment. 'The suspect – a registered sex offender by the name of David Calderwood – was seen in the area of the park at the time of the abduction, and given his history and proximity to both the park and the Kennet, he felt like a solid choice. However, he denies the allegation, and a search of his property has located no traces of Lydia's DNA.'

'Maybe he cleaned the place,' Joe interjected. 'There are videos on the internet teaching lay people what chemical cocktails to use to remove even blood traces; it's what you hire crime scene cleaners to undertake after a murder, right? How do you know he didn't clean his place up?'

Andrews ran a hand through what little hair still remained on top of his head. 'Those cleaning companies are highly-trained specialists, Joe. For an ordinary person to manage to remove every trace of DNA would take a great deal of time and luck. There was no sign that your daughter ever stepped foot inside his house. Believe me when I say I wish it was different.'

Joe struggled to contain his frustration. 'But you said he was at the park when she disappeared, right? What was he doing there?'

'He was walking his dog. We have footage of him at a corner shop minutes later on his own, with no sign of Lydia.'

'That doesn't mean he didn't take her though,' Joe snapped, squeezing his fists involuntarily. 'Maybe he has a partner of some kind, and maybe they took her somewhere that wasn't his house.'

Andrews raised his palms in a calming gesture. 'I promise you we've explored every avenue as far as Calderwood is concerned, and we don't have enough to pursue anything against him at this time.'

'Tell me where he lives, and I'll get a confession out of him,' Joe growled.

'Please, Joe,' Meg interjected, sensing his blood was up, 'let's just listen to what Detective Andrews has to tell us.' She offered Andrews a look of encouragement. 'I'm sorry, I'm sure you can understand that isn't the news we were hoping for.'

Andrews forced himself to smile at them both. 'Of course, and I know that there's probably a part of you that wishes you could get David Calderwood in a room and physically hurt him, but I have to advise you both that such acts won't bring us any closer to the truth.'

Joe didn't want to admit what was running through his mind in that moment, and resented how placid and understanding Meg was appearing to be. Couldn't she see that Andrews and his team had failed them? Where was her anger and urge for revenge?

'I know it's hard for you to hear,' Andrews continued, keeping his gaze on Joe for longer than was necessary, 'but now is the time when you need to trust us more than ever. Lydia's killer is still out there, and so is the evidence of their guilt. We will give everything to find it and bring the right person to justice.'

Joe couldn't tell who Andrews was trying to convince more: them or himself. Either way, Joe wasn't buying it.

'Do you have any further questions?' Andrews asked, slapping his hands against his thighs, ready to leave.

Meg looked at her husband, her eyes willing him to

shout or scream, or whatever he needed to do just to open up, but he turned his back and stared out into the garden instead.

'I'll show you out,' Meg said, standing and walking Andrews out of the room, closing the door to as she went.

Joe ground his teeth as he pictured Lydia's killer out in the open, breathing the same air when all he deserved was to be strung up. It was all Joe could do not to march after the detective and demand the suspect's address. He remained rooted to the spot, waiting to hear the front door being closed so he could have it out with Meg about why she wasn't angrier with their lot. Seconds passed, and still the front door didn't close.

Moving to the ajar lounge door, Joe heard the low grumble of voices as he was about to pull it open, and stopped himself when he heard Meg's voice.

'You don't need to worry about Joe. He isn't the confrontational type.'

'I wish I shared your confidence,' Andrews muttered back dismissively.

'He's just frustrated with this whole situation; he feeds off his anger, rather than opening up to me so we can deal with it together. I hate seeing him beating himself up like this, but nothing I say or do seems to get through to him.'

'Will you do me a favour, Meg? If you sense that he … that he might try and take things into his own hands, will you let me know? With everything the two of you have already been through, the last thing you need is for Joe to get into trouble too.'

'As I said, Detective Andrews, it isn't in Joe's character to be confrontational. Take last year for example. It was our wedding anniversary and we went out for dinner, just the two of us. And even though we'd reserved a table, we were forced to wait for twenty minutes before we were seated, and then when our food was brought out, mine was cold in the middle, and to top off the *perfect* evening, the waiter then spilled wine on my dress. Joe was as annoyed as me, but he refused to say anything to the waiter. Instead, he wrote a carefully-worded email to the restaurant manager the following morning. My husband is heartbroken, but he isn't reckless. He's better than that.'

Joe moved away from the door, resenting his wife's doubts about his capabilities. She might not believe it, but he was certain that if he ever had the opportunity to meet his daughter's killer, he wouldn't hesitate to act.

Chapter 9

Joe

Having checked on the beagle who is still snoring peacefully atop my hoodie, I return to the basement. The camcorder is switched off to preserve the battery, but he's had long enough to come to terms that this is happening, and that I won't stop until I get answers from him.

I lift the glass of water to my lips so he can definitely see the smile on my face as I take a long drink of it. He wets his lips with his tongue, but doesn't ask me for a drink. He's starting to realise that his only way out of here is going to be compliance; if he wants a drink he's going to have to give up something in return.

I take another sip, and then move behind the camera, switching it on, and adjusting the zoom until the screen is focused on him lying against the bars. He looks defeated, but it's only been a few hours, and I'm not prepared to underestimate him again. I've learned from the mistake at the boot.

Twenty minutes of asking him why he killed my daughter over and over, and even I'm bored of the question. It's time for a fresh approach. His response to the question has remained: "I had nothing to do with her death," but is he emphasising the "I"? Is it possible he has a partner in all of this? Someone who …?

My eyes widen as I picture the white-haired brute forcing the girl into the van, and the look of terror on her face as I looked in through the rear doors. Connections fire in my head, and I need to watch my body language as David's eyes are on me the whole time. It can't be a coincidence that he just happened to be walking his dog at the recreation ground where the girl was snatched.

I start the recording, but step away from the camera, projecting a calm exterior.

'Who's your partner?'

He doesn't move a muscle, but continues to stare.

'I'm not naïve enough to assume that you didn't have help with abducting and holding Lydia. There was no trace of her DNA inside your house, which means she must have been held elsewhere; who's to say she wasn't at your partner's house. Is that what I should call him, the guy who helps you? I mean, he's not your *boyfriend* is he?'

He straightens his body against the bars, and I'm now convinced the sad look in his eyes and the apparent lack of strength in his upper body is just an act to lull me into a false sense of security.

'No,' I conclude, 'he looks too butch to be your type. I saw him tonight, you know. Right after I'd put you in the boot. I saw him snatch the girl just up the road from us.'

His right eyelid opens and shuts twice in quick succession. He's doing everything he can not to give anything away, and yet his body is betraying him.

'Big bloke,' I continue, picturing the man I saw.

'Looked like a rugby player. You know, like a prop in the front line of the scrum. Enormous arms, much bigger than yours. Certainly not the sort of bloke someone like you would go for. Too strong and manly. You'd definitely be the receiver in *that* relationship.'

'I ...' he croaks, 'I know what you're trying to do, and it won't work. You can't rile me into confessing something that isn't true.'

'Is that what you think I'm doing? I thought we were just chatting.'

He licks his lips again, but I won't offer the water. For him to fully submit, he needs to instigate the request, and then I will negotiate for what I want.

'He was surprisingly agile on his feet for one so well built. I gave the police his description when I reported the abduction. It was lucky I was there, otherwise the two of you would be ruining another family's lives right now.'

'I ... I don't know what you're talking about.'

'Sure you do, David. Your partner who drives the van.' I recite the registration number I gave to the police. 'Ring any bells now? Tell me; is that the same van you used when you snatched my Lydia?'

'There was no van. I don't know what you're talking about.'

'Wait a second,' I say clicking my fingers, 'is that the way the two of you took my daughter? Just snatched her up like she was a feather and threw her in the back of that van before anyone saw?'

The question is genuine. This whole time Detective Andrews was focused on pinning Lydia's murder on just David, but what if there is someone else involved.

It would certainly answer some of the evidential anomalies.

He pushes his body away from the bars, but remains on the floor. 'How many times do I have to repeat the same thing? I DID NOT KILL YOUR DAUGHTER!'

I watch him without allowing his shouting to affect my demeanour. I suppose if he's told himself that lie often enough, at some point the brain might begin to believe it as truth. I walk slowly to the bars and crouch down so that our eyes are level.

'Who's the guy with the van?' I whisper to counter his aggression.

He reaches out a hand, a lame attempt at an olive branch. 'Listen to me,' he pleads, 'whoever this man is, I don't know him, but maybe you're right about one thing. Maybe he *was* the person who snatched your daughter. Come on, think about it: you didn't know me before any of this, did you? I didn't know you until the police showed me your picture and explained why I'd been arrested. I'll tell you what I told him: it's a case of mistaken identity. You've got the wrong man.'

He pushes himself onto his knees, as if seeking my absolution.

'I understand why you would assume it's me. I did some bad things once, and I was seen in the area where she disappeared, but I'm not that man anymore. I'm horrified by what that monster has put you through, and I can absolutely understand why you'd be so angry, and want to inflict that rage on me, but I swear on my life that you have the wrong man.'

I remain where I am despite the temptation to grab his lapels and slam his head into the bars over and over.

'Think about it, Joe. You've *seen* this man abduct a girl tonight, so you *know* he's capable of it. Just take a moment to consider what I'm saying. You're wasting time holding me here when it should be him that you're interrogating. You could let me go, and we'll say no more about it, and then you could go in search of him. You don't have to worry about me: I won't say anything to the police or anyone else about this place.'

For a second he almost had me convinced that maybe I have made a mistake, but then he slipped up.

'Why should I believe you?' I whisper back through the bars.

'Because I'm telling the truth,' he says meekly.

'Like you were when we first arrived here, and you claimed to have no idea who I was? You've just admitted the police showed you my picture when you were arrested and explained exactly who I was. You've already lied to me, so why on earth do you think I'd BELIEVE YOU NOW?'

The roar frightens even me, and he scurries back across the cage, fearing my retaliation. I stand and move back to the camera.

'Tell me what you did to her.'

He doesn't respond.

'Tell me where you took her.'

He's silent.

My watch beeps: the alarm I set to give me enough time to get home before Meg wakes. I have to go.

I switch off the heater, and am about to stop the recording when he scuttles back towards the bars.

'Where are you going? You're not going to leave me here?'

I fix him with a hard stare. 'Are you going to confess to what you did?'

'I can't confess to something I didn't do.'

'Then I'm out of here.'

I step out from behind the camera.

'No, wait, don't go without leaving me something to drink. Please? I'm thirsty.'

I lift what's left in the glass and down the water.

'What are you going to do with me?'

'I'm going to do everything you did to my daughter, so you'll know exactly how scared she was at the end.'

I stop the recording and switch off the camcorder. I should have just enough time to get home and grab a few hours' sleep before coming back and doing what is necessary. Hopefully when he sees how serious I am, he'll start talking.

I head up the stairs, but the moment I open the door back into the kitchen, the beagle comes pacing over, whimpering. I can see the bowl of water I left for her is empty, and there's every chance she needs to go out.

'What are you doing to my dog?' David shouts from the basement, but I ignore his question, put on the beagle's leash and take her out through the back door and into the garden. It's pitch black out here, and so I make encouraging noises, keeping tight hold of the leash. She sits down at my feet, and looks up at me expectantly. There's a fine mist in the air that does a great job of waking me up.

'Come on, wee-wees,' I say, and am relieved when a moment later she trots off to a ceramic plant pot and squats beside it.

I don't have anything resembling a treat, and crouch

down, rubbing her ears playfully. 'Good girl, well done.'

Leading her back into the kitchen, I place her back on my hoodie and tell her to sit.

'Don't hurt my dog,' David calls up. 'Please, she's just a puppy.'

I'm not monster enough to harm an animal in exchange for a confession, but put a pin in the idea of using the threat of violence to stimulate conversation later.

'She's diabetic,' he shouts up next.

I move to the doorway. 'What?'

'She's diabetic. She has to have a shot of insulin before her meals.'

I had an aunt who was diabetic and dependent on needles, and something in the back of my head validates that dogs can develop the illness, but I don't know why I would know that. He could be lying, but I can't see why he would, as it doesn't serve any obvious purpose.

'Where is her insulin?' I shout down to him.

'In the fridge at my house. Listen, if you're planning on taking her to a shelter, you need to tell them that she's diabetic and is intolerant to wheat. She has a special dietary food supplement each meal time.'

I look down at the beagle, willing her to tell me that he's just trying to complicate my life, but she just stares back at me.

'What's the name of this food?'

'I can't remember the name … I get it from the vet. Look, there's a ton of it at my place. Please, don't hurt my dog.'

'I'm not going to hurt the dog,' I shout back at him. Maybe I'll be able to use the prospect of him seeing the dog again as a carrot to encourage him to open up later. Either way, I can't take her home with me now; Meg will ask too many questions, such as how did a beagle appear at our house when I've been asleep in bed all night?

'Where is the food at your house?'

'In the kitchen. There should be a big bag of it just inside the utility room, and the insulin is in the fridge.'

I don't want to debate it with him anymore, and close the door to the basement. I crouch down and rub the dog's ears again.

'You be a good girl for me, okay, and I'll be back in a bit to give you some breakfast.'

She rolls onto her back, and thrusts her paws into the air. My hand moves down to her belly, and I give it a playful rub.

How can someone so brutal and vicious be capable of showing affection to a dog? I can't let my doubts about David cloud my mind; that's probably exactly what he's hoping to do.

Chapter 10

Hazel

Hazel remains perfectly still as the beam of his torch continues to move about inside the frame of the window. He's toying with her. She keeps her head buried, her breath held so tight that she's worried she might suffocate if she doesn't allow fresh air into her lungs soon.

Just go away and leave me alone, she wills.

The beam finally fades, and she allows herself a tiny breath of new air. Maybe he thinks she's fallen asleep and will just leave her there until morning. It's freezing cold in the back of the van; no insulation from the late autumnal chill outside, but somehow that feels safer than being close to him.

Metal scrapes against metal, as he inserts the key in the door's lock, and eases the handle until even colder air washes in to the back of the van, causing Hazel to gasp at the bitterness. The suspension whines as he presses one heavy boot onto the step and climbs in; the floor shifting under his immense weight.

Still Hazel doesn't move, now too scared to even look. But she hears everything: the excitement in his heavy breathing; the squeak of his leather gloves as he slowly rubs them together; the clump as he takes another step towards her.

'I know you're awake,' he says, his voice deeper than even her dad's, but with no discernible accent. 'I can see you shaking, but you don't need to be scared of me ... not if you do as I tell you.'

She doesn't believe him, but if she wants to survive long enough to escape, she's going to have to at least pretend to play along.

Steadying her breathing, she silently summons every ounce of courage, and pushes herself up and into a sitting position. The figure crouched before her is wearing a large dark brown leather jacket, a black polo neck sweater and black jeans. But where his face should be are just two small eye holes cut out of the black balaclava. She can see strands of white hair poking out of the bottom at the side of his neck. He is even larger than she'd realised, and she senses that the bulging arms beneath the jacket are packed with muscle rather than fat. That said, muscle is heavier than fat, and she thinks that if she could just get past him and out of the van door, she could outrun him, not that she has any idea which direction she would head.

He must see her looking at the door, because he turns and quickly pulls it shut.

'What do you want from me?' she asks through chattering teeth.

'Who was the guy in the car?'

The question throws her. What guy? What car?

She shakes her head in confusion. 'I don't know what you're talking about.'

She's sure she can see his black eyes narrow through the holes in his mask. 'Don't lie to me. He followed us after I put you in here. Was he your boyfriend? Your dad? Who?'

'I swear I don't know what you mean. I was on my way home.'

'I thought it was coincidence to start with, but he kept coming, even when I tried to shake him off. And then at the lights he pulled up next to me and I saw him doing something round the back of the van.'

The man at the window, she suddenly recalls. *So he isn't the man I'm speaking to now.*

She doesn't know why but this thought brings her fresh hope. If someone witnessed her being taken, then maybe he's reported it to the police, and there are people looking for her right now.

'I don't know who that was,' she admits, even though there is still that familiarity she can't place.

Is he one of the parents of someone at school? No that's not it.

'Don't lie to me,' he growls.

But if he did see her being taken and chased after the van, where is he now?

'I'm not lying, I swear I don't know who that is. What did you do to him?'

He tilts his head. 'Nothing. He stopped following when the cop cars turned up, but I lost them at the petrol station.'

There were police cars? Does that mean the stranger did call the police? Are they searching for us now? Is that why he's stopped the van?

She gulps at this last thought.

The figure in black extends his arm and splays his gloved fingers in her direction. 'Give me your hand.'

She doesn't move. Somehow the back of the van

feels safer than being outside in the middle of nowhere with him. If he's going to kill her, she thinks he's less likely to do it in his van where he could leave DNA traces of her. She presses her hand down and touches the floor, rubbing her hand to ensure she leaves some kind of skin particles that he might not be able to wash off.

'Give me your hand, Hazel.'

She freezes at mention of her name. She'd assumed her abduction was a random act of chance; bad luck on her part. But if he knows her name, then what else does he know about her? Was he waiting at the park all along? How could he have known she would be there?

He loses patience and shuffles forward, grabbing her wrist, and even though she digs the heels of her trainers into the floor, he doesn't struggle to drag her out. His breath is acrid, and added to the body spray he's overused, it makes for a rancid cocktail. He wraps one of his arms around her middle and lifts her, tucking her there as if carrying a ladder and proceeds to move across squelchy mud. The smell of it fills her nostrils, and although she wriggles and kicks, she does little to slow his movement towards wherever he's planning to take her.

Closing her eyes she silently prays that death will take her before he does.

Chapter 11

Joe

I don't have time for this. Meg could wake at any second, realise I'm not in bed – haven't even been to bed – and suddenly my alibi for tonight will be up in smoke. I should just drive home, get in to bed and ensure my safety. But then I see the beagle's face in my mind's eye, and suffer a guilt overload at the prospect of inducing a diabetic coma or severe complications, and I keep heading in the same direction.

I don't take as convoluted a route from the old house as I did on the way. I'm still careful to avoid as many traffic cameras as possible, but I don't worry about doubling back or going out of my way to reach my destination. The Lexus has plenty of fuel, and there is a spare canister of unleaded in the footwell beneath my seat that I will use to top up. I can't afford to make a pit stop and have both the car and my face on a forecourt recording with the date and time when I should be tucked up in bed.

That means only using the heater in the Lexus sporadically. To be honest, it's probably safer keeping the temperature cool to keep me from falling asleep behind the wheel. The adrenaline has definitely worn off, and the ache now gripping my muscles won't be fixed by anything but rest. The thought of getting home and crashing in bed is almost enough to convince me to think twice about this detour for pet food and medication, but I'm only five minutes away, and it will save me having to come back later.

I hope a bit of solitude for a few hours will help shape David's frame of mind too. I sense he doesn't yet see me as a threat, and that is something that needs to change quickly if he's to tell me what I want to know. I have left a box of apparatus on the counter in the kitchen – items that might be used to encourage compliance – but if I am to use them, I know it will take me to a place from which there will be no return. When I first conceived this plan in Mike's office, I told myself that I was prepared to cross that line for the right reasons, but now that I'm faced with the prospect, I can't deny I'm nervous. Wait, scratch that, I'm terrified.

I used a VPN to research modern methods of torture, and have deleted my internet history as best I can but what I found has left a permanent mark on my psyche. I googled fingernail extraction, and the videos have now changed the way I look at pliers. One administrator described the act as more painful than amputation of a limb. And having heard the banshee-like wailing exhibited by the victim in the video, I can believe it. Am I really going to be able to tighten David's wrist in a vice while I individually pull out his thumb and fingernails? My hope is that the mere threat will be enough, but he could already have given me what I want to know and he's chosen not to. Even though he knows his recorded confession won't be enough to convict in court, he's shown he's prepared to play the long game and hope for the chance of release without caving. For the second time tonight, I have to accept that I've underestimated him.

The digital display in the dashboard tells me that it will be nearly five by the time I make it back home. None of my neighbours should be waking to head to work until five at the earliest – Mel across the road walks her prize-winning Shih Tzu before showering and leaving for the tube station at five to six – but I don't want to risk them hearing my engine and happening to glance out of the window. The cover of darkness has been my friend so far, and I'm hopeful for one more favour before I give in to my fatigue.

I'm less than a mile from David's house when I spot the first police car drive past in the opposite direction. I avert my eyes, and keep my head bent low just in case, but there's no way they should have been able to see in through the windscreen. I put it down to coincidence that there happens to be police so close to where I'm headed. When I spot the second car behind me, and then see a third parked up with its blue lights flashing further ahead, I know there is trouble brewing. Indicating, I pull into a Pay and Display car park on my left and park up, quickly reaching for an A-Z, holding it up to the window as the police car from behind continues on its way. I watch it as it joins the second, and also switches on the roof-mounted blue lights.

I remain where I am, willing the ball of anxiety in my stomach not to grow any larger.

They appear to be turning other cars away from the road, and as I look beyond them, I can already see a stream of small lights marching across the fields beyond them. The rotary blades of a helicopter pass by overhead and a spotlight shines on the fervent activity.

They're looking for someone.

It's probably not me, I tell myself. There's no way they can know that I was the one who abducted David, nor that I would be stupid enough to return to what is practically the scene of the crime. I'm certain nobody saw me subdue and bundle him into the boot. And even if they did, there's no way they could have identified the figures as David and I. At best they would have seen a hooded figure attack an old man with a dog. There's nothing to connect me to whatever is unfurling less than a mile from his home. And what are the chances anyone even knows that David is missing yet, let alone has reported it to the police? It's been less than four hours since I spotted him approaching my car.

No, I just need to breathe, and quell the anxiety. There probably is an alternative route I could take to David's house right now, but I'm too tired to think straight, and I can't run the risk of having to explain to a police officer why I happen to be driving around so early in the morning when I have no reason to be here.

Putting the car into first gear, I exit the car park, but turn right, and away from the sitting police cars. My eyes stay glued to the rear-view mirror, checking I'm not being followed, but the road is virtually empty, and they're soon out of sight, and the tension in my shoulders begins to alleviate.

It's four fifty-five by the time I kill the engine on my driveway. A check of the windows of the houses within viewing distance confirms nobody is yet up, and I'm hugely relieved. Unlocking the front door, I tiptoe into the house, careful to reclose the curtain over the front door behind me. Sliding off my joggers and t-shirt, I fold and carry both upstairs, only stopping to use the toilet, and taking a long drink from the cold tap. Pushing open the bedroom door, a gap in the curtains bathes the bed in the glow of the street light outside the window. Meg is still fast asleep, the remnants of the packet that had held her migraine medication still atop her bedside table.

Quiet as a mouse, I pull the duvet back and slide in beside her. She stirs and murmurs something, but I don't respond, rolling onto my side so I'm facing her. Her face is wrinkle-free, all the pain and tension of the last few months gone as sleep allows her to forget what's happened. I envy her: I wish my dreams would let me forget.

I'd argue she looks more beautiful in this moment than when we first met twelve years ago. Back then, her brown hair was cut much shorter, hanging just below her chin, and straightened to within an inch of its life. She was out celebrating graduation, and I was in the club for a friend's birthday. I still remember Cupid's arrow striking as our eyes met across the bar, and I knew in that moment I'd never see anyone as beautiful for as long as I lived. When she smiled coquettishly at me it was like someone had sucker punched me in the chest.

I was twenty-four, and Meg a year younger. I was working in a call centre, but planned to progress within the company, until redundancy forced me to reassess my options. By that point I'd plucked up the courage to speak to Meg, and although she was planning to return home to Leeds, we committed to taking it in turns to travel to see each other at weekends. Within six months she'd moved back to Reading and into my poky one bedroom flat. We were happy; it felt like nothing would ever be able to tear us apart.

But no amount of marriage guidance can prepare you for the shock of losing a child. There is no quick-win or Band-Aid to repair that kind of damage. She has told me not to blame myself; that we were both culpable of complacency, but I should have made sure she was watching Lydia when I went to buy the ice creams. It would have taken seconds to have called her name and tell her my intentions. Frustratingly, it wasn't even that warm that day, and to this day I don't know what made me go and queue up. I'm not even that big a fan of ice cream.

Lydia was though. She always used to insist I ask the man in the van to put a second chocolate Flake in the soft ice cream for her. In the end, I'd buy a second ice cream for myself, and just transfer my chocolate Flake to her cone. The sacrifice was worth it to see the look of pure excitement and joy on her little face.

If only I hadn't ...

No, I won't do that to myself now. I'm too exhausted, and it doesn't serve any benefit.

'Hindsight is the devil's cruellest trick,' my mum used to say.

She also used to remind me that there is no point in having regrets, but how can I not regret everything that happened that day?

Meg's brow furrows ever so slightly, and her lips twitch as if she's trying to say something, but I think she must be dreaming. I wish there was more I could do for her. She gave up work after her compassionate leave ended, and I haven't once complained that I'm now the sole breadwinner. How can I? If I hadn't gone to that bloody ice cream van, we wouldn't have lost our little girl.

I want to hold Meg to me and tell her that I will do everything in my power to make things better, but I'm terrified she'll reject me. She says we should seek help to save our marriage, but if we really love each other, then we shouldn't need the advice of a stranger to keep us together. Even though we share a bed, it's more out of convenience than anything else. The woman that I've been in love with for twelve years is now virtually a stranger.

And it is this troubling thought that stays with me as sleep takes hold.

Chapter 12

10 weeks ago

From the outside, the house looked like any regular two bedroom end-of-terrace. A small lawn at the front made it look welcoming, but aside from the colour of the door, it looked no different to the half dozen properties beside it. Joe wasn't even certain this was the right place. He'd found it against the name 'D. Calderwood' in the phone directory, but there could have been more than one in the Reading area.

Joe switched off his engine, but kept the stereo on, needing background noise to serve as a distraction, and uncertain how long he'd have to wait to get a look at the man suspected of taking everything from him. He'd all but convinced himself that if he could just look into the eyes of David Calderwood, he'd be able to see whether the police had been right to focus their investigation on him.

A battered blue Mondeo pulled up and parked directly in front of Joe blocking the drive of the immediate property. Joe silently cursed as he recognised the registration number, and was about to start the engine of his old Lexus and drive off when Detective Andrews rolled out and walked towards him.

Too late, Joe thought.

Andrews opened the passenger door and climbed in,

rubbing his hands together, and blowing into them.

'What are you doing here, Joe?'

'Detective, fancy meeting you here of all places. Maybe you can help me out. I am supposed to be collecting something from a house on Maybush Avenue, but I'm lost and not sure what road I'm on.'

Andrews smirked, sensing the deceit. 'Well, Maybush Avenue is about four roads over in that direction.' He pointed out of his window. 'But I imagine you – one of the city's leading estate agents – would probably know that. In fact, I'd go so far as to say you probably know the inner workings of these roads as well as a police officer and taxi driver would. Why don't you try again?'

'I-I don't know what you mean,' Joe stuttered. 'I only pulled over so I could check my phone for directions.'

Andrews's face remained passive, his thin lips pulled in a tight grimace. Turning his head slightly, he nodded through the windscreen at the house across the road. Joe looked over and saw a man in his mid-sixties stepping out of the property he'd been scrutinising moments earlier.

'That's him, is it?' Joe commented, no longer seeing the point in keeping up the pretence.

'You know I can't possibly answer that question, Joe, but then I get the impression you probably already know the answer.'

Joe had tried searching for Calderwood's name online, and had found a photograph of him from a newspaper article about his trial in 2006. He looked much younger then, and Joe had seen a darkness behind his eyes that he couldn't see in the older man with the shopping bag tucked under his arm now.

'Nobody would blame you for wanting revenge. Losing a child is hard enough to deal with, without the knowledge that someone chose to take her from you. I get it, Joe. The things I've witnessed down the years … Well, let's just say they'd break even the toughest person's heart. But there's a huge difference between yearning for justice and acting out revenge. And vengeance doesn't bring the relief you might think it would. I've seen people in similar situations to your own who've chosen to take the law into their own hands, and they've admitted to me afterwards that it didn't heal the pain.'

Joe wasn't really listening, keeping his glare on Calderwood as he moved quietly down the street, without an obvious care in the world.

Andrews rested a cold hand on Joe's knee. 'Listen, Joe, the best thing that you and Meg can do right now is be there for one another. Don't let your mind taunt you with images of what you might do if you ever came face-to-face with Lydia's killer. That path leads to nothing but misery. Let me and my team handle things, and with a bit of luck, we'll find you the closure you so desperately want.'

'It isn't fair,' Joe shouted, as the first tears splashed against his cheeks. 'He took everything from us, and yet he's free to move around as if he's done nothing wrong.'

'There's no proof that David Calderwood had anything to do with Lydia being taken, other than circumstance. I cannot say hand-on-heart that he is the person we're searching for.'

Joe's head snapped round. 'But you feel it in your bones, right? There must have been a reason you first started to look into his movements on that day; why you were prepared to arrest and interview him.'

Andrews sighed. 'It doesn't matter what I think, all that matters is what I can *prove*.' He sighed again. 'Don't do this to yourself, Joe. Go home and be with your wife. She's grieving too, and needs you more than ever.'

Joe could feel every tear falling from his eyes, as if they were icicles stabbing at his pupils. 'Lydia was the glue holding us together. Without her … we're just one gust from toppling.'

'I don't agree, Joe. I appreciate something like this would put a strain on even the strongest of relationships, but you and Meg need to be there for one another. Your marriage is worth saving, surely?'

Joe didn't know whether Meg really wanted their marriage saved, but didn't admit as much. She'd mentioned guidance counselling again last night when he'd got home from work, but he hated the thought of conveying his feelings to some stranger with a notepad being paid to scrutinise their every word and action. Maybe he'd just be better off offering Meg the divorce that would allow her to move on with her own life.

'You need each other right now,' Andrews continued, 'and you need to allow yourselves to love again. I know you're hurting, but you could try something small to begin with. I don't want to sound condescending, but there's a lot to be said for the restorative effects of adopting a pet.'

Joe wanted to slap the detective across the face for comparing his love for his beautiful angel to that of a pet owner, but kept his hands still. Maybe Meg was right about his fear of confrontation.

Andrews reached for the door handle, ready to leave. 'I must warn you though, Joe, if I catch you here again, stalking David Calderwood, I'll have no choice but to arrest you. Am I making myself clear?'

Joe nodded, but turned his gaze back on the house, unable to ignore the prospect of the secrets it held within.

Chapter 13

Joe

I jar awake with a start. I'm still lying on my side, but the space where Meg was is now empty, and when I run my hand beneath the duvet and the sheet is no longer warm. Sitting up I check the clock on her bedside table and see it's just gone eight. I'm surprised at how alert I feel after barely three hours sleep. Meg's running gear is no longer in its usual pile beside the bed, so I assume that's where she's gone.

A memory stirs in the back of my head: the sound of Lydia laughing in her bedroom. At first I almost believe the sound is real, and my brain is caught in that moment between sleep and reality where the lines blur. If Lydia is alive, then her disappearance, murder and funeral were all just part of a vivid and painfully intense nightmare. Deep down my brain is already undermining the sliver of hope that none of this is real, but then I remember the fear of sitting in my car and waiting for David to arrive. I can still feel the jarring of the stun gun in my hand as I drove it into his chest. I stay still for a moment longer, willing Lydia's laughter to prove my conscience wrong, but there is no sound over that of my breathing.

Stretching my arms over my head, I inhale deeply. I probably should try and catch a few more minutes sleep, but I'm conscious that I still need to collect the dog food and insulin from David's house before I return to Harrington Manor.

The sound of the helicopter's propellers fire somewhere in the back of my mind, and I switch on the television, and wait for the local news to start. It's a relief, but not a total surprise when there is no mention of David's abduction, and I have to hope that the early morning police activity near his house was totally unrelated. Maybe they were chasing down a joyrider or raiding a drugs den. Nothing would surprise me these days. Whatever happened to the majority people obediently obeying the law rather than looking out for number one? I'm sure I don't remember there being such a deluge of crime and antisocial behaviour when I was growing up. Or maybe my parents just sheltered me from it better.

Heading to the bathroom, I check my phone for notifications in case Meg has sent me a message about where she's gone today, but there is nothing other than a Facebook notification that someone I barely remember is celebrating their birthday today. I didn't celebrate my last birthday, and although Meg bought me a card and present, I asked her to return them. Birthdays should be joyous occasions, but there hasn't been any of those since we lost Lydia.

Showering, I dress in last night's joggers and t-shirt, and grab a fresh hoodie from the wardrobe. I head downstairs and have just switched on the cold kettle when there's a knock at the door. Assuming Meg has forgotten her keys I don't even check who's there before I open it to a man I vaguely recognise in a bomber jacket and faded jeans. He must be about my age, maybe a year or two older. He looks confused by my presence here.

'Hi, can I help you with something?' I ask when he doesn't speak.

'Um, is Meg in?'

He's scouse, and the more I study his face, it seems all the more familiar, but I can't place where I've met him before. His head is shaved razor-thin, and his small ears are elf-like. He's wearing horn-rimmed spectacles, which aren't in keeping with the more informal attire. They're covered by a thin mist of rain, enlarging the pupils behind the lenses.

'Uh, no she's not. Sorry. Think she went out for a run. Sorry, do I know you?'

'I work with Meg. Neil Cooper.'

He holds out his hand, and I shake it. Suddenly I'm transported back to Meg's office Christmas party, which must have been nearly three years ago. I can picture him in an all-black tuxedo and a bright red cummerbund and matching bow tie.

'Of course it is. Hi, Neil, sorry I'm awful remembering names.'

'No worries. Listen, do you know when she's going to be back? I need to talk to her about something urgently.'

'I don't, I'm sorry,' I say, embarrassed.

Even if I knew where my wife had gone running, I have no idea when she left or when she's planning to return. She doesn't know I've taken today off work, and might be waiting for me to leave so there isn't an awkward exchange when she returns.

'If you leave me your number, I can ask her to call you. Or if you want me to pass on a message, I'm happy to do so.'

He looks out to his left and then right and I can see he is jiggling his left leg slightly, almost as if he needs to use the toilet. When he looks back at me, there is hurt behind his glasses.

'Is everything okay?' I ask. 'Do you want to come in and wait for her?'

He hesitates, before stepping in. I lead him through the hallway and into the kitchen. The jiggling of his leg is worse, and has now extended to his arms.

'Neil, seriously are you okay?'

He pulls off his glasses as tears splash against his cheeks. 'Listen, I'm sorry, I shouldn't have come here, it's just ... I haven't seen our Hazel since last night, and I know that she and Meg are close, and I ...' he lowers his head and sobs replace his voice.

I place my hands on his upper arms and direct him onto one of the stools at the breakfast bar. He doesn't resist, but squeezes the bridge of his nose in an effort to quell his tears. The kettle boils behind me, and I fill two mugs with steaming water, dropping two heaped teaspoons of coffee in each. I slide one of the mugs across the breakfast bar to him, adding the sugar pot and carton of milk beside them. I drink from my mug without additions. I pass him the roll of paper towel from beside the sink. He tears off a strip, wipes his eyes, and blows his nose.

'Thanks. Sorry.'

'Hey, don't worry about it,' I reply, uncertain how to react to this virtual stranger breaking down in front of me. This is definitely Meg's area of strength, rather than mine.

He opens the sugar bowl, and drops in three spoons before stirring and leaving it on the counter.

'The thing is …' He breaks off as fresh tears threaten to fall. He takes an audible deep breath. 'Did our Hazel stay here last night?'

I'm assuming Hazel must be his wife or partner, and if Meg and she are as close as he suggests, I suppose it's an obvious leap to think she might have stayed here after an argument. Of course, I can't say for certain that she didn't stay here last night, and I'll need to check with Meg before amending my alibi for David's disappearance if this Hazel did turn up after I'd gone out.

'Not that I'm aware of,' I say loosely.

Meg hasn't mentioned a friendship with anyone called Hazel, but then it's been awhile since I asked her about her life, and I've been too preoccupied with setting things up for David's captivity to have noticed a new face about.

He fixes me with a sincere stare. 'Please, pal, she isn't in any trouble, it's just me and her mam are worried sick. We've had the police out looking for her all night.'

The blue flashing lights and helicopter's propellers instantly fill my mind. But, there's something else scratching at the back of my conscience that's more worrying.

'Sorry, who exactly is Hazel?'

'Listen, I know I shouldn't be asking, what with what you both went through, but we just want her home. She went to bed at eleven, but we think she must have snuck out to meet her boyfriend Matt.'

I don't want to ask, but I feel compelled to.

'Do you have a picture of her?'

He pulls a phone from his pocket, unlocks the screen, swipes at it, and then turns the phone so I can see it.

I swallow my breath. The golden hair, tiny upturned nose, and smattering of freckles: it's the girl from the back of the Transit van. My legs almost go from beneath me, and it's only the fact that I'm leaning on the breakfast bar that stops me crashing to the floor.

'Do you recognise her?'

I look him in the eye, and I so desperately want to tell him that yes I do recognise her; that I saw a large man with white hair grab her around the waist and force her into his van before driving off. But instead, I keep staring at the image.

'H-How does Meg know your daughter? You said they were close?'

He looks temporarily confused. 'The private tuition that Meg's been giving her … She's been helping Hazel study for her Maths and French exams.'

There's a part of me that wants to correct him and say that he must have mixed up my wife with someone else, but for all I know, maybe Meg has started offering private tuition. I know she used to do it in her spare time when she was at university. Money has been tight since she gave up work, so maybe the tuition is her way of contributing, or maybe it's just a distraction from the deafening silence of the empty house.

'Oh, of course,' I say instead. 'And you said you last

saw her when sorry?'

'She headed up to bed around eleven, but when her mam went to check on her at one, she wasn't in her room.' He wipes at his eyes with the crumpled tissue. 'Between the two of us, it isn't the first time she's snuck out to meet her boyfriend. He reckons he didn't see her last night, but I don't know where else she would go. I wanted to ask Meg whether Hazel had said anything to her yesterday after school.'

I don't understand how she can still be missing if the police intercepted the van. They definitely joined the chase on Mayberry Road. Not only did the 999 operator tell me as much, but I saw it with my own eyes. They had a description of the van and licence plate number, so how could they have lost him?

'You said you've spoken to the police?' I clarify, taking a sip of my coffee so he won't see the guilty look hanging from my eyes.

'Yeah, they've had men out searching near our place all night, but there's no sign.'

'And sorry to state the obvious, but have you tried phoning her?'

'Of course, it was the first thing we did, but her phone's switched off. The police are checking to see where it was last used, but they haven't updated us yet.'

The blood drains from my face. It's happening again: another innocent life in danger because I didn't stop it. Why didn't I just crash in to the van, or done something to run him off the road? Maybe if I'd kept pursuing him, rather than worrying about my own selfish motives, I'd have seen what the police missed.

He must have turned off somewhere after he went through the red lights at that junction. How long after was it before I saw the police car? Seconds only surely. Could a van that size really disappear so quickly?

'Hey listen, pal, I'm sorry, I shouldn't be putting any of this on you after what you two have been through with your little one. You're pale as a sheet. I'm sorry I should have thought this would bring up old emotions.'

He takes a large gulp of his coffee.

'Listen, can you just ask Meg to give us a call when you see her?'

I nod, unable to speak, and watch helplessly as he shows himself out. I can't just sit idly by and watch another family go through what Meg and I have suffered; not when I know the location of someone who may be able to confirm exactly where that brute took Hazel.

Unlocking my phone I open the CCTV app, and look down at David in his cell. I didn't tell him about the tiny camera I stuck in the corner of the ceiling so I can keep an eye on him when I'm not there. He's standing, pressed up against his cell, shouting for help, but there's nobody will be able to hear him in that sound-proofed cell.

Standing, I feel his house keys in my pocket dig into my leg. If he does know anything about the abduction of Hazel, then there may be clues as to the identity of his partner at his house. I'll have to be careful getting in there, but I need to move quickly if I'm to help the police track her before it's too late.

Chapter 14

Hazel

She didn't notice the tiny red LED when he dragged her in here, but she hasn't been able to take her eyes off it since waking. She's still inside the sleeping bag, her head on the flat pillow, and she hasn't moved since opening her eyes, but she's watching, listening.

She'd been too scared to really take in the surroundings as he'd carried her from the van, across the field, which had seemed to drag on forever, then in through some door, across a floor that stank of cattle and then into wherever she is now. He'd told her she'd find a mattress and sleeping bag, and that he'd return with food and drink later.

The room had been as dark as the van, and whilst not as cold, she'd quickly located the sleeping bag and climbed in. She'd cried herself to sleep thinking about her mum and dad and the inevitable moment they'd discover her empty room. She silently willed them not to give up on her.

She must have fallen asleep at some point under the weight of pure exhaustion. But now she is very much awake, and trying to gather as much information as possible. The red LED suggests some kind of surveillance or camera. What it doesn't tell her is where it's connected to, or if he's watching her all the time. He hasn't been back to the room since leaving her here, which is probably more of a blessing than she realises in this moment.

She needs to explore the space around her, but she's conscious that he could now be watching, and she doesn't want to give him reason to suspect that she will do whatever she can to escape. She hasn't spent much time in his company, but the voice of reason in her head is screaming loudly that she doesn't want to get on the wrong side of him. His strength alone tells her she is no physical match to him; throw in the fact that he knows her name, which probably means he's been planning this for a while; and then the fact that he knew exactly where she was going to be last night. It all adds up to someone she should be very afraid of.

So she lies still under the sleeping bag, gathering her thoughts and trying to figure out her next move.

When she was searching for the mattress, the floor felt cold, but not hard like concrete. She wants to guess it is wooden, and that's good because wood can be broken with enough force or scratching. Mud would have been ideal so she could find a means of digging her way out, but there's no point pining over something she doesn't have.

The room doesn't appear quite so dark now that her eyes have adjusted, and she can just about make out the wall to her right. It's maybe a metre or so from the edge of the single mattress, and as she allows her gaze to slowly climb the wall she can see there is a small gap where the wall meets the roof, and it is through this gap that she can now see an orange glow which is providing the light for her to see. She wants to say it's sunlight, but it could just as easily be artificial from a power source just outside the room.

There is a window about two thirds up the wall, but this appears to have been boarded up with something from the outside. Keeping her head perfectly still she now allows her eyes to follow the edge of the roof, and sees that the uneven join with the top of the wall is as a result of what the roof is made of. It appears to be corrugated metal of some kind, which strikes her as odd, though not necessarily of any benefit. The range of her gaze stops just before she reaches the outline of the door through which he carried her. She has no choice but to move her head a fraction, hoping he isn't watching.

The doorway is too far away to see properly, but she estimates it's maybe three metres or so from the foot of the mattress. She can't see a handle or how it is secured, and that will require further investigation when she feels safe enough to do so. And then she comes back to the red LED. She can't see a camera from where she is lying, but she can't think what else it would be. But unless he has a team of people stationed by the screen it is linked to, at some point he will have to stop watching to sleep. For all she knows, he is asleep right now, and although the camera is recording her every move, it's possible he won't be able to watch everything she does in here.

There's only one way for her to be sure. With a deep breath, she rolls onto her back and then onto her left side. The wall here doesn't look any different to the one on the other side, but it's much closer to the mattress, allowing her to gently push her hand out of the sleeping bag and touch it. Her fingers tremble as she stretches them and brushes against the cool wooden veneer.

The wooden floor, the veneer on the walls, and the corrugated roof, it reminds her of the temporary classroom she spent Year-7 in when her junior school was having building renovations undertaken. The porta cabin had been erected in the playground, away from the main body of the building, and although her current confines are much smaller, she is almost certain that's the type of place he's holding her in. Now she just needs to figure out how that information helps her.

She holds her breath as she hears a gentle rumbling growing from outside the cabin. At first she thinks it is thunder, but it is drumming out too regular a beat to be anything but heavy footsteps. She rolls back onto her back and stares at the door, knowing he's coming. It's only as a bolt is slid back and the door is thrust open that she notices that the red LED has disappeared.

Chapter 15

Joe

Finding a route back to Riverside Terrace that avoids coming into contact with the police isn't easy, and I end up driving out of my way just to come back to David's road. It's less than a mile from last night's abduction site. Although P.I. Edie Sinclair had told me Stable Road was part of David's regular dog walking routine – which is why I was waiting for him there in the first place – I can't help thinking that he must have known what the other man had planned.

I did a lot of research into child abductions in the UK in the days after Lydia was taken, trying to get my head around what would drive someone to snatch a vulnerable child. I was shocked to learn that children go missing *all* the time. As in, not just in creepy books and films, but like *all the time*. Last year alone there were more than 200,000 reported incidents of missing children to the UK police. For context that more than 500 reported cases *every* day. It was only diving deeper that I learned the vast majority of those incidents were resolved swiftly within 24-hrs, and that some of those children were reported missing on more than one occasion over the course of the year. But that still leaves 2% of cases that aren't resolved within a day, and often remain unresolved.

Lydia is no longer considered a missing child because her remains were discovered, but her murder remains unresolved, and until a person is charged the cause of her abduction also remains unresolved. And I know in the darkest recesses of my soul that David knows a lot more than he's told me and the police so far. The fact that he just happened to be walking his puppy along the same road where Hazel was snatched is too coincidental. For all I know, he only bought the beagle to give him an excuse to be so close to the recreation ground so late at night. And that's another thing: who walks their puppy at one in the morning? Maybe you'd take them around the block for one last wee, but you wouldn't walk more than a mile in the darkness for that.

There is too much about David's story that doesn't add up.

I'm parked across the road from his small three-bed end-of-terrace now. I wonder if his neighbours realise that they have a registered sex offender living next door to them. The police will generally notify the head teachers of any nearby schools, but aside from that only doctors and those running youth-organised activities would be told. The chances are that they don't know. I can only assume that Hazel's parents didn't know David would be walking his dog so close to their home on the night she snuck out.

David's picture and name were not reported to the press at the time of his arrest four months ago, so his neighbours probably don't even realise that he is considered the prime suspect in my daughter's abduction and murder. It's so tempting to send them all a notification letter, but I've been warned I could face prosecution if I do. Detective Andrews has said such an act could also give David's solicitor grounds for appeal at court if he was convicted. For now, I'm supposed to sit tight and keep my mouth shut.

I never was very good at doing that.

Pulling the hood of my top up, I push open the door of the Lexus, and slide out. I can't see anyone on the street, but I know I'm taking a risk in coming here in broad daylight, particularly once the police become aware that David is missing. Locking the car, I break into an easy jog along the road, up one side, crossing at the end, and then jogging back on the side of the house, turning off when I reach the public alleyway that I know will take me around to the back of his house. Keeping my head bent, I sprint along the alley until I reach the end, and then checking in both directions, I shimmy up and over the fence, landing on my feet in a squat position. I glance up at the neighbour's windows, and am relieved to see the curtains are still drawn.

David's garden is longer than I expected with a shed immediately to my left, and beyond it a plastic pond base dug into the ground. There's no water in the pond base, and the weeds around it look trampled on. The lawn that stretches the length of the garden is overgrown, but I'm careful to follow the flagstones at the side of the lawn, keeping my head bent below the level of the neighbour's fence.

My pulse is racing as I make it to the back door, and press myself against it. I've always been a law abiding citizen, but I'm about to break the law for the second day running. I catch sight of Lydia in her yellow party dress staring into the empty pond. She looks back at me and smiles.

'This is all for you,' I whisper and blow her a kiss, before turning my back, and trying David's keys until one slots in and the patio door opens. Stepping through I'm immediately hit by the overpowering scent of lemon and honey, forcing me back outside for a breath of fresh air, before I head back in. There are two air fresheners standing on opposite sides of the room, one beside the television on its stand, and the other on a bookcase. In front of the bookcase is a hard plastic dog's bed and cushion, and an open packet of puppy training pads.

The lounge is big enough for a small two-seater sofa beside the narrow bookcase, and a cupboard unit beside the television stand, a small aquarium atop it. Grabbing the pot of fish food I study the directions, before dropping a pinch of orange nuggets into the top. That ought to keep them from going hungry for a couple of days. I'll have to think of a different plan if David's absence is prolonged.

I open the doors of the cupboard unit, but all it contains are board games and puzzles. Moving through to the kitchen, I scan the pages of the calendar hanging on the back of the door, but there are no entries save for a dental appointment scheduled for tomorrow morning, which he is not going to make. I need to find clues to the identity of the white-haired man who grabbed Hazel, but it isn't easy in a house you're unfamiliar with. I open each of the drawers and cupboards in the kitchen, looking for any kind of address book, or exchange of letters, or anything that will tie David to being at the recreation park last night, aside from my testimony.

The kitchen draws a frustrating blank, and so I head upstairs, careful to keep my hands tucked inside the cuffs of my hoodie. There are four rooms up here: a bathroom which takes under a minute to check, a master bedroom, an office and a spare. I freeze when I look in the spare room, and see that the single bed is made up with a pink floral duvet set and pillow. There are a bunch of lilies in a vase on the dressing table. But what is most alarming are the bars on the window of the rear-facing bedroom. The room isn't dissimilar to Lydia's untouched room at home, and I dry retch, until I compose myself long enough to leave. Andrews was adamant that no traces of Lydia's DNA were discovered in this house, but this room definitely suggests David was planning for someone to stay here. Maybe he was planning to hold Hazel here before his partner panicked and drove off.

I force myself to leave the room, but make a note to question David about it later. The main bedroom is also a bust, but in the office, I'm relieved when I find a computer at a desk in front of the window. It is an old-fashioned desktop and monitor, and as I press the on button with a cuff-covered thumb, I'm disappointed to see a password is required to access it. Opening the top drawer of the desk, I rifle through the contents of pens, paperclips, and Post-It notes, but there isn't anything obvious to reveal his password. The second drawer down is an equal bust, just filled with an open pad of paper. Flipping through the pages, there are no imprints of previously written notes, but as I'm about to return the pad, I do spot the little brown, leather-bound book still in the drawer. Snatching it up, I return the notepad and close the drawer. There must be at least fifty names, addresses, and telephone numbers listed, which will take some studying, but at least it's a start.

Quickly scouring the rest of the room, there is nothing further of interest, so I head back down to the kitchen to collect the dog food and insulin. I've just moved to the fridge by the sink when there's a knock at the door. Looking out the front-facing kitchen window, I can see a woman in a smart dress suit on the doorstep. She must be early thirties, her chestnut hair tied in a bun, and her face red with rage. I drop to the linoleum just as she starts turning to look in my direction.

I don't think she saw me, but I'm not going to be able to move until I know she's gone away. There's no reason to assume she's a detective; she could just be a neighbour on her way to work; or a Jehovah's Witness for all I know.

She knocks at the door again.

My back is pressed against the cupboard beneath the sink, and my knees are tucked in tight to my chest, so she shouldn't be able to see me even if she comes closer and presses her face to the glass. But I can't risk crawling across the floor in case she does happen to look in. No matter who she is or what she's doing here, if she spots a hooded figure trying to sneak away, her first call will be to the police, and then I'll be in no end of trouble.

Thirty seconds pass with my breathing as quiet and shallow as I can manage. At some point I'm going to have to risk a second glance to check she's gone, and I certainly can't remain here all day. I shouldn't have come. I should have just tied the beagle to the fence at the animal shelter last night on the way to the house, and then I wouldn't be in this mess.

The letter box rattles, and then I'm sure I hear the sound of heels stomping on stone. I hold my breath for a count of sixty, and then slide my bottom along the floor to the doorframe, and dare myself to peer out and around to the front door. A folded piece of paper is now sitting on the internal doormat, presumably having been posted through the letter box. There's no shadow being cast through the frosted glass panels in the PVC door, and so I sneak over and scan the note. The relief causes me to chuckle. It seems David's next door neighbour isn't happy that he keeps allowing his new puppy to defecate on her front lawn, and she's threatening to report him if it continues.

Sliding back into the kitchen on my hands and knees, I feel more confident as I approach the sink, and slowly bring myself up until my eyes are in line with the bottom of the windowpane. The woman in the dress suit is gone, but I can't rest on my laurels: I need to get the food and insulin and get back to my car.

Crossing quickly to the fridge, I open the door and peer in. It is fairly well-stocked with shop bought cheeses, meats, pickles, yoghurts, and pies. In fact, it reminds me of a delicatessen counter. To think what he did to my daughter, but rather than serving his punishment behind bars, he's living like a king. Let's see how well he does on basic bread and water rations for a few days.

I move the packages and jars about, but there is no sign of insulin anywhere. He definitely said it was in the fridge. I double-check, but there is no insulin anywhere, and I can't imagine he would have simply run out. A feeling of dread passes over my back. Closing the fridge door, I move into the small utility space, and locate a single bag of dried puppy food. It's a supermarket brand, and makes no mention of the wheat intolerance that he told me about. I circuit the kitchen once more looking for syringes or other dog food varieties but come up empty handed. He lied to me *again*.

I shouldn't be surprised: he's been lying since day one. And if he's willing to risk pissing me off by lying about something as silly as dog food, then I'm even more certain he's lying about everything else. It's time to crank up the pressure, as he's not going to give me a straight answer without fear.

Shoving the bag of dog food under my arm, I return to the back door, lock it and hurry to the end of the garden. The upstairs curtains of the neighbour's house are now open, but I can't hang around here any longer. Scaling the fence, I keep my head bent as I jog back along the alleyway turning left at the end, and then left again. I hurry across the road to the Lexus, dropping the bag of dog food on the back seat beside the spare tyre and jack that I've yet to return to the boot. I get into the driver's seat and am just about to start the engine when I see the familiar sight of Detective Andrews's Mondeo pulling up directly in front of me.

It's too late to drive away and pretend I wasn't here. Maybe the neighbour did see me at the kitchen window after all, and called the police. I shouldn't be here. He's warned me before. I've not known fear like this since the moment Lydia disappeared in the park.

Chapter 16

9 weeks ago

'Have you got the keys for that studio above the tandoori in the precinct, Joe?'

Joe quickly minimised what he'd been reading and turned to face Esther who was moving towards him. 'You mean the place on Duckhams Road?'

The bifocals around her neck rattled against her necklace as she nodded.

'Think I put them back in the safe,' Joe said, pointing at the locked key safe on the wall at the back of the room, obscured from view by a pillar.

She continued moving towards his small desk. 'No, I checked in there. I wondered if you'd forgotten to put them away.'

She stopped and leaned over him, rummaging her outstretched hands amongst the mess, and looking under papers until she found what she was looking for.

'Here we are,' she cooed, snatching up a key-ring, much to Joe's surprise.

'I'd have sworn I put those away,' he said, his forehead creasing with hurt.

Esther stepped back and frowned with empathy. 'It's an easy mistake to make. Don't worry about it. I won't mention it to Mike.'

Joe nodded his thanks as she made her way back to

her desk. Turning back to face his monitor, he surveyed the bombsite of his desk, but couldn't be bothered to tidy it, instead clicking back on the internet window he'd been reading when Esther had come over. He checked left and right that nobody could see what was on the screen, and proceeded to study the article about David Calderwood. This one was a small piece by a local news office, but pretty much appeared to be a lift and shift of what he'd already read a dozen times on a number of other sites. Where was the originality and unique spin he craved?

'Joe, can I have a word?' Mike shouted from the back of the room.

Joe looked across to check whether Esther had already broken her promise, but she was busy with a client and nowhere near Mike, so this had to be something else. Locking his screen, Joe stood, and took another look at the mess before him, choosing to follow Mike into his office.

'Close the door will you?' Mike asked, sitting in the enormous faux leather chair behind the much larger desk.

Joe obliged, and then sunk into one of the much smaller plastic chairs across from his manager.

'How are you coping?' Mike asked with barely a trace of sincerity. Compassion was not a strength.

'You know ...' Joe replied; the standard response he'd adopted for such questions, allowing the enquirer to internalise without bogging them down with unwanted detail.

Mike was actually looking straight at him, which wasn't his usual approach, and Joe felt compelled to look away.

'The whole team can see how much you're struggling ... Have you thought about taking a few days off to get your head together?'

Joe's eyes filled from nowhere, and as he tried to compose himself his shoulders began rocking of their own accord, and when he opened his mouth to speak, the only sound that escaped was the sob strangling his words. Joe's gaze turned to meet his manager's sudden discomfort.

Mike instinctively reached for the packet of tissues he kept in his locked bottom drawer for emergencies, and tossed them across the pristine desk. Joe pulled one from the packet and spread it across his sodden eyes. It did little to quell the flood, and he soon reached for a second, and then a third. He was grateful Mike had insisted on him closing the door.

'There, there, mate,' Mike cringed from across the desk, recoiling as much as the limited space behind the enormous chair would allow.

'I ... I just feel ... so redundant,' Joe sobbed.

'With everything you've been through that's to be expected, mate.'

There was that word again. *Mate*. They'd never so much as been for a pint after work together.

'Nobody blames you for feeling a bit down,' Mike continued, now regretting asking Joe to close the door, and hoping Esther might break the office rule and come in even though it was closed. 'And nobody would think twice if you wanted to take a few more days at home –'

'It ... feels ... so quiet ... without her there,' Joe

stuttered as his chest continued to shake.

He took several deep breaths, closing his eyes, forcing his breaths to stay in for longer each time, until his shoulders settled.

'I'm no longer needed for anything, and I feel so lost.'

'It's understandable to feel that way, mate,' Mike offered, as if reciting from some out-dated handbook on dealing with emotional team members.

'It doesn't feel like Lydia got the justice she deserved, and I've failed her as a father.'

Mike settled more into his chair. 'Well, I for one am amazed at how well you've coped given everything. If I was in your shoes, I reckon I would have been arrested for attacking that suspect they let go. Imagine the secrets he'd spill under the right conditions, am I right?'

'I know so little about him,' Joe admitted, wincing as though he'd been kicked in the gut.

'Ah that's a pity, because monsters like that deserve to be strung up and castrated, if I had my way.'

Joe nodded in agreement, but he was certain that if Mike was faced with similar circumstances, he'd be equally as unresponsive.

'Anyway,' Mike said, elongating the vowel sounds in an effort to conclude the meeting, 'think about what I said about taking a few days to get your shit together. Okay? Then we can get the old Joe back, firing on all cylinders. Yeah?'

Joe nodded, even if he did think the sentiment was misplaced. He stood and began to reach for the door.

'Oh,' Mike interjected, 'I just wanted to add that

we've had all the paperwork back through for Harrington Manor. Lady Violet has signed everything, so how are you getting on with finding a suitable tenant for the old place?'

Joe counted to five before turning back to break the news. 'Still searching to be honest. There doesn't seem to be much call for period places amongst locally-based film companies.'

Mike frowned. 'Really?'

Joe grimaced. 'Well, let me rephrase. There aren't any local companies who can *afford* the rent she's asking for.

Mike nodded his understanding. 'Well, stick with it. Seems such a waste to have a grand place like that left empty when it could be so much more.'

Joe froze, as the embers of an idea began to slowly spark.

Chapter 17

Joe

Detective Andrews is wearing dark grey suit trousers, scuffed brown shoes, and a camel-coloured overcoat. The only thing that's missing are bright red braces, otherwise he'd be a strong contender in a Del Boy lookalike contest. His round face and rapidly shrinking hairline aside, he looks older and more tired than I remember when we first met six months ago. Back then I'd have described him as bright-eyed and bushy-tailed, or maybe that had just been wishful thinking. The last person you'd want in charge of investigating your daughter's disappearance is a washed-up wheeler-dealer.

Andrews doesn't wave as he approaches the front of my car, immediately diverting for the passenger side, and pulling on the handle until I lean across and unlock it. He climbs in without a word, and the disappointment is radiating off him in waves.

'Andrews,' I acknowledge quietly. 'Fancy meeting you here.'

It's a poor attempt to lighten the mood with humour, but it's the best my terrified brain can manage under this level of scrutiny. I'm trying to determine whether he's here because he knows what I did last night, and wants me to drive him to the manor to collect David, or whether that nosey neighbour did spot me and phoned to report a hooded figure in David's house. I've never been arrested, and the prospect of cuffs and the shame of being marched into a police station have frightened me since I was a child. I suppose that's the curse of having a mum who served in the police for more than twenty years. She raised me to stay on the straight and narrow. I wonder what she would make of what I'm doing now.

I glance into the rear-view mirror and catch Lydia smiling back at me. I'd swear she's mouthing, 'Stay calm, you got this.'

Andrews draws out a long, loud sigh. 'What are you doing here, Joe?'

I pause. If he doesn't know about David being abducted, and that neighbour *didn't* phone, then how did he know I was here? My mobile is at home, still plugged into the charger so I can fall back on the, 'Oh I must have forgotten it,' excuse, knowing it won't be tracking my GPS coordinates when I go back to Harrington Manor.

I suppose it's possible that Andrews didn't know I was here until he arrived, in which case I need to quickly think of an excuse as to why I would be parked across the road from David's house having been explicitly told not to come anywhere near Riverside Terrace.

'Um …' is the best I can do to buy myself some time.

'I thought we'd already discussed this a couple of months ago,' he says, sighing for a second time, in case I hadn't picked up on his disappointment. 'I told you what would happen if I caught you here again.'

'I'm not breaking any laws,' I say with a determined air. 'I'm just parked in my car.'

Andrews turns to face me and he cocks his eyebrow. He isn't impressed by my petulant response, and I can't blame him.

He looks from me to David's quiet house across the road. 'And of all the streets in Reading where you could have parked, you just happened to choose upon this one to park for a rest?'

I know now that he isn't going to follow through with his warning, but I also sense that this will be the last time he's so lenient.

He sits back in his seat, and rests his palms flat on his knees. 'I get it, Joe. Believe me, I understand how frustrating this all must be for you and Meg. After what the two of you have been through, I can absolutely understand how difficult that would be to process and live with. I've seen many couples experience similar things, and not many survive it in the way you and Meg have.'

Survive – is that what we're doing? – I don't ask. It certainly doesn't feel like we're surviving. Something about the way Neil only wanted to speak to Meg earlier is jarring with me, but I can't yet figure out why. Now isn't the time to relive the intricacies of that strained conversation.

'But what did I say to you about being here? Can you tell me what I said last time, because I want to check our memories of the last conversation we had here aren't different?'

'You said I shouldn't come here.'

'It was a little more than that, wasn't it?'

I can feel his eyes burrowing into my head, as if he's trying to expose my thoughts to read them. I turn my head towards the window, but I'm not really looking at anything, just trying to avoid looking at his disappointed face.

'You said I wouldn't get any benefit from watching ... *him*.'

I can see him shaking his head in my periphery. 'I believe I told you to leave the policing to the real police.'

'We did that and where did it get us?'

The words are out of my mouth before I can stop them. I know it isn't Andrews's fault that the evidence wasn't strong enough to charge David with her abduction and murder, but he's the only police officer I know that I can blame. I feel like I should offer an apology, but I remain tight-lipped in case I let anything else slip out. The less I say, the less chance there is to reveal the lengths I've gone to over the last few weeks and days.

'You have every right to be disappointed by the outcome of the investigation. Hell, *I'm* disappointed too, but that doesn't mean I'm going to spend every night camped outside the lead suspect's door hoping for a miracle. Like it or not, David Calderwood has rights too. In British law he is innocent until proven guilty, and we haven't got that far yet, but I've not given up on achieving the burden of proof required to re-present the case to the CPS.'

I tilt my head back so I can see his face when he answers my next question. 'So you still think he's the man responsible?'

Andrews opens his mouth, but quickly closes it again. 'He is still considered a person of significant interest in the case.'

'That wasn't what I asked,' I push. 'Forget about what you can or can't prove. In your opinion, did he do it?'

'Look, Joe, what I think is neither here nor –'

'Just answer the goddamned question!' I interrupt. 'Why can't you just give me a straight answer?'

'It isn't a question that I can answer.'

'Bullshit!'

I'm allowing my frustration of the past six months to boil over, and I really need to reign it in or risk exposing everything I've done, but in truth he's never given me a straight answer on what he thinks. David was identified as a suspect very early on, and was the primary focus of the investigation as far as I'm aware, but Andrews has never formally told me whether that was his call as SIO or someone else's suggestion. Given what I plan to do to David today, I need the reassurance that Andrews is as certain of David's guilt as I am.

'I just want to know whether your gut instinct – that little voice in the back of every police officer's head – is screaming that this man is the one responsible.'

Again he opens his mouth as if he's finally ready to answer the question, but thinks better of it. 'What good will it do? It doesn't matter what I think, only what I can *prove* beyond a reasonable doubt.'

'It will *help* me,' I grizzle. 'I can't rest until I know who did this to us; who …' I summon the strength to say the words, 'abducted and murdered my little girl.'

'I understand that Joe, but I don't think you should put so much reassurance on what *I* think. I'm just one man, and my opinion is worth nothing.'

'You're a serving police officer with years of experience; I'd argue that your instincts are worth a hundred times that of the average Joe on the streets.'

I point at myself as I say this, because I am the average Joe on the streets trying to pick a path through the mire of bullshit I find myself in.

He looks away for a moment, and I sneak a glance back to the road to check there are no other police cars heading towards us, and that the detective isn't just trying to keep me talking while he waits for back up to arrive.

'That's what most people don't understand about the police,' he says with a heavy heart. 'They see all these televised shows where the hero is driven to go against the rules in order to find out the truth, but reality isn't like that. We have procedures and protocols to follow. Before a suspect can even be declared a person of interest, it has to be agreed by more than just the SIO, and it certainly isn't based on gut calls.'

'But you did make David your prime suspect though, right? If that wasn't based on your intuition, what specifically led you to him?'

He shakes his head. 'I can't tell you that, Joe, and before you argue, my hands are tied with that. There were reasons – good reasons – but they weren't good enough according to the CPS, and so we continue to work at it.'

This is getting us nowhere, but something fires in the back of my mind.

'Did you ever consider the prospect that he was working with … say, a partner?'

The detective's head snaps around, and he narrows his eyes. 'I already told you: I can't discuss the intricacies of the investigation with you.'

'Just humour me for a minute,' I press. 'You said there wasn't any of Lydia's DNA found inside his home, but what if he wasn't holding her there? What if he was working with someone else and they were keeping her at his place?'

His eyes narrow so much that I can no longer see his pupils. 'Where's this coming from?'

I shrug as nonchalantly as I can manage as my pulse quickens. 'Just a theory is all. There must have been something that made you suspect David to begin with – aside from the fact he's on the Sex Offenders Register – and so the logical next step is that somebody was helping him.'

'I can assure you that every angle was carefully examined, and will continue to be until we can bring you the resolution you deserve.' He pats his legs. 'But for now, Joe, all of *this* needs to stop. Do you hear me this time? I don't want to happen along this road again and find you camped out here. Do you really want David Calderwood pressing charges against you for stalking? How is that going to look if we're ever able to bring a case to court? He was threatening to complain about harassment when we kept interviewing him the first time around. If he cottons on to the fact that you're watching him, and having Private

Investigators running background checks on him ...'

He leaves the line hanging. He knows I hired Edie Sinclair to find out information about David, but does he know what she told me, or the excuse I gave her for running the checks. She did warn me she might have to let the police know if she suspected my intentions weren't forthright, but I didn't think she'd actually go through with it.

'Don't waste your money hiring so-say Private Investigators when you already have a team of professional, and very hard working detectives doing the job for you for free. It won't help, Joe, and I'm telling you this as a friend. Okay? I told you last time, but I'm going to repeat it in the hope it sinks in: I won't rest until I can work out what happened to your daughter and have charged the persons responsible.'

He reaches for the door handle.

'Is that why you're here today?' I ask, again, my curiosity getting the better of me. 'To question him again? Is there new evidence?'

He grimaces. 'I can't tell you why I'm here, other than to say it has nothing to do with Lydia's investigation.'

I hear Neil's words in my head: *We've had the police out looking for her all night.*

'Is it because of that other girl who's gone missing? Hazel Cooper?'

His eyes widen. 'How do you know about that?'

It's my turn to act sheepish. 'Her dad Neil ... He's friends with Meg and called round to ours this morning to talk to her. He said she snuck out last night and didn't come home. Do you think David has taken her?'

He shakes his head, but I can see from the slight watering of his eyes that I've hit the nail on the head. In fairness, he told me once before that when a child is reported missing and can't be located, it is standard practice for the police to contact known sex offenders in the area.

He opens the door and climbs out, but pauses as he spots something on my back seat. 'What's with the dog food?'

It had slipped my mind that I'd put David's dog's food on the back seat rather than in the boot.

'I didn't think you guys had a dog,' he continues.

'We don't,' I say, instantly regretting it, and clamping my eyes shut. 'B-But we're thinking about getting one,' I say.

What is wrong with me? Why not just say we've bought one, or that I picked it up for a friend, or was planning to make a donation at a shelter?

Andrews looks back at me through the open door.

'You said yourself that it might help fill the void left by Lydia,' I say as my mind races to establish some control. 'Meg and I discussed it and we're considering adopting a dog from an animal shelter, but we had to pick up a few bits and pieces before they'd agree to letting us bring one home for the weekend.'

I'm making it sound like we're planning to test drive a new car, but he doesn't question it.

'Well, I'm glad you're at least following some of my advice,' he says resting his hand on the frame of the door, looking pleased with himself. 'About the other thing, Joe, please just let me and my team handle it. Okay? For the last time: don't let me catch you here again.'

With that, he slams the door, but remains where he is on the pavement, until I start the engine and pull away. I can only hope that when David's door goes unanswered, he doesn't put two and two together and come looking for me. Either way, the clock is ticking if I'm to get the answers I need from David. It's time for me to step up.

Chapter 18

Hazel

He is wearing the balaclava again, but the leather jacket has been abandoned. A small brown paper bag hangs from his wrist, as he stands there, surrounded by such a bright light that Hazel has to close her eyes to ease the burning sensation. He remains where he is, little more than a menacing shadow.

'I brought you something to eat,' he eventually calls into the room. 'Are you hungry?'

She doesn't want to answer, wanting him to still believe she's still asleep, naively thinking he'll leave her alone if she isn't awake.

The brilliant white light framing him must be from some industrial-sized bulb, and even with her eyes clamped shut, she can still feel it burning into the room, like staring at the sun during a solar eclipse.

'Answer me, or I'll take the food away and leave you to starve,' he calls next.

He must have been watching when she'd rolled onto her side, and that's what triggered this visit, but for all she knows he was watching for a long time before that and saw her eyes open.

She has been too scared to think about food or drink, but if she is to escape, she needs to keep up her strength.

'Yes,' she mutters, her throat drier than she'd realised.

'Yes, what?' he fires back like a disapproving parent.

'Y-Yes ... p-please.'

The cabin shakes as he steps into it, the floor seeming to bend as it supports his full weight, in the same way the van did when he climbed in last night. It feels like that's significant, but she can't concentrate on the thought for long enough, because he is now tipping the contents of the bag on sleeping bag over her legs. She wants to wince with the pain, but grinds her teeth instead in case he changes his mind and takes the food away.

The mattress shakes on the floor as he turns to leave.

'Th-Thank you,' she ventures.

He stops still and looks back at her.

'Good girl, Hazel. I'm glad to see you're learning already. The sooner you realise that compliance is more rewarding than resistance, the sooner I'll let you out of here.'

He's given her an in. Without considering the implications, she pushes the sleeping bag off her body and stands before him on the mattress.

If he wanted to kill her, she reasons, he would have done it by now. This isn't about killing for him, though she doesn't doubt he's capable of it. She is playing a hunch, which could massively backfire, but she figures she has little to lose at this point.

She squints as best she can at his shadow trying to see the face beyond the balaclava, before raising her hands high into the air above her head, knowing it will straighten and accentuate her slim figure. She twirls her hands together and gently sways to the rhythm of the song in her head.

'Is this what you want?' she croaks. 'You want me?'

He doesn't answer, but she can feel his eyes moving from her hands, down her arms, pausing as they reach her thin face and long blonde hair. She can practically hear his arousal as his eyes study the outline of her breasts and continue down to her feet.

Yes, she thinks, this is precisely what he is after. She continues to move rhythmically, trying to entice him to move closer. She imagines Matt standing in front of her instead of him. She imagines the look of desire in his eyes as he relents and takes her.

But the man doesn't move, he just continues to watch.

That's okay though, she figures, while he's watching her, he isn't watching the door he left open. If she can get him to come close enough, maybe she can do enough damage to slow his ability to chase after her.

She lowers her right arm until it is perpendicular with her body, and then she beckons him with her fingers. She is playing with fire. If he suddenly grabs her hand and twists it behind her back, she'll be powerless to stop him taking advantage, but with him standing where he is at the moment, there isn't enough room to squeeze past him.

He makes no movement towards her hand, but his body is starting to sway slightly. He's forcing himself not to yield so easily, but he's clearly struggling with the fact that she's offering him exactly what he wants so soon.

Hazel bends and twists as she lowers herself to her knees on the mattress, but like a coiled spring, she's ready to leap forward as soon as she spots her opportunity. Her heart is racing so fast that it feels like it might pop out of her chest like in those lame cartoons she used to watch with her dad. She shakes thoughts of him from her mind; she needs to focus.

'Don't you want me?' she whispers seductively.

One of his feet shuffles forwards slightly as he struggles to contain his desire, but it's all she needs. Quick as a flash she's up and diving forwards, escaping his last minute swing to grasp her. The light is so bright that she shields her eyes with her forearm, driving towards freedom, but she's barely made it out of the doorway and down the three steps before she feels something tug at her, and then suddenly she's falling, crashing forwards, the putrid-smelling straw on the ground coming up to meet her face. Her forehead smacks the ground first sending a shooting pain behind her eyes. She tries to ignore it as she scrabbles to get up, but her right leg won't bend as it should, and despite her best efforts to crawl towards the light, instead she is being pulled backwards by some invisible force. It's only when she turns onto her back that she sees the thin rope wrapped around her ankle, being pulled back towards the stairs by the figure in the balaclava.

Chapter 19

Joe

The beagle's muted barks greet me as I open the door at Harrington Manor. I can only just make out the sound once inside, but there wasn't a peep when I was parking the car, which means any screaming David has done since I left earlier today will have been wasted. I've parked the car to the side of the main house, so it won't be visible from the wrought iron gates at the bottom of the drive. Lady Violet told me that nobody was due to stop by whilst they were away, but I don't want an eagle-eyed neighbour to spot my car and raise the alarm. I didn't pass anyone on the private road as I was driving up to the property, but I'm more conscious of just how much brighter it is during the day. My activities certainly feel less clandestine.

Opening the kitchen door, I'm immediately greeted by the smell of faeces, and I have to pull my hoodie up over my nose. The beagle is sitting by the back door, shaking, maybe sensing that she could be in trouble for the small packet she's left beside her water bowl. Lowering the bag of dog food to the table, I grab her leash, and hurry opening the back door, and allowing her to pull me outside, where she quickly crouches and urinates on the paving slabs. The poor thing must have been barking for hours, waiting for someone to let her out while I was sleeping at home and searching David's house. It doesn't feel fair leaving her here to fend for herself, but I can't think of a better alternative at the moment.

Putting her out in the garden here doesn't feel adequate for a breed this size, and even though she's still only a puppy, exercise is an essential part of her routine. She comes over and rubs herself against my ankles, and so I stoop to one knee and run my fingers over her big droopy ears. She pushes her head closer into my hand, and seems to snuggle into the warmth. She certainly is a cute puppy, and very affectionate even though her only experience of me is attacking her owner in the dead of night. Maybe there could be more to what Detective Andrews had suggested about a pet helping to bridge the chasm left by our loss. I'm not suggesting that a puppy or kitten could ever replace our daughter, but we owe it to her to allow our hearts to love again.

The sound of her tummy grumbling has me back on my feet and leading her inside. It's close to ten and feels wrong feeding her breakfast so late in the day. Reading the packet, there are directions and a table telling me how much I should feed her, but I don't know enough about the breed to determine whether she'll become a medium or large breed size, nor do I know how old she is or how much she weighs, so I can't be certain what is for the best. There's also no obvious sign of a scale in the kitchen, so I grab a second bowl from the cupboard where I borrowed one for water, and drop two handfuls of food into the bowl and place it on the floor near the back door, while I go in search of something to clear up the mess she left. Five minutes later, with the poop flushed, and the floor wiped with toilet roll and washing up liquid, I make a mental note to bring some floor cleaning wipes from home the next time I come.

Opening the door to the basement, there is no screaming coming from below, and for a brief moment I'm concerned that David might have found some way to escape and has already left the property in search of the authorities, but as I head down the stairs, I hear movement, and as I hurry down the rest find him sprawled against the bars, looking half dead, but blinking.

'Water,' he croaks, barely louder than a whisper.

He doesn't look well. His skin is grey and dry, his eyes bloodshot, and his tongue practically hanging out of his chapped lips. If I found him looking like this anywhere else, my instinct would be to call for an ambulance, and move him into the recovery position, but then I think back to his lies about insulin and specialist dog food, and I won't be so easily duped this time. I pull over the chair and sit down, watching him silently.

'Water, please?' he tries again, this time straining up a grey hand and wrapping his fingers around one of the bars.

Still I don't move.

'You lied to me,' I say eventually.

He blinks slowly, but doesn't offer any kind of apology. We both know he lied about the insulin and wheat intolerance, but part of me doesn't want to give him the satisfaction of my anger. He's playing games, and I don't doubt that this act of feebleness is just another of them. Well two can play that game!

Leaning over, I open the fridge door and extract one of the small bottles of mineral water, cracking open the top and pouring a liberal quantity into my mouth. The cool relief on my tongue is welcome.

'P-Please?' he croaks.

I look straight at him, and put the bottle back to my lips, adding a satisfied sigh as I swallow it, and licking my lips.

'Mm, so refreshing,' I add for good measure.

He sits up slightly, his weakness suddenly less evident.

'Please, Joe, show some mercy. I'm so thirsty.'

'You didn't show my daughter any mercy did you?'

'Please? I'll do whatever you want, just give me a drink. I think I'm dying here. I think there was blood in my piss. I have a condition. I shouldn't go too long without a drink.'

Whether that's true or not, I'm not going to dignify it by going to check the bucket. The background report compiled by Edie Sinclair certainly didn't mention any underlying medical conditions. It's probably just another lie, a means of making me pity him.

I place the cap on the bottle, and stand, moving behind the tripod, switching on the camcorder.

'You know what I want from you. Confess to what you did to my daughter, and I'll give you a drink of water.'

I start the recording from where I left off yesterday.

'What do you want from me? I told you yesterday that any confession obtained through oppression is inadmissible in court.'

'And I told you that's not what this is about. Tell me how you took my daughter and what you intended.'

'I've already told you it *wasn't* me.'

There is more colour in his cheeks as he pleads his innocence, and he seems less frail as he sits up straight, looking at me and the camera.

I remove the lid of the bottle again, and take another drink.

'Alright, alright, but I can't confess to something I didn't do. What if I give you something else? How about that?'

I keep the camcorder recording, but am all too aware that this could be yet another fabrication.

'I'm listening.'

'Okay, okay, give me some water and I'll tell you.'

I step out from behind the camera and raise my eyebrows. 'Do you really think I am that gullible?'

'You have to give me something. I'm dying here. It's been hours since I had anything to eat or drink. Please?'

I shake my head. 'Give me what I want and you can have as much water as you want.'

He eyes the bottle in my hand and then stares straight at the fridge door as if willing it to open and magically fly towards him.

'If I tell you what I know, I have no guarantee that you'll give me a drink.'

'You have my word.'

'What if I tell you about the information I have to prove its worth, you give me a drink, and then I give you the information after? How about that?'

I nod for him to continue.

'You were asking me about an accomplice, right? You wanted to know about the man with the van; I can tell you who he is.'

I picture the pain in Neil's eyes, and think about Andrews knocking on the door of the empty house. Hazel Cooper is out there somewhere, and there is a very real possibility that David knows where she's being held. On the other hand, I told him about a girl being taken by someone in a van, so he could just be using my words against me. I can't take a chance on the fact he might be telling the truth.

Putting the bottle to my lips I drain it until there's about a quarter left, before sealing the lid and rolling it across the stone floor towards the cage. He drops to his knees and gathers it up, pulling it through the bars, tearing off the cap and draining it in one large gulp. He didn't even bother to wipe the mouthpiece.

'Well?' I ask. 'Who is he?'

'Give me a whole bottle, and I'll tell you.'

'No, you tell me first, and once I've verified the information, then I'll give you more. That's how this works.'

'Screw you! Fine, you don't want to save the girl, don't, it's no skin off my nose.'

I can feel the heat rising to my face. 'You really are one despicable human being, aren't you? Where is the girl?'

'Give me a bottle and I'll tell you.'

'Oh sure, I give you a bottle, and then you reveal that you don't know anything. Tell me something else about him to convince me you're not spinning me a line. How do you know him? What's his name? How long have you been working together?'

He folds his arms.

My hands ball into fists, and it would be so easy to go into that cell and attack him, but if I do I may not be able to stop myself, and then we won't get the confession. He clearly still thinks he's the one in charge, and that needs to change before he'll be more compliant. As frustrated as I am, I need to remain patient. Extracting a confession is going to take time. I knew that when this started.

The beagle's barking catches David's attention.

'What are you doing to her? Why is she barking?'

'She needs walking.'

'Bring her down to see me. She's probably missing me.'

I shake my head. 'No way. But tell me one thing: what's her name?'

He looks me flush in the eye. 'Why, her name is Lydia, of course.'

The red mist descends, and I'm not in control as I charge towards the cell, but he takes three quick steps backwards, and as I strain to get my arms through the bars to get at him, he's just out of reach.

'Now, now, Joe, temper, temper.'

He's laughing, and the pallor of his skin has softened to a gentle hue. He's no closer to dying than I am to getting to the truth.

'I swear to God, you *will* tell me what I want to know, or so help me I'll leave you down here forever, and as you're screaming in agony as your vital organs shut down through lack of food and drink, you'll meet

Satan knowing you had the key to your freedom the whole time and refused to see it.'

I peel myself from the bars and hurry back up the stairs, yelling back over my shoulder. 'I'm going to walk the dog. You'd better have answers for me when I get back, or you'll never see the light of day again.'

Chapter 20

8 weeks ago

The offices of Sinclair and Associates was not what Joe was expecting. A grey shutter in a unit of an industrial park didn't shout espionage and undercover work, but then maybe that was the point. To the casual observer, this looked no more than any other small business struggling to make ends meet. Joe double-checked the address provided in the email, before stepping to the small door at the right of the shutters, and pressed the bell.

A moment later a slide covering a window in the door opened and a girl with blonde hair, who looked no more than sixteen, appeared. 'Name?'

Joe stooped and put his mouth close to the hole. 'Hi, I'm Joe Irons. Here to see Edie Sinclair? I have a ten o'clock appointment.'

The girl closed the shutter and began to remove half a dozen bolts securing the fire door, before pulling it open. She nodded for him to enter, before glancing left and right outside of the door as if expecting an army to lay siege, and then closed and fastened the bolts back in place.

The office space inside was no bigger than Joe's living room, with a desk front and centre, a laptop plugged in to its charger, and several graphite-coloured filing cabinets lining the walls. A door cut into the far wall was closed and blocked off by a chair that the girl now pulled around and pushed towards Joe.

'Take a seat,' she said, making herself comfortable in a hard-backed chair behind the laptop.

Joe could only assume the girl was Edie's assistant on some kind of work experience or apprenticeship scheme, and so sat as instructed. Taking in the rest of the room, Joe spotted small semi-spherical bulges in each of the corners of the ceiling, presumably CCTV transmitting wirelessly to the laptop. A halogen fire glowed orange beside the girl, but did little to warm the rest of the room.

'Will Miss Sinclair be long?' Joe asked, glancing at his watch.

'I am Edie Sinclair,' the girl responded, reaching into the top drawer of the desk and pulling out a framed picture of her holding her credentials.

'Oh I'm sorry,' Joe quickly backtracked. 'Can I ask –?'

'How old I am?' she cut him off. 'Twenty-four, but owing to my mum's Scandinavian roots, most people assume I'm a teenager. You'd be surprised at how much that helps when I'm on an undercover assignment.'

Joe considered her again in light of this news, and now that he studied her face closer could see how most would replicate his mistake.

'I'm sorry,' he said again.

'Don't sweat it. Now, you said in your email …' she trailed off as she opened the email on the laptop and skimmed it again. 'You want me to find out information about a man called … David Calderwood?'

'That's right, Joe responded, silently reciting the story he'd concocted to explain his interest in Calderwood.

'Can I ask why the interest in him? Do you suspect him of sleeping with your wife? Or is he an ex-boyfriend threatening to spill intimate details about your sex life online?' Both questions were delivered with no trace of humour.

'No, nothing like that,' Joe clarified, though both would have been better reasons than what he'd come up with. 'I own my own business and this guy is a potential new investor, but I want to make sure I do due diligence on him before signing on the dotted line. Does that make sense?'

She nodded, and began typing into the laptop. 'And the address in your email puts him in Reading?'

'Yes, but he may own other properties. I believe he's only renting that address. I'm keen to know whether he does own anywhere else in the UK.'

Her head popped out from behind the laptop. 'Any particular reason why?'

'I want to ensure there aren't international tax implications, that's all.'

She ducked back behind the screen and continued typing, as Joe let out a small sigh of relief. So far so good.

'I can recommend some other private investigators a bit closer to Reading if that would help? Save you having to commute here to Southampton to meet with me.'

Joe had deliberately picked an agency outside of the county so that his own history with Calderwood wouldn't become apparent. There probably weren't many in Reading who wouldn't have heard about Lydia's abduction and murder. At least driving an hour further south might buy more anonymity.

'You came highly recommended,' Joe replied.

'Oh yeah? Who by?'

Joe hadn't anticipated her expecting him to drop a name, and changed his approach. 'Look, do you want the business or not?'

Her eyes appeared from above the top of the laptop. 'Of course, of course. There's a standard hourly rate for work of this kind, but at the end you'll receive a file detailing everything that's been found along with an itemised invoice conforming how the time was spent locating the information. Is there anything else you specifically want me to look for? It's easier if you say now rather than waiting until I complete the assignment.'

'You do undercover work and surveillance, I presume?'

She narrowed her eyes suspiciously. 'Not usually for this type of work. It'll be checking databases of all varieties.'

'Could you though? I want to understand more about this man. What are his likes and dislikes? What does his daily routine look like? Who are his friends? Anything unusual.'

She raised her eyebrows. 'Paranoid much?'

'I just want to be sure about who I'm going into business with that's all. I don't like nasty surprises.'

She lowered the laptop screen. 'That's interesting, Mr Irons, because I don't like nasty surprises either. You're telling me that you want me to research a potential business partner, but I sense there's more to it than that. You don't want to tell me the truth? That's fine. All I'll say is if it turns out that *this* is something else and something happens to this David Calderwood, I will have no hesitation reporting this conversation and activity to the police. My work is governed by the same laws as you have to follow, so I won't become embroiled in any kind of legal activity. Am I making myself clear?'

Joe nodded as the lump in his throat wouldn't let him speak.

Edie printed off the contract and slid it across the desk, indicating where he should sign. As the pen scratched at the surface of the page, he couldn't help feeling he was signing his own death warrant.

Chapter 21

Joe

Leaving the beagle at Harrington Manor was never going to work long-term. It isn't fair on her to restrict exercise and defecation to the small patio outside of the kitchen, and there's too much risk of being spotted if I walk her around the rest of the grounds. The safest option is going to be to take her to an animal shelter, but before I do, I need to nip home and collect my wallet, and check my emails. It's one thing to leave my phone at home so the GPS signal puts me there rather than at Harrington Manor, but I need it to look like I've been there using it too.

I shouldn't leave the beagle in the car while I go in for five minutes. There's no sign of Meg's car, so I should be safe. Lifting the beagle from her seat, I glance at the tag on her collar, but there's only a telephone number, and no name.

The echo of David's insipid laughter fills my ears.

Why, her name is Lydia, of course.

I bite down on my finger to break my anger transforming into a sob. The bastard! I'm sure he wouldn't have been twisted enough to name his puppy after my little girl, but to even suggest it, just to stick in the knife, fills me with hate.

The beagle sits up and nuzzles her nose into the

crook of my neck and then proceeds to lick and nip at my ear. When I try to extract her, she pushes herself into me more, and her whole body jiggles with excitement.

'Whoa, whoa, whoa,' I say in a firm voice. 'My ears are not for nibbling.'

Her eyes look bright as I stare into them, and the residual resentment I have towards David slowly disappears. She really is a cutie.

I glance up at the rear-view mirror, and catch Lydia's reflection staring back at me. I can almost hear her laughing and clapping her hands together in excited anticipation of me bringing a dog home. I look back at the beagle.

'My daughter would have *loved* you. I wish …'

My heart thuds long and slow as only regret can make it do.

'I wish I'd granted her wish. I wish …'

I don't resist the sting of the tears, allowing my eyes to fill as my brain switches into sorrow mode and I unlock Pandora's Box.

'I wish I'd known there was a registered sex offender within walking distance from that park. If I'd known, I never would have dreamed of taking you there, my sweet, sweet girl. And if I'd known David was going to become the prime suspect, I'd have grabbed him sooner, and forced the truth from his lips *before* he killed you. I wish I'd told you how much I loved you, and that I would have given my life for yours without a second's thought. I wish …'

The beagle has leaned over and is now licking the tears from my cheeks. Extracting her face from mine, her eyes are now full of concern. How can a dog read my emotions and behaviour better than I can hers? Which of us is supposed to be the more evolved?

Crying over things I can't change isn't going to get me what I need. Lifting the beagle, I tuck her into the crook of my arm and climb out of the car, hurrying to the door before any neighbours spot her. Opening the front door, I close it with my bottom, and head through the house and into the back garden, where she can run about and do what she needs. She races across the grass, stopping when she spots the stalks of Meg's now flowerless rose bushes, where she proceeds to squat.

'Don't let the owner of those bushes catch you doing that,' I call out playfully.

The beagle finishes and pads back over to me. No, it's alright, you can stay out here and have a run about,' I tell her, before realising she can't understand a word of what I'm saying.

She hops up the step and back into the lounge, before sitting at my feet. Oh well, if she really doesn't want to stay outside then who am I to argue? Leaving the back door open, I proceed through the house to the kitchen where I find my phone plugged in to the charger where I left it. Unlocking the display, I scroll through my emails, deleting two which are discount vouchers for restaurants we used to visit with Lydia. Whenever we had something to celebrate as a family – birthday, anniversary, good school report, etc. – we'd always visit one of three places where we knew Lydia would find something she'd be happy to eat, and where Meg and I could have a treat too. I don't think it would be the same to go back there now. Even if my wife was engaging in conversation with me, I think it would just be too painful to be reminded of the enormous hole in our family.

Closing the app, I do a quick scan of Facebook, Twitter, and Instagram, but I'm just going through the motions. How much time did I waste glued to my phone on apps like these when I should have been cherishing every moment with my beautiful daughter? Everyone warned me that she'd grow up too quickly, and they were right, but I took for granted the prospect of having more time together. Instead of making the most of every day with her, I was more caught up in presenting an image of a happy family to the world through photographs and posts that didn't truly reflect how absent I was from her life. She never complained – she was too well-behaved – but I shouldn't have waited for my child to tell me to be more involved. I am the adult and should have taken responsibility.

An image of Lydia catches my eye from a Facebook memory. It's two years ago, when Meg and I took her to her first fireworks display. We'd bought her noise-cancelling headphones as she hated loud bangs, but her face was such a picture that night. In the image she's sitting on my shoulders, eyes wide with expectation as a red and green display hangs in the sky over our heads. Meg took the picture, and it was one of a dozen I uploaded that night to show forgotten friends and colleagues what a picture perfect family looks like. The next image is me chomping on a hotdog. I'm mid-bite and the ketchup and mustard is just starting to ooze out of the other end, about to drop on and stain my favourite trainers. I remember Meg resisted the urge to pull her, 'I told you so,' face right after when I was cursing myself for not wearing my older muddier pair.

We really did look happy that night. Lydia didn't like her sausage, so gave it to me and chewed her sub roll as we walked home together. It was such a dark night, but surprisingly mild for November. She didn't stop chattering the whole way home, but the second she was changed and in bed, she was asleep within seconds, probably dreaming of all the wondrous colours she'd witnessed on the sky's canvas.

What I would give to go back to that night and relive it again.

The sound of a key turning in the front door, has me locking the phone and hurrying to the kitchen door. Meg looks equally surprised as our eyes meet.

'Oh, you're home?' she says, with confusion in her tone.

'Yeah, I forgot my phone,' I say, lifting it into the air.

She frowns as she eyes my tracksuit bottoms and hoodie. 'You not working today?'

Before I left this morning I packed my suit and work shoes into a satchel and stashed them in the boot. I'd planned to change before coming home tonight, but hadn't even thought about it just now.

'I, um ... I wasn't feeling very well when I woke up so I told Mike I'd take the day to rest and recover.'

She seems to accept this as a response, but doesn't ask how I'm feeling now. Instead, she closes the front door, drops her keys in the dish on the table beside it, and heads past me into the living room, carrying a couple of glossy magazines.

'You weren't here when I came back from my run, so I assumed you'd gone to work.'

'How's your migraine?' I ask to deliberately force the conversation from the topic of my presence here.

'Gone now I think.' She drops into the single armchair and looks back at me, before her eyes suddenly widen with shock. 'Who's this?' she asks, her voice a pitch higher, and staring at the beagle who has just trotted in and is now standing between my legs.

I can feel her tail bashing against the backs of my knees.

Meg is no longer looking at me, but is pulling faces at the beagle whose tail is flapping harder. I move my left leg, and she pushes on past, padding over to where Meg is now bent over, her arms and hands extended to greet her. Meg lifts the beagle up and onto her lap, and immediately begins to rub her tummy, causing the beagle's right leg to twitch involuntarily.

'Well aren't you just the cutest little puppy,' Meg coos, and it's as if I'm not even in the room anymore.

When Lydia first started asking us to get a dog, Meg agreed that it wasn't practical for us to get one, but she never said whether she liked the idea of us adopting a pet. She's smiling and laughing and I genuinely can't remember the last time I saw either. I'm half-tempted just to leave them to it, but the plan was to take the beagle to the shelter.

'So who is she?' Meg asks, finally making eye contact with me again, the beagle now lying on her lap, resting her chin on Meg's knee and enjoying the gentle stroke of Meg's hand on her back.

I'm about to answer when I suddenly consider the

prospect that David might have had her microchipped, and if he did the shelter would probably try and return her to him, which could lead them to realise he's missing and notifying the police.

'Um, she ... belongs to ... a ... friend at work,' I say as my brain struggles to come up with anything remotely plausible. 'He and his girlfriend had to go away suddenly and they couldn't put her in kennels, so I said I'd watch her for a few days for them. Is that okay?'

Meg is staring back at the puppy again, and nuzzles her face into her neck. 'Is that okay? Of course it is, though I'm not sure I'm going to want to give her back at the end.'

I'm staring at the woman I fell in love with all those years ago, and it fills my heart with a warm glow. Maybe there is more to what Andrews said about the power of a dog's restorative love helping to overcome pain and grief.

'Can I take her for a walk? Does she have a dog lead and things?' Meg's voice sounds so much like Lydia's that my tears nearly return.

'Um, yeah, she does, and of course you can. That would be great.'

Meg lifts the puppy into her arms, and stands, still pulling silly faces.

'What's her name?'

Why, her name is Lydia, of course.

'Um, she's called ...'

Come on brain, think!

'She's called Lola.'

I'm cringing that the first girl's name that came into

my head belongs to the first girl who ever dumped me, but am relieved that Meg doesn't make the connection.

'That's a sweet name, and she looks like a Lola. Come on then, Lola, do you want to go for a walkies with your Auntie Meg?'

I follow them out to the kitchen and pass Meg the leash I left on the counter. This couldn't have worked out better. The beagle can live with us for a few days, with Meg watching her while I'm at Harrington Manor, and I won't have to worry about any more accidents on Lady Violet's kitchen floor.

I'm about to pour myself a glass of water from the tap when Meg calls out to me.

'What's up?' I ask joining her at the open door.

But she doesn't need to answer, as I can see what's caused her alarm. It's the uniformed police officer walking up our driveway.

Chapter 22

Hazel

How had she managed to miss the fact that he'd tied a rope around her ankle to prevent her escaping? She had no memory of him doing it, and she hadn't felt it when she'd been lying inside the sleeping bag, but now that she thought about it, she could remember zipping up the sleeping bag when she'd first climbed into it, and yet when she'd woken the zip was open. How had she missed that too?

She'd been so consumed with playing teenage detective that she had missed the most obvious fact: this isn't his first rodeo, as her dad would say. She'd ignored the fact that the mattress had clearly been used by someone before her, that the sleeping bag even smelled like another girl had slept inside it previously. He'd been so assured when he'd grabbed and pushed her into the back of the van. When they'd arrived at his place, he hadn't seemed nervous or worried about what he was doing. It had to be because, unlike her, he'd experienced this before.

When he'd lifted her back inside the cabin, he'd warned her that he wouldn't tolerate disobedience, and had slapped her hard around the face. Even now, sometime after, it still stung to touch. He hadn't taken away her provisions, but she had yet to tuck into the sandwich packet, bag of crisps or small bottle of water. Obviously a meal deal from some petrol station or convenience store, but could she trust that he hadn't tampered with the food? The sandwich packet was sealed, but had yesterday's date on it, and given he'd chosen prawn cocktail, she wasn't sure that eating it wouldn't cause food poisoning. The packet of cheese and onion crisps also appeared to be sealed, but the cap on the bottle of water had already been snapped open. She desperately wanted a drink, but the more she thought about it, she couldn't think of any reason he would have opened the bottle unless he'd put something else in with it.

A police officer had visited school only last month to warn the year group about the dangers of drugs whether voluntarily ingested or not. The officer had warned them never to leave drinks unattended when out as the latest date rape drugs are colourless and tasteless. What if he's spiked the water so she'll pass out and then he can have his wicked way with her? The officer hadn't said how much of the drug needed to be consumed for the paralysing effect to take over. Would she be okay if she only drank half the bottle? Or maybe only a quarter would be better. Or a sip every hour might be safest altogether. In truth she doesn't know, which is why the bottle remains untouched.

The red LED came on several minutes after the slap, and she now wonders whether he makes a conscious decision to switch off the camera when he is coming to see her. If he's streaming or recording the footage, maybe he doesn't want his distinguishable figure to appear. She has made a note to casually glance towards the LED every now and again to test her theory. If he does switch it off when he is on his way, it offers her a tiny window to do things when nobody is watching. It isn't a lot, but it stirs the embers of hope.

She looks back at the food items in her lap. She can't stand prawns, but relents and opens the packet, separating the slices of bread and using her finger to scrape the prawns back into the packet, shuddering with disgust. Putting the slices back together she bites into the wholemeal bread. The remnants of the sweet sauce on the bread aren't pleasant, but holding her breath, she's able to swallow it down, and soon half the sandwich is gone. She decides she will save the crisps for later s they will give her something to look forward to, and stave off the boredom of being trapped inside a cabin.

She finally reaches for the bottle. Standing she holds it up to the orange glow bleeding out of the gap in the roof, but even shaking the bottle doesn't reveal any hidden narcotic. Can she take the risk? For all she knows he's spiked the drink and once she drifts into an induced sleep he'll be back to assault her. The thought is enough to have her drop the bottle back to the mattress.

Sitting again, she tucks her legs beneath the sleeping bag and reaches for the rope around her ankle. There's so little light in the room that there's no point in looking at the knot directly, and at least under the cover of the sleeping bag, he won't be able to see what she's up to. She tries to tug at the strands but it's stuck fast. There is a slight gap between the rope and her skin, big enough for her little finger to slip through, but not nearly wide enough to get it over her ankle and heel. She tries anyway, pulling it as hard as she can, twisting her ankle and foot as she does, but it's a waste of time.

If only she could find something sharp to try and cut the rope. She glances down at the edge of the sandwich packet and runs her finger along it, but she doesn't think it will work. The crisp packet is even more flimsy. The plastic bottle won't help, unless she can empty and squash it down to form a sharp point with the sides. It's a long shot, but it's better than just sitting and waiting for him to come again. Unscrewing the lid of the water, she takes a gulp, swilling it around in her mouth, trying to detect any difference in flavour or consistency, but there's no clue to what it might contain. She swallows and replaces the lid. Lying back on the pillow, she concentrates on how her mind and body feel, waiting for any sign of change.

Chapter 23

Joe

I don't have time to think about why there's a police officer approaching our house or whether we have time to pretend we're not home, because Meg has already opened the door, holding the beagle back on her lead as she strains to meet the stranger.

When Detective Andrews received no response from knocking on David's door, is it possible he gained entry to the property and now knows he's AWOL? Would he suspect I could be involved in his disappearance? After all I was parked outside the property and had a rock solid motive.

Sweat prickles at my hairline as a gust blows through the open door, and I unzip my hoodie.

The officer shows us her identification tag. 'I'm PC Stef Greenhouse, and my team and I are asking for the public's support in relation to a local girl who went missing last night. Can you spare me a couple of minutes to answer some questions?'

I look beyond the officer in her dark uniform, but can't trace any other officers knocking on any of the other neighbours' doors. I'm also surprised that they'd venture this far out considering we're almost two miles from the Stable Road Recreation Ground.

Meg's hand moves to her mouth in surprise, and she

glances at me, but I don't meet her stare.

'Can you please confirm your names?' PC Greenhouse asks. 'Incidentally, the bodycam will record the conversation, so I don't need to write any notes.'

I can't help but stare at the small round lens protruding from her uniform, creating a permanent record of whatever statement we make. I can feel it burrowing into my soul, searching for answers about what I've done, until I force myself to look away. At least she won't be able to see just how uncomfortable I am from the doorstep.

'I'm Meg Irons, and this is my husband Joe. Would you like to come in?' Meg replies, stepping away from the door, and picking up the puppy in one motion.

Why, Meg? Why invite this woman into our home?

'Thank you, yes, it would be good to get out of the cold.'

Meg has to pull me away from the door, as anxiety has turned my legs to stone. PC Greenhouse moves past, following Meg through to the living room, patting the puppy's head as she does.

'What's his name?' PC Greenhouse asks once we're settled.

'She's a she,' Meg corrects, 'and her name is Lola. Joe's looking after her for a friend.'

Greenhouse looks straight at me and my back feels like someone just sprayed it with a hose. Why did Meg have to tell her that? She didn't ask whether the dog was ours or how long we'd had her. Why is my wife so willing to give away unnecessary detail to someone who could restrict our freedom if she discovered the truth?

'Oh, my mistake,' Greenhouse apologises. 'How old is she?'

Meg frowns, and then looks to me.

'I-I don't know,' I answer honestly. 'She's a puppy so a few months I guess. I didn't ask.'

'Well, she's very cute. My partner and I were thinking about rescuing a dog, but with my hours and her allergies, it's just not the right time. I'm not sure I'd get anything done either, and just spend all day playing with her.'

I'm staring at that bodycam lens again, now realising that it's recording evidence of David's dog in my house while he is missing. It's like I just painted a huge target on my back.

I clear my throat, keen to move things along, and regain some level of control. 'The girl who is missing … I presume you're talking about Hazel Cooper?'

Meg gasps 'Wait, what? Hazel? Hazel is missing?'

Of course, I realise now that I haven't seen her to pass on Neil's message. Greenhouse is also giving me a curious look.

'Her dad Neil called by this morning, asking whether she'd stayed over here last night.'

Meg's cheeks flush. 'You never told me that.'

Now is not the time to show our marital discord, so I face Meg, and rest my hand on hers, willing her to read between the lines.

'You were out on your run. Sorry I meant to leave you a note before I went out.'

'You do know the Cooper family then?' Greenhouse asks bluntly.

'I tutor Hazel,' Meg admits, making no effort to apologise to me for not sharing this detail sooner.

'What subjects?'

'Maths and French.'

'And how long have you been tutoring Hazel?'

Meg puffs out her cheeks. 'Um, let's see ... Three months? Maybe less? Hold on, it's on the calendar, I'll just go and check.'

She passes me the beagle, and heads out of the room. Greenhouse's eyes don't leave me the whole time, and so I pretend to be distracted by the dog as a long and uncomfortable silence descends. I know she can't read my mind, but my brain won't stop confessing.

No, I had no idea that my wife had started offering private tuition.

Yes, I am worried about what other secrets my wife might be keeping from me.

Yes, I did see Hazel being abducted last night.

No, I don't know where she is right now.

It's a relief when Meg returns to the room, clutching the calendar, and showing it to Greenhouse. 'There we go, I started the lessons on September third.'

'Thank you,' Greenhouse says with a thin smile, and Meg re-joins me on the sofa, scooping the puppy back onto her lap.

'Can you tell me how the private tuition came about?'

'Um, sure, yeah.' Meg says, but there is a fresh reluctance to her tone, as it dawns on her that she hasn't shared this story with me. 'So ... I used to work with Neil – Hazel's dad – but I stopped working about six months ago, after ... Well, anyway ... I was chatting to a mutual friend – Sally – and she mentioned that Neil was looking for someone to tutor Hazel in Maths and French, and she thought it might be of interest to me, as I used to do tutoring in my spare time at university. I was reluctant at first, but then, I thought it would be good to have something to focus my attention on, so I agreed to meet with Neil and his wife Ruby, and they introduced me to Hazel, and she seemed like a good kid, so I agreed to do it.'

Have I really been so distracted by planning David's demise that I missed my wife's new joie de vivre? No wonder she chooses not to leave me a note when she goes out running these days.

'How frequently do you tutor her?'

'Twice a week, Tuesdays and Thursdays for about an hour at a time. She comes here straight after school, and then I drop her home after the session.'

'And how has it been working out?'

Meg glances at me momentarily as if she might offer an apology, before thinking better of it.

'It took a couple of sessions for us to settle in to a routine, but yeah I'd say it's going well. I know Hazel has a ... A bit of a reputation, but deep down I think she's a lot smarter than people give her credit for.'

'What do you mean by her having a bit of a reputation, Mrs Irons?'

Another temporary glance at me.

'Just that I know she had some trouble at school with one or two of the other girls, but I don't think she's malicious, just mixed up like most fourteen year-olds are.'

'When did you last see Hazel, Mrs Irons?'

'Um, it would have been last Thursday.'

'Okay, and how was she when you last saw her?'

'Fine … The same as usual.'

'There wasn't anything troubling her?'

'No, not that I can think of.'

'She didn't mention running away, or that she was unhappy about anything whether at school, or at home?'

'No, I'm sorry.'

'What about Hazel's boyfriend Matt? Did she ever discuss him with you?'

'Not specifically. I mean, I'm aware she has a boyfriend, and that he goes to her school, but that's about it. Sorry, our relationship is very much teacher and student.'

'What about you, Mr Irons? How would you describe your relationship with Hazel?'

I don't appreciate the bluntness of the question, but I understand why she phrased it that way. I picture the look of terror in her eyes through the van window.

'I don't know her,' I say with greater affirmation than I'm feeling in that moment. 'I'm always working when Meg gives her classes.'

I pat my wife's hand for solidarity, making no show of the animosity I'm feeling.

'So Hazel didn't stay here last night?' PC Greenhouse asks next.

'No, absolutely not,' Meg replies firmly. 'Is that what Neil thinks? Oh gosh, they must be fraught with worry. I remember when … Well, will you pass on my best wishes?'

'Of course. Forgive my next question, but can I ask where you both were last night?'

'I had a migraine,' Meg says, 'so I took one of my pills and went to bed around eight I think.'

'And you, Mr Irons?'

Here we go, time to record my rehearsed lie for the camera. I need to sound confident, and believe the words I'm about to speak, because one day this interview might be analysed and any waiver in my voice will be picked up on.

'I watched the football, which went on until about ten, and then I watched the news and headed up after that, so must have been about eleven.'

'No, that's not right,' Meg interrupts, and my heartrate slows to a virtual halt. 'I woke and went to the toilet at half eleven, and you weren't in bed then.'

I can't believe she's just plunged this knife between my shoulder blades. It's one thing to question my version of events, and quite another to effectively point the finger and shout, 'Liar, liar, pants on fire,' while we're being interviewed by a police officer.

'Um, really? Are you sure?' I try, stalling for time.

'Yeah, I remember it because I was surprised you were still up.'

I can feel Greenhouse's stare burning into me.

'Oh, I remember now,' I say quickly, certain my hair must now look like I've just stepped out of the shower, 'I was planning to come up after the news, but I must have dropped off on the sofa. I remember waking suddenly and there was some black and white movie on, so I turned it off and headed up. I didn't look at the time to be honest.'

'Well you were snoring your head off when I got up at half seven,' Meg adds to my relief.

PC Greenhouse stands and extends her hand, passing Meg a business card. 'If Hazel *does* get in touch with you, please do call as soon as you can. Her parents are understandably worried, and just want her home.'

Meg passes me the beagle, and follows Greenhouse out to the front door. I can hear them speaking, but can't make out what's being said. The front door closes, and Meg hurries back into the room, scooping the beagle from my lap, and hugging her close.

'I can't believe you didn't tell me Hazel is missing,' she says, her brow furrowed with worry.

'You're one to talk,' I snap back unkindly, as I fail to control my own frustration. 'When were you going to tell me you'd started giving private tuition again?'

She looks shocked by my outburst. 'I'm sorry, I didn't … I mean, I thought I had mentioned it.'

My cheeks flush as I suddenly question whether I'm the one in the wrong, and it was my lack of active listening that left me in the dark.

'None of that matters right now,' she says, cuddling the beagle closer. 'What if she didn't run away, and was taken like our Lydia?'

I wish I could tell her what I witnessed, how the man with white hair grabbed Hazel and forced her into his van. But then I'd have to explain what I was doing there, and why I didn't do more to stop him escaping.

'I need to go and see Neil and Ruby,' Meg says next, lowering the puppy to the floor. 'Maybe there's something I can do to help. Do you want to come with me?'

I don't think I'd be able to meet Neil's gaze without being consumed with guilt.

'I can't, I'm sorry,' I tell her. 'I have something I need to do.'

I don't add that I'm planning to go straight to Harrington Manor and have it out with David once and for all.

Chapter 24

7 weeks ago

Nearing the gates at Harrington Manor, Joe felt as nervous as when he had first come to visit Lady Violet seven weeks earlier. Even though she'd given him the code for the gate, and had dropped the set of spare keys at their office, he still felt as though coming here today was tantamount to breaking and entering. He sensed he wouldn't have felt so guilty had he actually managed to locate a prospective client to take on the letting agreement.

Lowering his window, he studied the small card she'd given with the key code, and proceeded to type in the digits, exhaling when the LED turned green and the motors revved into life. The estate looked more daunting than he remembered with the trees overhanging the lawn edge casting claw-like shadows in the late morning sunshine. And with no sign of life inside the old building, Joe was transported to black and white horror films he remembered watching as a child late at night when his parents thought he was asleep. Suddenly, the allure of the estate he'd envied on his last visit vanished.

He had yet to hear back from the private investigator, though Edie Sinclair had warned him it would take her at least a couple of weeks to carry out the surveillance he'd requested. And just because she was digging up dirt on David Calderwood didn't mean he had to go through with the plan that had been slowing forming in his head since that moment in Mike's office. Technically he hadn't broken any laws yet, as planning a crime wasn't in itself a criminal offence. And his visit to Harrington Manor today was part of the agreement to ensure the upkeep of the grade-II listed building while Lady Violet and her husband were abroad.

Such lies did little to ease the grumblings in his gut.

Parking outside the front door, Joe hurried inside, suddenly aware that although he couldn't see any of the neighbouring properties, it didn't necessarily mean they couldn't see him. Once inside, his pulse returned to a normal rate, and he made his way upstairs to see which of the rooms had been left unlocked and were theoretically available for him to use.

Unsurprisingly, he found the master bedroom was locked, as were the doors either side of it. The three bedrooms that were unlocked each contained a double bed, built in wardrobe, and chest of drawers unit. None of the beds were made up, though Lady Violet had made reference to a linen cupboard near the top of the stairs. There certainly wasn't anything inspiring Joe as to how he could keep David contained if he was to bring him here. He didn't want it to feel like a vacation.

Heading back downstairs, he scoped out the drawing room, dining room and kitchen, but found all remaining doors locked. A door inside the kitchen was also locked, and he could only hazard it leading into a larder of some description. Lady Violet had told him that none of the regular staff would remain at the property during their time away, which suggested they probably employed a cook and he couldn't imagine Lady Violet vacuuming the long hallways.

Looking at the floor plans he'd managed to download, he couldn't work out where the larder could be as the dining room backed onto the kitchen, and there didn't appear to be sufficient room for anything larger than a broom cupboard. Turning on the light on his phone, he crouched down and shone the beam beneath the edge of the door, but still couldn't see what was inside. Standing, he was about to leave when he saw Lady Violet's name appear as an incoming call. Panicking, he quickly answered it.

'Joe?' her voice called with urgency. 'I need you to go to the house as the silent alarm has been triggered.'

Joe wasn't aware that the house had any kind of alarm; it certainly hadn't come up in any conversation between them that he could recall.

'I'm at the house now,' Joe said to reassure her. 'Sorry, it must have been me that triggered the alarm. I'm sorry, I wasn't aware there was an alarm.'

Her voice muffled as she shared the admission with someone nearby.

'That explains it then! You'll have to go to the closet beneath the staircase on the ground floor to reset it. Can you go there now and I'll give you the code?'

Joe left the kitchen, darted through the drawing room and to the cupboard beneath the stairs. Inside a large metal box on the wall was flashing red.

'Okay, I'm here.'

'Type in eight, seven, four, one, and then press

enter.'

He did as instructed, and the red flashing stopped immediately.

'Okay, it's stopped now,' he relayed.

'Good. So you're at the house, have you managed to secure us a tenant yet?'

'I have a viewing this afternoon,' he said to cover his real reason for being there, 'so I thought I'd come up and just make sure the place was as you'd left it.' He paused as inspiration struck. 'The thing is, Lady Violet, while I was in the kitchen mopping the floor, I accidentally spilled some of the cleaner and it's gone under the locked door there. Is there a way for me to open the door and just clean up the spillage? I'd hate for the smell to put off prospective clients.'

'That's the door to the basement, Joe. I'd rather you not go down there if it's all the same to you.'

Joe's pulse quickened as he thought about the possibility of keeping David locked in a windowless basement.

'I'd hate for the cleaning product to lie there until your return though. There's no telling what kind of damage it might do to the floor. I'd really like to get it cleaned up for you. I promise I'll lock up as soon as I'm done.'

He heard her sigh, but no response was forthcoming.

'Lady Violet?'

'The thing is, Joe, the basement … it isn't something I want the public to see.'

Joe couldn't understand what could be making Lady Violet so reticent about giving him access.

'I promised you I would keep the place in good order, and if that liquid is allowed to congeal, I don't think I would be living up to your expectations. You can trust my discretion, Lady Violet.'

Another sigh, this was louder and tainted with a frustrated groan. 'Okay, well first you must promise me that you will clean up where necessary, and do not go down the stairs. There are … My husband … There are things down there that would be … highly embarrassing for me should their existence ever be revealed.'

Intrigued, Joe reassured her that he would simply clean up the mess and lock up behind him. Lady Violet relented and explained where he could find the skeleton keys for all the locked doors, and described the basement door key to him. Once she had gone, he unlocked the door, and immediately headed down the stairs, gasping when he saw the prison bars of the sex dungeon Lady Violet had so desperately wanted to keep a secret. He immediately set to work clearing out the makeshift cell, moving the apparatus to one of the locked rooms upstairs where it could remain out of sight until he'd concluded his business in the basement.

Chapter 25

Joe

Lydia's eyes stare back at me in the mirror, urging me to do what is necessary to save Hazel Cooper, as I race back to Harrington Manor. It's almost as if I can hear her voice repeating, 'Not again, Daddy,' over and over.

I can't fail her. Not again.

Parking the car at the side of the house, I tear through the living room and kitchen, taking the stairs down to the basement two at a time. David is lying prone against the bars, but he must sense my anger, as he quickly scurries across the cage to the apparent safety of the inflated mattress, but he doesn't realise that I'm beyond shouting.

Fumbling the key in the lock, I can't keep my hands from shaking, as anxiety and dread mix toxically with adrenalin. The keys clatter to the floor.

'W-What are you doing?' David croaks from inside the cell, his eyes firmly fixed on me. 'Are you letting me go?'

I stoop to collect the keys from the cold concrete, and pause long enough to answer his question with a glare. If I was a braver man I'd already have the answers I crave. I need to be stronger. For Lydia. For Hazel.

My hands are so clammy that it takes two attempts

to actually grab hold of the keys. I straighten and wipe the sheen from my forehead and eyes with the back of my sleeve. Is it always so hot down here?

The key squeezes in, and with a twist to the left, the metal lock grinds apart, and I yank open the door. David's eyes are white spots in the darkness, but I've seen that look of terror before. It's the same look that's been staring back at me in the mirror for these last few weeks.

We wouldn't be here – none of this would be happening – if he hadn't taken Lydia, I remind myself. *This is all his fault.*

'Where is she?' I roar, giving him one last chance to come clean.

'I don't know,' he whimpers, and it's all the motivation I need.

Swallowing the distance between us in three strides, I grab tufts of his shirt in my balled fists, and heave him up off the floor. He's lighter than I'm anticipating, but not light enough that I can actually lift him into the air. Eye to eye will have to do.

'Tell me where she is,' I growl.

'I-I told you: I don't know what you mean.'

'Where is Hazel?'

There's a glint of recognition behind the fear in his pupils.

'Oh … her … well … um, let me see.'

He's stalling. He's waiting to see whether I have the courage to deliver the violence that will wrench control of this situation back into my grasp. He's not the only one with doubts.

'Tell me where she is, or I swear to God, I'll kill you

right now. Where is Hazel?'

He doesn't answer, daring me to go against every instinct in my body. I charge him backwards with all my strength until we crash into the brickwork at the back of the cage. Even I feel the force of the move, despite using his body to cushion the blow. His shoulders sag, as his torso weakens.

'Where is Hazel?' I yell again, to reinforce the message.

'I don't know who she is,' he spits back.

Lifting him temporarily from the wall, I slam him into it a second time and he grows limper in my hands.

'Stop lying to me! You know where she is.'

I slam him into the wall for a third time, but I have to be honest, my sweaty grip on his shirt is weakening as lactic acid burns in my forearms. He must sense this, because although I accepted his breathlessness to be genuine, he suddenly tautens, and tries to push back against me, but I plant my right foot behind me, and heave back.

His head lifts and he looks straight at me, but the grin breaking out across his face is the only truth he's provided since we got here.

'You fucking coward! Look at you, Joe. Just look at yourself. You have me at a disadvantage. I'm locked alone in this cell, and you have the freedom to do whatever you want, but you don't have the cojones to go through with it, do you? You threaten to harm and even kill me, when we both know neither will happen.'

I push my fists harder into his chest, but he barely moves this time.

'When your little girl needed you to do whatever it

took to save her, you couldn't, instead leaving it to the police to fuck everything up. Where were you when she needed you, Joe? Buying fucking ice cream of all things. You're pathetic.'

The little voice in the back of my head is screaming that he's playing a game, and his putdowns are nothing more than manipulation, but my imagination pictures him leading Lydia away from that park, and something snaps. I loosen the grip of my right hand, clench the fist tight again, and swing it at his face. It connects with his cheek, the sound reminiscent of a wet fish slapping a counter.

David laughs at me, his face barely moved by the action.

It was a weak punch, made by someone not practiced in the art of boxing. I take a deep breath and try again. This time I feel every knuckle connect with the bone in his nose, and as he doubles over, I'm the one who yelps as the burn between my knuckles fires.

'That's the spirit, Joe,' he pants, bent at the middle. 'I mean, it's pathetic by any normal standards, but good for you for finally stepping up to the plate.'

I turn my back, holding my right wrist to my chest, watching my fingers as I try to straighten and move them, checking for any signs of a break. The sharp pain begins to dull slightly as my fingertips play an invisible keyboard.

I hear his movement, but I'm too late to take evasive manoeuvres. David's shoulder slams in to my back, sending me hurtling towards the floor, my outstretched hands breaking my fall. But he's underestimated the move and also crashes to the floor a couple of feet ahead of me. Our eyes fall on the open cell door at the exact same moment, and we both scrabble to our feet, but age is in my favour, and as I tear past him, I'm able to kick his arm out from beneath him just as he's attempting to push himself up, and he slumps back to the floor again.

I can't believe I didn't even think to close the cell door behind me. Reaching through the bars, I extract the key, and pull the door closed, so that it locks us both in. Pocketing the key, I allow myself a moment to get my breath back and regain my composure. David remains slumped on the floor, but this time I'm not going to assume that his apparent weakness is anything more than illusion.

It would be so easy to walk over to him and kick until he begs me to stop, but in spite of knowing exactly who this man is, and what he's capable of, I can't get past the tiny voice telling me that there is a one per cent chance that he's telling the truth and didn't kill Lydia. If I could just silence the doubt, this would be so much easier, but he hasn't wavered from his story once.

He makes no effort to sit up, and challenge me again, but if I was him I'd be biding my time as well. I need to show him that he's wrong to underestimate me.

Summoning all my willpower, and with the pain in my hand slowly easing, I move forward, and step over him, planting one foot either side of his ribs. His back and shoulders tighten at my touch. Bending my knees, I carefully lower myself, wary of any move he might make to lash out. Then, when my hands are only inches from the back of his neck, I quickly pull my arm out and slide along the front of his throat, pulling his head up as I do, arching his back. His hands instantly shoot up to my forearm, but it's too late; I have him exactly where I want him. Pressing my right knee into the base of his spine, I could easily strangle him in the nook of my elbow.

He must realise the perilous position he's now in as his bony fingers claw at my arm, and then try to reach up and scratch at my neck and face. I tilt my body back and out of his reach, in turn bending him up further. He coughs and splutters.

'I'm only going to ask you once more, I sneer. 'Tell me where your partner has taken Hazel, or I'll keep squeezing.'

I can feel his Adam's apple bobbing against my arm as he gasps for any breath, but my grip is tight enough to prevent any inhalation. I hold him there for a count of thirty, but he still makes no attempt to speak. If we remain in this position for much longer, he'll pass out, or worse.

What is wrong with him? Why can't he just come clean? He has nothing to gain by dying in this cell.

His arms drop from their squeeze on my forearm, and his body goes limp. This could easily be just another of his tricks, but I can't risk actually killing him. Reluctantly, I extract my arm from around his neck, and his torso sags to the ground. Standing, I move away from him, back to the bars, but this time I keep my gaze on him. I need to know whether he's still alive, but the cell is so gloomy that it's impossible to see if he's breathing.

I hold my breath, listening for his, but my heart is

beating so fast that I can't hear anything else but its thud, thud, thud.

Relenting, I cross the room, and roll him onto his back. His eyes open and he stares up at me, and then that sickening grin breaks out across his face again.

'I knew you didn't have it in you,' he splutters.

I back away until I crash into the cell door, and then I fumble the keys into the lock, slamming it behind me. His laughter echoes off the walls, as I tear up the stairs and burst into the kitchen. I can still hear him laughing as I push the basement door closed and lock it, and as I turn I see Lydia staring back at me, deep sorrow in her eyes.

I fall to my knees in front of her, and the tears burn my eyes as they flow freely for the little girl I continue to fail every day.

Chapter 26

Hazel

She's lost track of time, but she doesn't think it has anything to do with the two gulps of water she digested. She guesses that it must have been at least twenty or so minutes since she last swallowed some, and she hasn't noticed any of the effects the police woman warned them about. No dizziness, no loss of inhibitions, no nausea.

Fear is the only thing she feels.

He's out there somewhere now sitting behind a laptop screen or television set while she lies motionless on the bed. Where is the entertainment in that? She remembers her mum telling her about the television show Big Brother where cameras filmed the lives of a group of captive volunteers, editing it to a highlights package that had viewers glued to their screens for series after series. Hazel hadn't been able to understand the appeal, and having watched Love Island still doesn't see how the mundanity of one person's life can bring entertainment to the masses. Especially when she's the focus of this "show" and has done little more than lie in bed all day.

She continues to check on the red LED every few minutes now seeing its presence as reassurance that he isn't headed her way. She opens the bottle of water and takes a longer drink.

Her ankle is red raw from her tugging and twisting the rope but it's still not any closer to coming off her foot. Maybe if he's planning to bring her more food later, he might mistakenly supply her with cutlery that she could use to try and cut it off, though something tells her he won't make that mistake. She realises now that he left the door open to test whether she would make a break for it, and she'd fallen into his trap. She needs to remember that he has probably held other girls here before her, and will anticipate her every move.

Fresh hope flashes through her mind. If she isn't the first to be held captive here, then maybe one of the previous occupants might have left some kind of clue to help her. She doesn't know what this might be, but her heart is fluttering with the prospect, and so she pushes back the sleeping bag, and stretches her legs out, before standing, and feeling her way along towards the back wall. The rope around her ankle just about allows her to reach the wall with her fingertips stretched out. It is covered in the same veneer as the wall beside the mattress, but this is stirring another memory in her mind.

It was two years ago, and her dad was converting their spare bedroom into a makeshift office for when he worked from home. He bought a second-hand desk online and went to collect it, but when it came to building it at home, he couldn't get one of the dowels to fit properly. In a fit of rage he slammed the top of the desk, thinking brute force was the answer, but instead, an unseen screw penetrated the veneer top of the desk. Angered at his own impatience, he explained that the desk itself was made of chipboard – wood shavings glued together – and that the veneer was just a thin strip of wood providing a smarter finish.

Could it be that the walls of the cabin are built of something equally flimsy? Could enough pressure in the right spot allow her to break through?

She buries the idea for now, figuring it is best to wait until the LED is off before exploring that possibility. Continuing to follow the wall with her fingers, she stubs her toe against something made of hard plastic which falls and rolls away.

Crouching she looks at the bucket, swiftly recognising why it has been left for her in the corner of the cabin. It makes sense that he wouldn't want to have to take her to use the facilities. Lifting the bucket, she looks for any area in the room away from the gaze of the LED, but there are no hiding places; no privacy. He wants to see everything.

She is tempted to stand before the camera and demand he switch it off while she uses the bucket, but she has no idea whether the camera is also fitted with sound, or if he's even currently watching.

She hadn't realised how much she needed to go until she kicked the bucket, but now she can think of nothing else. She considers trying to stand the flimsy mattress on its side to create a makeshift cubicle, but as soon as she starts to lift it, it flops at the edges, and won't do the job unless she holds it around herself.

Instead, she places the bucket back where it was, turns her back to the camera and wraps the sleeping bag around her middle, allowing her to lower her trousers without the camera catching sight of her bottom. He won't have the satisfaction of seeing her face either.

The plastic rim of the bucket is cold against her skin, but she pushes the discomfort from her mind, carefully perched, gripping the side, and worried about the prospect of slipping and spilling the contents all over the floor. Draining the rest of the bottle, she figures she'll have a couple of hours before the desire to go will return.

She's about to stand when something cool blows against the toes of her left foot. She instinctively pulls her foot away, but then realising that there is nothing else in the cabin with her, gives in to curiosity. Keeping her body perfectly still, she slides her foot out against the cool floor until her heel is as far as it will go. Sure enough a cool pocket of air blows against her toes from what appears to be …

She focuses her stare, willing her eyes to see through the gloom and darkness.

Yes, she's not mistaken, there is a crack in the floorboards in this corner of the room. The slight breeze coming from beneath the floor is evidence that there is air circulating beneath the floor, and now as she thinks back to the moment she made her break for freedom, she remembers the three steps down to the straw-strewn floor. And then she remembers how the floor seemed to shake when he climbed the steps and entered the cabin. It has to be suspended above the ground in some way, and if it is and she can widen this crack, there's maybe a way out of the cabin without using the bolted door.

Shifting her body weight slightly so that the end of

her left foot will be hidden from the camera, she raises her foot as much as she dare, and quickly drives her heel down to the floor. She winces against the burning sensation, but can't help smiling at the sound of splintering.

Chapter 27

Joe

I wake flat out on the kitchen floor, I don't know how long later. I wasn't even aware I'd fallen asleep. I'm alone, save for the monster trapped in the basement, but he can't do any harm down there. He must be hungry by now, and I'm surprised that someone so used to fine dining hasn't kicked up a stink about his lack of provisions. It leaves me with a difficult decision: if I believe I can find the strength to break him, then I'm going to have to provide him with at least basic sustenance. But if I don't cave, and allow human instinct to kick in then might he break under the threat of starving to death?

Thus far, I've somehow allowed him to control this situation, even though he's the one trapped in the cell. There's no logic to it in my mind. If I was in his position, I know I would have broken by now, and told him anything he wanted to hear, even if it wasn't true. And that's the thing that annoys me the most: why won't he give me the confession I've demanded, even though he could lie if it wasn't true? He's lied about everything else, so why not that? He must sense that I don't have it in me to kill him, though exactly how this can end any other way has yet to occur to me. One of us is going to end up in prison or the ground, but it's too early to determine which yet.

I wish I was stronger. Maybe I should have researched and hired someone to do the necessary deed for me. I don't know how one goes about hiring a hitman, but there must be ways and means.

In the meantime, I'm going to need to get in touch with the darkness that I know lurks deep. I never thought I'd actually be able to jump David with the stun gun and get him into the basement, but I managed it. I've even managed to throw my first punch – albeit meekly – so maybe I am capable of more.

Pushing myself up from the floor, I stretch out the ache in the muscles in my back, neck and shoulders, and cross the room to the tool box I left here last week. Unlatching the lid, I run my fingers through the tools within, until I feel the hardened plastic handle of the hammer. Screwdrivers and pliers scatter, as I shake the hammer free, and pull it out, holding it above my head, calling on the might of Thor to give me the courage I need.

I'm about to carry it down to the basement to see David's reaction to me coming to a fight tooled up, when I feel something sharp poking into my leg. Reaching into my pocket, I remove a small brown notebook, which I don't recognise at first, until I realise it's the address book I took from David's house this morning. It had totally slipped my mind, but as I hold it in my left hand, and the hammer in my right, I know which route of investigation will be easier to stomach.

Returning the hammer to the tool box, I move across to the window, flipping open the book, studying the names, addresses and phone numbers scrawled inside. It's possible that one of these names identifies the white-haired brute who snatched Hazel, and it deserves to be looked into before I reach the last resort.

I read each name, and where there are addresses I try to picture where the address is in relation to David's house and the Stable Road Recreation Ground. But I soon draw a blank because my mobile is still at home, and I have no means of getting online to look up these people without it. I would assume Harrington Manor has internet access, but I don't know where the router is, or the Wi-Fi code, and have no device to connect either way.

I know if I had my phone, I could look up each named individual to see if they have social media accounts and would quickly be able to see whether any of them look like the white-haired man. David's phone was basic without internet access, so I can't use that either.

Pocketing the address book, I know what I need to do, leave the house, and drive to the Reading Gate Retail Park. Thirty minutes later I'm sitting in the car park of Curry's PC World. Reaching into the glove box, I pull out the baseball cap I keep in there for sunny days, and wrench it low over my forehead, peak pointed down. With a deep breath, I exit my car, keep my eyes on the ground, and hurry across to the shop. Once inside, I hang around the televisions and tablets, before slowly making my way to the mobile phones, when there is more of a crowd there.

'Can I help you with something, sir?' a young woman in a black short sleeve shirt and wearing a badge that says 'Here to Help' asks.

I avoid looking at her directly. 'Just after a couple of Pay-as-you-go phones,' I say quietly.

'Sure,' she replies, 'any particular device taken your fancy? Most of our phones can be bought as SIM-only, and we offer a range of Pay-as-you-go SIMs depending on your needs.'

'I just need a basic smart phone for … My kids are going on a school trip, and I want them to be able to call in an emergency.'

I don't know why I've lied to complicate matters. She hasn't asked what I intend to use the phones for, but my paranoia feels the need to explain my otherwise out-of-character behaviour.

'Do you know whether your children will be using them for basic internet and social media browsing as well, or are either of them into gaming at all?'

This is taking too long, and my head feels like it's on fire beneath the baseball cap. If she sees me sweating, she's bound to figure out there's something wrong, and potentially tip off the security guards to keep an eye on me.

'Just general browsing. Listen, I'm sorry to be a pain but I'm in a bit of a hurry as they're shopping with me today, and I want this to be a surprise. I just need two phones that aren't the cheapest of the cheap, but don't cost an arm and a leg. Are there any deals on at the moment?'

She points to a laminated poster on the wall. 'Our Samsung phones have twenty per cent off when bought with a 5GB SIM card on any of our networks.'

I study the poster, and point at a mid-price device

and hold up two fingers.

'Fewer arguments if they both have the same one,' I add, again for no apparent reason.

Having paid in cash, I hurry out of the shop and collapse into my car seat, removing the baseball cap much to the relief of my clammy brow.

Unboxing the first phone, I insert the SIM card and switch it on, skipping through the settings menus as quickly as possible. The device takes two minutes to boot up, and is fifty per cent charged so I plug the charging cable into the car's cigarette lighter, so the phone can start charging once we get moving. I don't plan to use both phones, but I figured it was better to buy a back-up now, rather than having to go through this routine again at a later date.

I count through the names in the address book, immediately discounting eighteen who bear women's names. That isn't to say that he's using some kind of cryptic code in the book or has listed his partner under a woman's name, but I'm playing the odds here. If none of the other names produce results, then I'll have these eighteen to come back to at a later date. There's no reason to assume he has codified the address book, as there's no way he could have suspected I'd break into his house and try to use it to find Hazel. I jot the names into a draft text message in the phone as a back-up.

Then studying the addresses, I preliminarily rule out a further nine whose homes are at least two hours from Reading. That isn't to say that these men wouldn't travel down from Birmingham, Manchester, Edinburgh or up from Plymouth, but it will take too much effort to visit each of their addresses on the off-chance that they drove here, grabbed Hazel and then returned home with her. I can't explain why, but my gut says the white haired man is more local than that. To have been out in the middle of the night at the recreation ground and able to evade the police so quickly suggests local knowledge.

The Facebook app has come preinstalled as it often does these days, and so I sign in to my account, waste five minutes proving that I am the person trying to access my account, and finally begin to look up the remaining twenty names. I'm forced to scroll through five pages of Will Spencers, but only two of them live in Berkshire, and neither profile image looks like David's partner. I continue to search ruling out another seven names, but that still leaves twelve names where I can't locate a Facebook profile, or the profile picture isn't available or distinguishable.

Of the remaining twelve, seven don't have an address, and only a phone number, so I'm not sure how to begin finding out whether they could or couldn't be the man I'm looking for. I try writing one of the numbers into a search engine, but I don't get more than a provider's name. I could pass the book to Detective Andrews and tell him what I saw that night, and that I believe one of the people listed in the address book is the man responsible for abducting Hazel, but he'd probably have me sectioned or arrested for wasting his time.

A fresh idea strikes, and I sign into my Gmail account on the phone, drafting an email to Edie Sinclair. I thank her for the information she was able to dig up on David, and promise this will be the last request I make of her. I type in the names and numbers of the seven, and ask her to supply basic information: age, address, employer, etc. I sign the email promising to pay whatever it costs, and asking that she action as a priority. Hopefully, I didn't burn all my bridges with her the last time we met.

And that leaves me with five names and addresses within a thirty minute radius of where I'm currently sitting. Typing each address into Google Maps, I work out a route that will allow me to drive to each address without having to double back on myself. I then check each address using Street View, looking for the presence of the grey van, but to no avail. Turning over the engine, I start the directions.

Chapter 28

6 weeks ago

'There he is!' a voice went up from somewhere within the throng of heavy metal music, shouted conversations, and clinking of glasses.

Joe could barely see beyond the body directly in front of him, but strained his neck, trying to hear where the shout had come from.

'Over here, Joe,' the voice shouted again, somewhere off to the right.

Joe had followed the signs inside the busy student bar towards the promise of a beer garden, but the closest thing to a garden was a single ceramic pot stuffed full of cigarette butts that Joe had noticed as he'd stepped out into the cold reverie. The fact that the floor and steps were no longer carpeted was an indication that they were no longer indoors. A concrete monolith surrounded by high brick walls. Clearly the owners of the bar had determined that anything outside was classified as 'garden' to distinguish it from the rest of the venue.

It hadn't been Joe's idea to meet here, but beggars couldn't be choosers, and Joe had felt it necessary to see the man he'd come to meet in his natural habitat before determining whether he could trust him to join the enterprise.

A tug on Joe's arm pulled him through the crowd like a warm knife through butter, and in seconds they were away from the bustle and at a wooden picnic bench in the far corner of the garden.

'How long's it been?' Rhys asked as he settled onto his side of the bench, across from Joe.

Joe knew exactly how many years it had been since he'd last seen Rhys on graduation night, but made a show of trying to perform the mental arithmetic, pulling an awkward face, and staring blankly at the starless night sky.

'Must be twelve years, maybe?' Joe said, repeating the estimate as Rhys leaned closer, straining to hear over the noise of the live band performing on the concrete stage at the edge of the main building.

'Right, right,' Rhys confirmed, almost shouting. 'You graduated in 2009, right?'

Joe nodded, but didn't want to draw attention to the fact that Rhys had failed to graduate, yet had remained hanging around the same bars and venues they'd frequented more than a decade ago. Joe couldn't be certain if Rhys still saw himself as a student; he certainly dressed the part in a retro Blink 182 t-shirt beneath an open flannel shirt and ripped jeans. The shaved head was new, but probably a necessity based on the obviously thinning patches.

'You look well,' Joe offered, taking a sip of the lemonade he'd ordered at the bar on his way down to the garden. He wanted a clear head tonight.

'Yeah, you too, bro,' Rhys reciprocated, raising the pint glass of multi-coloured liquid, and clinking it against Joe's. 'I couldn't believe it when I saw your message on Facebook about wanting to meet and catch-up. Figured you were probably married with kids by now.'

Joe bit down on his tongue to keep the sting from filling his eyes. 'What are you up to these days? I think the last I read you were a tour manager for an up and coming band?'

In truth, Joe had scrolled through Rhys's posts before coming out this evening, but the post about the band was from 2018.

Rhys pointed at the three lads with guitars on the stage. 'That's my group. The fittie on keyboard is my missus.'

Joe had to strain to see the petite blonde slamming her fingers against the keys, but nodded at Rhys when he spotted her.

'They're …' Joe began to say, but didn't know how to describe the cacophony assaulting his eardrums. 'They're certainly popular with the crowd,' he settled for.

'Yeah, they're still building their repertoire, but we're hoping to cut an album later in the year and see if we can generate some real interest with record labels. I've got a mate who reckons he can put an album on the desk of one of the top execs at the company where he's temping, so fingers crossed …'

Joe raised his right hand and made a show of crossing his fingers for Rhys to see.

'So what are you up to these days?' Rhys questioned, leaning closer so he wouldn't have to shout quite so loud. 'The last time I saw you, you were planning on using your degree to set up your own business to develop housing projects, weren't you?'

That project had lasted for about six months before crippling student debts had meant he's had to take the first job that he'd found while trying to set things up in the background. As one year in the call centre had turned into a second and third, the business plan had gathered dust, and then marriage and eventually fatherhood meant that putting food on the table had become priority. Not that he regretted any of that.

'What can I say?' Joe shrugged. 'Maybe this time next year we'll both be millionaires.'

They'd been good friends sharing a house in their second and third years of university, bingeing episodes of Only Fools and Horses between lectures, while smoking whatever Rhys was experimenting with. To look at the pair of them now, they were polar opposites.

'It's good to see you, man,' Rhys said, his eyes glazed.

Joe could only guess at how many of these cocktails he'd already consumed prior to their meeting.

'I have to confess,' Joe began, leaning so close, his lips were practically touching Rhys's ear. 'There was another reason I wanted to meet. Do you still have contacts outside of the law?'

Rhys gave him a puzzled smile. 'I can still score weed, if that's what you're after?'

Joe shook his head. 'Not weed, but something a bit more specialist. Hypothetically, if I needed to get my hands on a gun, could you sort me out?'

Chapter 29

Joe

It's after two by the time I make it to the third address on my list of five, and to say I've seen the best Reading and its surrounding towns have to offer would be an overstatement. It's all very well having an address for potential suspects, but what I hadn't considered was how I would actually be able to find out who lives inside the property. I was lucky with the first address on the list, as Barry the owner was outside washing his vintage MG racer.

In his mid-forties at a guess, the bungalow, overly-elaborate quiff, and of course the soft-top car were all clear indicators of a man going through a midlife crisis. Whilst guilty of poor taste, he was clearly not the white-haired man I witnessed abducting Hazel. To confirm my suspicion, I approached him, claiming to be looking for someone called Glenda whom I was supposed to be collecting a purchase from. Barry was very accommodating, telling me – bearing in mind he'd never met me before – he lives alone, that he inherited the bungalow from his late mother, and his ex-wife can go to hell.

The second property – a flat on the sixth floor of a high rise – and inhabited by Ed Cox was more difficult to rule out. The problem with searching for a specific person, when in all likelihood they might recognise me from the other night, is that it's not as easy as just walking up to the front door and knocking on it. In that situation, if the white-haired man did answer the door, I'm not sure what I'd do, nor what he would do. I could put distance between us and phone the police, but what if he had Hazel inside and killed her on account of my turning up out of the blue? Or worse, what if he dragged me inside too and killed us both?

These were the exact thoughts running through my head, as I placed the empty mobile phone box beneath my arm, and climbed up the six flights of stairs, the baseball cap once more pulled low over my eyes. Without my own phone marking my GPS coordinates, nobody would know I'd ventured to the tower block, so if I did vanish, I'd be untraceable. I had checked the parking bays around the block for any sign of a grey van, and maybe wouldn't have been so audacious had I spotted one, but still it was a huge risk knocking on the door of flat 6F.

The door was answered by a man in his sixties, but I'd have said his hair was more a silvery-grey than white, and the skin hanging from his bones was in stark contrast to the heavyset frame of David's partner.

'Yes?' he'd asked, a strong smell of weed emanating from the hallway behind him.

'Delivery for Mrs Marshall,' I quickly lied, keen to get going.

'Nobody by that name lives here, son,' the man said, smiling, leaning into the door like it was all that was holding him up. 'You want to come in anyway? It gets very lonely up here. I have poppers, and a host of other goodies.'

I made a show of looking at the imaginary address on the box. 'Is this Flat 7F?'

He shook his head, disappointed. 'Wrong floor, son. You want the next one up. You hurry back though, I'll make it worth your while.'

Embarrassed, I thanked him for his help, and sprinted back to the stairs, not daring to stop and look back until I felt safe in my locked car. Removing the baseball cap, I then burst into hysterical laughter. I couldn't remember the last time I was propositioned, and it now makes me very wary about going to the door of any other addresses on my list. Maybe it was naïve to think I'd have what it takes to narrow the search for Hazel, but what choice do I have?

Lydia's clapping hands greet me when I look into the rear-view mirror. I can't say why, but I sense she would approve of this insane approach.

The third property on the list is just up ahead, and as I stare out of my window, trying to read the numbers on the houses left and right of me, I quickly realise that 22 Fairway Avenue is three doors away, and that there is a dark-coloured Transit van parked facing out in the driveway. My mouth dries instantly, and my breathing quickens. The van isn't grey, but I'd describe it as a metallic cyan, with more than a hint of silver. Parking my car on the opposite side of the road, a few houses up, I turn and study it through the rear window.

It's not dark grey, but then the sky is much brighter today than it was in the middle of the night with limited street lighting. Is it possible I made a mistake? Is that why the police gave up their pursuit, because I told them the van was grey when it was more bluey-grey? I can't see the licence plate from where I'm parked, but I'll be taking a hug risk to move closer to look at it. If only I'd brought the beagle with me I'd have the perfect excuse to be walking along the road, casually glancing at houses and vehicles as I went. There's no sign of life on this residential street, and so I'd stick out like a sore thumb.

Opening my wallet, I pull out the business card for Detective Andrews. The ink is starting to fade, and the corners are fraying slightly, but his number is still legible. This is my chance to phone him and confess everything. I can tell him how I took David in a moment of temporary insanity, but how I saw Wayne Jennings abduct Hazel on Stable Road and drive away. Surely my statement would be enough to allow them to apply for a warrant to search his property and seize the van. It would only take a single source of Hazel's DNA to have him banged to rights. But, of course, what would that mean for me and for David? I'd face prosecution and he'd get to walk away unpunished for his involvement in Lydia's murder. It would be too big a chance to hope that Wayne Jennings would implicate his partner in Lydia's death.

I turn the card over between my fingers, searching for alternatives, but none readily present themselves. But what if I'm wrong now? What if that isn't the van I saw the other night? It's too difficult to be certain from this distance, but I did get near enough the other night that I'm sure I'd know if it was the same van if I got closer. Adding Andrews's number to the burner phone, I pocket the card and climb out.

Pulling the baseball cap low over my eyes once more, this time I keep the burner phone in my hand at my side, ready to call Andrews the moment I confirm the van is the one I saw. I start my journey on the opposite side of the road, casually glancing at the licence plate as I pass by, but I can tell in an instant it isn't the number I recited to the police. Temporary relief is quickly followed by paranoia as I consider that the plates on the van the other night might have been false, and that could have been how Hazel's abductor escaped. It would also explain why the van had still yet to be located and why the registered owner hadn't been arrested.

I continue for a hundred yards or so while different scenarios play out in my head. I picture the van as it pulled away, trying to focus on the exact shade of paint, but it was just so dark. Even when I see myself clambering up to look through the window of the van, my imagination is now making me see the bluey-tinge to the paint when I can't be certain if I did notice it the other night.

I have to be certain before calling Andrews and turning myself in.

Crossing the road, I double-back, making less effort to cover my tracks as I near number 22. The houses here are semi-detached of varying sizes, with the orange brickwork hallmarks of properties built in the early eighties. As far as I can see all of the neighbouring properties have double-glazing installed, but number 22 still has single pane sheets, probably from the original build. There is a large sycamore tree dominating the small area of green lawn which partially blocks the view of the front window from the kerb.

At the bottom of the driveway, I glance around me to make sure that nobody is watching, before sneaking up to the front of the van and resting my hand on the bonnet. The hood is cold, suggesting it hasn't been driven recently. Sneaking along the side of the van, away from the front window, I squeeze myself between the garage and rear doors. Stepping up onto the bumper, there is just enough room to lean so I can peer inside the van, but it's so dark that I have to flick on the torch on the burner phone to actually look inside.

I'm surprised to see the inside is full of various panels of wood that certainly weren't there the other night. Shining the beam around, I close my eyes as I try to picture Hazel's terrified face, but the inside of this van is much darker than what I saw the other night. In fact, now that I'm properly concentrating, I do remember something else about my peer through the window. Whilst Hazel was sprawled on the floor of the van, I realise now that the floor and walls were insulated with fixed plastic panelling. This van has neither, and as I step down, my relief is tempered with disappointment. On the one hand, I don't need to turn myself in and drop a grenade on mine and Meg's future, but I'm still no closer to finding David's partner.

'Oi, you,' a deep voice booms. 'Stop right there!'

I look up and see a red-faced man in khaki trousers and a flannel shirt glaring at me. The vein at the top of his shaved head is throbbing as he leaps from the front door, and it's all I can do to make it down the driveway before he's coming for me.

'You bloody thief!' he yells after me. 'Think you can steal from me again? I'll bloody kill you!'

Something tells me that stopping to explain why I was really looking into the back of his van won't end well, and I break into a sprint, heading away from my own car, but hoping I can go for long enough that he'll give up his pursuit. Whilst I don't doubt he is stronger than me, the extra weight he's carrying around his middle won't be easy to sustain for too long.

Chapter 30

Hazel

She wakes to find herself in a sitting position, with her neck sore from her head having been hanging for some time. The muscle and skin burns as she slowly raises her head with all her strength, but she's still feeling woozy as she does, and she daren't open her eyes as she tries to recall the last thing that happened.

She can remember feeling angry that there was no privacy for her to relieve herself; she remembers squatting over the bucket, the plastic rim cold against her bottom; she remembers finishing the bottle of water; she remembers nothing else.

So he had drugged the bottle after all, it had just taken longer than she'd expected for it to take effect in her system. But where was she now? With her eyes still closed, and the pain in her neck too much for her to look down, she scrabbles around with her fingers, feeling a metal frame. There are thin legs leading down to the floor, a strip of wood supporting her bottom, and another supporting her back. She is sitting on a chair, but that wasn't here when she explored the room before. Which means he has been back in here while she was passed out. She freezes at the thought, and the pain in her neck slowly starts to ease as ice fills her veins.

But the chair isn't the only thing that's different. She hadn't noticed it at first, but now it's painfully obvious. The Jack Skellington costume is gone. Instead, she is wearing what feels like a dress. The bodice is tight around her middle, but as her legs jiggle with nervous energy, the loose material dances over her knees. She dares to open her eyes, as her fingers catch on the smooth material over her legs. It has a satin feel, and offers little resistance as she grips a handful with her right hand.

She has no memory of him removing her Halloween costume, nor of him manhandling her into this costume. The violation fills her eyes with hot tears, which quickly escape. If he changed her clothes, what else did he do?

She doesn't want to think about the answer, but she knows she must. Scouring any flashes of memory, she searches for clues as to what has happened in the last hour or so, but only darkness greets her. Forcing her hands to search the rest of her body, she wills her brain to move past the feelings of disgust and panic, and focus on what her body is telling her. There is no pain in her groin, or in her legs. Although her neck and shoulders ache, there is no pain in her back or lower down. She tries to stand, and despite her legs feeling like they're made of jelly, she manages to grip the chair in her hands, and force herself up. There is no other pain, and as she stumbles back towards the mattress, her legs give way, and she crashes back to the sleeping bag, quickly wrapping it around herself, as her body shakes as the sobbing takes control.

She hears the crash as the chair tumbles to its side

on the floor, but she doesn't care about the noise or mess. She just wants to return to the dreamless sleep where he can't get at her.

'Mum,' she whispers, 'where are you?'

There is no response, but images of her mum and dad flood her mind, and she clings to them, playing out happy memories against the backdrop of the tears soaking he cheeks in their salty warmth. She wills the endorphins to flood her mind with their gentle affection, and eventually her shoulders stop rocking uncontrollably.

He did this to you, she reminds herself. *This isn't your fault.*

The words help to steady her breathing, and as she lies on her side beneath the sleeping bag, her legs curled into her body, a calmness returns, and she begins to lash out at the person who has forced her into this position.

You won't die here, she tells herself. *You will keep him subdued until your escape is guaranteed.*

She remembers the crack in the floorboards by the bucket, and hope begins to filter into her mind's eye. She needs to wait until darkness returns to the room and he is likely to be asleep, and then she will return to work. That is the key to her escape.

Chapter 31

Joe

The fourth name and address on my list is equally as fruitless as the previous three. This time the woman who was kneeling in the front garden weeding was only too happy to speak to me about her late husband Jasper. Lung cancer had got the better of him eight months ago, and when she showed me a photograph of him, his dark skin instantly crossed him off the list even if he hadn't been dead. I thanked her for her time, but asked how her husband had known David Calderwood. The look of disgust as she spoke about my daughter's killer reassured me that the world is a little bit safer with him off the streets.

It is nearly four and the light is fading fast as I finally arrive at 16 Grosvenor Place, and my heart sinks when I see the driveway is empty of any vehicles whatsoever. Despite the enveloping darkness, there are no obvious lights on inside the house either. Again, it's another three-bedroom semi-detached house, not dissimilar to those on Fairway Avenue. Roads like this are ten a penny in and around Reading and Berkshire. Even Meg and I live on a similar road.

Parking up across the road, I kill the engine and login to my emails looking for any response from Edie, but she has yet to reply to my email about the names without addresses. That could be because she's on another job, is weighing up how to reject the request, or has totally washed her hands of me after dishing the dirt on David. So far, this search has been a total washout, and again I'm reminded of the fact that David might have been smarter than leaving his partner's details in an address book the police would undoubtedly seize in a raid.

Would he be less careful with leaving incriminating evidence on his computer? If there was some way I could bypass his password and gain access to the hard drive, would I find something there? I'm fairly tech savvy, but I'm no expert. If I asked David to confirm the password in exchange for provisions, would he oblige? I doubt it, and unless I brought the computer to Harrington Manor, he'd probably set me on a wild goose chase with dummy passwords in an effort to keep control.

I look out of my window at number 16, and can now see that a light has come on at the back of the property, highlighting the top of the roofline. I can only assume it's some kind of security light on the back garden, but if it's been triggered, then it's possible that someone is home. I've come too far not to check, and so I climb out of the Lexus, cross the road, and head up the driveway. Entrance to the property is at the side of the building, and I now see that there is a garage door back here too, obscured from the road. Tiptoeing past the door to the property, I approach the garage door, and try to look through the gap at the edge. It's too dark to see whether there's a van hidden inside, so I use the burner phone's torch to shine light inside. There's no van, but the garage is full of clutter.

Turning, I head to the entrance and ring the bell. I can see a glow through the frosted glass panel as if lights are on in a rear room of the property. A moment later a light fires in the hallway and a small figure approaches the glass. I hear a security chain being slotted into place, and then the door opens a crack.

The woman huddled behind the door has a dark grey bob, framing her tired and chamois-like face. Her brown eyes are untrusting, and when she speaks, her weak voice is barely more than a whisper. 'Yes?'

I relax my shoulders and plaster on my most welcoming smile. 'Hi there, I'm Joe, and I'm looking for Francis McAdam?' I keep an edge of uncertainty to my tone, reflecting her vulnerability.

'I'm his mum, what do you want?'

Great, another bust!

'Um, I'm kind of an old friend of his, but I haven't seen him in years, and wasn't sure whether he still lived here or not.'

'Are you police?'

The question strikes me as odd, but piques my interest.

'Um, no ma'am, I'm not with the police.'

'You a reporter then?'

'No, ma'am.'

'Because if you are and you don't tell me, I can sue you for harassment. It's time that people like you just left my boy alone. God knows we've been through enough.'

I play a hunch and move forwards so my head and shoulders are more in the light of the doorway. 'I promise you, Mrs McAdam, I'm not a police officer or a reporter, but I really do need to speak with Francis urgently. Is he home?'

She narrows her eyes. 'No, he's away on business.'

That potentially explains the empty driveway, but not why the hairs on the back of my neck are suddenly standing.

'Can I ask when he's going to be back?'

'I don't know. A few days, a week, maybe? I can't remember. I get confused.'

I nod empathetically. I need to get into this house so I can find a picture of Francis McAdam, but I don't want to frighten this woman unnecessarily.

'Would it be possible for me to come in and use your facilities? I travelled a long way to see Francis today, and it's a long way home.'

She doesn't budge, but her fingertips are white from gripping the door's edge. 'You didn't say how you know my Francis.'

I play a second hunch. 'I know him from … From when we were both inside.'

She doesn't immediately slam the door in my face, and she doesn't immediately question why I would believe Francis had been in prison.

'Forget I asked,' I tell her, stepping back. 'Maybe if I leave my number, do you think you could ask Francis to call me when he gets home? It's been a few years since we last caught up, and I might have a bit of work for him. Legitimate work,' I add for good measure.

I remain where I am, willing her to yield, and a moment later, she removes the security chain and opens the door wider.

'Come on in.'

She points at a pad of paper beside the telephone on a small table at the end of the hall.

My eyes dart left and right as I cross the carpet, looking for any photograph to confirm Francis's identify, but the walls are bare, save for the flock wallpaper. I scribble a fake number on the pad.

'You know I feel quite honoured to meet you, Mrs McAdam,' I say, handing her the piece of paper. 'Francis spoke a lot about you when we were … you know. He said that it was your belief in him that helped him get through it all.'

Her cheeks flush slightly.

'To be honest,' I continue, 'I'm glad my mum wasn't around to see how I turned out. She'd have been disappointed with some of my earlier life choices, but I'm working hard to put that right now. Hopefully, I'll make her proud of me again one day. Francis should know how lucky he is that you've stuck by him for all these years.'

'Where did you say you'd travelled from today?'

'Wolverhampton,' I reply as it's the first town name that enters my head.

'You can use the toilet down here,' she says, nodding at a door beneath the stairs.

I don't realise how desperate I am until I lock the door behind me and switch on the light in the poky broom cupboard. When I emerge I can hear the kettle boiling and as Mrs McAdam is nowhere in sight, I head through to the kitchen where I find her just removing the lid of a cake tin.

'You'll stay for some tea and cake won't you? It's

homemade. Apple and cherry, my Francis's favourite. It'll only go to waste with him away.'

I see now how lonely Mrs McAdam must be to have invited a stranger to share tea with her, and the smell of the almond and cinnamon from the tin has me salivating, and given I didn't eat lunch, I warmly accept.

'Make yourself useful and fetch me a pair of cups from the cupboard, would you?' she asks as she cuts a generous slice from the round cake and drops it onto a plate.

Opening the cupboard she's indicated, I extract two cups and saucers from a dusty stack towards the back of the cupboard, and can't help but notice the brown envelope stuffed with cash in the corner. I leave it where it is, but my pulse quickens.

'Is it just you and Francis living here?' I ask, as I close the cupboard door and carry the cups over to the counter.

'That's right. Francis's dad passed when he was still a nipper, God rest his soul. I'm sure our Francis wouldn't have got misled as he did had his dad been around. But I was working all hours, and barely making ends meet, so it wasn't all Francis's fault.'

She looks up and smiles at me as I pour kettle water into the cups and swish around the teabags.

'But that's all in the past now,' she continues. 'God knows Francis has done more than enough to make up for all that silly business. But you try telling that to all them I used to know at the church and bingo hall; people like that won't let you forget, you know. I'm sure you've probably experienced something similar.'

'Once a criminal always a criminal,' I echo, and the irony of my current actions aren't lost on me.

Mrs McAdam hands me a tray and places the plates of cake on top, and I carry them and the tea through to the back room, where a halogen fire glows orange beside the French window.

'It's a wonder anyone can turn over a fresh leaf,' Mrs McAdam picks up once we're seated. 'Every time a child runs away the police come knocking here. Always the same ones, always with the same excuses, always full of doubt that Francis could be perfectly innocent.'

My feet tingle, and so I make fists with my toes to keep from leaping out of the seat, and demanding to see a picture of Francis. I try to allow my eyes to casually take in the whole room, but she's watching me very carefully, not yet totally trusting me.

'I know what you mean,' I nod with empathy. 'As I said, Francis is very lucky to have you championing him on.'

'Have you got much family in Wolverhampton, Joe?'

I shake my head. 'Only child, and I was taken into social care when Mum passed when I was ten. I didn't know my dad.'

I silently pray that Mum and Dad will forgive my betrayal and understand that I'm only doing this to try and help Hazel and her family.

'I don't know what I'd do without Francis here,' she says, breaking off a piece of sponge and putting it between her lips. 'It was hard when he went away the first time. This old place always feels so big when he's not here. I don't bother with the gas heating when it's just me as it costs an arm and a leg to heat the whole place. I use the electric down here and extra blankets when I go up to bed. People don't seem to understand that the pension only covers so much, you know?'

I don't mention the envelope of cash in the cupboard as it flashes through my mind again. I can't see how she doesn't know it's there, but then maybe she's been warned not to use it.

'Has Francis been away on business for long?' I ask, taking a sip of my tea.

'Two days,' she nods, 'so you're unlucky to have missed him.'

'And did he say when he would be back? If it's only a couple of days it might be worth me hanging around in Reading for a little longer rather than waste another journey home and back again.'

'He didn't say, luv,' she replies.

'And I don't suppose you can let me have his new number so I can call him? The number I have is out of service apparently.'

She puts her plate down and quickly leaves the room without another word. I don't know how long she'll be gone for, but I might not get a second chance. I stand, and follow the line of the wall, looking at the small pictures hanging in frames from the wall, but they're landscape reproductions of paintings rather than holiday snaps. How is it there are no photographs of Francis anywhere?

I cross the room and peer through the door into the kitchen, but Mrs McAdam has her back to me and is bent over a drawer. I hurry over to the bookcase and scan the shelves without success. I daren't head anywhere else for fear of getting caught and end up sitting back in the armchair and shovelling the remains of the cake into my mouth. As I'm returning my plate to the coffee table, I see there is a Mills & Boon paperback upturned near her chair, and poking out of the back is a shiny corner of a parrot. Sliding my hand across the table, I pinch the corner of the photograph and gently ease it out, my eyes widening as they fall on the round face and brilliant white hair of the six foot tall, barrel-chested man hugging Mrs McAdam.

Snatching up the image, I charge into the kitchen and slam it down on the counter in front of Mrs McAdam.

'Where is he?'

She starts at my appearance and sudden anger, and immediately slams the drawer shut.

'W-What do you want? Who are you really?'

'Tell me where Francis is, Mrs McAdam.'

'H-He's away on business.'

'Give me his phone number.'

'H-He doesn't have a mobile.'

'But he drives a van, doesn't he? A grey van.'

'Well, yes, that's for his business.'

'What business does he do, Mrs McAdam? Where did he tell you he was going?'

'I-I don't know … I forget.'

Taking the picture with me, I show myself out, finding Andrews's number in the list of contacts, and I'm about to call him when I have second thoughts. I need him to consider Francis McAdam as a suspect in the disappearance of Hazel Cooper, but it would be better if he doesn't hear it from me. Hurrying back to the Lexus, I call Crimestoppers instead, covering the mouthpiece of the burner phone and adopting an Australian accent (it's the only one I can do for any length of time). I ask the operator to pass the message on to Detective Andrews and then I speed away back to Harrington Manor. I now know that Francis McAdam took Hazel, but I need to know whether he was also involved in what happened to my daughter.

Chapter 32

5 weeks ago

This time, Joe had insisted Rhys meet him somewhere more low key. Whilst Joe had no doubt that the students in the beer garden either wouldn't have been able to hear their conversation, or would have been too drunk to recall it, he didn't want to take the risk. Of course, given how drunk Rhys had been, Joe couldn't be certain his former housemate would recall any of what they'd discussed either.

Now, with the sun long since set, he was nestled beside the bottle banks in Waitrose car park, waiting for Rhys to arrive. It certainly wasn't where Joe had pictured having the conversation he planned to hold imminently. The supermarket was long since closed, with shutters down, but there were still a slew of cars parked near the entrance, and he could just about make out light inside the building allowing the cleaners to do their work, and the overnight staff to replenish the shelves. Hopefully none would emerge before Joe and Rhys's business was complete.

Joe had brought a couple of empty bottles in a cardboard box, which were currently snuggled behind the passenger seat on the off-chance that an inquisitive police car turn up unannounced and questioned his motivation for being here so late at night.

A set of headlights now pulled onto the strip of road leading to the car park, but Joe couldn't yet determine the make and model, not that he knew what car Rhys drove. The headlights slowed as they entered beneath the height restriction bar covering the entrance, seemed to remain still for several seconds, before slowly completing a circuit of the car park, and then stopping not far from the other cars near the entrance.

Joe let out the breath he'd been holding in. It had to be another staff member arriving for their night shift. Joe turned his attention back to the car park's entrance, awaiting the next arrival. It was already after ten, which meant Rhys was late, and it wasn't helping Joe's nervous disposition. He wasn't cut out for cloak and dagger work, and if Rhys didn't arrive soon, he'd have to find a tree to relieve himself behind.

A minute passed but there was still no sign of another car turning up, and Joe's gaze fell back on the car that had arrived earlier. The occupant still appeared to be sitting in the vehicle, but Joe had no way to message his former housemate and ask where he was, as Joe had decided to leave his phone at home so his movements couldn't be traced.

Joe continued to watch the figure in the other car, waiting for them to go into the shop, but still the occupant sat and waited. Curiosity and the urge to wee finally got to Joe and he climbed out of his car and ducked behind the bottle bank, before crossing the car park towards the stationary vehicle. The cloud of smoke inside the car made it difficult to see the figure beyond the glass, and as Joe tapped on the window, there was an explosion of shouting and cursing, before the window lowered and Joe instantly recognised the curious smell.

'Jesus Christ!' Rhys exclaimed. 'You gave me a blood heart attack. Where the hell have you been?'

'Me?' Joe protested in a loud whisper. 'You told me to meet you by the bottle bank at ten. I've been sat waiting for you to show up for ten minutes.'

Rhys took a draw on the joint, and then burst out laughing. 'Oh, did I? Never mind, you're here now. Get in.'

Joe studied the car park and entrance to the shop, making sure no eyes were on them, before opening the door and sliding in. The smell of the weed was even more overpowering inside the car, so Joe kept the window open a crack to funnel some of it away. It was a risk that the smell of the smoke might draw unwanted attention to them, but he didn't want to get high through passive smoking either. It would be hard enough to explain to Meg why his clothes stank of weed.

'You want a tug?' Rhys, asked, offering him the joint, and there was a time when Joe wouldn't have thought twice, but he shook his head. That was a different life, and less complicated; it suddenly dawned on him why Rhys might want to prolong the Peter Pan lifestyle.

Joe reached into his inside jacket pocket and extracted the sheets he'd printed off, and passed them to Rhys.

'What's this?'

'Just read them,' Joe said, looking out of the window, knowing it would be easier than saying the words.

Rhys picked up the first sheet and studied it, pausing only to take another puff of his joint. Joe could feel his stare burning into the back of his head when he finished the first page, but refused to acknowledge Rhys's new insight.

'Holy fucking Christ,' Rhys gasped when he reached the end of the second page. 'Jesus, Joe, I'm so sorry, mate. I had no idea this was anything to do with you. I … I'm so fucking sorry, mate.'

Joe ground his teeth, willing himself not to react to the sympathetic tone; he didn't want Rhys's pity, just his help.

Turning to meet his friend's stare, Joe nodded. 'So, we were having a hypothetical conversation last week, and now I want to continue it.'

Rhys squashed the joint into the car's ash tray and gulped audibly.

'Hypothetically, if I wanted to take action against the man mentioned on the second page … would you be able to help provide what I need?'

Rhys squashed himself back into his chair and ran a hand over the stubble on his chin and cheeks. 'What did you have in mind?'

Joe had spent the last week trying to determine how much of his plan he should share with Rhys. On the one hand, Rhys was an unreliable, immature friend from a former life, and the last thing Joe wanted was to put him at risk of trouble. On the other hand, Rhys was someone with connections unavailable to Joe directly, and probably the last person who would go blabbing about their discussions and Joe could do with a sounding board for his plan.

'I want to take him by force, and do whatever it takes to obtain his confession.'

Rhys coughed as something irritated his throat. '*You*? No disrespect, matey-boy, but you're hardly cut out for something like that.'

Joe tried to keep the frustration from his voice. 'I'm capable of a lot more than you think, Rhys, but humour me for a minute, would you? If you were planning something like this, how would you do it?'

'Hypothetically speaking, right?'

'Absolutely.'

Rhys took a deep breath and slowly exhaled it through his nose. 'If you ask me, I'd say it's a two man job really. I can't exactly tell from the image on the printout, but let's assume he's a typical man in his mid-sixties, I think it would be safer to have the threat of two men to ensure he cooperates and gets in the car. After that, I don't know. Most men will admit to anything when faced with death, so I guess I'd take him somewhere like a cliff top and threaten to push him over the edge.'

'I don't want him to just tell me what I want to hear though,' Joe countered. 'I want him to tell me the truth about what he did to my little girl.'

'That'll probably take longer. Can you get access to a lock-up or somewhere you could keep him quiet for a few days?'

Joe pictured the cell in the basement. 'Then what?'

'Then, withhold food and drink until he cracks, and you feel certain you've got the answer you want. But there are still no guarantees. And if you don't manage to get him at the right time or in the right place, it could escalate very quickly and then you'll be up shit creek without a paddle.'

'And if I want to do this on my own, how would you suggest I get him to cooperate.'

Rhys's eyes took on a fresh sadness as he spoke. 'Then you're going to need a gun, and you're going to have to be ready to use it.'

Chapter 33

Joe

If at first you don't succeed …

That's what they say, right? To try, try again?

In truth, I don't think I'll ever have what it takes to inflict the necessary damage to break David's will. And he knows I don't, which means he isn't threatened by any of my attempted intimidation.

Standing at the basement door, I am greeted by the stale odour of sweat and flatulence drifting up to where the air is fresher. The downside of holding him in a windowless room beneath the ground was always going to be the smell. I can hear him whimpering at the bottom of the stairs, and given I can no longer see the back garden through the darkness beyond the kitchen window, I can only imagine how desperate for food and a proper drink David must be.

Maybe there is another way.

Extracting the loaf of bread from the box on the side, I snatch up a slice, and carry it down to the basement. The moment my feet hit the stairs, I hear David wincing and scurrying over the cold concrete floor, before the distinct popping sound of him clambering onto the inflated mattress against the far wall. I'm sure this feigned panic is all an act for my sake; to lull me into a false sense of security, but for once he's the one wasting his time. There's no way I'm going back into that cell; everything I need to say and do can be done out here.

I can barely see him, hidden in the shadows of the cell, but I know where he is, and stare off in that direction.

'I'm not an unreasonable man,' I say into the darkness. 'Considering what you've put me through this last year, I'd say I've been more than accommodating to you. However, a man's got to eat, am I right?'

I hold the slice of bread up to the light so he can see it.

'I could easily leave you down here alone without provisions, and watch as your vital organs slowly shut down while you squirm in agony, but that doesn't benefit either of us, now does it? So,' I reach down and pull out one of the small bottles of water from the fridge, and quickly snap off the lid, 'I'm going to show some faith, and let you have these.'

Avoiding looking at him, I place the bottle of water just inside the bars, balancing the single slice of bread beside it.

'These are for you,' I say, forcing eye contact. 'You should take them.'

He doesn't move, his mind working overtime as he tries to calculate what game I'm playing, or how the trap will spring.

I shuffle back to the chair, and drop into it, but David doesn't budge.

'You must be hungry by now. Even if you had a snack right before you left home to walk the dog, it's at least sixteen hours since then. Go ahead and eat, and then we can talk.'

He remains still.

'If you'd rather starve yourself to death, be my guest.'

The air bed protests as David slides off it and slowly slides across the floor on his hands and knees, grasping the bottle of water first and downing half the contents. I remain where I am, poised, but with no intention of going anywhere. David rests the bottle on the floor, and dares to move his fingers towards the bread, pinching it between thumb and finger, and tearing back to the inflated bed with both his finds.

Back in the shadows, I can't see him eating, but I can hear the dry slapping of his dehydrated mouth as he chews and tries to swallow the crust.

My voice echoes in the darkness as I begin to speak again. 'I think we can both agree I'm not a violent man. I thought I was – God knows how many times I've imagined myself beating you to within an inch of your life – but I realise now that I'm just not built that way. What I am though is patient.' I pause to allow the admission to sink in. 'Patient enough that I could happily keep you locked in this basement on basic rations for the rest of your life.'

I lean down and remove a second bottle of water from the fridge, but this one I drink myself.

'You've repeatedly told me that you had nothing to do with my daughter being taken and killed, and whilst I don't believe you … I'm now prepared to listen.' I pause again. 'Convince me that I'm wrong to doubt you.'

His lips chap together, and he coughs to clear his throat. 'If I tell you, you won't believe me.'

'Convince me, David.'

The air bed strains under his movement, and he emerges from the shadows, crawling to the bars, and placing the empty bottle of water back where I'd left it between the bars.

'And if I do tell you what you want to hear … will you let me go?'

I don't immediately respond so he'll think I'm considering the question. The truth is I can't let him go because as soon as I do, he'll contact the police and report me for what I've done, and Meg will never forgive me for trying and failing. I'm not cut out for a life behind bars, whether I deserve it or not. But what's the alternative? I don't have it in me to take a human life. Ultimately that would make me as bad as him, and if he deserves to die in prison, then so do I. I can't let him go, and I can't kill him. With Lady Violet due back in the next couple of weeks, I certainly can't keep David here indefinitely. How did it all become such a sodding mess?

'If you can convince me that you truly aren't the man responsible for abducting and killing Lydia, then I'll have no choice but to let you go.'

'Is that thing still on?' he asks, nodding towards the tripod.

I shake my head.

'Well put it on, and let's get this over with once and for all.'

I stand, and step behind the camera, switching it on and adjusting the zoom until David's head and shoulders fill the tiny screen. He is sitting cross-legged just behind the bars, shoulders back, and for a man deprived of food and sleep, he looks surprisingly well.

The red LED flashes on to indicate the recording has started, and I retake my seat off camera.

'My name is David Calderwood, and I am of sound mind and body. The date is ...' he trails off, looking at me for an answer.

'First of November,' I tell him.

'The date is first of November, and there is nothing forcing me to make this statement.' He takes a deep breath. 'I am not responsible for the murder of Lydia Irons, but I am here today to explain why.'

For the briefest moment I thought he might actually give me the confession I'm so desperate for, but I shouldn't have been so naïve. Whatever drivel he's about to spew is pointless, but if I'm quiet, he might just give me enough to hang him from later.

'In 2006, I was convicted of sexual assault on a minor and imprisoned for a decade. She was someone I met online, and although I knew it was wrong to be engaging in that kind of activity with a fifteen year-old, she was very mature for her age, and I believed we'd fallen in love.'

My stomach turns but I remain perfectly still, ignoring every instinct in my body.

'You must remember what it was like being in love, Joe, don't you? That feeling like there's nothing in the world that can destroy what the two of you have together. I genuinely believed she loved me, and when she suggested we meet, I thought we'd run away together and live happily ever after. That's what the jury never understood at my trial … Despite what she told them about being scared of me and feeling duped when she realised how much older I was, she only said those things because her parents pressured her to do so. If anyone had seen what we were like when we met up, they'd have realised that it was all lies, and that she loved me as much as I loved her.'

I can't tell if he's deliberately trying to make me uncomfortable or if he really believes this bullshit. Maybe he's spent the last fifteen years convincing himself it's true. Or maybe it's just more lies as he continues to play games, trying to buy himself time to escape.

'I know I hurt her because I didn't tell her my real age until we met that first night, but I swear to you, Joe, she forgave me. We were all set to skip the country when she bottled it last minute and told the port authorities that I'd abducted her.' He pauses and his eyes shine. 'She broke my heart in that moment, but I forgave her instantly. It was wrong of me to assume that she could turn her back on her friends and family for a lifetime in a foreign country with me.'

I sit forwards, and rest my elbows on my knees. 'What does any of this have to do with my little girl?'

'She was only six, right? Your little girl?'

My throat tightens. 'Yes.'

'Well there you go, you see. Too young for me. Not all sexual deviants are the same, Joe. Terms like predator and paedophile get thrown about so easily, but not everyone on the Sex Offenders Register want to defy the law. Take me for example; I fell in love with someone I met online. That first day we met, she didn't tell me she was only fifteen. It was only a few weeks later that she admitted to being under sixteen. By then, I was already in love with her. She had such a unique outlook on the world, you see.

'Then of course, there are those who genuinely get their kicks from fantasising about children. These are the monsters you read about in the news who are opportunists. They spot a vulnerable child alone and pounce. Now, I can't say for certain, but based on what that detective told me, your little girl was abducted from a park or something, right?'

My heart skips a beat as I recall that moment I turned from the queue at the ice cream van to see that Lydia wasn't where I expected.

'If I had to guess, I'd say that whoever took your daughter, just happened to be at the park, waiting for an opportunity to strike. It could have been any one of the children at the park that day, and you and your daughter were the unlucky victims in what happened. Check that file you have on me. Have I been arrested on suspicion of abduction or for any reason since I came out of prison?'

I don't need to check the file Edie prepared to know that he's right on that point, but it doesn't mean he wasn't responsible.

'I signed the Sex Offenders Register because I fell in love with the wrong girl at the wrong time. I am not someone who would go to a park and snatch the first child not being supervised by her parents, especially not one so young.'

He folds his arms and falls silent.

I blink several times, surprised that his argument

has ended so quickly. I'm tempted to ask if that's it, but I sense that it is. My opinion of him hasn't changed, and yet there is logic to his argument.

I close my eyes and try to picture Lydia in the park that day. I can see her calling my name from the top of the climbing frame, and when she was at the top of the tallest slide; so proud of how brave she was being. I've tried visualising the faces of everyone else who was in the park that day, but they're just a blur of colours, because the truth is I wasn't looking at any of them. I couldn't hand on heart recall how many people were in the park that sunny day, let alone what they looked like.

My eyes snap open, as something does stir in my mind. If I'm to accept his argument that Lydia was too young for him, the same can't be said for Hazel Cooper who just happened to be snatched near where he was walking. Opening the refrigerator, I take out another bottle of water, remove the cap and replace the bottle between the bars.

'If not you, then who?' I ask. 'What sort of person should I be looking for? Do you know anyone capable of such an act? Help me find the person responsible.'

Chapter 34

Hazel

She remains where she is until the red LED blinks off. Her entire body tenses at the possibility, and she begins to silently count.

One potato, two potatoes, three potatoes, four potatoes.

She gets to twenty potatoes before she hears the faint sound of his boots. It's thirty potatoes before the stomp is louder and he nears the door. Forty-one potatoes before she hears the bolt being drawn back, and the door being prised open. Still she remains on the mattress, her knees tucked into her chest beneath the flimsy protection of the sleeping bag.

'I've brought more food,' he calls out, this time not waiting to see if she is awake.

The floor bends beneath his weight as he enters the cabin, but she remains where she is. She hears the squash of plastic as he places something at the foot of the mattress.

'You should eat to keep your strength up,' he says, so close that she gasps beneath the sleeping bag.

She makes a nodding gesture, hoping the movement of the sleeping bag will show him the compliance he craves without the need for her to speak. She begins to silently count in her head again, willing him to leave, but the floor doesn't shift, and he remains where he is.

He rips the sleeping bag from her clutches and her fringe dances with the gust of air created. It crumples against the wall, and he throws a sandwich packet and chocolate bar onto the mattress beside her.

'Eat now,' he says moving away and lifting the chair into a sitting position by the door, before dropping onto it.

The beam of light behind him is less intense than it was yesterday, but she still can't make out his features beyond the shadow. She gathers the items, and slides to the end of the mattress, and uses the wall to prop herself against. She tears into the packet and puts the sandwich in her mouth without even checking what's in it. She tastes wholemeal bread, and cheese, much to her relief. She chews, but her throat is dry, and it is difficult to swallow. Her eyes dart to the mattress but she can't see that he's provided more bottled water. She tucks her tongue beneath her lower teeth, until saliva fills her mouth, and the she takes a second bite of the sandwich. She's so thirsty, but is too scared to ask him for a drink. The quicker she consumes the meal, the sooner he will leave, and she can try to use the forty-one seconds before the LED returns to work on the hole.

She isn't sure what she can use to make it bigger as her heel is still throbbing, but she will pound the wood with her fists if necessary. Limbs will heal once she's free.

She finishes the first half of the sandwich, but it feels stuck in her throat because of the lack of fluid.

'Please,' she whispers, 'I-I'm thirsty. C-Can I have

a drink?'

He is watching her in absolute silence, legs apart, and hands resting on his knees.

'Please?' she tries again.

His head tilts against the light, and then he stands, and exits the cabin, leaving the door open. He disappears from view, returning ten potatoes later, carrying a bottle. He climbs back into the cabin, the ground swelling, and sits before throwing the bottle towards her on the mattress.

She made no attempt to leave, as the rope would have stopped her getting further than the steps, and she still hasn't figured out how she's going to get free of it and into the hole she's going to dig, but her desperation to get away from this place is blurring those questions in her mind.

She picks up the bottle, immediately noticing that the seal is intact. Either he's chosen not to drug this one, or he simply didn't have time. She opens it with a satisfying snap and takes a long drink.

'Thank you,' she dares herself to whisper before replacing the cap and starting on the second half of the sandwich.

'You're welcome, Hazel,' he says quietly, hands back on his knees.

She wills herself not to react hearing her name on his lips, and instead pulls her dry and chapped lips into an uneasy smile.

She can't see if he's smiling back beneath the balaclava, but is pleased with herself for extending this olive branch, and hoping that in doing so she's shown herself to be trustworthy. Her long-term survival and escape plan is based on earning his trust.

He didn't go very far to collect the water, she thinks now. Either he brought it with him and chose to leave it outside the cabin, or he has some kind of supply of bottles there. The water is a fraction cooler than room temperature, suggesting it isn't being kept in a fridge. If there is a supply just beyond the door to the cabin, then when she does make her escape, she might have access to supplies before heading out.

She realises now that escaping the cabin is just the first part of what she needs to consider. She has no idea what is beyond the door of the cabin, or where they are, and what direction to head in for the quickest means of seeking help.

Finishing the sandwich, she reaches for the Mars bar and savours the sweetness on her tongue as she takes her first bite. There is no point in her worrying about those additional details just yet; her focus has to be on getting out of the cabin. And as he stands to come and collect the empty sandwich packet, she realises that he has already brought her the perfect tool for breaking through the wooden floor: the chair legs.

Chapter 35

Joe

I pull out David's small brown address book, and hold it up to the light, making sure he understands exactly what he's looking at.

'I found this at your house when I was looking for the dog food,' I say.

'Oh yeah?' he replies casually. 'And?'

'And I want you to tell me who I saw abducting Hazel Cooper last night.'

'Who?'

He's back to playing games; just when I thought we might be making some headroom.

'The blonde girl in the Jack Skellington costume who your friend forced into the back of his van.'

'This again? I told you I know nothing about some girl being taken last night.'

'Really, David? Is that how you want to play this? Pretend like you have no idea what I'm talking about?'

I stand and move away from the camera, making a show of opening the address book and flicking through the pages, calling out random names.

'Is one of these your friend?' I say at the end. I've deliberately not mentioned Francis's name, and am not surprised that his expression is one of calm as he stares back at me.

I reach into my back pocket and pull out the photograph I took from Mrs McAdam's book. Walking purposefully to the cage, I hold the image up so David can see it clearly, but far enough away that he can't reach out and snatch it.

'Talk to me about Francis,' I say calmly.

He definitely tenses at the name.

'Who?'

I smile at his lame attempt at amnesia. 'The man in this photograph, David. The same man who was on Stable Road last night abducting fourteen year-old Hazel Cooper.'

'Is that who you saw then?'

'We both know it is. Cut the crap, David.'

'You really do have such a low opinion of me, Joe. If you're telling me that Francis McAdam is the man you saw up to no good, then you ought to report him to the police.'

'I already have,' I say with a smile, hoping that Detective Andrews has heard my message and is close to bringing in McAdam. 'What I want to know is whether he's also the man responsible for harming my daughter.' I pause. 'I mean, if I'm to believe your claims that you had nothing to do with my daughter's abduction, perhaps you know if Francis McAdam was involved.'

I don't know how Joe will react to the suggestion. On the one hand, if he truly wants me to accept that he isn't the guilty party I know him to be, I'm giving him the opportunity to throw McAdam under the bus. On the other hand, he may fear me seeing him as guilty by association; after all, the address book is evidence that he knows McAdam. He could hold his hands up and deny any knowledge of McAdam's activities to hedge his bets instead. I can almost hear the cogs turning behind his eyes as he considers his options. The fact that he's even thinking about it tells me everything I need to know: only a guilty man would have to think so carefully about his answers.

'I don't know Francis well enough to say for certain whether he could have been the man responsible for abducting your daughter. I'm not saying it's impossible, but I don't want to deliberately mislead you, Joe; not after everything you've already been through.'

I bite the inside of my cheek to keep from bursting into laughter at this last statement. Does he really believe he's doing me a favour here? This guy is beyond belief!

'What can you tell me about your friend Francis?' I ask, sitting down, about a foot from the bars, barely far enough not to be overwhelmed by the smell of B.O. hanging in the air between us.

He glances up at the camera. 'I wouldn't exactly describe us as friends.'

'You have his name and address in your little brown book, so you must at least be on first name terms. His mum suggested you're at least acquainted.'

He tilts his head in surprise. 'You spoke to his mother? Quite the detective you're turning into Joe. How is the old battle-axe?'

'She told me he is a good man who doesn't deserve to have his past constantly dragged up when the police are looking at crimes relating to minors.'

'Yes, well, what is it they say about mothers being blind to their offspring's misdemeanours? She has no idea what he's capable of.'

Andrews never mentioned who else they had in the frame for Lydia's abduction and murder, and only told us about David Calderwood after his arrest. I can't help wondering why McAdam wasn't also brought in for questioning or consideration given his background and what I witnessed last night.

'I met Francis inside, but I wouldn't describe us as friends. He was a means to an end.'

'In what way?'

He narrows his eyes. 'I take it you've never been inside a prison, Joe?'

I shrug. *Not yet.*

'A lot is made about how easy prisoners have it these days, particularly in the Category-B and C prisons. Televisions and games consoles in their cells, three meals a day, work opportunities, and access to gym equipment. And probably for most, it isn't quite the punishment it maybe once was. For those convicted of sexually-motivated crimes, there's more to it than that, especially when those crimes involve children. Even the most criminally-minded have strong feelings about those kinds of crimes. When I was imprisoned in 2006 after signing the register, I was admitted to hospital four times in my first three months alone. And nobody ever sees a thing. A slip here, a trip there, bones get broken, and nobody bats an eyelid when the injury is inflicted on a sex offender.'

I feel no sympathy for him, though I am surprised that such abuse is ignored behind bars, and yet I'm glad it is.

'I soon realised that if I was to survive inside, I needed protection. That's where Francis came in. Even though he was also on the register, he was bigger and stronger than most, and he had this air about him. If anyone was considering jumping him, they were warned against it. What can I say? I sided with the devil to keep myself safe. There were still minor skirmishes after I attached myself to him, but none requiring hospital admission. When I was released I never anticipated coming into contact with him again, but then he turned up on my doorstep one day wanting me to repay the favours he'd done for me inside. Against my better judgement, I gave him cash and a place to crash whenever he needed a breather from his mum.'

'What was he convicted of?'

David sucks in his cheeks like I've just asked him something offensive. 'You mean you don't know?'

I shake my head, wondering just how much of these lies I can continue to stomach.

'Well, Francis is a depraved individual, which is why I've done my best to distance myself from him since leaving prison.'

'I'd argue anyone who preys on children is fairly depraved,' I counter.

'More so than someone who attacks, abducts and imprisons an innocent man?' He laughs at this. 'I'm only teasing you, Joe. But yes, I'd argue that amongst offenders, what Francis did is far more savage than my crime.'

He pauses and reaches for the open bottle of water,

taking a long drink, giving me the chance to look at my watch. It's already after seven, and Meg is bound to be wondering where I am. I should probably go soon even if just for appearances sake.

'When Francis was arrested in 2005, it was shortly after he'd abducted a ten year-old boy from a shopping centre. Francis is one of those opportunist predators you see. He knows what he likes, but he doesn't have the patience to build a relationship. He acts on the hoof, and so now the more I think about it, yes, Joe, I believe Francis McAdam has all the traits of someone who *could* have abducted your little girl. You're looking for her killer, and I'd say he would be as good a place to start as any.'

Andrews must have looked into Francis McAdam if David's summary of his modus operandi is to be believed, and yet he's never mentioned him to me. Could it be that I targeted the wrong man last night?

I shake my head at the thought and stand, switching off the camera and hurrying up the stairs without another word. My mind won't accept that David just happened to be on the same road as McAdam when he snatched Hazel Cooper. But what if I was only half-right when I snatched David? What if my daughter's actual killer is still out there now? I'm just going to have to hope that Andrews responds to my message and reaches the same conclusion.

Fixing the peanut butter sandwich, I carry it back to the basement and open a second bottle of water for David, before switching off the camera.

'Get some rest, and I'll bring you more food tomorrow if you're prepared to open up and help me find the evidence of Francis McAdam's guilt.'

I don't look back as I head back up the stairs, locking the door behind me.

Chapter 36

4 weeks ago

Edie Sinclair was already seated at the small, square table outside Starbucks on the high street when Joe arrived. Dressed in a black leather jacket and with her face well made-up, she looked less like the adolescent he'd met almost a month earlier. He was grateful as at least their meeting wouldn't look so out of place. The large black sunglasses she was wearing, despite the lack of sunshine, was the only thing out of place.

It had been her choice to meet here, noticeably public, and Joe was surprised she was so willing to discuss such affairs in public. He'd offered to drive back to her office in Southampton, but she'd insisted. The fact that she was five minutes early for their appointment didn't surprise him either. Pulling out the chair across from her he sat.

'How's things?' he asked to break the ice.

She lowered her glasses. 'You're not getting a drink?'

She already had a latte glass between her fingers, and he wasn't thirsty.

'No, I'm fine. Are we going to talk about business here, or do you want to go somewhere a little more private?'

There was only one other person sitting outside, two

tables away and with her head buried in a book.

'I prefer to hide in plain sight,' she replied, pushing the glasses back up her nose, before reaching into the large shoulder bag between her feet and extracting an iPad. Switching it on, she slid it across the table to him. 'You'll be emailed a digital copy of this once I'm back at my office.'

'You found him okay then?'

She didn't answer at first, wiping lipstick from the rim of her glass. 'Did you think I wouldn't figure out why you really wanted information about David Calderwood, Joe?'

He had yet to pick up the iPad, suddenly conscious of just how exposed their location made him. Was Detective Andrews or one of his team lurking nearby waiting to pounce and arrest him for what he'd been so carefully planning?

'I don't know what you mean,' he blagged, but not even he could be convinced by the weakness in his tone.

She glanced away. 'What was the phrase you used in my office? Due diligence, that was it.' She turned back and stared straight at him from behind the lenses. 'Well I do my due diligence too, Joe. I know about what happened to your daughter, and I am sorry for what you and your wife have been through. I'm heartbroken for you, but what you're doing here, it isn't right, and it isn't healthy.'

He was about to plead ignorance again, but decided against it and closed his mouth.

'I'm guessing Calderwood is the man the police arrested, and questioned, but released without charge, right?'

He nodded, bowing his head at being caught in the lie.

'I figured as much when I came across his criminal record, and then learned that he'd been made to sign the Sex Offenders Register. Just because he has offended before doesn't automatically make him guilty this time. You realise that, right?'

'I figured there was no harm looking into the man suspected of killing my daughter.'

'You're right, there's no crime against that, so long as this is where it ends. I warned you last time, Joe, that if Calderwood comes to any harm, I am legally obliged to reveal our arrangement to the authorities. If you're planning to do anything with the information you've paid for, then I'll have no choice but to turn you in. I cannot be held as an accessory.'

So that was why she'd chosen such a public place; maybe she suspected he might be capable of threatening to harm her in exchange for her silence. She'd be the first to believe him capable of such a threat. Meg and Rhys certainly didn't see him that way.

'I didn't mean to put you in an awkward position,' Joe said, fixing her with an apologetic stare.

'It isn't awkward until you cross the line, Joe. And if something bad does befall this man, whether you're involved or not, don't you think you'll be the prime suspect given your motive? Just worth bearing in mind,' she added with a sigh.

'Right, you can read that or I can give you a summary of what I found.'

He was surprised she seemed so willing to still help,

and passed her the iPad back, figuring he'd be able to pour over the digital version when she emailed it over later.

'He's a bit of a loner from what I can tell. Doesn't have any friends stop by to visit him. He has a beagle puppy that he takes for walks twice a day. Usually he walks her to the local newsagents before nine, buys a newspaper and walks her home. They tend to be out for about half an hour to forty-five minutes, and then very rarely leave the house for the rest of the day. He takes her back out for a walk when it gets darker, often after ten o'clock at night, but on a couple of occasions he didn't leave until closer to eleven. Night time routes tend to vary, but I've highlighted two to three that he walks regularly. He buys his food at a delicatessen about ten minutes from his home, and goes there on a Wednesday and Saturday morning without the dog. And that's about as much I can tell you.' She pauses, and then goes again. 'Oh, and he seems to get a lot of online packages delivered to his house. I spotted a couple of Amazon boxes, but some came via Royal Mail, and others by nondescript delivery vans.'

Joe wasn't sure what he'd been expecting to hear, maybe something sordid involving David visiting dogging sites, or hanging out with other known criminals, but he would study her written report once he was home.

Chapter 37

Joe

There are no lights on at home as I push my way through the front door, and when I'm not greeted by the whine or bark of a dog, I make the assumption that Meg must be out walking her. There was once a time when my arrival home would be welcomed by a pair of warm arms around my waist and an effervescent summary of whatever had been memorable for Lydia that day. At the time I didn't pay much attention to whatever her latest best friend had told her in the playground or what book she'd managed to read without Meg's help. It wasn't that I wasn't interested, but as a parent I just took those moments for granted.

I would give anything to have just one more chance to actually listen to what Lydia had to say and appreciate her wanting to tell me. Is it really too much to ask for just one more day?

Dropping my keys into the pot on the table by the door, I head straight into the kitchen and pull open the fridge door. Light from the unit reveals no sign of dinner preparations on the counter or hob, and so I reach for a bottle of lager, and twist off the top. I drink it without drawing breath, but even as the last of the liquid gushes down my throat the medicinal properties have barely scratched the surface of the itch in my head, and so I immediately open a second bottle, but force myself to close the fridge door and step away.

When Lydia first vanished from the park, I didn't dare give in to the lure of alcohol's temporary absolution. I couldn't entertain the possibility that we wouldn't get her back, and turning to booze only felt like a step towards accepting the inevitability of heartbreak. I wanted to be sober so that if the call came to collect Lydia from wherever she was being held, I'd be sober and fully compos mentis to do what was necessary. I had to stay positive, as hard as it was to be patient; I told myself to trust Detective Andrews to do his job. I told myself that nobody in their right mind would want to hurt a six year-old, let alone kill her.

I lied to myself because it was the only way I could get through the days.

I kept my hopes higher than I should have, and when Andrews delivered the news of what they'd found dumped in the mud and leaves on the banks of the River Kennet, the legs were pulled from beneath me. I fell hard and fast, and as my heart shattered into a thousand tiny splinters, wine became my best friend, vodka a shoulder to cry on, and whiskey my confidante. I couldn't sleep unless I was so charged up I couldn't speak without slurring. Meg told me I was killing myself, but that wasn't enough to snap me out of it. Maybe her prediction would have come true had I not started on this alternative mission to find the truth.

Opening the cupboard beside the fridge, I find a tube of Pringles and pop open the top, snatching up half a dozen and cracking them in my mouth. They'll do until I can figure out what to cook.

Unlocking my phone, I'm disappointed not to see any messages from Andrews informing me that they've found and arrested Francis McAdam, but then I remember he won't know it was me who passed on the tip. Instead, I open the BBC News app and scan for any information about Hazel Cooper's abduction, but there is nothing. That must mean there hasn't been a public appeal yet. I suppose that makes sense given it's not even been twenty-four hours since he forced her into the back of his van.

Taking the tube of Pringles and bottle of lager with me, I head through to the living room, and put on the television for background noise. Those who've lived with children in their home don't realise how noisy it is, until the children are gone. This place has echoes of a cemetery these days, and it freaks me out being here alone. Resting the crisps on the table in the middle of the room, I drop into the reclining armchair. An episode of *A Place in the Sun* is just starting and the unnaturally tanned presenter introduces the two retirees who are looking to purchase a holiday home on the island of Crete where they honeymooned thirty years before. I always harboured the dream that Meg and I would be in that position one day. Not to go on a television show, but to have the funds to invest in a property in a warmer climate where we could go when the going got tough in the UK. Somewhere our adult daughter could take her own family during the school holidays.

My view of the screen blurs behind the mist in my eyes, and the lager is difficult to swallow past the lump in my throat. It's yet another future memory that was clawed away from us by the bastard who killed our little girl. How many other future memories were stolen from us in that moment? I can only hope that in some alternative universe there is a version of me who knows how lucky he is to still have his busy and noisy angel begging for his attention.

The front door opens and is followed by the sound of Meg struggling to hold onto the dog lead as Lola pulls and is eventually released and comes charging along the hallway and into the living room. She nearly knocks the bottle from my hand as she leaps up onto my lap and smothers my chin and cheeks with her tongue.

'Whoa there,' I say as firmly as I can muster, but deep down I'm grateful for the distraction.

I run my hand over her soft head, balancing the bottle of lager on the table beside the crisps. She settles into my lap, still in her harness, and if I didn't know better I'd say she's missed me.

'Oh good, you're home,' Meg calls out, as she heads into the kitchen and flicks on the light.

I remain where I am, waiting to see if she's going to add any more to that statement, but I can hear her opening cupboards and the crinkling and rustling of packets as she busies herself. Lifting the beagle, I take off the harness, and lower her to the ground, before making my way to the kitchen. In the sixty seconds since she arrived home, Meg has two pans on the stove, one containing pasta and water, and is busy reading the back of the jar in her hand. I wish I could be as pragmatic.

I don't want to disturb her concentration, and wait

at the door. She eventually looks up and over to me.

'I was at Neil and Ruby's,' she says, adding, 'The Cooper's,' when I stare blankly back at her.

'Oh, right. Have the police found their daughter yet?'

She bites her lip and shakes her head.

My heart drops. 'Wait, what? Are you sure? What's Detective Andrews doing?'

'I don't think he's involved. Neil said the Senior Investigating Officer is someone called Churchill.'

I suppose it was naïve to assume that Andrews would be made SIO after the failure to prosecute anyone for what happened to Lydia, but does that mean he won't follow up on the message I left for him via the anonymous call to Crimestoppers? At the very least, surely he'd pass it on to the investigative team, wouldn't he? Here was me thinking I'd done what was needed to get Hazel Cooper reconnected with her family, but from what Meg has just told me, she's still out there waiting to be found.

I'm half-tempted to drive straight back to Harrington Manor and demand David tell me where McAdam is holding Hazel, but I don't believe he'd tell me even if he did know. I could try phoning Andrews instead, under the pretence of a casual chat, and try to find out whether he received my message. It's risky though.

'Don't look so worried,' Meg says, and I realise she is watching me. 'I'm sure she'll come home soon enough.'

I frown at her certainty. 'What makes you say that?'

'Because deep down Hazel is a good girl. She won't

want to cause her parents unnecessary worry, and as soon as she realises the trouble everyone is going to, she'll be back.'

And that's when it hits me: Meg just thinks Hazel has run away like a tearaway. She doesn't realise how much danger Hazel is in.

'That's assuming she ran away and wasn't taken,' I counter.

I don't mean to be so blunt, but given what I know, I'm now worried that if this is Meg's thinking, it must also be the Coopers' thinking, and may also be what they've been led to believe by the police.

Meg's brow furrows. 'I don't think the police are ruling anything out at the moment. They've had her boyfriend Matt in for interview and apparently he's admitted to being with her last night, but claims not to know where she is now. She snuck out after she'd gone to bed to meet with him. They met up at the recreation ground on Stable Road, which is halfway between their houses. They hung out for about an hour and then went their separate ways – or so he claims.'

I guess that would explain what she was doing running past my car after I'd put David into the boot, but I can't ignore the doubt in Meg's voice.

'You think different?'

Meg hands me a packet of cheddar and the cheese grater. 'Would you mind grating this while I get changed?'

She leaves the room and heads upstairs. Turning, I see the beagle snuggled on the lino at my feet, already gently snoring. I don't understand why the police aren't treating Hazel's disappearance more seriously.

My 999 call last night described the abduction scene, and my tip-off to Andrews has identified the culprit responsible. Why isn't there a full search on for Francis McAdam? Why isn't his picture being shared and a demand being made for public support to locate him? Am I the only one who can see how much danger she's in?

If I was to take David at his word – and I'm not saying that I am – then Hazel Cooper was abducted by the same person who might have snatched and killed Lydia. What's to stop him doing the same to Hazel? Why can't anyone else see the risks ahead?

Meg glides down the stairs, but moves to the living room, rather than returning to the kitchen. I wipe the crumbs of cheese from my hands, and follow her through.

'What else did the police say?' I ask as Meg begins to fold the dry laundry from the clothes airer.

Her eyes are on the beautiful landscape of Crete's golden sands. 'What? Sorry.'

'The police: what else did they say about Hazel's disappearance?'

'I-I don't know. I didn't speak to the police directly; just Neil and Ruby.'

'I heard something about a 999 call reporting an abduction last night,' I say off the cuff, hoping Meg doesn't see through the lie.

She stops folding the shirt and looks at me. 'Really? Well, apparently someone did phone 999 and reported seeing a young girl being put into the back of the van, but they now believe it was a prank call, and not related to Hazel going missing.'

I can't keep the anger from my voice 'What? Why?'

'The caller didn't leave a name, and they've tried to trace the number that placed the call, but it's been disconnected all day. Police were dispatched to the apparent location, but there was no trace of the van or the person who placed the call. When they checked the registration details provided, they were false.'

'But if Hazel was last seen on Stable Road and the witness said the abduction was on Stable Road, why aren't they linking the two?'

I'm doing a terrible job of keeping my own insight a secret, but I can't believe that my efforts have been so easily dismissed.

Meg's eyes divert to the open bottle of lager on the table, and then she raises her eyebrows at me.

'I'm not drunk,' I insist too forcefully.

She doesn't react, and continues to fold the washing. 'I know it can't have been easy Neil coming here this morning to ask about Hazel, and I know it probably came as a shock to you to learn that I've been tutoring her, but allowing your imagination to jump to conclusions isn't the answer.'

She must recognise the confusion sweeping across my face.

'After everything we've been through, it's only natural to see links between things. Hell, I did the same earlier when that police officer came to our door and was asking questions about Hazel. My first thought was: what if history is repeating itself, but the situation here is very different to what we went through.'

'No, it isn't,' I snap. 'It's more similar than you realise.'

She stops folding again, and fixes me with a soft stare. 'Yes it is, Joe. Lydia was abducted because we took our eyes off her. Hazel had an argument with her boyfriend and has taken herself away for a couple of days to get her head together.'

But I saw her being taken, I desperately want to shout, but I can't get the words past my throat.

'I've just spent the afternoon with Hazel's parents, and when they told me what her boyfriend had relayed to police, it kind of made sense in my head.'

I reach for the bottle of lager and take a long drink to cool the heat rising to my neck. I nod for her to continue.

'Matt is sixteen, so almost two years older than Hazel. He told the police that when they met up last night, Hazel told him she wanted them to go to the next step in their relationship, but he refused, citing her age and the legality of what she was suggesting. They argued because she said she was ready and had spoken to her GP about going on the pill to be safe. He told her he loved her, but wanted to wait, and that's when she stormed off. When she was here for her lesson a couple of weeks ago, she was telling me about Matt, how he had told her he loved her, but wasn't the sort of boy to pressure her into anything. I think now in hindsight she was looking for my approval to have sex with him. Of course, I didn't encourage her, but I can understand how hurt she must be feeling now. When she comes to her senses, she'll come home.'

I want to tell her how naïve she's being; I want to tell her everything I've done in the last twenty-four hours, and how I know that Hazel hasn't just run away because of an argument with her boyfriend. I want to tell her that the best chance of Hazel being found alive and well is currently under lock and key in the basement of Harrington Manor. But to be honest, I'm not sure she'd believe me. One thing's for certain: I need to keep David onside if I'm going to get the answers I need; for all of our sakes.

Chapter 38

Hazel

She has no idea how late it is, but the orange glow is no longer bleeding through the gap in the wall and ceiling. It's impossible to keep track of time with no watch or phone, or window to view the sky. Assuming that the prawn cocktail sandwich and crisps were breakfast, and the cheese sandwich and Mars bar were dinner, then he shouldn't be back to disturb her again.

The sky was starting to get dark from four last week, with the sun gone from the sky by half past. Assuming the orange glow is daylight seeping through the cabin, then it must be after eleven by her estimates. And that's assuming he isn't manipulating the lights and meal times to keep her off-guard.

Since he last left, she's been trying to count minutes with potatoes, but fear of never seeing her parents or Matt again keep splicing through the rhythm, and now she can't be certain if it's five or six hours since he last brought food. Maybe it's more than that; maybe it's less.

The red light has remained there watching her the whole time. To stave off boredom she has stretched the rope as much as possible and paced the small space, trampling over the mattress and sleeping bag as she has gone. When she got bored of that, she tipped the mattress onto its side, propped up by the chair and performed star jumps and squat thrusts, though the exercise didn't last long. The important part of her routine is that she has now positioned the chair near the bucket purely by chance, or at least that's the way it should appear to him if he's been watching closely.

Of course, if he hasn't been watching then when he next looks he may question her motive for moving the chair and mattress to more surreptitious locations, but that's a chance she has to take. If he has got any suspicions, he certainly hasn't presented them by returning.

Maybe he's gone out.

It's the first time she's considered the possibility that she isn't the sole focus of his attention.

Does he have a job? A family? A partner or spouse?

It seems so naïve to have assumed that he's been nearby this entire time when she knows nothing about him or even the reason he took her in the first place. Aside from the physical abduction and locking her in the cabin, he hasn't done anything to harm her, apart from the slap for trying to escape. Sure, spiking her drink and changing her clothes are creepy, and less than endearing, but he hasn't sought sexual gratification.

At least not yet.

This final conclusion is all the motivation she needs to plough on with her plan. In her head, she believes it is late enough that he might be sleeping. She has no way to be certain, but everyone has to sleep eventually. If it wasn't for all the drug-induced naps she'd had today, she's certain she'd be suffering for yesterday's late night antics. There's been no sign that he has a partner watching the camera with him too, so she has to work on the assumption that he is on his own, and so probably can't be watching her activity all the time. Added to that the fact that it's too dark for her to see her own hand in front of her face, the chances are the camera won't pick up her movement.

Sliding slowly from beneath the end of the sleeping bag at the furthest point from the camera, she keeps her unblinking eyes on the red LED, her breath held to limit the sound of her movement. The sleeping bag crinkles slightly, and she freezes, waiting to see if the light disappears.

One potato, two potatoes, three potatoes.

The LED is still glowing through the darkness. She continues to slide out, wincing when her feet hit the cold wooden boards. She is now beside the mattress, obscured by the back of the chair, and moving towards the stale-smelling bucket. She gently slides it away, holding her hand above the floorboards until she feels the cool flow of air. Placing her left hand down on the spot where the crack in the wood is more apparent, she grips the metal chair leg with her right hand and pulls it slowly towards her other hand.

It scrapes against the wood, and she instantly stops, peering around the back of the chair at the red LED. It still shines through the black cloud.

She doesn't know if the camera is recording sound as well as picture, but any attempt to widen the crack in the wood is going to be noisy regardless of what she uses.

She is lying on her front, propped up on her elbows,

and drags the chair leg again. It sounds so loud this close to her ears, but that doesn't mean he can hear it too, she reminds herself.

Moving her left hand away from the crack, she positions the foot of the chair on it, and then stretches both elbows up and onto the seat of the chair, keeping her head ducked behind the chair back. She leans her weight onto her elbows, even lifting her knees from the floor on tiptoes.

The chair doesn't move, or make any additional break in the floorboard.

She lowers her knees back to the floor, and this time drives her elbows against the wooden chair seat. Her skin slaps against the seat noisily, but a quick glance back to the LED reassures her that she can continue.

The chair leg still doesn't appear to have made a dent, and so she moves swiftly to her next plan. Straightening her legs, she keeps herself bent forward as low as she can so her movement will be less perceptible to the camera. When she is standing just in front of the chair, she jumps back onto the seat with all her might, landing bottom first, and this time there is an almighty crack and the chair tips forward as the leg goes through the floorboard, knocking Hazel to the floor.

Her eyes dart up to the corner of the room, but the red LED has vanished: he's coming.

She pulls the leg back out of the tiny hole, and jabs at it again, trying to widen it as much as possible.

One potato, two potatoes, three potatoes.

She repeats the action over and over, prodding at the floorboard, gripping the edges of the wood and driving it at the board, no longer worried about how it looks or sounds.

Seventeen potatoes, eighteen potatoes, nineteen potatoes.

She doesn't know how long the LED has been off and whether he is coming because of what he heard or saw.

Twenty-three potatoes, twenty-four potatoes.

She can hear his stomps growing louder, and moves the chair away from the hole, but continues to hit out at the crack with her balled up fists.

Twenty-eight potatoes.

It's no use, she's not going to get through the hole before he arrives. Dragging the bucket back over the hole, she dives back to the mattress and pulls the sleeping bag just over her body before the bolt slides back and the door opens.

She doesn't move, not even to take a breath to settle her racing heart. She knows he's there, but this time there's no powerful light framing him. Instead he shines a torch beam around the room, finally settling on the mattress.

She waits for him to storm into the room and punish her for trying to escape again, but he doesn't move. Instead, he throws something into the room which lands with a splat.

'Eat and rest,' he tells her. 'You'll need your strength for tomorrow.'

With that the torch beam dies and she hears the door being closed and bolted again. She exhales, and takes quick shallow breaths until her breathing returns to a normal rate. She can smell pizza, and as she scrabbles to the end of the mattress she finds the still warm box and lifts the lid. Tomato, basil, and mozzarella fill the air and she doesn't think twice before ploughing into the feast.

This meal is a reward, she tells herself, *which means he didn't see what I was doing.*

She decides she'll eat the meal and then get back to breaking free. She doesn't realise how wrong she is.

Chapter 39

Joe

The sausage and egg McMuffin smells so good that I'm now regretting not buying one for myself too, though having eaten a bowl of porridge that Meg left for me before her run, I don't think I'd have fully appreciated it. Still, hopefully David will value the effort I'm going to in order to encourage his compliance. Whilst my original goal had been to obtain his confession about how he targeted and killed Lydia, finding Hazel safe and well has to take priority. Once she's safe we can revisit his personal attack on my family.

After dinner last night, I continued to interrogate Meg about what else she'd learned at the Coopers' house, but she wasn't able to offer anything that would help to convince me that their assumptions about Hazel simply running away were anything but wrong. After finishing the pasta bake she'd prepared, Meg told me she was feeling shattered and retired to bed to read, leaving me alone with only my thoughts. The problem with drinking alone is that's when the darkest thoughts pepper my tired mind. Thoughts of Lydia, alone in some dark prison, crying out for her mum and dad to come and save her; praying for salvation, only for those prayers to go unanswered.

And then I question my own inaction during those dark days before her body was located on the banks of the River Kennet. Meg and I put our total faith in Andrews and his team, and hung on everything the Family Liaison Officer told us, even though she was no doubt trying to determine our own possible involvement in Lydia disappearing. That's what they don't warn you about when the police launch an investigation into a missing child: the parents are the prime suspects. I bet Neil and Ruby Cooper don't realise that there is probably at least one officer currently investigating their recent history and possible motivation for wanting their daughter gone.

It riles me to think that all the time Andrews was telling us how hard his team were working to find Lydia, there was a part of him questioning whether we were guilty of more than just negligently looking away for a split second.

I should have done more to press him for more details on what his team were up to. I should have demanded to know who else was in his pool of suspects. I should have demanded to know how many registered sex offenders there were in the area and whether their current locations were being tracked. I should have been spending every waking minute looking for Lydia. I should have been kicking in doors and calling her name until I was blue in the face.

Instead I failed my daughter in her desperate hour of need.

I'm all that stands between Neil and Ruby Cooper ever being able to tell their daughter how much they love and miss her. I realised that in the middle of the night. With the police seemingly uninterested in finding Francis McAdam, I'm all she has. It's a responsibility that weighs heavily on my shoulders, but I can't allow David to see how desperate I am. I need to make him want to help me. Hence the cooked breakfast and fresh cup of tea.

I finish my coffee in the Lexus, clearing my mind of all the doubt and worry that has dogged me on the drive over.

What if he refuses to help? What if he is actually in cahoots with McAdam and chooses to ignore my plea for help? What if he's telling the truth and really has no idea where McAdam is, but strings me along with false information?

I can't allow these questions to weigh me down. I need to think positively. I need to believe that I will convince him to help, and that before the day is over, Hazel will be found and returned home.

Pushing open the door, I grab the brown paper bag of food and head in to the grand hallway. I'll have to squirt some air freshener before Lady Violet returns, as I'm not sure she'll appreciate the smell of fried food hanging over her antique furniture.

Opening the basement door, I hear nothing, and for a moment I'm worried that he might have passed away during the night, and then I see the mess, and hurry down the stairs. At the bottom, I can see the tripod knocked on its side, and the make shift rope he has constructed from the torn blanket hanging through the bars.

The two empty plastic bottles of water lie scattered amongst the mess.

'What did you do?' I yell.

I survey the damage to the camera, detaching it from the tripod and stuffing it in the inside pocket of my jacket. One of the pedal feet of the tripod has been unscrewed, and it looks as though he has been shaving the bolt end to fashion a key to work on the lock of the cell door, but his effort has been wasted.

I'd sensed he was stringing me along; only telling me what he thought I wanted to hear, but I'd underestimated that he might actually try to escape from the cell. Now the tripod and camera lie in ruins, and I'm furious for allowing myself to underestimate this man again. I am as guilty as Andrews for not breaking his will. The red mist descends.

Leaping up, I pull the keys from my pocket, and yank open the cell door. The stun gun feels heavy in my hand as I remove it from my pocket, but rather than jabbing it towards him, I drag him up and off the floor, and slam him against the brickwork at the back of the cell.

'What the hell is wrong with you? I was trying to help you!'

'I-I'm sorry, I was trying to get more water, that's all. I was thirsty, and I didn't know when you'd be back, if at all.'

He's lying, I can see his eyes dancing across the open cell door, waiting for his opportunity to distract me long enough to make his escape, but I haven't underestimated him this time.

I press the prongs of the stun gun against his neck and fire a jolt. His body instantly weakens and he drops from my grasp to a pile on the floor.

'You stupid son of a bitch!' I spit down at him.

I press the prongs into his neck again and hold the charge button for a count of five. He screams as he writhes at my feet.

'I brought you hot food!'

Another five second jolt, this time to the base of his spine.

'You were supposed to tell me how to find McAdam. You were supposed to help me find Hazel.'

I jolt him again, this time in his leg.

He's no longer screaming such is the shock to his body, but I almost don't care. I want him to know how much he's screwed everything up.

'What is wrong with you?' I shout at his prone body. 'I gave you a chance; a chance to come clean about what you did … About what you took from us.'

I jolt his leg again.

'Then I dared to believe that there might be some truth in the bullshit you were spinning me. Maybe I was wrong and you weren't the shit stain responsible for killing my daughter. I was even considering letting you go, but you've screwed that all up now. Do you hear me, you useless waste of space? You fucked it all up!'

It's pointless continuing to aim abuse at him. He's now unconscious, and God knows when or even if he'll come around again. Maybe I actually wanted to kill him deep down; some kind of vengeance for Lydia, I don't know.

Kicking his leg to check that this isn't another attempt to lull me into a false sense of security, I move back to the cell door and slam it shut. Collecting the brown paper bag of food from the floor where I dropped it, I squash it into the dustbin beside the fridge, and head back up the stairs. I need to get the camera home and hope he hasn't destroyed what I've recorded so far.

Chapter 40

3 weeks ago

The last place Joe ever thought he'd find himself was queuing to enter a prison on a dreary Saturday morning. The call from Rhys, advising Joe of his arrest and subsequent incarceration, had come as a shock, and Joe's first instinct had been to put as much distance between himself and his former housemate. But Rhys had appealed to Joe to come and visit him on the inside, and Joe had reluctantly accepted.

But as he stepped in line with wives and girlfriends, some with pushchairs, others without, he couldn't keep the voice inside his head from telling him to turn around and go home. Rhys had said he'd been caught at a gig with a bum-bag full of marijuana, and despite Rhys's claim it was for personal use, the volume was enough for charges to be pressed. Due to previous convictions he would be held on remand until his trial date.

What Rhys hadn't mentioned was whether he'd kept quiet about their conversation in Waitrose car park, and that was why Joe had agreed to come.

The rational side of Joe's brain told him that the police would already have been in touch with him had Rhys dropped him in it, and as that wasn't the case he should consider himself home and dry. And yet, the paranoid, cynical part of Joe's brain couldn't keep from imagining today's meeting was an elaborate sting operation with Rhys wired up to entice Joe's confession.

'Next,' the uniformed guard at the gate declared, waving Joe over. 'Name?'

'Um, Joe Irons.'

The prison guard scanned the two pages on his clipboard. 'I don't have a prisoner by that name.'

Joe's cheeks burned at the mistake. 'No, I'm Joe Irons. Sorry, I'm here to see Rhys Houseman.'

The officer checked his papers again. 'You'll need to show your identification at the front desk and deposit any personal items in the lockers provided. Next?'

Joe took the cue and headed in through the gate, across the tarmac and into the visitor's centre where he waited behind a mother with a screaming toddler. He couldn't help picturing Lydia at that age, not that she was prone to such public tantrums. She was always such a happy child, though Meg would probably paint a different picture.

Joe's nerves didn't stop even as the disinterested clerk behind the desk took his details and booked him in with barely a second glance. It was only once Joe was seated in the visitors' area, reminding him of a school canteen, that he allowed himself to relax a fraction. Rhys was led out minutes later, dressed in a grey, cotton tracksuit, but as Joe extended a hand to greet him, he was swiftly told there was to be no contact. The stern telling off from the prison guard was enough to stiffen Joe's shoulders and neck again.

'Hey mate, thanks for coming,' Rhys said once seated. 'I appreciate it's not the most welcoming of places. How you been?'

There was at least a two metre distance to the next table and pair of chairs, and although there were four prison guards moving between the rows of tables, they seemed more interested in preventing physical contact than listening too closely to the specifics of conversations.

Joe didn't know the correct etiquette, nor whether the tables could be wired with surveillance technology, so was reluctant to bowl straight out with the question searing his mind.

'Do I need to be worried?' he asked, when he could take the paranoia no more.

Rhys frowned, puzzled. 'What about?'

Joe looked around at the two prison guards closest to him. 'About us; you and me.' He lowered his voice. 'About what I told you in your car about …' He mouthed the final word, 'David.'

'Oh, that? No, no, this has nothing to do with *that*, Is that what you thought? No, I'm in here because I'd brought too much weed to a gig, that's all.' Rhys was making no effort to keep his voice quiet.

That wasn't what Joe had meant. He looked around nervously again, trying to pre-empt if and when the trap would be sprung.

'Have you told anyone about what we discussed?'

'In the car? Of course not! Nobody would be interested in a hypothetical conversation between two old friends anyway. Just relax, will you? You're making *me* nervous.'

Joe sat back in his chair, not quite ready to believe that there was no threat to his freedom.

'I only asked you to come because ... well, I don't have many *close* friends, and it gets lonely in here. That's what they don't tell you about places like this: all the solitude gives you too much time to think about what you've done or should have done differently. Imagine being locked up 24/7 with me talking nonstop. That's what I have to put up with in here,' he tapped the side of his head.

Joe had been planning to ask Rhys to be his number two, if and when he chose to make his move on David, but unless Rhys's trial date was imminent and the solicitor somehow managed to convince the court that Rhys wasn't selling the weed, there was no chance he'd be out in time.

Was it simply Joe's bad luck, or was fate trying to steer him away from a grave mistake?

Rhys waited for the guard to pass their table before speaking again. 'Listen, I have been thinking about your situation,' he said, using air quotes around the last word. 'I know you talked about arming yourself with something, and I thought you should consider getting hold of a personal stun gun. A couple of jolts would be enough to weaken his position.'

Joe's head snapped around as he feared the prison guard might have returned to listen in, but he was several tables away already. Joe glared at Rhys in an attempt to silence him.

'They sell them online,' Rhys continued. 'They're not illegal to own in this country, and it could help you overcome him if you *hypothetically* wanted to.' Rhys's attempt at a subtle wink only served to draw more attention to the potentially incriminating conversation. 'I'm sorry I won't be about to help you do it, but if you could hold off until I get released, I'd be happy to give you a hand. If you're right about this guy, then someone should do something.'

Joe didn't disagree, but could he really afford to wait until Rhys was released? Lady Violet would be back soon enough, and so the window of opportunity was narrowing by the second.

Chapter 41

Joe

The sound of the shower pumping and splashing tells me that Meg is already home when I return. The beagle makes a huge fuss of me as I walk through the door, but it only serves to remind me that she isn't ours, and a time is coming when I'm going to have to make a decision about her future, and that of her owner.

Considering the scene I've just left at Harrington Manor, it's clear I've been lying to myself about David's true motivations for pointing the finger at Francis McAdam. The only question that remains in my mind is how much of what he told me is true, and how much was a fabrication to steer me away from his own involvement.

I once read that the strongest lies are those based on a modicum of truth. It is human nature to lie when we think we believe we can get away with it, and to exaggerate the truth for our own benefit. I don't think I've ever written a CV that is a true reflection of my skills and achievements; I've certainly not included all the times I've screwed up in my profession. Instead, I've painted a picture of a competent, young professional who's never put a foot wrong, and again before two days ago I think I'd actually managed to convince myself that that illusion was at least partially true.

I know better now.

I know now that I *am* capable of planning a crime, and keeping it secret from the woman I love. I know what it is to feel the nervous energy fuelled by anxiety that flooded my system while I sat and waited for David Calderwood to appear beside my car. I know how energised I felt when I first struck him with the stun gun, and then smuggled him down to the cell in the basement of the old manor. And I know now how satisfying it was to make him suffer for knocking over the camcorder and damaging the tripod.

There is no coming back from the line I've crossed. The life course I was on has been altered, and is impossible to return to. I can only see two possible outcomes now: release David and face the inevitable consequences and feelings of failure.

Or …

If I can find the courage to kill him, I will be able to cover my tracks and he won't be around to tell the police or anyone else what I have done. But will I be able to live with his blood on my hands? I don't believe that to be possible unless I know for certain that he was responsible for what happened to Lydia.

Which brings me back to his most recent "confession". Do I believe that Francis McAdam is the monster he described? Someone capable of abducting and murdering an innocent child for kicks? I know he's capable of abduction from what I witnessed, but that doesn't necessarily mean he was the one who killed my daughter. Maybe he did, or maybe he was working with David.

I have to acknowledge the possibility that David's description of Francis's depravity could have been him simply projecting his own wickedness onto the patsy I presented him with.

If only I could find that one golden nugget of evidence to prove he is the one responsible, I believe I could do what is necessary.

My mobile ringing distracts me from playing with the beagle, and I answer as soon as I see Edie Sinclair's name in the screen.

'Edie, hi, how are you?'

'Good morning, Joe,' she says dryly. 'I am well, all things considered. Should I ask how you are, or is it best I not know?'

I know that she can't possibly know what I have done to David, and yet, can I really say for certain that she hasn't been somehow monitoring my actions? After all, it's her job to disappear in the shadows and keep watching. Maybe she's just trying to unnerve me to see whether I'll crack.

'I'm good,' I reply quickly. 'Did you receive the email I sent you? Have you made any progress with the list of names?'

I could waste time continuing with formalities, but I can't think of any other reason she'd be phoning.

The line buzzes as she sighs heavily into her end. 'Where did you get the list of names and numbers, Joe?'

'What does it matter where they came from, did you manage to do what I asked? What can you tell me about them?'

'No, Joe, that's not how this is going to work. I

warned you the other week that I wouldn't allow myself to become embroiled in some kind of vendetta.'

It wasn't clear from David's address book who the named men were or how David knows them, but her tone and concern would suggest they're more than just the butcher, the baker, and candlestick maker.

'Don't be so dramatic, Edie,' I say dismissively. 'That's not what this is.'

'Oh no?' she snaps back. 'Then why do you have me investigating seven ex-cons known for violent crimes?'

My chest tightens. 'What sort of crimes?'

'Tell me where you got the list of names from Joe?'

'What does it matter? Please just tell me what you know about them. Do any of them live close to Reading?'

The line buzzes again, and is followed by silence, as she awaits a response to her question.

I don't want to lie to her, but I don't want to embroil her in my current affairs either. The less she knows the safer for her, and if I tell her where I found the names, I know she'll refuse to give me the information.

What if I'm wrong about Francis being David's partner? What if it genuinely was a coincidence David being near the recreation ground when Francis struck? That doesn't mean David doesn't have a partner out there somehow. How else to explain why none of Lydia's DNA was found at his property? He had to have held her elsewhere.

Edie still hasn't spoken, and I pull the phone from my ear to check that she's still there. I hear the shower stop, which means Meg is going to be able to hear this conversation in a minute.

Pressing the phone to my chest, I hurry through to the living room, then out of the patio doors, closing them behind me.

'Okay, okay,' I whisper loudly into the phone. 'I believe these men to be associates of David Calderwood, but I'm sure you already know that.'

'What is it you're planning, Joe? God knows you can be forgiven for hating the man you believe responsible for killing your daughter, but digging up information about him isn't going to solve anything. There's nothing you can do or look for that the police haven't already considered. I should tell you that I did speak to the SIO in charge of your daughter's case after we spoke.'

I remember Detective Andrews's reference to wasting money on private investigators when we were sitting outside David's house, so this isn't news.

'I need to know if any of them could have helped him do … what he did,' I say evenly, opting for a slimmed down version of the truth.

I'm half-expecting Edie to hang up on me, but she remains silent on the line. Eventually she sighs again.

'I've just emailed you over a summary of what I found. I've not included their exact addresses in case you're not being totally honest with me. Two of the seven are currently behind bars, so I'd doubt they could have had any involvement, and only one lives within two hours' drive of Reading. Each of the men on the list have served time in the same facility as David Calderwood at one time or another, so I would assume that's how he has their contact details.'

I pull the phone from my ear, and check I've received the email.

'Thank you, Edie, I appreciate everything you've done for me.'

'I swear to God, Joe, if anything happens to anyone on that list, I will not hesitate to inform the police of our conversations and the information I provided you. Am I making myself clear?'

'I told you, Edie, it isn't like that.'

'Okay, well, I trust this brings an end to our business?'

A fresh thought strikes me like a locomotive.

'Wait, there's one final thing I need from you. Another of David Calderwood's former cellmates is in the wind, and I need to know where he is.'

'No, Joe.'

'Please, Edie, I swear I won't ask for anything else, but this is a matter of life and death. There's a girl's life in the balance.'

'Then speak to the pol–'

'I've tried,' I interrupt. 'I've told the police that I believe Francis McAdam is responsible for abducting a local girl who's currently missing, but they don't believe me. All I need you to do is find out his mobile number and where it last transmitted from.'

'Why?'

'I told you: I believe he has taken a local girl and her life is in danger.'

She snorts with derision. 'Then tell the police, and let them do their jobs.'

I put the phone to my chest, feeling as though I'm being watched, but when I glance up at the bedroom window, Meg isn't there.

'Please, Edie. Just find out whether he has a mobile phone registered in his name, and where it last connected to a network, and let me know. Please?'

'*If* I do this for you, Joe, you are not to contact me ever again, and know that I will also be sharing what I find with the police directly.'

'Good. Do that. I want them to know where Francis McAdam is.'

I relay McAdam's mum's address and Edie hangs up. Andrews will have to respond if Edie also pressurises him to do so. I just hope it isn't too late.

Opening the patio doors, I head back in, starting when I see Meg in the kitchen, her hair dripping onto the bath robe she's wrapped in.

'You made me jump,' I say at first, until I see what she's looking at.

When her eyes meet mine, they shine with tears, and I can hear the echo of David's voice through the speaker of the camcorder screen she's watching.

Chapter 42

Hazel

In the first few seconds of her waking, Hazel believes she is at home, in her own bed, waiting to hear her parents rise. Dad will be grabbing his tablet and heading to the bathroom for his *daily ablutions* as Mum jovially refers to it. Mum will be heading downstairs to put on the kettle as she 'can't function without my morning shot of caffeine.' She'll have a second cup on the go before she comes up to wake Hazel, and remind her that the bus to school is operating on a different schedule due to planned roadworks. The roadworks in question have been underway for three weeks already, so Hazel and the other students already have the new timetable and routes committed to memory, but that doesn't stop Hazel's mum from worrying.

Hazel will of course tell her all of this, before relenting and dressing, and if she has time, grabbing a piece of toast before rushing out the door because the argument over the timetable has ironically put her behind schedule. She'll forget to tell either of her parents that she loves them with all her heart, because complacency means she assumes they know.

Something stirs in Hazel's mind now as reality scratches at the surface of her imagination. The pillow beneath her head is thin and damp, not like the memory foam she is used to. And this thin covering over her legs and body is not her plush ten tog winter duvet. The image of her running to school in her uniform slowly melts away, and the flashes of memory from the last twenty-four hours rush back to the surface: her argument with Matt, rushing across the muddy grass at the recreation ground; grabbed and forced into the van; the terror; the cabin.

She isn't yet ready to open her eyes and see the orange glow at the edge of the roof, and the bucket of foul smelling urine, which is surreptitiously hiding the now obvious hole in the floor. She'd rather shut all of that out and return to dreaming. She pictures Matt's cute face, the way he has a bit of stubble on his chin and cheeks, but nothing on his upper lip yet. His brown eyes that she's been lost in too many times to recall. His chestnut hair with flecks of blonde inherited from his mum.

She'd told him she was ready to go to the next step, and she'd blamed him for rejecting her, when really she should have been praising his chivalry. Despite her protestations, he knows it is illegal for them to have sex because of her age, and he is doing the right thing by them both. Why can she only just see this now? Had she considered his feelings rather than her own desires, she would have allowed him to walk her home and then she wouldn't have been vulnerable to this monster's abduction.

She opens her eyes as they fill with warm tears. Even though she tried so hard to focus on her positive memories, her hostile reality won't allow her to forget.

At least she made good progress on the hole after finishing the pizza. She'd given up using the chair once the initial hole was widened, as it was noisy and impractical. Instead, she'd balled a fist, pressed it into her trainer and bashed with it while clawing at splinters with her other hand. Progress was slow, and she must have been at it for at least an hour, forcing herself to glance at the reassuring red LED every few seconds to ensure she wasn't disturbed. By the time fatigue took over she'd made a hole wide enough to fit one leg through. The wood scratched at her thigh as she dangled her leg through, but she will need to double the area if she is to squeeze through and down to the straw-covered floor below.

Where she will go after that she has no clue. Whenever the door is left open, she's not been able to see past the intense light. Were there other doors between the cabin and freedom? What if she escapes the cabin, only to find another locked door impenetrable without a key? She shakes the thought from her mind, choosing instead to focus on the positives. But even if there isn't another locked door, and she manages to get out into the open, where will she go from there? There have been no distinguishing sounds to suggest where she is being held, and assuming she leaves at night when he is less likely to be watching the camera, it will be even more challenging for her to find her bearings.

Focus on the positives, she reminds herself.

At least she will be out and away from his clutches. If she can make it into fresh air under the cover of darkness, there is no reason to assume she won't be able to run and find somewhere to hide until she can figure out her next steps. This thought has her stomach fluttering with anticipation.

Does she really have to wait until tonight before working on the hole? The sooner she widens the gap, the sooner she'll be ready to make her escape. She'll be taking a huge risk to go at it without the cover of darkness, but isn't it also possible that he is still asleep, or off tending to his normal life? Where had he been to buy the pizza last night, and why had he brought it so late? How much time has she wasted assuming he is watching her every waking minute of the day when in fact he's been away?

She's about to slide out from beneath the sleeping bag when a new thought troubles her: what if he *is* watching, and then sees what she's been up to and promptly comes to stop her? All her effort would be wasted. And what if he killed her for it?

Torn, she dares to subtly move her head and look towards the bucket, trying to determine if there is any way she can work on the hole without the camera picking up on her movement, but as her eyes fall on the floor, they widen at what stares back at her.

No, it can't be. How? When?

Her mind races to find a logical explanation for the piece of wood now housed beneath the bucket, but her mind is blank, and as she sits up on her elbows to get a better look and check it isn't a trick of the light, her head is woozy, and her vision blurs at the edges. She fights the wave of nausea, crawling towards the hole that caused the still sore welts on her thigh.

Impossible!

She runs her fingers against the rough edges of the off-cut that has been glued in place over the hole beneath the plastic bucket.

This has to be a bad dream, she tells herself, scratching at her arm to try and wake up, but still she finds herself on the cold, wooden floor.

But then she rolls onto her side and looks up to the corner of the ceiling, and her heart stops when she sees only darkness where the red LED should be. And that's when she hears the creaking of the chair over by the door and realises she isn't alone.

Chapter 43

Joe

The blood has drained from Meg's face, and her eyes look ready to stream.

'Give me the camera, Meg,' I say stretching out my hand.

'What is this, Joe?'

I can't be sure how much of the recording she's watched, or what she's heard, but the sooner I get it from her, the easier it will be to explain away what she's holding. Although, right now, my brain can't process events quick enough to even consider how to explain this as anything but what it is.

'It's nothing,' I say, blasé. 'Can I have it please?'

She makes no effort to hand me the camera, her eyes searching mine for answers that she doesn't want to hear.

'Is this …?' her words trail off.

I don't know how much she knows about David Calderwood. Although, Andrews told us his name, we were never shown his picture, and were told very little about him, other than he is registered on the Sex Offenders Register and is resident in the county. His picture and name never appeared in the press, as he was released without charge. It is only my due diligence, and the report prepared by Edie that brought me as close to him as it has. There is a chance Meg won't make the connection, but from the shock and hurt tightening the skin beside her eyes, I sense it's already too late.

I drop my arm. 'Yes, that is David Calderwood in the video.'

I lower my eyes, and turn away. It's like I'm six years-old all over again, and been caught stealing a cookie less than an hour before dinner.

Her breaths are fast and shallow. 'But how … when … why?'

So much for hoping to cover my tracks. The cat is well and truly out of the bag, and there's no way Meg will accept being fobbed off. Even if I tried to lie, she'd see through it as she's always been able to do. But in truth, I don't want to lie to her anymore. My conscience has been eating away at me, and now feels as good a time as any to tell her everything and unburden myself. I'm hoping that a problem shared might really be one halved.

I look up at the photograph of the two of us and Lydia hanging above the radiator. The three of us are gathered around her birthday cake on the day of her party, and the image fills my heart with love and warmth.

'I wanted to meet him,' I tell her, unable to meet the stare I can feel burning into the top of my head. 'I had to look into his eyes to understand if he really could be guilty of what they accused him of –'

'And?' she gasps.

'And I don't know. I thought if I asked him outright he'd feel compelled to tell me the truth. I thought if I threatened him he wouldn't be able to keep quiet, but,' I shrug at the camera.

'When?'

'I caught up with him a few nights ago. I found out where he lived and I've been watching and waiting for the chance to get at him. I did it for you, Meg.'

She grunts. 'For me? I just wanted you to open up to me. I never asked you for this.'

'You didn't need to ask, Meg. I've seen what losing Lydia has done to you; to us! I hate waking every day not knowing who I can blame for what happened.'

'It's *our* fault, Joe. We were the ones who were complacent.'

'No Meg! No. I've blamed myself every day for Lydia being abducted, but looking away for a split second should not automatically mean we're negligent. I will never forgive myself for taking Lydia's safety for granted, but we aren't responsible for what that bastard did when we were vulnerable. How many other children were in that park that day not being carefully watched by their parents? He could have chosen almost any child, but he didn't. He targeted Lydia, and I need to understand why. I need to know what *really* happened, and I thought if I could get him alone I could make him crack, but …' my head drops lower, and I feel tears on my cheeks. 'I failed. I failed Lydia, and now I've failed you, and I am so sorry.'

Meg doesn't speak, and it's only when I dare to glance up at her that I realise her tears are flowing silently.

'I couldn't go on without knowing,' I tell her, tiptoeing across the room, and placing one hand beneath hers, and the other on top of the camera.

Still she doesn't speak, and doesn't even stop me as I lift the camera out of her grasp and move it to the counter top across the kitchen. My secret is out, but it doesn't feel any less of a burden. I wish she would say something; shout at me if she's angry; shake her head if she's disappointed; but as much as I watch her, I cannot read what is going on inside her head. I know it's a shock, but there should be some initial reaction to that kind of message.

I open my mouth to speak, but I don't know what to say. There is no excuse or just cause for what I have done, and as much as I've been trying to convince myself otherwise, there is no way out of this.

'Please, Meg, just say something.'

She stares despondently at me. 'You think you're the only one suffering? You think I don't wake up every morning with the hope that it was all just a nightmare? Every day I pray for just a second more of her laughter, a second more of her scent. I would give *absolutely* anything for one more second with her, but no amount of praying or wishing will bring her back, Joe. We are doomed to live the rest of our lives with never-ending heartache.'

I cross the room to her and take her hands in mine. 'That's why I need to know who is guilty. I can't just accept that her death will never be pinned on the person responsible. Someone deserves to suffer for what happened –'

'That isn't your call to make,' she interrupts.

I press my hand to her cheek, and wipe her tears with my thumb. 'The police let us down, but David

Calderwood is the man they think is responsible. If I can just get him to admit what he did, I'll be able to start learning to live with our loss and grieve properly.'

Her brow furrows as her eyes study mine. 'You mean he's still alive?'

My expression reflects her confusion. 'Yes, of course. Wait, what? You thought I'd killed him? That's where I've just come from. He's the one who damaged the camcorder. That's the only reason I came home.'

Something changes in her expression. 'Where is he?'

I tell her about Harrington Manor and the sex dungeon I discovered in the basement.

'So that's why you've been leaving home without your phone?' she asks.

'I didn't want any evidence tying me to that place, and I know my phone's GPS would give me away. I didn't think you'd noticed.'

She wipes her other cheek. 'Are you kidding? You're never without your phone, and then a few weeks ago I saw that you'd gone out without it, and then I noticed you'd left it charging another day. And again. I thought …' She breaks off and moves to the window, her back to me.

'You thought what, Meg?'

'I thought you were having an affair.'

That's rich, I don't say.

'Are you going to tell the police?' I ask instead.

She continues to stare out of the window, but doesn't answer. I realise now that by telling her what I've been up to, I've inadvertently made her an accomplice, unless she immediately reports my actions to the police. I should probably find myself a solicitor with good persuasive skills who can help minimise the punishment I'll face. The sound of the prison doors sliding shut when I visited Rhys echo in my mind. I'll take my punishment on the chin, but if I can avoid a custodial sentence, I'll count my blessings.

'Meg?' I say, still awaiting her answer.

She slowly turns to face me, resting her bottom against the kitchen sink. 'I want to ask you something first: why didn't you tell me this is what you were planning to do?'

The question throws me. The honest answer is it wasn't a conscious choice that I made. It wasn't like I ever actually considered telling Meg what I had planned, because I know she would have told me I'm an idiot and that I was being selfish for flushing our future down the toilet. There have been times since the plan first formed in my head in Mike's office, where I've considered coming clean, but I still love my wife, and I can't stand to see the disappointment in her eyes that I'm seeing right now.

'I didn't want you to try and stop me,' I reply. 'I knew you wouldn't be comfortable with what I was planning, and wanted to spare your feelings.'

She looks up at the ceiling, shaking her head before looking back at me. 'You stupid, stupid man.'

At least her anger is finally coming out, and I'm not going to challenge the inevitable barrage of insults about to come my way.

'No, wait, you're not stupid,' she corrects herself, her head still shaking. 'You're selfish!'

'Meg, I'm sorry. I understand why you're angry,

and you have every right to –'

'You think you know why I'm angry?' she interrupts.

'You think I've messed up everything because I took the law into my own hands.'

She runs her tongue around her mouth in disbelief. 'You haven't got a clue, Joe. I'm not angry because you decided to abduct the man responsible for killing our little girl. I'm annoyed that you thought you should do it on your own!'

Her cheeks are flaring with fire, but this certainly wasn't the reaction I'd been anticipating.

'What gives you the right to use our shared grief to interrogate the bastard responsible? Do you think your grief is somehow worse than mine? Do you not realise how frustrated I was that the police let him go because they didn't have enough evidence? What gives you the monopoly on grief?'

'I'm sorry, Meg.' I don't know what else to say.

'You should have told me what you were planning. I would have helped you to arrange it.'

I don't want to ask her outright if this means she isn't planning to report me to the police, in case I'm misreading the situation.

'I have just as much right as you to look into the eyes of our daughter's killer, and demand the truth,' she continues. 'I want you to take me to this country house *now*.'

I remain perfectly still. I want to tell her that there's no point; that David isn't talking, and that if I couldn't manage to make him speak, there's little chance she'll succeed either, but such thoughts are hypocritical.

There's a calmness to her breathing that I envy, but maybe she will have more luck with him. Maybe coming face-to-face with Lydia's mother will be the trigger for David's empathy to kick in. It certainly can't hurt.

'There's something else you need to know,' I say. 'When I jumped him I think I witnessed Hazel Cooper being abducted by a man I now believe is somehow connected to Calderwood.'

Meg's eyes widen. 'You saw someone abduct Hazel?'

I nod. 'I didn't know who she was at the time, and I tried to intervene, but the guy got away. I reported it to the police –'

'You were the anonymous 999 caller?'

I nod again. 'I only gave up the chase when they said they were on the van's tail, but somehow he still evaded them. I think he still has her, but the police have so far ignored my efforts to explain that.'

I tell her about David's address book, about visiting Francis McAdam's home, and my anonymous message to Crimestoppers.'

'Neil and Ruby genuinely believe she's just hiding because Matty refused to have sex with her.' She pauses. 'Do you think Calderwood knows where they are?'

I shrug. 'Maybe, but I can't be sure if he's just telling me what he thinks I want to hear.'

Meg reaches for a tissue, wipes her face and blows her nose. She puffs out her cheeks. 'Right, here's what we're going to do. You're going to drive me to Harrington Manor now, and let me interrogate David.'

'Meg, he's a tricky son of a bitch.'

She fixes me with an icy stare. 'He doesn't know what's coming for him. I'll make him talk one way or another. Bring the camera with you. I want to see the rest of what he's told you.'

Chapter 44

1 week ago

The car shook as Meg slammed the door shut.

'Bloody hell, Joe!' she scolded. 'Was that really necessary?'

He didn't answer, nor did he make any attempt to start the engine. It hadn't been his idea to come to this damp and cold community centre to sit in a circle with others and 'talk about his feelings'. He'd told her beforehand that it would be a total waste of time, but then she'd pulled that face; the one that made him feel like he was the worst human being alive.

'I came; that's what you wanted,' he replied evenly.

'What I *wanted* was for you to participate in an activity designed to help us understand our feelings and deal with our grief. Sitting there in silence with your arms folded, and rolling your eyes whenever the group would offer supportive words is not what I would call participating.'

Had she really expected him to be any different? What was the point of talking about his feelings? How would it help to admit to a perfect stranger that he couldn't sleep for the anger burning inside of him? How every waking minute was spent willing karma to strike David Calderwood down for what he had done to them; for what he had done to *her*.

He could feel Meg staring at him now, presumably waiting for him to apologise, but in his head he had nothing to be sorry about. He hadn't told anyone in the room how pointless the whole exercise was. Instead he'd sat and pretended to listen, all the while picturing David at his feet begging for forgiveness.

'Every person in that room tonight was grieving for a lost child too, you know,' Meg continued, the hurt in her voice like a dagger to his heart. 'I thought it would help to be amongst people who understood what we're going through.'

His head snapped around as he could no longer bite his tongue. 'What we're going through? Not a single one of them knows what *we're* going through. They were lucky: their children died as a result of illness or accidents. There may be no rhyme or reason to their loss, but at least they know there was nothing they could have done about it. At least they have something to blame for their loss. They're not like us, Meg. Can't you see that? We all lost a child, but ours was taken from us, and we still have no clue why or by whom.'

Her cheeks burned bright under the brilliance of the street lights. 'Do you really think that will make it easier? If Andrews arrests and punishes the person responsible, do you really think that will bring you any peace? Don't kid yourself!'

But she was wrong. He knew deep in his soul that hearing David confess and beg for mercy would bring so much satisfaction. And he had no doubt that it would prove more beneficial to Meg than she realised.

He studied her face now, wondering whether he should just tell her what he couldn't stop imagining. If she knew what he had planned, would she realise just how much he'd been suffering? Would she see that they would both benefit from knowing the truth?

He opened his mouth to speak, but she stopped him before he had a chance.

'I don't think I can do this anymore, Joe.' Her eyes filled with tears, but she could no longer meet his gaze. 'I know you're hurting too, but I don't think *this* is healthy. I want us both to find a way to move on, but everything I suggest and try is met by you with derision. It's like two recovering alcoholics in a co-dependent relationship. It just doesn't work long-term. I can't help you grieve if you won't allow yourself to do so, and I can't keep clinging on to the past.'

His mouth dropped. 'You want to forget about Lydia and move on, just like that?'

The slap stung his cheek but his eyes didn't leave her face.

'How dare you, Joe? My heart aches as much as yours; more, if anything. I grew her, felt every movement inside of me. She was a part of me, and to not be able to tell her how much I miss her, and how a part of me died that day is excruciating. There isn't a single second that passes when I don't want to just end it all and be with her again, but I know she wouldn't want that. She'd want us to find a way to keep going, but it feels like you don't want to move forwards. You seem to be stuck in a void, and I want to pull you out, but you don't want me to, do you? You seem perfectly content to hold the whole world responsible, and I can't live like that.'

She opened the door and pushed her foot out onto

the pavement.

'What are you doing? Where are you going?'

She waited until she was out of the car before replying. 'I need some air to clear my head. I'll walk from here.'

'Don't be stupid, Meg,' he protested. 'It's at least a couple of miles home from here. Don't be ridiculous. Get back in the car.'

She leaned in. 'Go home, Joe. I think a bit of space will do us both the power of good.'

He was about to argue, but she slammed the door and strode away, wrapping her coat around her middle against the cold.

Joe remained where he was, waiting for her to realise her error and come back, but she didn't look back once, and was soon around the corner and gone from sight.

Leaning across her seat, he opened the glove box, searching for the charger for his phone, when something bright and yellow caught his attention. Stretching, he scooped out the small bracelet, the feel of the plastic beads so familiar, and yet he hadn't seen it in months. He could still recall the moment they arrived at the park that day and Meg insisted Lydia take the bracelet off, worried that she would lose it while playing. Lydia hadn't been happy, but had reluctantly passed it over, and they'd hidden it in the glove box for safekeeping.

Joe clenched his fingers around it, pressing his fist to his cheek as tears splashed against it.

Meg was right about one thing: he wouldn't be able to move on until he had the answers he needed. There were so many reasons he could think of for why he shouldn't go through with the plan, but he knew in his soul he'd never forgive himself if he didn't try. Rather than heading for home, he pulled out of the car park in the direction of Riverside Terrace.

Chapter 45

Meg

The house is bigger than I imagined from Joe's brief description. I wouldn't have even known the old place was here from driving past the private road, and it alarms me that he managed to find it in the first place. All he's told me is that the owners are away overseas, but there's an element of me that wonders whether that is just another lie on top of all the others he's been spinning these past few weeks.

I pinch myself as he parks the car. So many times I've imagined what it would be like to come face-to-face with my daughter's killer, and I can't be certain I'm not dreaming now. I pinch myself for a second time, but I don't wake in bed. This is really happening.

Joe kills the engine and removes the keys, but doesn't attempt to exit the car.

'You okay?' he asks, his face tight with concern.

Given what I've learned in the last hour about his deception, and what I'm about to encounter, actually yeah I am just about holding it together.

'It isn't too late for you to phone the police and drop me in it,' he adds, with no trace of humour.

I know he's only saying it to test the strength of my conviction, and to give me a way out, but I'm not as weak as he thinks. I've allowed myself to rely on him since we got married – it's been nice having the support – but I was strong and capable before we got together, and I haven't lost any of that guile, even if I have kept it hidden for a number of years. Giving birth to Lydia was my proudest achievement and the son of a bitch inside that house stole that from me.

Am I ready? You bet your arse I am.

I meet Joe's gaze with a firm nod. 'I wouldn't betray you like that. But no more lies, agreed?'

He nods vigorously. 'I'm sorry I didn't tell you before.'

I look out at the stately home. 'So am I Joe. Maybe if you had we wouldn't be in this mess now. But there's no time for regret. From here on in, we do this together.'

He picks up my hand and kisses the back of it. 'Together.'

We exit the car and hurry up to the front door. The wind is strong and I can feel tiny drops of rain blow against my cheeks. Over our heads the clouds are charcoal-coloured, and it won't be long until the brewing storm erupts.

I gasp as we step in through the door. The hallway is majestic, the ceiling so high, and the chandeliers so shiny that there is an air of magic to the place. This should be the home of a king or queen, not a prison for a registered sex offender and chief murder suspect. Joe leads me through the grand living room and out to the kitchen, putting a single finger to his lips, while pointing at a plain looking brown door cut into the wall.

Slipping the small handbag from my shoulder, I

place it on the counter top so I know where it is in case I need to quickly get to what I've hidden inside it. Joe isn't the only one who can keep secrets.

He reaches into the box beside my bag and extracts what looks like some sort of torch, but then he presses a button on the side and sparks of electricity fire out of the two prongs at the end.

'In case he gives us any trouble,' he says. 'A couple of jolts is usually enough to subdue him.'

I hand him the video camera. 'Be ready to record as soon as he gives us what we need.'

'Do you really think you can make him confess? You saw how I tried.'

I can't tell him why, but I know David will tell me what I need to hear. Taking the stun gun from his hands, I tell Joe to take me to him.

He unlocks and opens the door to the basement. The single bulb hanging just above our heads provides little light on the staircase down, but I can already smell the angst of what has come before me in this dungeon. It's reminiscent of the smell of a boys' changing room at school: testosterone mixed with sweat and fear. My stomach turns as I follow my husband down. I'm almost at the bottom of the stairs when I first see the iron bars poking from the concrete floor. It's not what I would expect in such a grand home, but it's a perfect prison for such a monster.

The grey haired man lying lifeless on the floor isn't what I'm expecting to see inside the cage either. He looks half-dead and weak. Where is the monster who's been haunting my nightmares? Where is the looming beast who lurks in the shadows waiting to strike?

The figure moves at the sound of our footsteps, and cranes his neck to look at us.

'Who's this?' he croaks at us, shuffling so he can get a proper look at me.

There's a sadness in his eyes, and I can't tell if he's putting it on for my benefit. But I can also see the cogs turning behind his eyes as he assesses what's coming next. He plants his hands, and forces his body into a sitting position.

'You must be Joe's wife,' he croaks again.

I swallow down my own fear, and tentatively step towards the bars, squeezing the handle of the stun gun in my hand. 'That's right,' I say less confidently than I'd intended. I clear my throat and try again. 'I'm Lydia's mum, and you're the bastard who took her from me.'

His shoulders straighten at the statement. 'No, you've got it wrong. I had nothing to do with what happened to your little girl, and you have to believe me when I tell you how sorry I am for your loss.'

I take another step forward. 'Stop talking. I don't want to hear your lies.'

He pouts, his eyes darting from me to Joe who remains a few steps behind me, quietly observing the exchange.

'You know that you're both breaking the law imprisoning me like this. So that's assault, abduction, false imprisonment, and … let's throw in a charge of actual bodily harm to boot.' He pauses and whistles through his teeth. 'They'll probably lock you up for a few years for that. How would your daughter feel if she knew that her parents were capable of such malice against an innocent man?'

I leap towards the bars and press my face against them. 'Don't you dare speak of what my daughter might think or feel? You stole the breath from her lungs, so you have no right. No right whatsoever!'

He could easily launch himself towards the bars and strike me if he wanted, and although I've taken a risk, I'm hoping that he takes the bait and gives me the excuse I'm looking for. Before I step into the cell, I need to know that he's capable of what he was accused of doing. He remains where he is, sitting cross-legged.

'I can see you're not scared of us,' I say, quieter now, projecting myself as meek. 'All we want to know is why you felt it necessary to kill Lydia. She was a good girl, and didn't deserve to die so young.' I allow my eyes to fill with tears, but force myself to look at him. 'As a parent, I just need to understand what happened and why you did it. Please, just tell us what we need to know and we'll let you go.'

David stands but doesn't charge towards the bars. Instead he puts his hands in his pockets. He's maybe an inch or two taller than me, but the clothes hang from his thin frame. If I had met him anywhere else, I'd have probably described him as a kindly old man; the sort of grandfather figure I might expect to see in one of those adverts for toffees. He doesn't look like a killer, but then I wouldn't have said he looks like a sex offender, and yet I know he's been to prison for his previous crimes. Can leopards change their spots? Have Joe and I really got it so wrong? My gut tells me we haven't, and we've already wasted too much time. Hazel's life is in danger, and we need to find her.

'Open the cell,' I tell Joe, and he moves to the door and inserts the keys.

'Are you sure about this?' he whispers.

I don't reply, moving to the door, and nodding for him to slide it open. He obliges, and the scraping of the metal sends a shiver the length of my spine. Stepping into the cell, my entire body feels suddenly cold as nervous energy floods my body. If I've underestimated David, he could quickly overpower me, and threaten my life to get Joe to do what he wants. Is he considering the same thing as he stands, watching me?

Joe begins to slide the door closed, and it's the only encouragement I need. I take two giant strides forward and swing my arm out, burying the prongs into the folds of skin in David's neck, and depress the switch on the stun gun.

David's body leaps into the air and crumples at my feet, but he manages to break his fall with his arms. I wrap my arm around the top of his head, pulling it back slightly so he can see the stun gun in my other hand.

'Tell me where Francis McAdam has taken Hazel Cooper,' I bark, 'or I swear to God the next shot goes in your eye.'

He looks far less confident, but I haven't broken his spirit yet.

'I-I don't know where Francis is. I told your husband he's just someone I knew from my time inside. He's a monster who I want nothing to do with. Please, I can't tell you what I don't know.'

I bring the stun gun closer to his face, and fire the trigger so he can see what is coming next.

'I don't believe you,' I tell him.

'P-Please, don't blind me and add GBH to your charge sheet. You can still walk away from this if you phone the police and tell them what Joe has done. There's no reason you both have to go to prison. Help me get out of here, and I'll tell the police you saved me. Come on, Meg, you're better than this.'

And that's the moment I know he's lying.

'If you're so innocent, then how the hell do you know my name?'

I don't wait for him to think of another lie, instead pressing the prongs into the space between his neck and shoulder, and holding the switch down until his eyes roll back into his head. I check his pulse as he crumples at my feet.

Joe quickly slides open the door and takes the stun gun from me. 'Now what?'

I extract myself from the cell and take several deep breaths to compose myself whilst he locks the cell door behind us and pockets the keys.

'Show me what else this place has. Clearly the stun gun isn't doing what we need.'

I don't wait for him to answer, hurrying back up the stairs to the kitchen, grateful as my nose acclimatises to fresher air.

'What did you have in mind?' Joe asks when he joins me in the kitchen.

I'm about to answer when I hear my phone ringing in my bag on the counter.

Joe looks disappointed. 'You brought your phone? That means you can be traced here.'

I don't recognise the number in the display, but answer anyway. 'Hello?'

'Mrs Irons? Hi, sorry to disturb you, but it's Detective Andrews. I'm parked outside your house and am looking for Joe. I don't suppose he's with you now is he?'

'Hold on, Detective Andrews,' I say for Joe's benefit, 'I'm driving, let me just pull over so I can speak to you.' I lower the phone and press it into my chest, looking to Joe for answers.

The blood has drained from his face, and his neck has a shade of green, like he might be sick.

'Oh perfect!' he exclaims crossing to the sink and gripping the edges. 'Now he'll be able to put you here thanks to GPS. What does he want?'

'He said he wants to speak to *you*.'

I don't think I've ever seen Joe look so worried and uncertain.

I press the phone back to my cheek. 'Hi, Detective Andrews, sorry about that. Um. Joe isn't with me, but I can ask him to call you as soon as I see him. Is there anything I can help you with? Is it an update on Lydia's case?'

He sighs. 'No, nothing like that, I'm afraid. Do you know where he might be? I tried his office but his boss said Joe's off sick, which is why I came to your house, but there's no answer at the door.'

'Well I have his car, so he might have just gone out for a walk. I'll try and phone him for you, and let him know you're waiting at the house for him to get back.'

I hang up before he can argue, and look at Joe.

'Take the car and drive home, but park somewhere else. Deal with whatever this is, and then get yourself back here.'

'What about you?'

'I'll be fine. David's passed out and is locked in the cell.'

'I don't want you going down there without me here. Promise me, Meg.'

'I'm not stupid, Joe. I won't go near him.'

Satisfied with my answer, he hurries from the kitchen, leaving me to go exploring for fresh ideas.

Chapter 46

Hazel

He is sitting forward in the chair, his elbows planted on his knees, hands clamped together, staring at her. For the first time she can properly see his face, the balaclava abandoned. His cheeks are round, but clean shaven. His white or silver hair shimmers beneath the orange glow of the roof. His nose is short but wide, with a bump at the bridge where it may have been broken once. But his eyes are as black as night, as is the tired skin pooled around them as he glares despairingly.

Hazel can barely keep herself propped up, as nausea continues to swirl in the cloud inside her head. She didn't drink the water last night, despite her desperate thirst and fatigue at having worked tirelessly on the hole. The only thing she'd consumed since the Mars bar was that pizza, and now as it threatens to rematerialize, she realises her fatal error. He must have dosed her food and waited until she passed out on the mattress before returning to block the hole.

She flinches as he reaches down between his legs and his hand disappears into a box between his parted feet. She watches in terror, waiting to see what weapon he will produce to punish her with, and starts as his hand emerges clutching papers of some kind.

Death by a thousand paper cuts, fizzes through her head, and she almost laughs, but her brain isn't functioning as it should be.

Am I dying?

She closes her eyes and tries to just focus on the art of rolling back onto the mattress, but misjudges how far she's travelled, and the back of her head crashes against the wooden floor.

'Dear Auntie Answers,' he reads, deliberately raising the pitch of his voice as if mimicking a teenage girl. 'I'm only fourteen, but I feel ready to take the next step with my boyfriend Matt. He's sixteen, and we've been together for six months, but I love him, and I know he loves me. I don't want us to get in trouble, but I can't get him out of my mind. Sincerely, Real_Chica_07'

It's like he's reached into her soul and plucked her deepest, darkest thoughts. Hearing her words on his lips increases the likelihood of regurgitation.

'Dear Real_Chica_07, love at your age can be a minefield to navigate, but you're clearly smart enough to understand the law, and to ask for help. I can't overstate how brave you are to be holding such an adult conversation despite your age. I think for your own protection it might be best if we take this conversation into a private chat space if you're happy to do so. The internet can be a dangerous place after all. Sincerely, Auntie Answers.'

Hazel lies still, recalling the moment she'd received that message from the Auntie Answers website, relieved that her question had not only been acknowledged, but that the legendary anonymous agony aunt was going to offer her the advice she desperately craved. How had her captor managed to get access to this private conversation?

'Dear Auntie Answers, thank you for helping. We're constantly warned about the dangers of online grooming at school, so it's such a relief to find a trusted site like yours. I've been reading some of the other posts and responses, but my issue seems to be a touch unique. I'll be fifteen in January, but I'm worried that Matt will lose interest in me if I don't have sex with him. If he was with a girl his own age, he'd be free to do what he wants. Everyone always says I'm mature for my age, but I don't want either of us to get in trouble if we have sex.'

She can almost recite Auntie Answers' response, but it doesn't make it any easier to hear her tormentor read it aloud. This is a private conversation that not even Matt knows about, let alone her parents. She forces her head up to look at him as he drops a page to the floor and begins to read from the next.

'Dear Real_Chica_07, you should only have sex with a boy if *you* want to, not because you feel pressured to do so. You say you love Matt and that you know he loves you, but has he told you that? Have you talked to him about sex? Do you feel he is pressuring you into wanting what he wants?'

She'd felt affronted by those questions, but after consideration, realised they were standard questions that a concerned counsellor would naturally ask a vulnerable young adult. If anything the challenges only reaffirmed how genuine Auntie Answers was. Fresh doubt now washes over her, as she realises there is only one way he could have got hold of the conversation.

'Dear Auntie Answers, Matt has told me he is happy to wait until I am sixteen before we take the next step, and if anything it is me who is desperate to have sex with him rather than the other way round. He tells me he loves me every day, and if you saw the way he looks at me, you'd know he means it. I know he's worried about my age, but I have no doubt that I'm ready to have sex with him, but how do I convince him of that?'

This last message is what she'd sent a week ago, and it was because of Auntie Answers' suggestion that she invited Matt to the clearing on Halloween.

'Dear Auntie Answers,' he continues, adopting a deeper, more masculine voice, 'I think my girlfriend wants to have sex, but how do I tell her I'm not ready without hurting her feelings? She's mentioned it a couple of times, and I know that I love her with all my heart, but I'm worried about the age gap between us. She's only fourteen and I'm sixteen, and I'm worried that if I say no she'll think I'm rejecting her and that I'm not crazy about her. What do I do? From M_and_M_and_M_and_M_05.'

He stops reading and smiles lasciviously at her, before returning his eyes to the page. She had no idea Matt had used the same site, nor that he was worried by what she'd been planning.

'Dear M_and_M_and_M_and_M_05, I'm messaging you privately due to the sensitive nature of what you've asked. You're right not to have sex with your underage girlfriend. You need to reject all of her advances, as failure to do so would constitute a serious breach of the law, and you could go to prison. At fourteen she is vulnerable, but more importantly why are you dating someone so much younger than you? Aren't there any girls your own age (or older) you could go out with instead? My advice to you is to meet with her and explain that she is too young for you, and you need to spend time with girls your own age. The law is there for a reason. Sincerely, Auntie Answers.'

So that was why Matt had so calmly rejected her at the clearing. Hazel is winded, but her captor isn't finished yet. He discards the pages to the floor, stands and moves to the end of the mattress.

'You don't want to be wasting your time with a wet blanket like Matt, Hazel. Not when there are real men out there who understand just how special you are and are ready to give you everything you desire.'

He reaches for his belt, and to her horror, begins to unfasten the buckle, but then stops as his eyes catch sight of the bucket and freshly glued board.

'But before we get to any of that,' he says turning his back and bending over the box, 'I need to make you understand that vandalising your room can't go unpunished.'

As he straightens, the orange glow catches on the blade of the secateurs in his hand.

Chapter 47

Joe

I should turn back. Screw Andrews wanting to meet with me. Where was he when I needed him?

I look up to the rear-view mirror and see Lydia in her yellow party dress staring back at me.

'I shouldn't have left your mum there with him,' I say to her, my eyes pleading that she confirms my suspicions and tells me to turn around.

She remains silent, just staring back at me with a look of pure love that it feels as though my fractured heart will explode.

He's locked in that cell, so as long as Meg doesn't open his cell, and stays out of the basement there's nothing he can do to her. Right?

But what if I'm wrong? What if he figures out a way to escape, and then I've left Meg at his mercy?

I'm practically home, but it isn't too late to go back there. After all, Andrews doesn't actually know I'm on my way yet. All Meg told him was she would *try* to get a message to me; he doesn't know if she's managed it.

I look back at Lydia's reflection, and reach for the burner phone, quickly typing Meg's number, keeping one eye on the road. It rings eight times, but there's no answer, and then the messaging service cuts in. I end the call without leaving a message.

She's probably just put it down, I reason with myself. *Or she's put it on silent and hasn't realised I'm calling.*

I nod at my own anxious eyes for reassurance, but it doesn't help.

What if she went back down to the basement to try and reason with him again, and he suggested letting him out and now he's overpowered her and escaped?

The burner phone comes to life in my hand, and I see Meg's number in the display. I stab the answer icon with my thumb.

'Meg? Is everything okay?'

'Oh, Joe it's you. I didn't recognise the number. Have you changed your phone?'

'It's a burner,' I quickly respond.

'I see. What's wrong? Have you finished with Andrews already?'

My heart flutters as the anxiety eases slightly. 'No, not there yet, I just … I had a bad feeling, and wanted to make sure you're okay.'

I can hear the frostiness in her tone. 'I told you I would be.'

'Yes, I know … I'm sorry, Meg. You're sure you're okay?'

'Yes, Joe. He's still in the cell, and I've not been back down there. Just do what you need to do, and get back here.'

'Okay, okay. I'm sorry for doubting you. I'll call again when I'm done so you'll know when I'm on my way back.'

'Good luck,' she adds, before hanging up.

Seeing the small Co-op at the end of the road, I pull

into one of the allocated bays outside the shop, lock the car, and jog back along the road, cutting through the alleyway that leads back to the estate our road is on. I slow my jog to a walk as soon as I'm on the road, and my breathing is halfway back to normal when I spot Andrews's car parked at the kerbside outside our house. I feign surprise as I near the vehicle and see Andrews in his brown suit squashed in behind the steering wheel, staring out at me. I nod in his direction and he lowers his window, and waves me over.

'Hi, Joe, sorry to drop around like this, but I was hoping I could have a word with you.'

I swallow my doubt and panic as best I can. 'Oh yeah? What about?'

'Do you mind if I come in with you? It feels like I've been stuck in this car all day. I could do with stretching my legs.'

The last thing I want is a trained detective snooping around inside my house, but I can't refuse without looking suspicious.

I step back from his car as he opens the door, and then lead him down the path to the front door, unlocking it and stepping to one side to allow him to enter. The beagle barks from behind the kitchen door to greet us. I open the door and give her ears a rub, hurrying her through to the back garden so she can relieve herself.

'Meg said you were off sick,' Andrews comments as he glances into the kitchen and gives it the once over as he passes.

Having listened to her end of the conversation, I know this to be a lie, but can't call him on it.

'Dicky tummy,' I reply dismissively, closing the patio door and allowing Lola to roam and investigate.

'There's a lot of it going about,' Andrews nods in acknowledgement. 'I find its worst when the kids first go back to school after an extended break. My two seem to bring home a range of colds and upset stomachs.'

'I didn't realise you had children,' I say honestly. 'You've never spoken about them.'

He looks at me and I realise through the silence of the glass-eyed stare that he probably prefers to keep his work and personal lives separate.

'Aside from a bit of gastroenteritis, how are things?' he asks next, now in the living room, perched on the edge of the armchair.

I reverse onto the sofa, reminding myself that he can't possibly know where I've just come from or what we've been doing at Harrington Manor. This visit is nothing more than coincidence.

'Things are as you'd expect,' I answer carefully.

He nods again. 'Good, good. Meg's not home?'

'She went for a drive,' I lie, sticking to her story.

'Ah, I see.'

Andrews isn't one for small talk, and Meg said he wanted to speak to me about something specific, and it's starting to worry me that he hasn't bowled out with whatever it is yet. Is that because he finds it awkward? Or because he doesn't know how to raise the subject?

'Cup of tea?' I offer, like having the police in my house is a totally normal occurrence.

'Thanks, but this shouldn't take too long,' he says, smiling.

I remain where I am, rather than ducking to the kitchen, and just wait for him to spit it out.

'The thing is, Joe, I need to check whether you've been back to Riverside Terrace since I saw you there yesterday.'

He is watching my reactions carefully, and I daren't give away what's been going on. I try to look confused by the question, whilst shrugging and shaking my head.

'You made it perfectly clear what would happen if you found me there again, so, no I haven't.'

He nods, looking around the room. 'How's the dog settling in?'

'She's as good as gold. Meg's fallen in love with her.'

'They're amazing animals. I remember having a German Shepherd when I was growing up, and he was my best friend. I still miss him to this day.'

Surely he hasn't come here to talk to me about the restorative power of a dog's love again?

'David Calderwood is AWOL,' he blurts out, and it takes me a moment to process the statement.

'AWOL?' I question, trying to add enough surprise to my voice.

He nods. 'I was calling in to speak to him about something when I saw you outside his home, but there was no answer. I've been back twice more since, and there's no answer. His mobile is switched off too, and he isn't answering his home phone.'

So, he knows David isn't home, and his first thought was to come knocking at my door. This isn't good.

'Maybe he's on holiday?' I suggest, my pitch higher

than I was expecting.

'One of the conditions of his release is that he has to tell his local police team if he's planning to go away for a few days, and there's been no word.'

'Have you tried the hospitals? Maybe he was taken ill suddenly.'

Andrews considers the question. 'He's not been admitted to any hospitals in the county.'

Is he waiting for me to confess? Has his detective's brain already started to piece all of this together? He found me outside David's house yesterday and has automatically reached the conclusion that I must be involved? Why is it suddenly so hot in here?

'I take it you haven't passed him in your travels?' Andrews asks next.

'Why would I?' I snap back, before adding, 'I've been home sick since yesterday lunchtime.'

'Of course, I was just curious as to whether you might have seen anything at Riverside Terrace yesterday.'

'Like what?'

'Well, I don't know how long you were parked there before I arrived. Maybe you saw him getting in a taxi, or being picked up by someone? We know he doesn't drive, and we're checking his bank details but it doesn't look like he's used any of his cards for a few days.'

I look off to the distance, like I'm deep in thought trying to remember what I saw. 'No, sorry, I was only there for a few minutes before you showed up, and I didn't see him there. Sorry.'

He continues to stare at me for what feels like

forever, before giving a quick nod, and slapping his hands on his knees. 'It was worth a punt.'

'Are you worried about where he might have gone then?' I say, unable to prevent the question escaping.

Why am I continuing to engage with him when I need to get back to Meg?

'I'm sure he'll turn up, but I'd rather know where he is.'

'This isn't anything to do with that missing girl, is it?'

He narrows his eyes. 'What makes you ask that?'

I give him a knowing look. 'A teenage girl goes missing at the same time as a known sex offender? I don't have to be a rocket scientist to see the possible connection. I mean, that's why you were calling around to speak to him, right? I remember when Lydia went missing, you said one of the first things you did was to interview known offenders in the area.'

'Well, I can't speak about an open case. I'm sure you understand.'

'I take it she's not been found yet?'

He shakes his head, his face downcast.

'Are there any other offenders in the area who could be involved?' I ask, keen to understand whether he's acted on the message I left with Crimestoppers.

'I assure you we're exploring every possibility.'

'It's just …' I stop myself, but frankly I've nothing to lose. 'It's just that when you couldn't find evidence of Lydia's DNA at Calderwood's house, did you ever consider whether he had a partner of some kind? You know, like someone he may have served time with who stashed her for him.'

'Predators like that don't tend to work with partners. They tend to be quite sociopathic and not good at building relationships, so it's unlikely.'

'But surely Calderwood isn't the only registered sex offender in the Reading area? What efforts are being made to question the others about this girl's disappearance?'

He stands, and straightens his suit jacket. 'I'm afraid I can't discuss the details of an on-going investigation with you, Joe. I promise we're doing everything we can to locate Hazel Cooper.'

This time I stop myself from asking whether David is a suspect in Hazel's disappearance, and allow Andrews to leave. Fetching Lola from the garden, I play with her in the kitchen while I wait for Andrews to pull away, but he just sits there for ten minutes, as if he's waiting to catch me sneaking away. I wait a further five minutes, before daring to poke my head out of the door to check the coast is clear, before dashing back to my car, knowing I've already been too long.

Chapter 48

Hazel

She tries to slide back onto the mattress and away from his outstretched grasp, but her limbs won't respond to the messages her head is sending them. Not that it would make a difference even if they would, he's already shown how much stronger he is. And now she accepts how much smarter he is too. For all she knows he was watching the entire time as she worked hard on the hole, devouring the pizza to keep her strength up, all the time weakening herself so she'd be powerless to stop him.

He snaps the secateurs together as he straightens in case she's missed his obvious intention. Her mum has a similarly sharp pair that she uses for cutting stubborn rose bushes. Images whish through her drug-addled mind: him cutting off her fingers; him cutting off her toes one at a time and then eating them; him driving the blades under her chin and cutting off her face so he can wear it.

He swallows the distance between them, trampling over the mattress in his heavy boots, the whole cabin seeming to shake as he nears. Still she tries and fails to slither away, but he's over her, blocking out the light in no time, and then he folds one arm around her waist, and lifts her into the air like a feather. Her arms and legs hang down, and though she manages to move her foot, the kick does nothing to stop his movement back towards the chair. He drops her onto it, and her lower back stings with the impact.

He then reaches down and lifts the rope around her ankle, following it back to the hook in the floor where it's attached and cuts it with one snip of the secateurs. He then gathers the rope, returning to the chair, and proceeds to tie the length around her second leg, and then her hands to the back of the chair. He's wasting his time, as even if she did want to fight back, her body is useless.

She feels his hot breath on her neck, and gags at the acrid stench as it drifts past her nostrils.

'You'll grow to love it here,' he tells her quietly. 'Once you realise that I'm not such a bad guy. I will show you what it is to be desired, and in time, you will learn to love me back. I know you're ready because you told me as much in your messages, Chica.'

And that's when the realisation hits her flush in the face: all of this is *her* fault. Had she just spoken to Matt about her wishes and fears, rather than seeking answers from some anonymous source, none of this would have happened. How many other innocent and vulnerable teens have fallen foul of this monster, or other monsters? How many more would suffer because she is too weak to stop him?

He grabs a handful of her blonde hair and puts it to his boxer's nose, inhaling deeply and audibly. Her gag reflex kicks in again, but this time she manages to twist her head to the side and throws up in the cardboard box beside the chair. He yanks her head back with the hair in his grasp, and curses as he surveys the mess on the floor.

'Stupid bitch!' he snaps, kicking the box away and rescuing the pages in its vicinity, in case she repeats the action.

Her throat burns, but her stomach feels empty already, and she hopes she won't throw up again. It's been hours since she had a drink, and her mouth is so dry, and now all she can taste is half-digested pizza.

He rests his hands on her shoulders, as he moves back behind her on the chair. 'One day you will learn that I saved you from making a terrible mistake with that insufferable bore, Matt. Seriously, what is wrong with the guy? If someone as gorgeous as you had approached me at that age, I'd have sold everything I own to buy you whatever you wanted to show you how much I desired you. Don't you see, Hazel, how far I went to bring you here? It wasn't easy, but you'll see my sacrifice was worth it.'

'P-Please,' she croaks, 'water?'

'In due course, my love, but as I said, I need to teach you not to vandalise your room. I can't trust you in my mum's house until I am certain you know how to behave properly.'

He grabs a handful of her hair again and yanks it forward so she can see the ends in her periphery. She hears rather than sees the secateurs snap closed, and then his hand is right in front of her face dropping the lengths of hair onto her lap.

She wants to cry. She wants to scream for him to stop.

Not my hair.

He grabs more of her golden locks at the back of her head and the secateurs snap shut. Again he drops them onto her lap, and they float down like dandelion seeds.

'P-Please,' she tries to gasp again, but he either can't hear or is choosing not to listen.

She closes her eyes as tears fill them with each snap, snap, snap.

Chapter 49

Meg

I'm not going to go down there. Joe's right. If David Calderwood is capable of pulling the wool over the eyes of a team of highly-trained detectives, then he's definitely capable of lying to me.

I snatch up my phone and look at the screen. Still no word from Joe to say he's finished with Andrews. What on earth could be taking so long?

I put the phone face down on the table, and stand, moving away from the small table in the kitchen, and move to the back door, staring out at the garden. Unlocking the door, I step out onto the small patio and take a deep breath of the fresh air. There must be an herb garden nearby because I can smell mint and rosemary, and maybe just a hint of basil. The patio stones are damp from the drizzle, but as I look up to the clouds and close my eyes, I welcome the cool splashes on my cheeks.

Is Lydia up there looking down at us now? She must be in heaven, because she was as good as they come. I just hope the angels are looking after her until I'm there to resume my maternal duties. Would she be disappointed by what we've done? Sunday school classes told me I should forgive and forget, but how can I forgive the man who stole my little girl and then ended her life in the most horrific way? Does he deserve my forgiveness if he isn't even prepared to admit what he did?

My phone bounces on the table top as it vibrates to announce an incoming call. I hurry back in and scoop it up.

'Joe? How'd it go?'

'He's gone, but they know David is missing. I think at the moment they just assume he's on holiday, so I don't think we're in the frame for anything yet.'

I sigh with relief. 'So you're on your way back?'

'Yeah, I just got back to my car. I won't drive direct in case I'm followed, but I'll make sure I'm not. How's everything with you?'

'I'm fine. I think he's starting to come around now, so you should get back here as quickly as you can so we can start again.'

'Sure, okay. We probably shouldn't keep talking in case anyone is listening in. I love you, Meg. See you soon.'

The call ends before I can respond, and it worries me that I'm so surprised by what he said. We've been married for ten years, so it shouldn't be a shock to hear my husband tell me he loves me, but I can't remember the last time I heard him say it. And shamefully I can't remember the last time I said it to him. Looking back on our relationship, our marriage took second place the moment Lydia was born. I don't think that's uncommon. As soon as children enter the mix, the roles change from wife and husband to mother and father. It's the most natural phenomenon, but since Lydia's murder, neither of us have made any effort to revert to our previous roles.

I think there was a part of me that thought his recent late returns from work and nights at the pub were just excuses to cover an affair. And I didn't blame him. I've not offered the affection or intimacy he deserves, and I think I was okay if he'd chosen to seek solace elsewhere. Now that I know he was planning all of this instead, it actually warms my heart to know he didn't stray despite everything we've been through.

Unlocking my phone, I open the photo gallery as I always do, and look at the last picture I took of Lydia. It was on the day she went missing at the park. It's not a particularly good image. She was on the swings, and was begging me to take the picture, but because of the movement of her legs, the image is blurred. I can make out bodies in the background, but the police poured over the image for days and couldn't identify any specific individuals who might have been able to help them understand what had happened. Pinching the screen with my fingers, I zoom in on that background detail, but the faces are a blur of pixels. The investigative team asked for other parents from the park to come forward and share any images they'd captured, but it was another dead end lead.

I wipe my eyes with my hand as they quickly fill. I would give anything to go back to this moment in time, take Lydia's hand and hurry home. How different our lives would now be had we done that instead of making the most of the warm sunshine and daring to believe she was safe.

I don't know how long I'm at the table thinking about that day, but a noise eventually disturbs me. A weak shout echoes from the basement, but I can't make out what is said. I move closer to the door, but don't open it, pressing my ear to the wooden panel instead.

'Hello?' the voice sounds again. 'Please? I need food and drink. I … I feel weak. Please?'

I look around the kitchen and spot a loaf of bread poking out of the box on the counter. Joe didn't tell me whether he'd fed David this morning, but it's now after one, and I know he didn't give him anything to eat when we arrived.

He doesn't deserve my empathy, but maybe if I show him a kindness and take him some food, he'll reflect it and tell me what we need to hear. Maybe it's just my optimistic side being naïve, but I have to try.

Moving to the box, I extract two slices of bread, but there is nothing else of use in the box. Opening the cupboards in the kitchen, I locate a plastic plate a teaspoon, and a jar of honey. I fix the sandwich and cut it unevenly with a dinner knife, and carry it to the door. I stop and take a deep breath. I need him to believe that I am not alone here, and that my act of human kindness comes at a cost. Projecting a confidence that I'm not feeling, I pull open the door and quickly move down the stairs.

'Oh, thank goodness,' he says when he sees it's me and what I'm carrying. 'There's bottled water in the fridge over there.'

I look at where he's pointing and see the portable fridge. I extract a bottle and tell him to move away from the bars. He takes several steps backwards, enabling me to place the bottle between the bars. I don't take my eyes off him, anticipating any possible lunge or attack, but he doesn't move. The bars are too close together to get the plate through, so instead I place it on the floor beside the bars and move away. He should be able to reach through and collect the sandwich.

'Help yourself,' I say when I am far enough away that he can't get at me.

He hurries to the bars, and drops to his knees, unscrewing the bottle and drinking half the contents in one go.

'Thank you, thank you so much.'

He reaches for the first half of the sandwich and shovels it between his lips. It's gone in two mouthfuls.

'I see you're more sympathetic than your husband,' he says, smiling at me while chewing.

My skin crawls, but I keep a straight face.

'We're not monsters,' I reply evenly.

He takes another long sip of the water, before reaching for the second half of the sandwich.

'I suppose you're going to expect some kind of information in return for this?'

'Seems like a fair exchange.'

His smile widens. 'Very well. What do you want to know?'

I'm conscious that no matter what I ask, he'll probably lie, but I have to try.

'Where's Hazel Cooper?'

His smile vanishes. 'As I've repeatedly told your husband, I don't know who she is or where Francis might have taken her.'

'You're lying,' I say back.

He tilts his head slightly. 'Why do you say that?'

'You have a tell.'

He suddenly erupts with laughter. 'Do I now? Remind me never to play poker with you then. May I ask what my tell is?'

He hasn't denied he's lying. I was bluffing, but that tells me something about him, and why Joe's right not to trust a word he says.

'If you ever hope of being freed, you'll have to tell us eventually.'

'I can't tell you what I don't know.'

'Why help him? If McAdam isn't your friend, and you weren't involved in Hazel being taken, why prolong this silence? Does human life mean so little to you that you're prepared to allow him to harm her?'

He finishes the second half of his sandwich in silence.

'Is that what you really want to ask me, Meg? Here we are, just the two of us, and you could ask me *absolutely* anything, and you just repeat the same nonsense as your husband. Don't you want to ask me about Lydia?'

I inwardly gasp at the sound of her name on his lips.

'Don't you want to know what her final words were?'

His smiling face blurs as my eyes fill.

'Don't you want to know whether she begged for you?'

I throw myself forwards, but he jumps back from the bars, leaving me reaching through, grasping at air.

'You sick bastard,' I shout between sobs.

He laughs mockingly, and my cheeks wet. Covering my ears, I hurry away and back up the stairs, slamming the kitchen door behind me, angry at my own weakness.

Joe catches me, and I fall into his arms, burying my face in his shoulder.

'What's happened? What's going on?' he asks urgently. 'Did he hurt you?'

I shake my head woefully, trying to contain my sobs.

'Did he say something? Tell me, Meg.'

I peel my face from his now damp hoodie, and take several breaths to compose myself.

'This … isn't … working,' I stutter. 'He's not … going to speak … until … he's scared.'

'We can use the stun gun on him again. Maybe if we do short bursts, it'll take longer before he passes out; cause more pain.'

I shake my head. 'I have a better idea.'

He frowns at me, so I take his hand and lead him from the kitchen, through the drawing room and upstairs to the bathroom I found on my earlier scouting mission.

'You want to give him a bath?'

I shake my head again, and point to the ropes I've tied to the handles in the bath, and the towel I found in the airing cupboard.

'No, we're going to water board him. When he knows how serious this is, he'll talk.'

Chapter 50

Hazel

He's left her untied, but discarded on the mattress like trash. Her golden locks are strewn in a circle around where she was sitting in the chair. It now looks as though a cat has made a snow angel out of the strands. He took the chair when he left; not one for repeating his mistakes, clearly.

She's cried so much that her eyes are as dry as the veneer on the chipboard walls. It's as if he has ripped the living soul from her body, and now all that's left is the offal that nobody can stomach. For six years she's been growing her hair, never losing more than an inch when she would visit the salon with her mum once every couple of months. Long blonde hair was what made her who she was.

She is the girl with the golden hair, like Rapunzel in that cartoon. Everyone knows that Hazel has the blonde mane. What are her friends going to think when they see her?

Will they even recognise me?

The question burns deep, but her eyes remain arid.

She gasps: *what will Matt think of me?*

No sixteen year-old guy wants to hang around a girl who looks more like a boy than he does.

They'll all think I'm a boy.

She hasn't dared to feel what is left, but her imagination is doing a pretty good job of heightening her worst fears. She knows how high his hand was gripping the hair when he snipped it with the secateurs. She'd wanted to struggle and fight – God knew she'd prayed for the strength – but the rope had been firm and her body limp from whatever she'd ingested on the pizza last night.

What if Mum and Dad don't recognise me?

She shakes her head to dismiss the thought, but it feels weird not having the brush of loose hair swatting against her cheeks and chin. Never again will she be able to twist her hair into a makeshift scarf and coil it around her neck; brush it all forward to perform her impression of It from *The Addams Family*; tie it in a loose ponytail when her mum wants her help to cook.

As each of these memories from her past life plays out in front of her eyes, she realises just how integral a part her hair has played in her life. And now, like a best friend struck down with terminal illness, it's gone.

She doesn't even bother to check whether the red LED is glowing or not. Her only means of escape has been boarded up, and after what he's done, she has no doubt just how evil he is. Who else would steal a girl's hair for any reason than to exercise his control over her?

The hair will grow back eventually, she tells herself, *but it will never be the same again.*

And who's to say he won't cut it again at some point in the future, depending on how long he plans to keep her trapped here. When he'd finished reading the email exchange between her and Auntie Answers, he'd told her: *there are real men out here who understand just how special you are and are ready to give you everything you desire.*

Had he meant that? Did he really believe that despite the considerable age gap, she would become his girlfriend? What kind of boyfriend locks up his girlfriend and chops off her hair? Not one that she would want to be associated with. Besides, she'd have to be pretty desperate to consider an oaf like him; she doesn't even know his name.

She takes a deep breath and tentatively raises her right hand towards her head. Her entire hand is shaking as she dares to push it towards the tips of her hair, as if they might singe her skin somehow.

She closes her eyes in the way she would when a scary alien was about to appear on *Dr Who*, and inhales slowly, then jabs her hand at her head. She gasps again as she feels her scalp almost immediately. She pulls her hand away, this time sitting up on the mattress, and raising both hands towards her head. It stings as she feels the space where her long locks should dangle. It's even shorter than she'd feared, and as she bravely runs her fingers across her head, she realises just how uneven the cut is too. Not only will she resemble a boy, everyone will assume she's a boy who cut his own hair.

She lowers her hands and pictures the monster who did this to her. He wasn't wearing his balaclava when he was in here, which tells her one way or another, he won't be letting her go. She can identify him now meaning he either intends to keep her locked up, or plans to kill her.

Sorrow and remorse quickly subside to resilience.

This whole time she's been planning to try and escape while he isn't looking and sneak away, but that was never really an option. She was avoiding the prospect of having to confront the monster, but that's the only real way to break free of a nightmare.

She didn't deserve what he did. She doesn't deserve any of what is happening right now. Her blood simmers beneath the surface, as she imagines him falling at her feet and begging for forgiveness. She's never wanted to see someone suffer as much as she does in this moment. So focused on plotting her revenge, she doesn't even hear the bolt being slid back and him returning to the room.

Chapter 51

Joe

I stare at Meg, waiting for the skin around her mouth to tighten into a smile, but it doesn't.

'You're serious?' I ask, unable to comprehend how her suggestion could be anything but a joke. 'You want me to help you drown him?'

'All but,' she clarifies, fixing me with a hard stare. 'The idea is to take him to the brink of drowning. To him it will feel like he is as his lungs fill with water, but just as he's on the edge, we'll pull him back.'

I turn away from her, shaking my head in disbelief. 'What the hell do either of us know about water boarding someone? That's actual torture.'

I know I'm the last one who can pass judgement, given my part in how David wound up here, but what she's suggesting is beyond what I ever intended.

'I found a video online which showed the different stages of what we have to do. Once he realises how serious we are, and how painful the experience will be, he'll tell us whatever we want.'

I don't share her confident tone. 'And if he doesn't? Then what? Pulling out his fingernails? Thumbscrews? When does it stop?'

She moves around me until our eyes are locked once more.

'Whatever it takes,' she says.

This isn't right. I want him to tell us the truth about what he did to Lydia, but if he was going to come clean, I'm sure he would have done it by now. He has no intention of confessing, and why should he? If he admits what he did, he's going to realise that it won't end well for him. Why bring further trouble to his own door?

I take her hands in mine, and search her eyes for the woman I knew who wouldn't harm so much as a spider. 'But what if we're wrong about him?'

'We're not,' she answers instantly, and I sense she's already had this internal debate while I was dealing with Andrews. 'Do you think he isn't responsible for what happened to Lydia?'

'No, but …'

'There's no buts, Joe. He's either innocent or guilty. I believe – no, wait – I *know* he's the one who killed her.' She pats her chest. 'I feel it in here. Lydia is telling me he's the one responsible.'

'But don't you think it's possible that we *could* be wrong? What if he is innocent and we torture him; what does that make us? And what if we go too far and accidentally kill him? Then what?'

Her shrug is emotionless. 'Then fate will have shown us the way.'

My eyes widen. 'What the hell is that supposed to mean?'

She rolls her eyes. 'It means he will have got what he deserves. How did you picture all of this ending, Joe? We all go our separate ways and live happily ever after? There's only one way this can end, and we both know it.'

My face and neck are suddenly frozen, because I know exactly what she's getting at, and I'm not ready to face that question yet. I've been putting it off since I first started planning all this. And I suppose I thought that obtaining David's confession on video would have been enough to guarantee his silence. Once he'd unburdened himself, and I had the evidence of his complicity on video, he wouldn't dare to tell the police what I'd done.

'I'm not a killer, Meg, and let's stop beating about the bush; that's what you're suggesting isn't it?'

She breaks free of my embrace, and crosses the bathroom, staring out of the window at the garden below. It's stopped raining for now, but the sky is still a carpet of grey.

'Tell me something, Joe,' she says, without turning, 'has he given you *any* reason to doubt his guilt? He's been here for two days? He's had every opportunity to come clean and tell us what we want to hear, but has he?' She pauses, as if expecting an answer, but then continues. 'No, he hasn't. I took him a sandwich while you were out, and he asked me whether I wanted to know if Lydia begged for her life. He's been playing us both and the system for months. Well enough is enough!' She slams her hands against the edge of the basin.

I think back to what he told me about Francis McAdam being a more likely suspect, and although the argument he presented was convincing, it felt like he was stringing me along. But therein lies the problem for me: I'm ninety-nine per cent certain that he killed

Lydia, but there's still that one per cent element of doubt.

Meg slowly turns to face me. 'If you're not comfortable with what I'm proposing, I'm happy to do it alone. All I need is your help in getting him up here and securing his wrists and ankles to the bath.'

I look down at the scraps of rope she has fastened to the handles and taps, and I've no idea where she found them.

'Don't forget, there's still another missing girl out there,' Meg adds, touching my arm. 'Remember how it felt when we were waiting for news about Lydia? Remember how soul destroying it was, not knowing where she was or who'd taken her? That's what Neil and Ruby are experiencing right now. If someone had offered us the chance to get her back at the cost of torturing a convicted sex offender, would you have thought twice about it then? He knows more about McAdam than he's told us. At the very least, we need to know what he does about where McAdam has taken her.'

What choice do we have? Let David go and allow another innocent child to be harmed? Meg's right: I can't allow that to happen.

I follow her downstairs, and take out the stun gun while she unlocks the cell door. David must sense what's coming because he cowers by the far wall, adopting a defensive position with his arms, but he can't fend me off for more than a minute before I have the prongs against his neck, and he drops to the floor. Our hands under hit pits, we drag him from the cell, and up the stairs to the kitchen before resting for thirty seconds and continuing until we make it back to the bathroom on the first floor. He's already coming around as I secure the second cord of rope around his wrist, before moving on to his feet. We give him a further minute to realise where he is and what we have planned, but rather than terror, he laughs mockingly at the pair of us.

'I'll see you two rot in jail for this,' he spits.

It's actually a relief to cover his face with the large towel; at least I don't have to see that sneer. Meg reaches up and lifts down the shower head, fiddling with the taps until a steady stream shoots out of the end.

I stick out my hand. 'I'll do it. I'm the one who got us into this mess.'

She considers the offer, before reluctantly placing the shower head in my hand. I check the temperature of the water to ensure we won't scald him, and then I point the spray at the towel. He jerks and writhes as the towel absorbs the water and tightens around his jaw and nose. I allow my eyes to wander around the room, unable to watch as he shakes and sputters. I'm hoping for a glimpse of Lydia's reflection somewhere to show me that we're doing the right thing, but we're alone.

'Stop,' Meg warns, pushing my hand to one side so she can lift the towel from his face.

He coughs and spits out water.

'Tell us where Hazel Cooper is,' Meg says evenly.

'Fuck you!' he grizzles back.

Meg doesn't ask again, stretching the towel back across his face as he gasps and takes a deep breath. I twist my hand back to its original position and keep it pointed at the towel for a count of forty-five seconds. Meg reaches for the towel again, and I point the stream down at his chest. His upper body is already soaked through, but that's the least of his troubles right now.

'Where is Hazel Cooper?' Meg tries again.

'Go to hell!'

She slaps the towel back over his face, and this time snatches the shower head from me, and points it at his face.

'We can do this all day, David,' she warns. 'Tell us where Hazel is, and I promise we'll stop.'

This time I get to sixty in my head before she steers the stream away. I oblige in lifting the towel from his face. His skin is decidedly white, and he is gasping for breath, as water spills from the edges of his mouth.

'Okay, okay,' he pants. 'I'll tell you … I'll tell you.'

He doesn't look well, and if he suffers a heart attack in this moment, we're going to be left with an entirely different problem.

'McAdam has access to a farm,' he sputters. 'He works there sometimes. If he's got her, then he must be there.'

'Where's the farm?' Meg asks.

'Bracknell.'

'Where in Bracknell? What's the name of the farm?'

'I can't remember,' he pants, staring at the two of us.

He's playing games again, hoping his lies will convince us. I begin to lower the towel to his face again.

'No, wait, please, I'm telling you the truth. I can't

remember the name of the farm, but I have the address on my computer at home. Take me there and I'll show you. I swear!'

Meg twists off the taps and heads out of the room without another word, leaving me chasing after her.

'Surely you don't believe that crap, do you?' I say.

She shrugs. 'I don't know what to believe any more.'

I close the bathroom door, and lead her along the corridor so that we're out of hearing range. 'He knows we can't get the computer out of his house and here without drawing unnecessary attention to our actions. That means he knows we'd have to take him with us to check the computer. I have a really bad feeling about this. He's had days to think of a way to instigate his escape, and mentioning his computer could be part of that plan.'

'I don't see that we have any other choice. We have no other way of tracking where McAdam took Hazel.'

'And if he's lying, and tries to escape? Then what?'

Meg narrows her eyes as if she's about to reveal some dark secret, but instead she heads back to the stairs and hurries down them. I'm compelled to follow her, calling out her name, but she doesn't stop until we're back in the kitchen, and she's reaching for her handbag. She unzips it, and a moment later her hand is gripping a semi-automatic.

'Where the hell did you get that?' I exclaim, pointing her hand down to the ground in case it accidentally goes off.

'I told you before: I've spent months thinking about what it would be like to come face-to-face with my daughter's killer as well. I've imagined pressing the barrel of the gun to his head and pulling the trigger. I wasn't sure I'd ever get the opportunity, but I wanted to be ready. I ordered it through the dark web.'

Who is this woman before me now, and what happened to my sweet and innocent wife? I don't want to think about how long she's been in possession of the weapon, or where she's been keeping it at home. I also don't want to think about the reality that she chose to bring it with her to the manor today without telling me.

Chapter 52

Hazel

She starts as he closes the door to, and when she turns to see what torture he has planned next is surprised to see he is carrying a laptop computer beneath his arm.

He considers her for a moment, tilting his head, before shaking it. 'Damn,' he says, whistling through his teeth. 'I really did go a bit overboard with the trim, didn't I? I suppose it'll grow back eventually. We have plenty of time.'

She doesn't respond, still crouched on the mattress. It is pointless for her to try her hand at this moment in time. Her arms and legs are still shaky from whatever was on the pizza, and he's already shown how much stronger he is. Her time will come, of that she is certain, but this isn't it. For now, she is powerless to resist whatever his intentions are.

'I'll bring you some breakfast in a bit, and then I think the two of us should chat about some ground rules. In case I didn't make it obvious, your little stunt with the chair and the floor was very disappointing. I don't want you to think such behaviour is acceptable, Hazel. Now, I know it's still early in our relationship – and hey, maybe you didn't realise just how upset that would make me – so I'm happy to let bygones be bygones, and move on from this.'

His chin rises as his lips stretch into a friendly smile, as if he's the one making the sacrifice. Her face remains devoid of emotion, though she'd love to wipe the smile from his face.

She flinches as he steps towards her, whipping out the laptop, opening the lid and resting it on the mattress before her. She recognises the launch page on the screen and her email address in the user ID box.

'If you could type in your password that would be great,' he says calmly.

She stares at the screen for an age, trying to work out what cruel misery he has planned next.

'Hazel, your password,' he says, sharper this time.

Still she stares at the screen, daring herself to ask, 'Why?'

He exhales loudly, making sure there's no doubt how frustrated he's becoming. 'Because right now your parents and half the world doesn't know where you are. And unless we let them know that you're safe and well, they'll continue to worry.'

She remembers the feel of her new spikier hair, and almost smirks at the term *safe and well*. It isn't how she'd describe her current state of health.

'You want me to email my parents?' she asks.

'Exactly. I want you to tell them to stop looking for you.'

No, she wants to scream, but grinds her teeth instead. 'Why would I do that?'

He sighs loudly again, the smile now gone from his face, his eyes glaring instead. 'Do you really want them to lose sleep over what might have happened to you? Are you really that cruel, Hazel? They must be worried sick about where you've run off to, as I'm sure your wet blanket of a boyfriend is too. So, you're going to type in your password, and I'm going to send them both an email to let them know you're safe and have decided to stay with me from now on. That way they'll have peace of mind that something horrible hasn't happened to you, and they can all move on with their lives.'

It takes all her resilience not to smirk. Does he really believe the shit that just tumbled from his mouth? Does he think she's chosen to stay with him? Has he repressed everything that's happened in the last forty-eight hours?

'No,' she tells him with an air of calm she hasn't anticipated.

'Type in your password, Hazel.'

'No.'

'Type in your password, Hazel,' he repeats through gritted teeth and his words cloaked in a low rumble.

'No. I don't want my parents to stop looking for me.'

'You *will* type in your password, Hazel. You don't want to anger me.'

In her head she tells herself there's nothing he can do to hurt her any more than he has, even though she hopes he won't test her certainty.

'No.'

His hand whips out and slaps her cheek before her eyes have even registered the movement. She collapses to the mattress, shooting a protective hand to her cheek. He is down to his knees, and pushes her back onto the mattress so she is perpendicular to his body.

His fingers are chubby and warm as they wrap around her neck, his palms pressing against her voice box.

'You will type the password, or I will kill you here and now.'

She doesn't believe that he will have gone to all this trouble if he's prepared to kill her over something so small, but then she remembers he probably has more victims available to him via the Auntie Answers page.

He's squeezing hard enough that she can no longer inhale breath, and she begins to choke on spittle in her throat. She tries to cough it free, but she can't exhale either. She tries to swat his hands away, but his arms remain firm, the pressure growing. Her face begins to flush, and she can't swallow. She swats harder, even trying to scratch at his neck, but he continues to press harder, squeezing the life from her young body.

She thought he was bluffing, but as spots appear at the corners of her vision, she suddenly has no doubt that he does see her as replaceable, and that nothing she can do will prevent him from finishing her off. Fear now takes control of her mind: she doesn't want to die, even though her immediate future offers nothing but pain and terror.

She bats at his arms again, the lactic acid building in her muscles, making it more difficult to keep them elevated.

'O … K,' she mouths.

He keeps his hands where they are for a second longer, before releasing, and allowing her to roll onto her side and inhale deeply while simultaneously coughing. He gives her a few seconds to recover, before pushing the laptop closer to her.

'Password.'

She's temped to say no again, but she thinks if she does he will actually throttle her and not stop. She types in the password and hits the enter key, before collapsing back on the mattress. He drops into a sitting position beside her head and scoops up the laptop. She hears his fingers dance across the keyboard as he quickly types the emails. He doesn't tell her what he is typing, nor does he offer to read the content to her. Two minutes pass, and then he slides the laptop from his legs onto the mattress, nudging her arm in the process, and then rests his warm palm on her tender cheek.

'Let's not make a habit of disappointing me, shall we? If you do as I say, we will get along just fine.'

Is this really what she fought back from death for: a life where he dictates the future and she suffers?

He releases her cheek, and rolls slightly to his side so he can press his hands into the mattress and prepare to push himself up. The closed laptop bumps against her arm again as the mattress shifts beneath his weight. Without a second's thought she grabs it with both her hands, flips to her knees, raises it high over her head, and then brings the thinnest edge crashing down on the back of his head.

Chapter 53

Meg

David still looks soaked through despite our efforts to pat his clothes dry. I can see him watching me from the rear-view mirror, and I have to admit I'm spending more time watching him than I am the road. Joe insisted he sit in the back with our prisoner, and to be honest I'm grateful that he did. I don't think I'd be able to remain so calm sitting beside such evil.

The handgun is back in my handbag in the footwell of the passenger seat. Although we belted David in to his seat, I'm not prepared to trust him to sit still, even though Joe has the stun gun primed against his rib cage. All it would take is an elbow to the bridge of Joe's nose and then a lunge to the front seat and we'd be in all kinds of trouble. That's why my eyes have yet to leave him.

Joe's right to question whether to believe David's claim that he just happens to have the address of the farm on his computer, but as I argued: we have no choice but to take him at his word. He knows now what we're capable of, and if necessary I *will* use the handgun. I wasn't lying when I said I've imagined being able to kill my daughter's killer. It's all I've dreamed about since Andrews first broke the news. I've wanted to know who was responsible not for emotional closure, but so I can exact a mother's revenge.

If it wasn't for Hazel being lost out there somewhere, I already would have squeezed the trigger. It doesn't make me a bad person to want revenge; it's basic human instinct.

Of course, there could be all manner of reasons why David wants us to take him home. Maybe he's hoping he'll be able to call to a neighbour for help; or maybe he thinks he'll be better able to overpower us both on familiar territory; or maybe he's just fed up of the site of the cell at Harrington Manor. Only time will tell whether we've made a huge mistake in playing along.

If his plan was to try and jump out along the way, he didn't take into account the fact that we still have the child locks engaged on Joe's car. It seems silly, and I'm sure we could have switched them off by now, but neither of us has had the heart to do it. It's the last remaining remnant that we had a child requiring them.

'Pull in up here on the left,' Joe calls from behind me. 'His is the one with the grey door.'

I do as instructed, and then allow my eyes to wander to the house of the monster who has haunted my dreams. It looks so ordinary. I don't know what I expected: maybe something more gothic, or run down. The property looks like all the others immediately around it. I hate that it looks so much like our own place. How can a predator and murderer live a life as ordinary as ours?

I apply the handbrake and kill the engine, instinctively reaching for my handbag, and extracting the weapon. I told Joe that it's only loaded with blanks, because he looked so nervous about me handling it, but if David forces me to use it, Joe will see that I was lying. I grasp the cool, graphite handle and slowly slide it out, quickly turning it on David.

'Any funny business, and I won't hesitate to put a bullet between your eyes. Am I making myself clear?'

Joe is sweating anxiously, but doesn't undermine my statement verbally. David raises his hands loosely into the air. Putting the gun into the pocket of my anorak, I keep my hand coiled around the handle and climb out of the car. Moving to David's door, I open and hold it open, pointing my pocket in his direction, and as he unfastens his belt he slowly climbs out, quickly followed by Joe with the stun gun still pressed into David's side.

The small strip of lawn looks recently mowed, and there are only a few odd weeds in the flower bed that sits beneath the kitchen window. If I didn't know who lived in this house, I wouldn't have any reason to think such a monster lived here. How many of his neighbours just assume he's a kindly old man who can be trusted? I feel like painting the word monster on his front wall, just to warn others: keep your children away!

'Nice and easy,' Joe says, closing the door and walking beside David, up to the front door, with me following behind.

Much to our relief, David makes no attempt to call for help, and I'm certain that even if a passer-by did notice the three of us, they'd think we were nothing but friends catching up. Once the front door is closed behind us, I pull out the gun again and show David that

I mean business.

'Where's my dog?' David asks, looking at Joe.

The question throws me. How didn't I connect the dots? I thought something was odd when Joe suddenly turned up with Lola the beagle, but I hadn't made the connection that the dog belonged to David. My cheeks burn with embarrassment, but I remain tight-lipped.

'She's safe at our house,' Joe says, glancing at me with an apologetic shrug. 'Take us up to your computer?'

'I want to see my dog.'

'That's not possible right now,' Joe counters. 'You give us McAdam's location, or I will stop restraining my wife from doing what she's so desperate to do.'

David's eyes flick to me and I can see him trying to read whether I am capable of squeezing the trigger. If only he knew.

He must see something in my eyes as his head drops and he places his foot on the first step of the staircase. He moves slowly up with Joe following behind, but as soon as he reaches the top, he kicks out his foot, and drives it into Joe's knee, and he is suddenly falling towards me. I have to adjust my balance to catch him, but we both nearly fall backwards down the stairs. Joe leaps forwards just in time to see David disappearing into a room, and closing the door, but Joe doesn't break stride as he plants his foot on the door, and sends it crashing in, flying off its hinges.

David is over by the window, the net curtain raised up and over his head, but by the time I arrive I can't tell if he's trying to get the window open or just signal for help. Either way, he soon drops to the floor as Joe fires the stun gun into his leg. A wet patch spreads out across the groin area of his nearly dry trousers.

'Try anything like that again, and I won't hesitate to shoot you,' I snap at him, pressing the barrel of the handgun against his temple. 'Now give us that address.'

He blinks rapidly, but nods his compliance.

The room we're in must be used as some kind of office as all that's in here is an antique-looking desk, a monitor and desktop PC. David raises himself onto his knees and switches on the device. It whirs and beeps as it comes to life and the monitor flashes and comes online. David types in his password, but his fingers move too quickly over the keyboard to make out what he's typed.

He points at the screen. 'There! That's it: Hunter's Farm in Bracknell. He does part-time work there at harvest time, but they allow him use of one of the old barns for storage at a reduced rate. If he has the girl that must be where he's holding her.'

It's just an address and postcode, and it isn't obvious that it has anything to do with McAdam. I don't want to think what could be waiting for us there.

Joe makes a note of the address on his phone, and then tells David to back away from the computer. I keep my gun hand trained on him, but pull Joe over, keeping my vice low.

'What do we do?'

'We phone Andrews and tell him that's where Hazel is being held,' he says.

'But what about when he asks where we got the information from? And what if she isn't there and we send the police on a wild goose chase?'

His brow furrows, and I can practically read his mind. There's only one way to know for certain, and that's to go to the farm, but the thought of transporting David anywhere else in the car fills me with dread. He's already made a break for it here, and there's no knowing what he'll do if we try and take him with us, and it turns out he is lying.

'One of us needs to go and check out this address. If she is there, we phone the police anonymously and report it. And if she's not, we go back to the manor and finish what we started.'

It's a logical plan, but the question is: which of us stays, and which of us goes.

'I'll go to the farm,' I say.

'But what if McAdam *is* there, and catches you looking? He's a big bloke, Meg, and I hate the idea of sending you into the lion's lair like that.' He pauses and looks round at David. 'But I hate the thought of leaving you here with this snake just as much.'

David is looking at the two of us, and opens his mouth to speak, but thinks better of it when we both glare.

'I can handle this snake,' I tell him. 'We can tie him up so he can't cause any trouble, and I have this if he tries anything on,' I lift my gun hand. 'You go to the farm, check out the lay of the land, and as soon as you have confirmation McAdam is there, phone me, and the police.'

Joe's eyes suddenly widen as inspiration strikes. 'Wait, I have a better idea.' He ducks out of the room, and scrolls through his burner phone until he finds what he's looking for, and puts the phone to his ear.

'Edie? It's Joe Irons, have you managed to locate that person yet?'

I frown at the name. I don't know anyone called Edie, but wait for Joe to finish his conversation.

'Wait a second, Edie, can you just repeat that for my wife?'

He puts the phone out on his palm, and I bend my ear closer to the speaker.

'I found the number for Francis McAdam, and it last pinged on a mast in the Bracknell area. I can't be much more specific than that.'

'That's great, Edie, thank you,' Joe says, ending the call. 'She's a private investigator I hired,' he quickly explains. 'There we go, she says he's in Bracknell, the address of the farm is in Bracknell. What more do we need?'

I don't want to point out the obvious, but don't have a choice. 'We know that McAdam is there, but that doesn't mean Hazel is.'

He sighs, but nods. 'Okay. Let's get David tied up and then I'll be as quick as I can. If all goes to plan, we'll find Hazel and the police will get McAdam.' He pauses and turns back to look at David. 'And then we can figure out what we're going to do about him.'

Chapter 54

Hazel

Her arms shake as the edge of the laptop halts its trajectory on contact with the crown of his head. He topples forwards, crashing to the floor at the edge of the mattress with a thud, nothing to break his fall.

Hazel gasps at what she has just done, and allows the laptop to slip from her hands and back to the mattress. She's expecting him to reach up and rub the red bump that is already beginning to show through his white hair. But he doesn't move. He doesn't even scream out in agony.

Her first thought is she's killed him, but that was never her intention. But then what was her intention? She'd known what she was doing when she'd grabbed the laptop and swung it over her head. She'd even had the foresight to twist as she brought it down so that the sharp edge would connect and would likely cause more damage than the flat base.

I only meant to incapacitate him, she tells herself, but isn't convinced by the lie.

Does it matter what her intention was? He isn't moving, which means he is no longer her prison guard. Her eyes dart to the door. She doesn't remember hearing him lock it, but she's thinking that any sudden movement might stir him awake, and then he'll retaliate in the most callous way.

Holding her breath she delicately climbs off the mattress and tiptoes to the door. She knows checking for a pulse will confirm his health one way or another, but she doesn't want to get that close to him in case he's faking. She keeps her eyes on his prone body as she reaches for the thick metal handle on the door.

It doesn't move. She pulls harder, but it is stuck still. Whether he locked it or it has an automatic locking mechanism, it is locked now. She looks back at him, trying to sense whether he's moved at all since his face crashed against the floor. She holds her own breath as she tries to determine whether there is any rise and fall of his back to indicate if he's breathing or not, but it's so hard to tell with his jumper the colour of the night sky and the fading orange glow from the roof doing little to penetrate the darkness.

I don't have a choice, she determines. *He has the keys to the door. I can either risk waking him trying to find them or wait for him to come around. The net result is the same.*

Slowly exhaling, she takes one deep breath quietly through her mouth and tiptoes back towards him, trying to work out where he would have put the keys to the door. He isn't wearing a jacket, so logic tells her she's going to have to check his trouser pockets.

Crouching down, breath still held, she moves her trembling fingers towards his hip, conscious that any touch or sound could wake him. Her fingertip brushes the edge of his black jeans, and she jerks her hand back.

You can do this, she tells herself, and perilously extends her arm again, opening her first and middle fingers like a pair of pliers, and slowly prising them into the pocket. Her eyes don't leave the top of his head, certain he'll feel the movement, come to, and reach for her throat again.

Her fingertip brushes something round and hard, and her eyes widen in excitement, as she hooks her index finger through the small ring, and gently jiggles the key ring out of his pocket, catching the two keys in her palm before they can jangle.

Slowly standing, she steps back, all the while staring at him as she makes her way back to the door. The only time she looks away is to line the key up with the lock and slide it in. The fit is smooth, and she quickly turns the key counter-clockwise. The bolt inside the door snaps back so loudly that she's certain he must have heard, but she doesn't have time to think about it. Pulling on the round metal handle, the door opens and she dives out towards the huge bright light. She involuntarily checks there is no other restraint about to trip her up, even though she knows the rope is gone.

Darting behind the light she spots a small plastic bottle of water, and is reminded of how thirsty she is, but she can't trust the possibility that he hasn't spiked it with something that would ultimately slow her journey, and as desperate as she is for refreshment, she leaves it where it is.

She stops at the next door, which again she finds is locked. She thinks about the second key on the ring. Of course she should have thought that two keys would suggest two locked doors, but she left it inside the lock in the room.

Cursing under her breath, she creeps back to the cabin, now better able to see in with the door open and the brilliant light highlighting the interior. He is still face down, but she is almost certain his position has moved slightly, though she can't pinpoint why she thinks this.

Tiptoeing up the stairs, she keeps one foot outside the cabin, while her hand reaches around the edge of the door and tries to extract the keys as quietly as possible. Although it slipped in easily, it doesn't seem to want to come out. She pulls harder, but the key is stuck fast.

Maybe it can only be extracted when the locking bolt is engaged.

Twisting her wrist quickly, the bolt shoots out of the door with a bang, and as the key begins to slip out of the lock, she hears a roar that chills her to the bone.

Chapter 55

Joe

It's getting dark by the time I arrive in Bracknell, which makes it more difficult to read road names and signs. Twenty minutes have passed since leaving Meg at David's house, and I'm keen to get back there as quickly as I can. The Satnav has left me in the middle of nowhere, and so I have to look for any bearings to help me locate the entrance to the farm.

I eventually reach a mud track, which has a weathered, painted sign reading "-UN-ERS –A-M", so I'm hopeful this might be the place. There is a long iron gate blocking my entrance to the actual farm, and parking up outside it, I can see the gate is padlocked. Despite the full beam of my headlights, it's impossible to see anything beyond the gate from this distance, and the edge of my lights disappears into the low fog that seems to have arrived with nightfall.

Exiting my car, but leaving the lights on, I move closer to the gate to try and get a better look, but I can't see the barn David referenced, and there's no sign of the grey van I saw McAdam pushing Hazel into the back of. There's nothing to confirm they're here, but likewise there's nothing yet to confirm they're not here. It's too early to call the police, but it's too soon to leave. I'm going to have to vault the gate and continue my quest, but I'm also conscious it's been too long since I spoke to Meg, so I climb back into the car, and make the most of the warmth being pumped out by the heater.

I locate Meg's number in the redial menu and call her. She answers on the fourth ring.

'Hi,' she pants.

Her breathlessness instantly has me on edge. 'What's going on? Are you okay?'

'Yes, everything's fine. I went up to check on David, and he'd managed to get one of his wrists free, and was working on the other. I used the stun gun on him until he passed out, and re-secured his wrists. I found some cable ties beneath the sink in the kitchen and used those. They should be firmer than the cotton threads we used initially.'

I knew it was a risk leaving her at his mercy, but she was adamant she'd be fine. I'd hoped to be back with her before he woke.

'Are you sure you're okay? You're out of breath.'

'I was upstairs and my phone was in the kitchen that's all.'

I'm not convinced by her response, and I sense she's holding back, but there's nothing I can do from here.

'Does he still have the gag in his mouth?'

'He'd managed to get the tape off and had spat out the sock. I've replaced the tape, but was concerned he might choke on the sock so have left that out. I'm going to sit outside the room so I'll be able to hear when he comes to again, and if he tries anything. Have you made it to the farm yet?'

Her attempt to change the subject isn't subtle.

'Yes, I'm here, I think, but there's no sign of life. I'm going to try to get a bit closer before I head back. Looks like he might have been stringing us along again. At least when we leave with him it'll be under the cover of darkness.'

'Oh some woman came knocking on the door, and almost gave me a heart attack! Snooty-looking woman in a business suit, I saw from the bathroom window, but she didn't hang around for too long.'

I picture the neighbour who disturbed me the last time I was there. Hopefully she didn't see the three of us arriving at David's house. We took a risk in bringing him back there, particularly if the police have to launch a missing person investigation and a witness is able to give our descriptions to the police.

'Keep out of sight just in case,' I warn her.

'I will. I'll stay upstairs until you get back here. Are you okay? There's no sign of McAdam?'

'No, not yet, but I'll keep you posted. I'll phone again if there's any sign of them.'

Meg ends the call before I can tell her I love her, and as I lower the phone, my eyes fall on the rear-view mirror, but there's no sign of Lydia offering the moral support I need.

In hindsight, I should have brought the huge torch we keep in our garage, but when we left home this morning, I never envisaged I'd find myself in the dark and fog looking for a missing teenager. Removing the keys from the ignition, the surrounding area falls into dark gloom, and I can't even see the gate and weathered sign from the safety of the car. I can't escape the sense of foreboding as I push open the car door and step out into rapidly-cooling air. Switching on the torch light of the burner phone, I point it at the ground so I'll be able to see if I'm about to tread in manure once I'm over the gate.

Passing the weathered sign, I point the beam up at it, trying to make out what the missing letters once were, and I gulp as I read the 'Trespassers will be shot,' notice beneath it. I can only hope the farm's owner meant it tongue in cheek.

Planting my foot on the first rung, I hold the phone between my teeth to allow my hands to get a better grip, and then swing my trailing leg up and over the top of the frame, and down into the soft squelch of mud. Shining the torch down, I can see the track from here is churned up by rain and tractor tracks. There's no way I'm going to make it out of here not covered in mud. Choosing my steps carefully, I follow the track as it begins to descend into some kind of valley, and my breath escapes me in plumes of steam.

I can smell cattle somewhere, but there's no sound of life. I can no longer hear the hum of traffic from the M4 which I know to be less than a mile from my present location. Keeping the light pointed at the ground, I bury my free hand in the pocket of my hoodie, regretting not bringing a coat to protect myself against the winter climate.

I can almost picture David laughing to himself when he realises we fell for his lies again. He must have suspected that we wouldn't choose to bring him to Bracknell with us, which means he only has one guard to overpower instead of two. And of course Bracknell was close enough that we'd feel obliged to check out the address before passing it on to the police. In fact, the more I think about it, the more convinced I am that this is just another of his games. He offered up the address to stop the flow of water over his face, and we fell for it hook, line, and sinker. For all I know, this farm is long since abandoned. Surely if it was still in use I'd have at least heard or seen some kind of life by now. I've been walking for at least five minutes.

There isn't even a farmhouse anywhere nearby. Waving the beam back along the track I've descended, I can't see more than a couple of metres, and I'm beginning to wonder whether I'll be able to find my way back to the car as the blanket of dark fog is so thick.

Pointing the beam ahead again, I continue to move forwards and do finally see a thin outline of yellow light framing some kind of building up ahead. Slowing as I near, I'm very careful with my footsteps to avoid squelching, and when I'm barely a metre away, I take a moment to compose myself, before killing my torch light, and following the light emanating from beneath the barn.

It smells strongly of varnish, and if I didn't know better I'd say it's not long had a fresh coat, though when I press my fingers to the wooden panels, they come away dry. Holding my breath, I strain to hear any activity inside, but there's nothing beyond the sound of the breeze blowing past my ears.

I try to remember what David claimed about McAdam's use of the farm. He said something about McAdam being employed here during harvest in exchange for using the barn for storage, but what could he actually be storing out here, so far from home?

Continuing to follow the edge of the barn, I've completed three quarters of the perimeter before I come across anything resembling a door. Trying the handle, I'm not surprised it is locked, but there's a slight gap in the panels, and I'm able to bend and peer through, spotting the glow of straw across the floor, and several cows lying down off to the left. It surprises me that the farmer will have left the light on for them, but at least that suggests there is life here amongst the gloom. No sign of McAdam's van though, and I'm tempted to give up this pursuit, when I hear what sounds like a man's muffled shouting somewhere in the darkness beyond the barn. Slowly moving closer to the sound, I see there is a second barn beyond this one, and again flick on my torch light to cut through the mud as quickly and quietly as I'm able.

My body is shivering against the cold, and I think if a farmer suddenly appears with a shotgun, looking for trespassers, I'm not going to have the adrenaline to get away. The shouting has now stopped, but it had to have come from this second barn, and as I near it, I quickly locate the door, and my pulse quickens as I try the handle and it yields. I only open the door a crack, but amongst the straw I can see tyre tracks, and the breath catches in my throat when I see they belong to a mud-streaked grey van. The registration plates are different, but otherwise I'd say it looks very similar to the one I clung to that night at the traffic lights.

If the van is here, then does that mean …?

The door is suddenly yanked from my hand and a figure crashes headfirst into me.

Chapter 56

Hazel

Her first thought is that the man waiting outside the barn door is one of her captor's friends, who is coming to help him as she attempts to escape. She puts her arms up in a defensive position to cover her face and torso, and pummels at his chest as he tries to reach for her.

'Stop, wait,' the man cries out, wincing with each hit. 'Hazel? Is it you?'

He doesn't sound certain, and his eyes are looking at her short spikes of hair, searching for reassurance. His voice triggers a memory somewhere in the back of her mind, but she can't quite see what it is.

'I'm not going to hurt you,' the man says, before unzipping his hoodie and wrapping it around her shoulders as she continues to resist. 'I'm here to rescue you.'

She lowers her arms a fraction, long enough to look up at him. The light from inside the barn highlights his face, and she gasps as she recognises the kind eyes, soft cheeks, and slightly receding hairline of the face she saw at the van's window the night of the abduction. She knows this is the same man, but what she doesn't know is what he happens to be doing at the farm where she's been held for the last few days.

She doesn't have time to weigh up the pros and cons of trusting him, as her captor bellows again from within the cabin. She'd managed to get the key out of the door as he'd tried to stand but woozily crashed back to the floor, screaming her name. The blow to the back of his head may not have killed him, but it's certainly weakened him. But with every passing second his strength will be returning, and with it, fresh anger at her further escape attempt.

'We need to go,' she tells the man who looks cold without his hoodie.

'I have a car back up the track, but it's quite a trek.'

She spots the phone in his hand, its beam shining down at the muddy floor now staining her feet. 'Phone the police. Tell them where we are and that they need to come and arrest this guy.'

He frowns and shakes his head, showing her the lack of bars. 'There's no signal down here. If we can get back to the car, we can phone them from there. And Meg, she'll be over the moon to hear you're safe.'

'Meg?' Hazel pauses as the jigsaw puzzle pieces slot together in her mind. 'You're Mr Irons, Meg's husband.'

He nods. 'Yes, I'm Joe. I saw McAdam snatch you the other night, and we've been searching for you ever since. It's a long story. Come on let's get you back to the car.'

McAdam bellows again, and this time she hears his boots stomping down the stairs of the cabin, at the far side of the barn. She grabs Joe's hand and follows as he leads her away from the barn into the all-consuming darkness. Her feet squelch and splat as she breathlessly tries to run, but her progress is slow. She hadn't thought about trying to find her trainers before getting away from the cabin, and with no fluid having passed her lips in more than twelve hours, she doesn't know whether she'll have the strength to make it to Joe's car. They've barely been running for a minute, and she wants to stop.

The light from Joe's phone bounces and darts over the muddy terrain, but even he's struggling to keep going, pulling on her hand, almost dragging her with him. The ground feels as though it's sliding away from her, and she nearly loses her footing a couple of times. She pulls back on her hand, and brings Joe to a stop.

'I-I can't,' she pants, huge plumes of steam rising from her mouth and nose.

'I'm not leaving you here,' he pants back, unlocking the phone, and checking for signal, even waving the device over his head, but there are no bars of signal.

She looks back the way they've just come, and can no longer see the barn, but there are two headlights emerging and turning to point straight at them. It's not possible to estimate just how far away the van is, but it won't take McAdam long to catch up with them. If the car is as far as Joe estimates, they'll never make it, and then he'll have them both cornered.

'He's coming,' she warns, pointing at the lights. 'We need to find somewhere to hide.'

Joe looks back down the slope, and nods his agreement, turning in a circle, and shining the torch light around. It barely lights up more than a metre of space in front of them.

He pulls on her hand again. 'Come on, I remember

seeing some bushes separating one of the fields. We should head there and catch our breath, and then try to plot a different course back to my car.'

He nods in the direction of their travel, before switching off the torch, so that McAdam won't see their change of direction, and the fact that they're no longer scaling the hill back to the entrance of the farm. She is placing a lot of faith in the man by her side, but she refuses to consider the possibility that he is in league with McAdam, and is taking her to the bushes to await the van's arrival. She remembers seeing a photograph of Meg and her husband, laughing as they danced with their daughter, hanging on the wall in their living room. She knows the tragedy they've experienced, and wonders if that's Joe's motivation for coming for her.

They reach the side of the track, and the mud is replaced by cold grass. The frost-covered blades poke and tickle her soles as they hurry across it, until they find the leafless hedgerows Joe spoke about. They don't immediately duck, instead hurrying for several metres before crouching down. Joe pushes her into one of the bundles of sharp twigs as far as they will allow, and then puts himself between her and the track. She can only hope McAdam won't think to stop and check this spot as he passes.

She can't see the track from where she's hunched down, and it's less than a minute before the freezing air swirling around has her teeth chattering. They can't stay here indefinitely, and she's about to tell Joe that they should move on again, when the sound of an engine fills the air. It's being over-revved, and as she sees the track lit up by the beam of the headlights, she sees the grey van shoot past them, but skidding across the track, as McAdam struggles to keep control of it.

'Come on,' Joe says, standing as soon as it's passed and the red taillights shrink into the distance.

Her breathing has yet to return to a regular beat, but she feels less pressure knowing that he is now ahead of them, rather than in pursuit. There's a chance he'll double-back when he reaches the top of the track and finds they're not there, or he might wait to try and attack them both, but hopefully Joe's phone will get a signal before they reach that point and they'll be able to hide out until the police arrive.

They walk slowly, but stick to the frosty grass, as it provides more grip than the track, so they still make better progress than they were before. But after a couple of minutes, Joe extends a protective arm across her, urging her to stop. She doesn't see what's concerning him at first, but then she spots the lights of the van, and ducks behind Joe's arm. The lights aren't moving, and she can see one yellow, and one red light, suggesting the van is parked at an angle. The engine is still turning over, as they creep closer, but Joe tells her to wait while he approaches to look for a way around it.

At first she's only too happy to keep distance between herself and McAdam, but as Joe's light gets swallowed by the darkness, the isolation becomes too much for her, and she quickly hurries forward, taking his warm hand in hers again.

Safety in numbers, she tells herself.

The van is stationary and as they reach the side of

it, they can see that the van has crashed into a stone wall, and McAdam is slumped over the wheel. He must have lost control, but they choose not to hang around and wait for him to wake, continuing up the track until they make it to an enormous iron gate.

'My car is the other side,' Joe tells her. 'Wait here.'

This time she obeys, watching him vault the gate, open the boot of his car, and fiddle about in it for a minute, before returning.

'Take this,' he says, handing her an identical phone to his. 'It's an unregistered pay-as-you-go. Call the police and tell them you're at Hunter's Farm in Bracknell in Berkshire. Tell them who you are and that your abductor's name is Francis McAdam. Please don't mention my name, or that I helped you. As far as anyone is concerned, I was never here. Is that okay? Will you do that for me and Meg?'

She is confused why he wouldn't want recognition for helping her escape McAdam, but she nods anyway, and switches on the device, relieved when she sees two bars of signal appear on the display. She dials 999 and relays what Joe told her, before handing him the phone back.

'No,' he tells her. 'Keep hold of it. If they ask where you got it from, tell them you found it inside the barn when you were making your escape. Hopefully they'll send paramedics out too. Are you okay? Did he … Um … Did he …?'

'He didn't rape me if that's what you mean,' she says with a reassuring smile, which seems to ease the strain in Joe's tired eyes, as if a weight has been lifted.

He remains with her until they both hear sirens in

the distance. She hugs him as he tries to leave, thanking him for coming in her hour of need, and promising to keep his secret. She still refuses to believe her nightmare is over, even as the two uniformed officers come rushing to her aid, telling her she's safe and that there is an ambulance on its way. She tells them where McAdam crashed, and when a second police car arrives, they head down to find him.

Joe has disappeared by this point, and for the rest of the night she wonders whether he was ever really there, or just a figment of her imagination sent by an angel to protect her. She offers a prayer of thanks to the angel just in case, knowing how close to death she came.

Chapter 57

Meg

Squashed up against the corner between the wall and door of the bathroom, I could almost fall asleep. It's been a long and stressful day, and with the lights off inside David's house, it's dark enough to encourage sleep. Not that I want to sleep, but it's taking all my willpower to keep awake without making any kind of noise to alert David to my presence just outside the door of the office. If my heavy eyelids win the battle, I might miss the tell-tale sound of David attempting to break free of the cable ties. I used two per wrist, but I've no idea if it will be enough. He doesn't look particularly strong, but Joe and I have both been guilty of underestimating him before.

I start as I realise my head is dipping forwards, and I rub at my eyes, hoping that the pain will keep my mind alert. Turning over my phone, I stare at the screen, willing Joe to phone and tell me whether the journey to Bracknell has been a waste of everyone's time. It must have been at least half an hour since he last called, but I daren't ring him in case David hears.

I've spent most of the last twenty minutes trying to work out what else we can do to get the truth out of David. If it turns out the farm in Bracknell was another lie, then our efforts at waterboarding will have been a waste, and I don't believe he'll admit the truth under any method of torture. And what does that leave us with? A suspected murderer who will tell the police what we've done and ruin both our futures. I can't allow that to happen. There's a line Joe isn't prepared to cross yet, but I am.

At least, I think I am.

I hear a scratching just inside the office, and freeze. It could have come from outside, but I need to be certain before I allow my breath to escape.

There it is again. There's definitely movement inside the office door. David is waking.

I have the stun gun beside me, but I think it must be running out of charge, because when I last used it on him, it took longer than before for him to yield. I don't know if there is enough juice left in the batteries to stop him if he manages to get free again.

'H-Hello?' he calls out weakly.

I don't respond, don't move a muscle, even as I feel cramp starting to claw at my aching buttocks.

'Hello?' David calls out again, louder this time. 'Meg? Are you there?'

He could just be checking whether I'm close so he can begin to try his escape. I wish Joe would phone to let me know what's going on, and when he'll be back. I could hear from his voice how worried he was when I told him about catching David breaking free of the original bindings. It's possible he's already on his way here, and just forgot to call in his desperation to get back to me.

'Meg? You are there, aren't you? I can smell your perfume nearby.'

I slowly try to exhale through my mouth, but saliva catches in my throat, and I can't stop myself from coughing.

'Ha! I knew it. You don't need to be afraid of me. In fact, if anything, I should be the one afraid of you. After all, you're the one with the gun and the … uh … cojones. That's how they describe courage in prison. I can say with some conviction that you'll survive longer in prison than Joe.'

I don't respond, having seen from the video how he taunted Joe, and sensing he's just trying to get a similar rise out of me. I glance at my phone again, but Joe still hasn't called. I unlock the screen and begin to type him a message.

'I can see you're the one who wears the trousers in this family,' David continues. 'You know, Joe actually believed that imprisoning me and a few days of hunger and thirst would be enough to make me confess. Pathetic!'

I ignore the jibe and continue to type the message.

'At least you had the brains and guts to genuinely put me in fear for my life. I never would have thought you had it in you when I first saw you at that park.'

My fingers freeze over the screen.

What did he just say?

'You remind me of her, you know. Facially, I mean, I can see where she got her fair skin and bone structure from.'

He's lying to me, I tell myself. This is a man who has resisted every opportunity to do the decent thing, and what he's saying now is all in an effort to manipulate me.

'I always wanted a child of my own, and when I saw her that day in the park, and she turned and smiled at me, I knew I had to have her. Of course, she wasn't actually smiling at me, she was smiling at you, but I knew that with time and gentle persuasion, I could teach her how to love me in the same way as you and Joe.'

I close the message, and open the voice recorder app on my phone. Even if he is lying, I need to make a copy of it for Joe.

'Are you still there, Meg? Isn't this what you wanted: my confession?'

'What do you want me to say,' I reply, my voice barely more than a whisper as the sob catches in my throat.

'She didn't want to come over to me at first, but as soon as she saw my dog, she came running over. I was sure you or Joe would see her wandering off behind the trees where I was standing, but your face was buried in your phone, and I could see Joe striding towards the ice cream van. It felt like destiny had brought us together in that moment, and her to me.'

The tears escape, but I make no effort to wipe them away, instead sliding the phone closer to the gap beneath the door.

'She didn't want to come with me, and she tried to scream when I took her hand, but then Francis was able to quickly cover her mouth and put her in the back of his car before she had the chance to call anyone over.'

I don't want to listen to these cruel lies, but I can see it playing out in my mind's eye.

'I continued on my journey to the shop, knowing

that the security camera inside would capture my face and the time, giving me the perfect alibi. How could I possibly have snatched young Lydia, when minutes after she disappeared, I can clearly be seen tying my dog outside the Co-op and entering alone?'

'You're lying,' I manage to whisper.

'I'm really not, Meg, and I think before you are locked up for assault and false imprisonment, you need to know the truth about what happened to Lydia, and why despite my best wishes for her, she became too much of a liability to keep around the place. When you first entered my cell earlier today and immediately went for me, I could see where Lydia got her disobedience from too.'

Joe's name appears on the screen of my phone as it vibrates, but I don't snatch it up to answer, because I need to hear the rest.

'You're just telling me what you think I want to hear,' I say.

He doesn't answer at first, and I'm starting to believe I've caught him in a lie, but his next words chill me to the bone.

'I can prove it to you.'

I think back to that day when Andrews told us they were releasing their prime suspect due to a lack of evidence. Even if he had used McAdam to help fabricate his alibi, if Lydia had been in this house, there would have been some kind of DNA evidence to prove it. But they didn't find any trace of her inside the house or on any of David's clothing.

'How?' I croak back at him.

'Let me out of this room, and I will show you

irrefutable proof that she was here with me.'

There we have it, what he's been after since we got here: he wants me to let him out.

'No way,' I snap back.

'No? So you don't want me to remove the nagging doubt from your mind? You don't want to see where little Lydia cried for you?'

I stand and back away from the door. The best thing I can do right now is go back downstairs and wait for Joe. David is using my desire for the truth against me in the cruellest way, and all so he can escape.

'If you let me out, Meg, I'll show you where she died.'

My heart explodes with pain, and I fall to my knees as the stress of the last few month's bubbles to the surface.

Don't listen to him, I tell myself. *This is all just an elaborate game to him.*

'She begged for you, you know, as I smothered her with that pillow. I'd tried so hard to convince her that you and Joe had been killed and that I was going to be her new daddy, but she refused to believe me. In the end, she left me no choice. I'm sorry about that. Leaving her body on the banks of the Kennet just felt like the quickest way the two of you could be reunited.'

I know he's lying, and that if I cave, he's going to do whatever he has planned, but I'm helpless to resist the temptation that there might be more truth to his words than I want to give him credit for.

Crawling to the door, I unlock and open it. He's still exactly where we left him, his wrists chafing where the cable ties are binding his hands to the radiator pipes.

'The police found no evidence that she'd been in here,' I challenge, curious to hear how he'll explain away such an undisputed fact.

'Yes, I know, but did you really think I'd be so stupid as to allow her in my house before she'd accepted my version of events? Go and see for yourself: I set up a room for her, but I couldn't let her see it until she stopped screaming and crying for you.'

I spin and look at the closed door at the end of the landing. No longer caring about neighbours seeing lights on in the property, I flick the switch and bathe the landing in a yellow glow. Prising the door open, I gasp when I see the delicately painted flowers on the wall, the pink-coloured bedspread, and the handful of dolls lying against the perfectly pressed pillow.

'I think she would have liked the room, don't you?' he calls from the office.

I know she would have loved it, and for that reason alone, I need to know the truth.

I charge back to the office and lean over him, pressing the handgun against his temple. 'Tell me where you kept her.'

'I'll do better than that: I'll show you, but you have to set me free. I won't give you any trouble, you have my word.'

He must think I was born yesterday if he thinks his word has any credibility with me, but that doesn't stop me reaching for the cable cutters, and unclipping his hands and feet. He rubs at his wrists, but makes no effort to disarm me.

'We need to go downstairs,' he says dryly.

I take several steps backwards, out of the room and

across the landing to the stairs. I usher for him to stand and join me, but I will make him go first so I can keep the gun trained on him. He winces as he stands, and hobbles to the stairs.

'Sorry, I just need to get the blood circulating again.'

He takes several breaths and then slowly places his feet on the first step, beginning his descent. I wait until his is four steps down, before I follow. At the bottom of the staircase, he turns and heads in the direction of the living room at the rear of the property. Once there, he pauses, and waits for me to agree to him opening the back door. The garden beyond the patio door is too dark to see anywhere a terrified six year-old could have been held, so I push the barrel of the gun against the back of his head.

'Wait, tell me where before you open the door.'

He raises his hands in surrender. 'I have a pond in the garden. It's empty at the moment, which you would be able to see if it wasn't so dark out there. Once we're outside, the security light will come on, and then you'll see it.'

'You kept her in a pond?'

'No, beneath it. Once we lift the plastic base, you'll see a hatch which leads to an underground bunker. One of the previous owners was obsessed with the prospect of nuclear war breaking out and had the shelter fitted. It's soundproofed and undetectable from ground level unless you know what you're looking for.'

I reach around him, and unlock the door, pushing it open, but keep the gun pressed to the back of his head. He steps out into the cold night air, and I feel it bite at my burning eyes, but I don't relent. The security light douses us in its beam when we are three steps away from the door, and then I see the empty pond, just as he described. I nod for him to pull off the plastic cover, and the moment he does, I see the wheel sticking out of the top of the bulbous hatch, and my blood runs cold.

I know now that he's telling the truth, but I'm beyond caring about the whys and wherefores, I just need to be close to my daughter. I tell him to open the hatch and then step back so I can see inside. And that's when I feel the force of something crashing against the back of my neck, and I tumble into darkness.

Chapter 58

Joe

I wait in my car, parked back up the track, and hunched down behind the steering wheel, until I see Hazel being driven away inside the ambulance. She's safe now, and that's all that matters. God only knows how things might have turned out had she not run into me as she was making her escape from the barn. She may have been perfectly able to escape into the darkness, and somehow evade McAdam, but then what? According to the thermostat on the dashboard, it's already minus one outside, and she was only wearing a thin dress. Adrenaline would have kept her body temperature up for only so long. She gave me the hoodie back while she waited for the police to arrive.

I had wanted to stay with her until the police were by her side, but to do so would have meant admitting how we found her. Hazel has agreed to keep my name out of her statements to the police. And as far as they're concerned, she overpowered McAdam, escaped her prison, and managed to call for help. McAdam didn't see me with her, so unless Hazel lets it slip, there's nothing tying me to the farm.

A part of me wants to phone Neil and Ruby, and let them know that their little girl is safe and on her way home, but I'm sure the police have already made contact with them. I hope they will realise how close they came to losing her, and make the most of every extra moment they'll now have to show their daughter how cherished she is. I just wish there had been somebody battling in the same vein for Lydia. Glancing up to the rear-view mirror, I'm relieved to see she's back there smiling at me, and she does look pleased. I'm certain she'd have been proud of what her mum and I have managed to achieve today.

Straightening my spine and rotating my aching shoulders, I dial Meg's number to let her know I'm on my way back, and to share the good news about Hazel. When she doesn't answer, the tension immediately returns to my back.

Don't panic, I tell myself. There could be any number of logical reasons why she didn't answer her phone.

I hit redial as I join the A329(M), but it rings until the answerphone cuts in.

She's probably just left her phone downstairs, I tell myself. That's possible. And if she's put it on silent, she'd have no idea it was ringing. But would she really leave her phone so far away?

Maybe she's just nipped to the toilet, and will call back in a minute.

But a minute passes and there is no return call. I press my foot down harder on the accelerator, willing the traffic to part and allow me through. I dial her again, and this time when the answer service cuts in, I leave a message:

'Hi, Meg, I'm on my way back. Hope everything is good with you? Can you call me when you get this?'

Another thought strikes, and it's the one I've been trying to silence in my head: *what if David has broken free and subdued her, and that's why she's not answering?*

I should be concentrating on the darkness of the road ahead, but all I can now see is images of Meg in his clutches. If he escaped, would he have called the police? Is there an army of police waiting for me at his house? Do the police have Meg's phone, and they're not allowing her to use it in case she tips me off? No, surely they'd want her to encourage me to come back and face the inevitable arrest.

What if he's killed her?

My heart skips a beat, and I almost lose control of the car. Looking up to the rear-view mirror, there's no sign of Lydia offering a reassuring smile in return.

This whole time we've been assuming that David is the man who abducted and murdered Lydia, and yet neither of us has truly considered just what else such a monster might be capable of. Although there was no evidence in what Edie supplied me with that he'd ever been arrested on suspicion of murder before, that doesn't mean he hasn't killed before. Lydia's murder might not have been his first. And at this rate, it may not be his last.

My mind is racing, sending assertions and contradictions with each second slipping away.

Why is this journey taking so long?

This is all my fault: if I'd never allowed myself to believe that abducting David would bring us the closure we needed, neither of us would be in such peril now.

Maybe if I'd left things up to Andrews, he one day would have uncovered the vital clue needed to pin her murder on David. They have McAdam in custody now, and along with Hazel's testimony, should have all the evidence they need to charge and prosecute.

And what if they also discover evidence that McAdam was the one who snatched Lydia and was holding her in that cabin in the barn as well? Is it possible David was telling me the truth in the basement? Why didn't I check Hazel's cell for myself? Maybe I would have found some clue that she'd been there. But if she was, then I've been holding an innocent man captive for days for no reason.

Suddenly I feel less vindicated by everything that's gone on. Torturing a monster to discover Hazel's whereabouts is easier to swallow than torturing an innocent man. And if he has managed to escape his bindings, he'll have every reason to want revenge on Meg.

'Wherever you are, sweetheart, I need you to go and keep an eye on your mum,' I say to Lydia, looking heavenwards. 'Tell her I'm on my way, and I won't be long. Tell her to hang in there.'

I never should have left her there alone. We tied up David, but what if he broke free of those bindings? We should have just taken him at his word, forced him into the boot, and the three of us travelled to Bracknell. At least then we'd all be together and my paranoia wouldn't be forcing my imagination to do cartwheels.

The brakes screech as I make it back to our parking spot outside David's house. There's no sign of police, which is a relief, but only a temporary one, as I don't know what I'm going to find inside. Meg insisted I lock them in and take the key with me, which I did, but that means I left her trapped inside with a killer.

My fingers are trembling as I try to line up the key with the lock, and the keys tumble to the doormat. It takes me precious seconds to recover them in the darkness, but this time I get them into the slot, and the door opens. I quickly close and lock it behind me.

'Meg?' I call out, willing her to appear at the top of the dark staircase.

I listen for any kind of movement, but the house is deathly silent. I take the stairs two at a time, and dart around the bend at the top. I flip on the landing light, and gasp when I see the empty office. There are broken cable ties littering the carpet where David should be. I can also see the broken strands of cotton we'd used to tie him to the radiator initially. Whatever has happened here, he's no longer tied up. There's no sign of any blood or disturbance, but it still doesn't explain where the two of them are.

I complete a circuit of the upstairs to ensure Meg isn't lying there unconscious somewhere, but freeze when I spot Meg's phone on the carpet. It's been recording something for the last twenty minutes. I crash to the carpet and scoop it up. There's a notification about my voicemail at the top of the screen. I stop the recording and play it back.

I don't think I take a single breath as I hear David taunting her about Lydia, telling her what he did, and offering to prove it.

'Tell me where you took her,' I shout at the recording.

'I'll do better than that: I'll show you,' David's voice replies, as if he's heard my question. But you have to set me free. I won't give you any trouble, you have my word.'

There is some background noise, and then: 'We need to go downstairs.'

I remain where I am, listening for any other noise or speech. I must be knelt there for a minute, but there's nothing but silence. The front door was locked, and they didn't have access to a car, so they must still be here somewhere. Tearing down the stairs, I flip on the light in the hallway, darting in and out of every room, and surprised to find them all empty. There are no hiding places here, so where has he taken my wife?

My eyes fall on the keys hanging from the patio door. It is pitch black beyond the glass, but I hurry to the door regardless, and it opens without turn of the key.

'Meg?' I call out into the darkness, but there's no response.

I step out, squinting, searching for any slight movement, listening for any hint of noise, but the garden is as deathly silent as the house.

'Meg?' I try again, in a loud whisper.

My footsteps trigger some kind of security light overhead. The plastic pond base has been left in the middle of the lawn, rather than buried where I saw it the other day. I hurry over to the hole, and can't process the small wheel and hatch about a foot into the ground.

I'm about to reach for the wheel when a blood-curdling scream ripples out from inside the hatch.

Chapter 59

Meg

The whole side of my head aches. It feels like I've been kicked in the face, but as I slowly open my eyes, and my fingers press against the cold, steel floor, the memory of me hurtling into the hatch returns. I try to assess whether any part of my body aches enough to be broken, but despite a burning in my right shoulder, I appear to have survived with just bumps and bruises.

The shelter isn't as dark as when I first looked into it. There is a dim, orange glow reflecting off the shiny floor, and bathes my immediate surroundings. At first, I think that David pushed me in here and has locked me in on my own, but then I hear a sound from somewhere behind me. I can't place the noise, maybe something being shuffled, but the sound in my right ear is muffled from the impact with the floor.

My throat is so dry, but I don't feel afraid. It's almost as if part of Lydia's spirit was trapped in here, and she's wrapped herself around me like a protective and comforting blanket. Assuming the person shuffling things behind me is David, I need to work out why he's brought me down here, and whether there's any way for me to escape.

I force my eyes to remain open, despite the overwhelming desire to close them and black out again. A fall and impact like I've experienced is bound to have caused some kind of concussion, and so I need to remain alert until I can at least get some kind of treatment.

Immediately in front of me, I can see what looks like two drawer fronts on the floor. They must be almost a metre wide, and half that again tall. I don't think I'll be able to open them without drawing attention to myself, and the longer he thinks I'm still comatose, the longer I'll have to get things straight in my head. There's no guarantee I'll find anything in them to help me.

A wave of nausea washes over me, as I try to move my head to see what else is in line of sight. I allow my eyes to close, and focus on breathing through the nausea, willing myself not to throw up. I've not eaten since breakfast, so it's only likely to be bile that comes up anyway. When the wave shrinks away, I try to subtly adjust my position, but this time I keep my neck still and use my hands and feet to change my viewing angle. I see now that the drawers are a part of a single bed, pressed against one end of the shelter. The steel wall stretches up and turns into the rounded ceiling without any visible join.

Rolling onto my back, the burning in my shoulder eases slightly, but as I look up expecting to see the hatch, I'm disappointed to find it isn't there. He must have dragged me to the opposite end of the shelter, which means he is closest to the hatch. Despite the roar of pain I turn my head so that I'm looking at him. He has his back to me, slightly leaning over something, his hands busy inside some kind of black, plastic tub. If he's heard any of my movement, he's showing no sign of it.

I can now see that the shelter stretches several metres, and I'd estimate it's the length of his garden. I don't want to picture Lydia trapped inside here for days, crying, and wondering why me and Joe weren't coming to save her.

After her disappearance in the park, I never gave up hope that she'd be found, and the world would make sense again. I could feel her alive in my heart, until that day Andrews came to the house to break the news. That morning something hadn't felt right when I'd woken. It felt as though I'd left part of myself in a dream-like state. Like one of my limbs was still asleep, but not. I can't describe the feeling properly, but the moment we saw Andrews pull up outside the house, I knew inside why: a part of me died with my daughter that day.

The police came to this house before her body was recovered on the banks of the Kennet, but they never thought to look beneath the garden pond for a secret underground shelter. I wonder now whether Lydia could hear them moving about overhead. Did she call out for them to help? Did she secretly believe it was Joe and I coming to the rescue, only to learn we'd let her down?

If I screamed now, would anyone hear it?

I don't think my aching head would allow me to scream even if I wanted to. I close my eyes instead, summoning the strength to lift myself into a sitting position, but something else plays with my senses. I can smell Lydia.

My eyes snap open, and I realise the folded duvet

on the mattress above me still has her scent. I have no doubt now that she was here. He wasn't lying, and no we have the evidence of what he did. All I need to do is phone Andrews and get their forensics team down here.

But of course, that isn't an option because I don't have my phone. I didn't mean to leave it upstairs, but I didn't think to collect it when he said he'd show me this place. But that isn't the worst part. The fact that he's chosen to show me this place, knowing that it incriminates him means he has no intention of ever letting me out of here.

I scream out loud, allowing all the stress and frustration to bellow out of my soul.

This is why he wanted us to bring him to the house. This is why he gave Joe the address in Bracknell. McAdam probably doesn't have Hazel there. In fact, it's probably a trap, and now my beautiful Joe is at the mercy of McAdam. David wanted me to be alone here with him so he could get me into this prison. And we walked headfirst into his trap.

How could I have been so naïve? So gullible even?

He stops rifling through the box, and glances back over his shoulder. 'Oh good, you're awake. For a moment there I was starting to worry the fall had killed you. Can't have that. At least, not yet.'

His head returns to the box, but he makes no effort to come over and restrain me.

'What are you going to do with me?' I croak, against the protest of the thunder roaring through my head.

'We need to wait for Joe to get back here first. What

I have planned requires you both.'

If he's expecting Joe to return, maybe that means McAdam wasn't lying in wait for him. No, scratch that, the private investigator confirmed McAdam's phone was in Bracknell. Maybe he means that McAdam will bring Joe back here.

'What makes you so sure Joe would come back here?'

He glances back at me, and gives a knowing smile. 'He wouldn't leave you here alone with me. Your husband is many things, but he wouldn't just abandon you.'

'You don't know, Joe, though,' I challenge, keen to keep him talking in the hope he lets something insightful slip. 'We may be married, but we haven't been a proper husband and wife for years. Lydia was the glue holding us together, and now we're just going through the motions. If you're waiting for him, you're in for a long wait.'

He continues to watch me, as if considering this last statement. Maybe he's trying to work out whether there's truth in it, or whether I'm just bluffing. All I hope is that Joe gets back here soon.

'He'll come. He's like a fruit fly attracted to a flame. Even though he knows it won't end well, he can't stop himself.'

'What's in the box?' I ask, without a beat.

His eyes fall back on the box, and leers sickeningly. 'Just a few trinkets.'

'What sort of *trinkets*?'

'You know, mementoes to help stir memories and feelings.' He pauses and reaches into the tub, lifting out a pair of children's underpants. They're white with a pink elasticated trim. I instantly recognise them as Lydia's. David holds them up to the light and then presses them against his nose.

I can't control my up-chuck reflex, and roll onto my side as bile erupts from my throat. The heat in my cheeks and the agony in my head is like a hot poker has been pressed to my face.

'She was wearing these that day in the park,' I hear him saying quietly behind me. 'They smell like her. Reminds me of the excitement I felt when she came over to stroke that stupid mutt, out of sight of you and Joe. The possibilities seemed endless. It was all I could do to control my anticipation as I walked to that shop to secure my alibi. I so desperately wanted to tell the young man behind the counter that I had a present waiting for me back here, but I resisted the temptation.'

I push my hands against the cold floor, and force myself into a sitting position to escape the small puddle of bile settling too close to my face.

'I thought you were worried about your dog?'

He carefully folds the underpants and returns them to the box, his smile widening. 'The dog was a means to an end. People see a man of my age walking in a park alone, and they become guarded, suspicious. An older man with a puppy on a lead just blurs into the background. She's been adequate companionship, but nothing more. I assume Joe took her back to your house?'

'Yes.'

'Oh well, if she starves to death there that's just something else for your conscience to deal with in your final hours.'

So he does intend to kill me. Then that gives me no choice but to defend myself. Pushing my hands down again, it takes all my strength to stand, and as I straighten, the room spins around me. I lower my eyes to the floor, willing my mind to focus on a single point to steady the room, but I end up reaching out for the edge of the mattress to guide me along the shelter. When I'm next able to look at my destination, I see that David has stopped looking at the box of my daughter's things and is pointing my handgun at me.

'You really don't look well, Meg. I think you should sit on the bed before you fall over.'

I don't move focusing on the gun as his face seems to spin in a circle. 'Let me out of here, David.'

'Sit down!' he yells, and the shock of the echo off the metal cocoon makes my legs give way, and I fall onto the bed.

I've never had a gun pointed at me before, and whilst I've no idea whether he plans to kill me here and now, I know that my sense of fight or flight is telling me to do whatever he demands to try and live long enough to escape. At the very least I need to live long enough to warn Joe not to repeat my mistake.

'What do you want from me?' I ask, hoping David doesn't automatically put one in my head.

He puts a finger to his lips, but keeps the gun pointing at me. His eyes are moving over the roof of the shelter as if he's listening for something. Is Joe here?

'If you're planning to keep me here as your prisoner, someone will find me eventually,' I say defiantly.

'I doubt that. The police never found this place and they did an extensive search of the house and garden. Of course, the pond was full of stagnant water at the time, which must have kept the sniffer dogs from picking up on Lydia's scent. But then again, this hull is built to withstand the effects of nuclear war, so the chance of anything escaping is slim. And if you're wondering why the police never lifted the pond, the person who had the shelter installed never sought planning permission to have it fitted, so it doesn't exist on any database or plans. So there really is no chance of us being disturbed any time soon.'

His eyes dart back up to the ceiling, and now I'm certain he must be able to hear some kind of movement above us. David takes a few steps backwards, and it's only now I see the retractable ladder in the ceiling, which he pulls down. He's planning to go out and bring Joe in. I can't allow that to happen.

Closing my eyes to keep the room from spinning, I charge at David, screaming as I do to try and disorientate him. My already sore right shoulder strikes something solid, and I realise now I've crashed into the ladder, but as I open my eyes, I see David is only centimetres from me. A shot ricochets off the wall to the side, and then I'm falling on to him.

Whatever I do, I need to get the gun off him. Hopefully Joe heard the gun shot and is taking evasive action above us. I don't care now if he phones the police and they charge us with what we did to David. There is enough evidence of Lydia in here to put him away for life.

He's stronger than I realise, and as I grapple at his hands, he drives the butt of the weapon into my collarbone. It's all I can do to regain my grip, but his slips as he tries to push me off him, and suddenly the gun is falling from both of our grasps. He doesn't delay, wriggling and shoving at my prone body, sliding out from beneath me. I'm straining as far as I can reach to get hold of the gun, but just as my fingers brush the handle, he spins me onto my back, his knees astride me. With no way to defend myself, he quickly slips his bony fingers around my exposed neck. His hands are so cold, that I gasp, but as I try to inhale again, he squeezes harder, and suddenly panic sweeps the length of my body.

I throw my arms out, swinging wildly, trying to connect with anything that will force him to release his grip. He's so much stronger than I realised, and I now imagine how terrified Lydia must have been when she faced him in this way. He buffets my arms with his shoulders, and his tongue pokes out as he squeezes even harder. He is going to kill me if I can't get free, and then he's going to kill Joe.

'I stretch my arms and hands out as much as I can over my head, trying to adjust my gaze so I can focus on reaching for the gun again. My vision is starting to darken around the edges. The pain in my head and shoulder urge me to stop fighting and face the inevitability of death, but then I see Lydia's ghostly figure appear beside me. Maybe this is the end, and at least I can be reunited with her once again. Although she doesn't speak, she shakes her head and her eyes urge me to keep fighting.

I strain, and it takes all of my rage to keep going. I finally feel the cold of the graphite in my palms, and bring the weapon to meet David, but he's realised what I'm doing, and releases my neck in order to stop my hands.

I gasp in fresh air to stave off the burn in my lungs and chest, but my body is so weak that he will soon wrestle the gun from my limp grasp. I shimmy left and right, as his dead weight body limits my movement.

And then there is the loudest bang as the gun goes off.

Chapter 60

Joe

The scream, though muffled, had to have been Meg's, based on the pitch and tone. But then the gunshot has me now fearing the worst. Despite her earlier claim that the handgun was only loaded with blank cartridges, I'm no longer so convinced. I can't draw any conclusion other than David must have somehow broken free of his restraints, overpowered Meg and forced her below the ground at gunpoint. I can't see any way she would have willingly climbed into an underground box with him.

The wheel on top of the hatch is stuck fast, so it must be locked from the inside. I've tried calling out her name, but there's been no answer. I never should have left her alone with him. If he's killed her, her death will be on my conscience now too. I was too late getting back here. Maybe if I hadn't hung around waiting to check that Hazel was safely taken to the hospital, maybe I would have made it back here before David got free. It's just the latest in a series of awful decisions I've made recently.

I freeze as I hear movement just inside the hatch. Someone is unlocking it and about to emerge. With all the will in the world, I hope it is Meg, but if it isn't I need to be ready. If David has just killed Meg, then he will be coming for me next. Armed. Considering what I've put him through in the last few days, I sense he won't hesitate to exact his revenge.

The security light is still radiating its light on me and the top half of the garden, but short of running inside to search for a knife – which there clearly isn't time to do – I'm going to have to make do with some kind of weapon from the garden. There's a gnome in one of the flowerbeds, but that's only a one use item; if I throw and miss, I'll be exposed. There's a hosepipe in a bundle on the floor near the back door, but it isn't connected to a tap, and I can't see a tap to connect it to.

The sound of metal grinding against metal, tells me the hatch will be open in seconds. Giving up on the idea of a weapon, I hurry around to the opposite side of the hole, and duck down. Based on how the hatch should open, when David steps out I should be behind him, and at least that should give me some element of surprise. Hopefully.

As I'm crouched, I spot a piece of plastic guttering discarded by the edge of the garden fence, and quickly pick it up. It's barely a metre long, but might just be enough to knock the gun from his hand, or get one good swing at his head.

There's a whoosh sound as the hatch opens and the airlock breaks. My heart is in my mouth as the security light switches itself off, clearly on some kind of timer. The garden is once again plunged into darkness, and the only thing I can see is the breath escaping from my nose, lit up by the moonlight overhead.

A figure emerges out of the hole, and the moment

the head and shoulders are above ground level, the security light kicks in again, and I drop the guttering as I realise it's my beautiful wife.

'Meg,' I call, and she swivels around, the gun now pointing at me. Her eyes are frozen in a look of terror, and I'm not convinced she won't fire.

'Meg, it's Joe. Oh thank God you're alive.'

The sound of my voice is enough to snap her out of the trance, and she continues up the remaining steps as I come around to meet her. I'm about to hug her, when I see the pool of blood on her top.

'Wait, are you hurt? What did he do to you?'

Her face is misshapen by swelling and her cheek is already starting to resemble a shade of banana. She looks down at the red stain on her top, and it's as if she's only just realised it's there.

'It's not mine,' she confirms quietly. 'It's …' but she doesn't finish the sentence.

She winces as I lift her chin with my finger so I can get a better look at her face. 'Are sure you're okay? What happened?'

She glances back at the hole. 'I need to show you something.'

I follow her back into the hole, and immediately spot David lying face down on the floor. There's more blood, slowly spreading out across the hard metallic floor, and the air is filled with the smell of copper. I don't need to ask if he's dead as there is no rise and fall of his back, and based on the amount of blood I can see.

'What happened down here?' I ask, trying to make sense of the scene before me. 'Did he attack you?'

She doesn't answer, shuffling past the body, careful to avoid treading in the bloody puddle. The hatch is about a third of the way along the shell of the room, but she leads me to the shorter end, where a black, plastic tub lies open on top of a drawer unit. Looking inside it, at first it resembles the sort of box of mementoes a parent might keep for a new-born. There are odd tops and trousers, pants and socks, a couple of stuffed toys, and a pair of trainers. I know because we have a similar box in the loft of Lydia's things: her first dummy, her first bib, the outfit we brought her home from the hospital in, including the tiny hat and gloves we'd put on her to keep her protected from the cool breeze.

I study the set of trainers closer, and my heart breaks. The white soles have specks of mud on them, and the outer layer of the shoe is yellow, with an image of a flying fairy holding a wand, from which a shower of glitter sparkles falls. They were the shoes Lydia was wearing that day in the park.

My vision blurs with tears, and when I try to speak, the words stick in my throat. 'Is this …?'

Meg nods, as her own eyes fill. 'He admitted everything to me. I managed to record –'

'I heard the recording,' I tell her, and pull her close to me, no longer caring about the transfer of David's blood to my clothes. I need to hold her, and provide the reassurance that everything will be okay. That is my job.

'You were right,' she whispers. 'He took her, and he … he killed her.'

I've longed to hear that admission for so long, and

yet it brings no relief or feeling of vindication as I'd hoped it would. Even hearing the recording on Meg's phone – the confession I'd set out to obtain – brought no level of joy; it simply confirmed what I already knew in my soul.

I kiss the top of Meg's head and then rest my face on the same spot. I'm not sure she'll ever tell me what really happened down here, I only hope I can bring her back from the edge with patient love and support. I feel like I should have been the one to stop my daughter's killer, but as I've slowly come to realise over the weeks of planning and the days he was in my custody, I didn't have the courage to do what was necessary.

'I found Hazel,' I whisper, but cling to her tightly as she tries to break free of my embrace. 'She was at the farm in Bracknell. He didn't lie about that. Francis McAdam is in police custody, and Hazel is on her way to the hospital to be examined. I spoke to her, and physically she is fit and well, though she's bound to need counselling to deal with the psychological trauma she's suffered.'

'But she's safe?'

'She's safe. We never would have … without you, she wouldn't be going home now. If you take anything from this experience, take that. You saved a girl's life.'

This time she does break free. '*We* saved her.'

I don't want to waste words arguing. 'We need to phone the police and tell them about this place. You should go home and get cleaned up. I'll tell them I came here demanding answers and he showed me this before we fought over the gun, and he was shot in self-defence.'

She starts shaking her head. 'No, Joe, I can't let you take the blame for my actions.'

I gently press my finger to her lips. 'I failed our daughter, Meg, I'm not going to fail you as well. Let me take the responsibility for what happened here. There's no need for us to both suffer for what this bastard did.'

Meg pulls away from me, making no effort to disguise her disappointment. 'And I'm not going to allow him to destroy our lives any further.'

It's my turn to frown. 'I don't understand.'

'The police couldn't prosecute David due to a lack of evidence. We now have that evidence, but think about how it was obtained. Even if they believed your version of events, what good will it do? He's dead, Joe, so there'll be no trial. Lydia's death will be attributed to him, but we already know that he did it. We have the conclusion we wanted: we know the truth, and this monster won't be free to hurt any other children. What good comes from our names being dragged through the mud just so Andrews can close her casefile?'

There's a resoluteness to her eyes that I haven't seen for a long time.

'What are you suggesting?'

'We leave him here, seal the hatch and move on with our lives.'

It sounds so cold, and feels like an easier way out, but I'm not sure I'll be able to live with the fear of the body being found one day and the police coming calling for us.

'But our DNA must be all over his house,' I challenge. 'When his body is found, the police will surely process the scene and realise what we did.'

'*If* they find the body. We can give the place a clean now to the best of our ability, and then go home. We'll burn these clothes and move on with our lives. *If* anyone ever comes looking, we'll deal with the fallout then.'

She moves away from me, and begins to climb the ladder.

'Meg, wait, where are you going?'

'To get what we need to clean the place. Trust me, Joe, this is the only way.'

I watch her leave, but I'm not convinced, and am certain it's only a matter of time before someone figures out the truth.

Epilogue

Three Weeks Later

We spent the best part of four hours scrubbing, wiping and vacuuming David Calderwood's house and inside the fallout shelter. We snuck out of his house, over the back fence and drove home at two in the morning, leaving the front door locked, with his key inside. The moment we got back to the Lexus, I was convinced that police cars with flashing blue lights and sirens would emerge and arrest us, but they didn't. We got home, bagged up our clothes outside to avoid blood traces transferring to the carpet, and stashed the bag in the shed. We both showered, and made a fuss of Lola the beagle who looked super excited to see us after most of the day on her own. She hadn't made a mess but emptied her bladder the moment she was let out into the garden. We stayed up playing with her, and headed to bed at nearly four a.m., but I didn't sleep properly, despite overwhelming exhaustion.

To be honest I haven't had a decent night's sleep in months, but it's been worse these past three weeks. When my mind does give in to the fatigue, the nightmares that greet me are so vivid that I wake in a cold sweat. Not nightmares about David per sé, but about the police suddenly turning up unannounced and hauling us away in chains. Leaving David's rotting corpse in that shelter doesn't sit comfortably with me, despite everything he put us through.

I think that's why Meg suggested this break away. She says I need to put it out of my mind and get some much-needed perspective. I'd argue that she's just as uncomfortable with our decisions that day as I am, and every now and again, I catch her gazing into space, and I'm certain it's because she's reliving the moment she took his life. When she catches me looking, she claims that everything is okay, and that she isn't suffering, but I know her better than she realises.

Rather than drawing attention to ourselves with a late night bonfire, we dumped the bag of clothes in our dustbin, and they were taken away by the council two days later, hopefully headed for some landfill from which they will never return. It's a huge risk, but I think there's a tiny part of me that hopes Meg's plan does unravel so that I can face the punishment I deserve to receive. I've hated the fact that my daughter's killer couldn't be prosecuted, but doesn't it make my a hypocrite to play the system in the same way as David did?

Lola the beagle is certainly making the most of our time at the beach. It's surprisingly mild for November, and although we're dressed in coats rather than swimwear, the beach walks and sea air are doing wonders for easing the stress and tension. Lola is yet another strand tying us to what happened to David, but she is now officially registered as our dog at the local vet's practice, with us paying for pet insurance, as well as a vet plan. Thankfully for us, David hadn't had her microchipped, so there isn't any paperwork tying her to him. Short of a witness coming forward and formally identifying Lola as the beagle David used to keep, she should be safe in our care. Of course, David did have that neighbour who complained about the dog messing in her garden, but she may just be relieved not to find any future presents left amongst her rose bushes.

Hazel kept to her word and hasn't mentioned the stranger who appeared in her hour of need and helped her escape the clutches of Francis McAdam. He was found still slumped over the wheel of the grey van with a major concussion following the incident with the laptop. He has recovered and is currently helping the police with their enquiries. Based on the evidence recovered from Hunter's Farm, the van described in the 999 call, and Hazel's statement, he's unlikely to be freed for the foreseeable future. When Hazel came to our house last week for her first tuition with Meg since her ordeal, Meg thought it only fair to formally introduce us. Hazel made no mention of us meeting before until Meg told her that she knew the truth, at which point Hazel wrapped her arms around my shoulders and hugged me tightly.

'I never got to thank you for what you did,' she said. 'You saved my life, and if you ever need anything from me, you've only to ask.'

I choked up at that to be honest, but have no intention of ever calling in the favour. At least it won't come as a shock to her if we ever bump into each other in Reading city centre at some point in the future.

We're on the beach now, and at this time of year, Lola is allowed on the sand with us. She's not so keen on the sea, daring herself to step into the wake as the waves shrink away, but leaping back as soon as more water approaches. It's funny to watch, and for the first time in weeks, I feel my body trying to relax.

Meg has been a huge part of that. It felt as if we'd almost become strangers, but slowly we're starting to open up to one another again. I know I shouldn't have kept my plan a secret from her, and maybe if I had come clean sooner, we could have found the answers we needed without it ending in David losing his life. I've replayed my actions in that week over and over in my mind, and tried to determine what I could have done differently to get to the truth sooner. I acted erratically at times, and in hindsight I'm not even certain of some of the steps I took and conclusions I drew, but that's the thing about grief: it makes you act in extraordinary ways.

As hard as it is living with the guilt of what we did, it feels easier with Meg sharing that burden with me. When it's all getting on top of me, I can tell her and know she won't judge me. No matter what happens in the future, this is an experience that only the two of us shared, and that means I will love her until the end of time, no matter what happens. In the grief that followed Lydia's death, I think we both lost sight of the fact that we vowed to remain a couple through the good and bad times, until death separates us. Lydia's birth and then death made us forget that once upon a time we were all the other needed in life. We're a long way from getting back to that point, but every passing day feels like a step towards it.

'We should probably head back to the hotel in a bit,'

I tell Meg with a huge yawn. 'All this sea air is exhausting.'

'Can we stay a little bit longer? Lydia always loved coming here, and it helps me feel closer to her. Just a little bit longer?'

How can I refuse?

'Why don't you go and buy us an ice cream from the stand over there?'

I look to where she's pointing. 'What do you fancy?'

'Something chocolatey, but if they have anything plain for Lola, get her a treat too.'

I pass the dog leash to Meg and begin to cross the sand to the small parlour just at the edge of the path. I study the image of ice creams on the board outside the stand, and I'm about to place my order when I see the blue lights coming towards us from the end of the road. The hairs on the back of my neck stand, and I try to convince myself that it's purely a coincidence that the unmarked Mondeo happens to be at the same strip of beach as us, but it pulls in at the edge of the road near the ice cream parlour, and I see Detective Andrews look straight at me as he climbs out of the car.

I look back to Meg, but she is oblivious to what is about to unfold, as she throws a stick for Lola to chase after.

I step away from the ice cream parlour, and adopt my most puzzled expression as Andrews nears.

'Fancy meeting you here?' I say light-heartedly, but it sounds so weak that I instantly regret the choice of words.

'Hi Joe, I'm sorry to interrupt your holiday, but

there's something I need to talk to you about urgently. Is there somewhere we can go and talk?'

His tone of voice tells me this isn't a request. I look back to Meg, who now glances up and stares straight at me. She shields her eyes with her hand, but she's quite the distance, so I'm not sure if she'll be able to recognise Andrews. I wave and blow her a kiss, before turning and following Andrews back to his car.

***

'I assume you have an idea about why I need to speak to you?' Andrews asks once we're seated in the small café further along the seafront.

Every nerve in my body is on edge, but I'm grateful that he's brought me somewhere informal to have this preliminary conversation. He's showing me the courtesy of allowing me to confess without the intensity of being cramped in a windowless room at the police station.

'Well the sign in the window did say this place does the best cup of coffee in Weymouth.' Again, my attempt at levity is misplaced, and Andrews makes no effort to smile.

'I want to talk to you about David Calderwood.'

My heart drops. I suppose we did well to carry on for three weeks, but I always knew this moment would come eventually. Despite Meg's assertions, I haven't been able to ignore the spectre of police interaction looming over us. And I already know what I will do to protect the woman I love.

'What about him?' I ask as the waitress brings over

two mugs of hot chocolate, mine with whipped cream and marshmallows.

'He's dead.'

He says it so bluntly that I don't have time to prepare a look of surprise or gasp of shock.

I cough. 'Right, I see,' I say, uncertain whether he wants me just to bowl out with my confession, or whether he has anything else to say first. I err on the side of caution and close my mouth.

'I assume you'll have heard that we've pressed charges against Francis McAdam for the abduction of Hazel Cooper almost a month ago?'

To be honest I wasn't aware the CPS had agreed to charges being pressed against McAdam, but I shrug as if I was.

'At first he refused to answer any of our questions, but once we presented him with our overwhelming evidence, he began to cooperate. He claimed that he didn't act alone, and that he only knew where Hazel would be because he was told by Calderwood. Apparently, McAdam said he'd done Calderwood a favour a few months ago, and in return Calderwood had found Hazel for him online. The details he gave were sketchy, but enabled us to obtain a warrant to search Calderwood's home, and although he didn't appear to be home, we collected his computer and uncovered several conversations he'd been having with minors online, including Hazel Cooper. Seems he was posing as some kind of agony aunt, answering teenagers' questions about sex. Hazel admitted to using the site. We found evidence on Calderwood's computer that he had been grooming several individuals, including Cooper on this site.'

He pauses and takes a sip of his drink, allowing me to think back to what he'd told me in the basement. Despite claiming to have little involvement with McAdam, it seems that was yet another spin of the truth. David took no ownership of having involvement in Hazel's abduction, and only gave us McAdam's location – playing his trump card – in order to separate Meg and me.

'We put out an All Ports Bulletin as we began to search for Calderwood, but there was no evidence of where he might have gone. He didn't have a phone registered in his name, and he hadn't used his debit or credit cards for several weeks. It was as if he had disappeared off the face of the planet.'

My stomach turns, as I realise where this is headed.

'And then I remembered our little meetings outside his house.'

He takes another sip of drink, as if expecting me to speak up at this point, but I remain silent, trying to choose the right words that won't paint me as a homicidal maniac. I'm about to open my mouth when he beats me to it.

'I figured if he'd really gone anywhere then you wouldn't have been keeping vigil at his front door for so long. And the fact that we had to break through his door to gain access to his property suggested he either wasn't planning to return, or hadn't left in the first place. The other strange thing that our search of the grounds discovered was that the backdoor was unlocked, and when we went into the garden to assess whether he might have scaled the fence at the rear of the property, we discovered that his pond was empty. Having checked the photographs taken by scene of crime officers when he was first arrested on suspicion of Lydia's murder, the pond had been full. On closer inspection, there was dislodged earth around the rim of the plastic casing, suggesting it might have been moved.' He fixes me with a sincere stare. 'We discovered a hatch which led to some kind of war bunker. We now believe that this is where he held your Lydia before she was moved to the banks of the Kennet. I'm so sorry, Joe.'

Even though none of this is news to me, I feel winded hearing the words spoken out loud. My eyes fill, and I fight to keep them at bay.

He reaches out and takes my hand. 'You were so convinced of his guilt despite everything, and I was blinded by the apparent lack of evidence. I can't tell you why nobody thought to look beneath the pond the first time we were at the property. If we had, we probably would have brought you the closure you needed sooner.'

'I wish you had too,' I say honestly.

'I'm sorry that we failed you, Joe. And Meg of course too. The bunker wasn't on any site plans of the property, and it was only when we interviewed the estate agency who'd let the property to Calderwood that they confirmed its presence there. We found Calderwood in a pool of his own blood surrounded by some items we've subsequently recovered traces of Lydia's DNA from. It isn't clear at this time what happened, but we recovered the gun used to kill him at the scene.'

I know we wiped Meg's prints from the gun, but we aren't experts in cleaning up crime scenes, and God only knows what other clues we left at David's house.

Andrews is about to speak again, when Meg comes bursting into the café with Lola in tow. She is breathless, and although she does her best to straighten her blustered hair with her hand, and control her panting, it's clear to see she's been looking for us for a while. Her arrival makes enough noise to cause Andrews to look back at her, before waving her over.

She glances at the waitress behind the counter, checking that she's allowed to bring Lola in. The waitress offers little more than a disinterested shrug.

I wish she hadn't come in as I'm certain she won't keep quiet when I offer Andrews my confession. There is no point in us both winding up in prison over David's death, and it was my action that led to us being at his house, so if either of us deserves to suffer, it's me.

Andrews waits until Meg has joined us, before continuing. 'Calderwood's death remains unsolved. I secretly suspect that McAdam killed his partner over some kind of disagreement, but he's refusing to comment on such a possibility. Unfortunately it looks like someone made a bungled attempt at cleaning up the place, but they did enough to prevent us getting a clearer indication of what went on and who is responsible.'

I realise I haven't taken a new breath in several moments, and slowly inhale through my nose.

Andrews looks from me to Meg and then back again. 'We're planning to close Lydia's case. Given what McAdam has told us about collecting Lydia from the park on Calderwood's behalf, along with the DNA samples recovered from the bunker, we're confident that Calderwood was the man responsible for abducting and murdering her. That's what I came to tell you today, and I'm sorry again for disturbing your break away. We may never know why he targeted her, or whether he intended to kill her from the outset, but at least you now know who was responsible. I'm so sorry we couldn't bring you that closure sooner.'

He sits back and takes a long drink of his hot chocolate.

I'm waiting for him to continue, but he remains silent. I don't understand. I was so convinced I would be led from here in handcuffs, and yet he doesn't seem interested in asking either of us any further questions about our involvement in what happened to David Calderwood.

'What about David?' I ask.

Andrews frowns. 'What about him?'

I glance at Meg. 'What happens about his death? Are you going to be investigating what happened?'

'He ... His death is unexplained, and his casefile will remain open and subject to further review, but right now I suspect we have his killer in custody. Off the record, I don't imagine it will ever be solved. It's just one of those things. Given what we now know he did to Lydia, I think karma caught up with him. Don't quote me on that of course.'

He smiles warmly.

I'm about to speak again, when Meg grabs hold of my hand and squeezes it. 'Thank you for letting us know, Detective Andrews, and for all you've done to bring us much-needed closure. We really appreciate it.' She glares at me, until I smile and echo her gratitude to Andrews.

He finishes his drink and stands. 'You've got my number if you have any questions later down the line, but I hope you both now have the chance to start rebuilding your lives.' He looks down at the beagle and his smile widens. 'And I'm pleased to see you decided to keep the puppy. She looks like she's enjoying her time with you both.'

Meg reaches down and picks up Lola. 'She's helping us rebuild our faith in love and kindness.'

Andrews nods and departs. I'm half-expecting him to turn back and realise he's made a mistake in not arresting us, but he doesn't look back. I suppose for him it's the closure of one case from his enormous pile of work. As much as my conscience wants to chase after him, and admit what we did, I stay where I am, savouring the warm touch of Meg's hand around mine. She meets my gaze, and leans forward, kissing me on the lips so tenderly that I feel like I might shatter into a thousand pieces.

'Come on,' she says, 'let's go home.'

The End

AUTHOR MESSAGE

Thank you for taking the time to read **WHAT LIES BENEATH**. If you enjoyed it, please post a review on Amazon or Goodreads and share the story with your friends. If a book is written to entertain, then the reader is the target audience, and I feel honoured that you chose one of my books to read.

Please don't be afraid to contact me via Facebook or Twitter to let me know what you thought of the story. There's nothing more joyful for an author than hearing from a reader who loved one of their books (believe me!). I really do respond to *every* message.

Thank you again for reading my book. I hope to hear from you soon.

Stephen Edger

www.stephenedger.com

/AuthorStephenEdger

@StephenEdger

ACKNOWLEDGEMENTS

I'd like to say special thanks to the following people, without whom ***WHAT LIES BENEATH*** wouldn't be in existence today:

Dr Parashar Ramanuj, my best friend for more than twenty years and my first port of call whenever I have strange questions about medical procedures and body parts. His knowledge of psychological illness was essential for this story, and any errors are my misinterpretation of what he explained.

Joanne Taylor who has been reading and providing feedback on my novels since the beginning. Thank you to Alex Shaw and Paul Grzegorzek – authors and dear friends – who are happy to listen to me moan and whinge about the pitfalls of the publishing industry, offering words of encouragement along the way. Credit to Paul for suggesting the title after I decided to change the original.

A special shout out now to a special group who agreed to beta read the novel (back when it was called 'My Daughter's Killer'). Their feedback and comments have helped make the story what it is today, and I'm eternally grateful to them: Jeremy Paris; Alan Rogers; Louise Gray; Lorraine Francies; Claire Lamont; Lindsey Gibbs; and Gary Peacock.

Away from publishing, I wouldn't be a writer if it wasn't for my beautiful and always supportive wife Hannah. She keeps all the 'behind the scenes' stuff of my life in order and our children's lives would be far greyer if I was left in sole charge. I'd also like to thank my mother-in-law Marina for all the championing of my books she does on social media.

And final thanks must go to <u>YOU</u> for picking up and reading ***WHAT LIES BENEATH***. You are the reason I wake up ridiculously early to write every day, and why every free moment is spent devising plot twists. I feel truly honoured to call myself a writer, and it thrills me to know that other people are being entertained by the weird and wonderful visions my imagination creates. I love getting lost in my imagination and the more people who read and enjoy my stories, the more I can do it.